M000164612

"Strange, infinitely sad, and ambiguously haunted, Verity Holloway's new novel is entirely its own creature. Edenwell – a WWı hydrotherapy retreat surrounded by ominous woodland and the scars of ancient mines – offers a deliciously spooky, folk horror-imbued setting for this Weird meeting of scars and secrets; fans of Lucie McKnight Hardy will be delighted."
Ally Wilkes, Bram Stoker Award-nominated author of
All the White Spaces

"This is a book of gentle strength, which works its magic by luring and inviting, without ever shouting. It will make you forget the world for a while, and then look at it from a new perspective. It is a story with a great sense of time and place, which also manages to be timeless and universal. Call it horror, call it fantasy, call it what you want, as long as you read it."
Francesco Dimitri, World Fantasy Award winner
and author of *Never the Wind*

"The absolutely convincing recreation of the past combined with a gradual, creeping dread make this a fascinating and frightening book. The prose is accomplished, the characters perfectly realised; rarely has horror been treated with such intelligence and attention to detail. Holloway is a major talent."
Alex Pheby, author of *Mordew*

"In *The Others of Edenwell*, Verity M. Holloway has woven a world of strange and secret treasures. It's a beautifully written novel that finds its way under your skin and makes a lasting impression."
A. J. Elwood, author of *The Cottingley Cuckoo*

THE
OTHERS
OF
EDENWELL

VERITY M. HOLLOWAY

TITAN BOOKS

The Others of Edenwell
Print edition ISBN: 9781803363950
E-book edition ISBN: 9781803363967

Published by Titan Books
A division of Titan Publishing Group Ltd
144 Southwark Street, London SE1 0UP
www.titanbooks.com

First edition: July 2023
10 9 8 7 6 5 4 3 2 1

This is a work of fiction. All of the characters, organizations, and events portrayed in this novel are either products of the author's imagination or are used fictitiously. Any resemblance to actual persons, living or dead (except for satirical purposes), is entirely coincidental.

A CIP catalogue record for this title is available from the British Library.

Printed and bound by CPI Group (UK) Ltd, Croydon, CR0 4YY.

For Edward, Fred, and Bill Urry
Who died together at Gallipoli
on the 12th of August 1915

THERE ARE THREE TYPES OF MEN

Those who hear the call and obey.
Those who delay.
And - The Others.
To which do you belong?

—PARLIAMENTARY RECRUITING COMMITTEE

"In some peculiar way great wars open up fresh channels for the psychic senses, and the physical struggle of great armies appears ever to have its counterpart on the spiritual plane."

—RALPH SHIRLEY, editor of
The Occult Review, 1915

PROLOGUE

THERE IS ONE surviving photograph of young Freddie, rescued from the bins of a Thetford charity shop during the 1970s. We glimpse him lined up with the rest of the hospital staff, shrugging against the wind rolling in from the flat Norfolk breckland. The photograph serves as a roll call for that hard year of 1917, when so many orderlies of sound body and mind had crossed the Channel to die. It is, in essence, a ghost image; of a young man on the cusp of a maturity that would never come, but also of a world beyond the frame of frail celluloid. Too much conspicuous absence. Too many women, standing with their backs to the fading grandeur of Edenwell Hydropathic Hotel.

It has been my pleasure these past thirty years to dedicate myself to the study of Alfred Ferry and the trail of breadcrumbs he left behind. Much has been said of the events of May 1917 in that hitherto quiet corner of East Anglia. I prefer to focus on Freddie's output; his puzzling, beguiling talent.

Surveying his body of work, collected here, what can one expect of the youth himself? Perhaps someone more striking than the figure at the back left of the photograph. Tall-ish, blond-ish, thin yet soft of face, he wears his rifle slung over his shoulder, mirroring his father beside him. These men were not soldiers, but groundsman and son. For young Freddie, there would be no sons. His energies were spent elsewhere, unbeknownst to those closest to him, let alone the art world. So strangely interrupted, so nearly lost.

We believe we know the world in which Alfred Ferry lived. Half blind, we squint into it each November on Armistice Day and convince ourselves we can see. We know the images Freddie left behind, impenetrable and unsettling, intricate and troubling. But we may never know the thoughts in his head. I believe he preferred it this way.

DR FRANCIS BYATT,
Norwich Academy of Art and Anthropology
Alfred Ferry: A Centenary of Strange Illusion

ONE

*Broken apothecary bottle. Pencil on
butcher's paper, 6×8in. C. February 1917.*

Oblong bottle, medicinal type, smashed in two. In the white
slash of reflected light, we see a speck. Something is coming.

A JACKDAW WILL TALK in his sleep, but Alfred Ferry
made little noise at all.

He dozed, his head wrapped in damp linen like a desert
explorer from *The Boys' Realm*. The warm bathwater rippled
with his breath, and in the dark of his drowsing mind he heard
the crows calling.

Out there, in conference without him, they teemed in the
pine trees, a raucous *Ha! Ha!* while gangs of rooks jeered and
wheezed, all pipe tobacco and spilled ale. The blue-tinged
magpies clattered musically like the man at the Red Lion playing
the spoons, and the jackdaws, always bolder, were the first to
break through the canopy to survey the Hydropathic. *Where is
the knave?* they were saying. *Where is he?*

11

"They're putting out the breakfast things, Ferry. Get on."

Nick Scole leaned over the bath as far as his bad leg would allow. Rough fingers clipped Freddie's nose, and the rooks blew away like coal dust. Freddie pulled the linen from his face and hauled himself upright in the tub. Gooseflesh prickled across his bony shoulders.

The Solarium had no clocks, but the wisteria foaming over the gallery windows was drowsy purple in the February half-light, signalling the late hour. Freddie was permitted to use the baths before the guests were breakfasted, and only on Doctor Chalice's prescription. Here he could lie with the sun reaching down through the glass roof, the potted ferns bursting green around him and the tiles gleaming like a Mediterranean lagoon. It was a ballroom once, Chalice told him, when Edenwell was a private house, long ago. It was part of his vision to keep the soul of the place intact. That spirit of gentle leisure and pleasure, so good for the body and the mind.

Freddie let his hands break the surface of the water and placed them over his heart. It felt more agreeable, if he wasn't mistaken.

"You awake?" said Scole. "Better be. When I was twenty-two, I was doing thirteen-hour days at the dairy."

If the Solarium walls were a lagoon, Nick Scole was an iceberg. His white uniform glowed. Some institutions required their male staff to wear little black dickie-bows, a palate cleanser to the starched tunic and trousers that so nearly said *hospital* and therefore *death*. At Edenwell, Doctor Chalice preferred more formal garb, verging on military. It lent the orderlies a most British authority, he said, which Freddie's father thought was quite astute for an American. As for Scole, the Edenwell tunic

12

and trousers were the closest he would get to a soldier's kit ever again. The silver Wound Badge shone on his chest. 'For King and Empire. Services rendered.' Freddie disliked how often he found himself looking at it, or at the orderly's shaved cheeks, the texture of shingle. *Rendered*, the rooks snickered. *Like tallow*.

"Get dressed," Scole said. "And wipe up after yourself, else I square you up."

He lurch-thumped away through the swinging doors and out into the gentlemen's changing rooms. Beyond that, in the main corridor, the maids could be heard, carrying mounds of white towels and pushing tea trolleys. Freddie could almost smell the breakfast kippers, though the building was judiciously laid out so no rogue odours could ever infiltrate the treatment rooms.

The guests would be stirring. Up in their suites, some availed themselves of the washbasins steaming with Edenwell water and lavender soap, while the wealthier visitors enjoyed private showers or steeled themselves for a morning massage from Katie Healey whose hands could subdue concrete. The fire was being coaxed in the library, the morning papers fanned out, the linen smoothed over the dining room tables. And in the groundskeeper's cottage, flung out on the edge of Choke Wood, Fa would be hunched at the hearth, preparing his, and Freddie's rifles.

Time to dry off, put on his overalls, and pretend he had never been there at all.

The breckland would look underdressed without a monument to the special water coursing beneath the black soil. If a stranger

13

had no idea they were standing on such a remarkable spot, Edenwell Hydropathic commanded respect by virtue of being the only building for miles, bar the odd shepherd's hut and bramble-bound hunting blind. Visitors had plenty of time to stare at the edifice, square and white and far too large, as they were drawn down the driveway through acres of patchy pines, interrupting the occasional cluster of deer. By the time they reached the front portico with its polished Grecian columns, they had already been treated to a wholly unnecessary jaunt around the four-layered fountain on the front lawn – the Well of Eden, the source of their hopes.

For the staff of Edenwell, Freddie included, the Hydropathic was about a different kind of hope: that of keeping the old girl afloat. Freddie tucked his broom under his arm and fumbled with the gaolers' ring of keys jangling on his belt. The North Wing had been shut off since a year after the war began. Freddie remembered the day they locked it, draping beds and tables, shutting the windows tight. The staff chatted nervously, filling the silence where once there had been the shuffling of slippers and the ever-present sound of water, pouring, spraying, douching. Doctor Chalice brimmed with optimism that day.

"When all this is over – and it won't be long, friends, I firmly believe it – what men will want is sanctuary. A little amusement. Imagine thousands of weary English soldiers disembarking at Folkestone, and the first thing they see is a billboard promising a pretty Norfolk nurse pouring a cool glass of healing water. And you and I? We'll be ready."

Freddie tucked the memory away, shunting open the door with one shoulder. They closed the North Wing because the lack of men meant a lack of staff, and soon a lack of guests to

14

run after. Putting half of Edenwell to sleep was required to keep the place alive. But an investor was just around the corner, Chalice promised them with one of his ever-ready grins.

"These things take time. Here, you people do business like you're dancing the two-step on a glacier."

Oh, and when this investor got his act together... a new sun terrace, an expanded tennis court with a refreshment stand, and fine refurbished bedrooms with views of the landscaped gardens. Maybe even a proper Turkish sauna fit for a sultan, with great cascading monstera plants from the jungles of Panama. Chalice told Freddie stories of the big London hospitals, where canaries were bred in gleaming aviaries so every patient would have a singing companion for the duration of their stay.

"Would you like that, Freddie-fella? You have a way with the birds. How'd you fancy conjuring me up some canaries?"

Canaries needed sand and cuttlefish bones. The birds he was used to laughed at the idea of cages. But he could manage it, Freddie said solemnly. Yes, he most definitely wouldn't let Doctor Chalice down.

When he told Fa, he received a fond slap. "You're a canary," Fa said. The idea was disappointingly never mentioned again, but Freddie took a scrap of butcher's paper and made a drawing of a golden palace on a rolling dune of pristine sand.

Soon. The word on everyone's lips.

Until then, it was Freddie's job to interfere with the North Wing, and it disliked him accordingly. Each day, he unlocked the double doors and slipped through, turning the key behind him so no stray guests could follow him in error. Though the living portion of Edenwell could be trying, with the guests' frank talk of bald pates and spreading waistlines, the North

Wing's emptiness rang loud with memories of those who came too late for the water's magic. Women drawn and brittle, men shaking too hard to drink their soup. Freddie didn't always notice guests as they arrived – in high season, Edenwell could expect up to twenty newcomers a day, sometimes together in a rowdy party – but when the most fragile visitors left, wheeled into private cars by manservants and white-capped nurses, Freddie often felt a nudge of personal failure.

There was a fat cobweb swinging in the draught caused by his entrance. Freddie swiped his broom at it, pretending it was a broadsword. The spiders loved the old Morton family crest, high up in the ceiling frieze. It had always frightened Freddie, that story. Given a few ales, Nick Scole was known to do a fearsome turn as the hermit Lord Morton, his brain softened by age and indolent living, swinging his hammer and turning every last coat of arms in the house to dust. Grief for his only son, killed by assailants unknown. The frieze in the North Wing was the only one to survive, being just out of Mad Morton's marauding reach. Missus Hardy the cook said he pulled up the kitchen flagstones and dug his own grave there. But servants would say anything to break up the monotony of the day.

Freddie made his apologies to the spiders and hurried on.

The North Wing was laid out in an open ward style, offering cheap, comfortable beds in opposing rows for Edenwell's cheaper, less comfortable guests. There were five fireplaces, spread down the centre of the long room to evenly heat the beds in the raw East Anglian winter. Freddie went to each one, knelt down, and felt about inside with the broom handle. It was his childish fear that one day he would dislodge a pair of

16

human legs, but there were no limbs that morning, just clods of chimney dust and the odd twig from the nests perched high above. It was not unknown for a pair of fighting jackdaws to slide all the way down a chimney, bursting out into the room, furious but unharmed. Freddie kept an envelope of stale bread in his waistcoat for that eventuality. Better to coax them out than chase them. They remembered that sort of thing.

The beds remained, stripped and empty, with a locker and washbasin each. Freddie was always thankful they had pulled back the dividing curtains before closing the wing. It was easy to succumb to uneasy feelings in such a long, silent room, and each time a stray breeze caught a curtain Freddie found himself thinking of the hikey sprites who moved with the sound of rustling leaves and *got you* if you left a candle burning at bedtime. But there were worse things to stumble upon, he reminded himself. Like Nick Scole with a girl.

Freddie got down on his knees at the fifth and final hearth, jabbing his broom handle about in the dark. Something plopped between his knees, showering him in dust and soot. His breath stopped in his throat as he brushed aside the crumbling dirt. The delicate architecture of a spine.

Drummerboy had been gone a month.

Outside, the rooks cackled. *A knave counts the days.*

"Stop that," he hissed.

Nothing but mouse parts: an owl pellet. Freddie swept it up. He heard the owl at night, screeching as he tried to sleep. Birds calling in the dark had always made him nervous. He supposed it was Fa's fault. When Freddie was small, his father took a fledgling jackdaw from a nest and locked it in a cage hanging outside the cottage door. Jackdaws had always been

17

friends of farmers and field-dwellers, he told Freddie. A tame one would loudly tell the master when a stranger approached. "A guard dog'll be bribed," Fa said, "but not one of these boys." Birds saw things men did not.

Young Freddie saw the cage and felt an overwhelming glee at having this wild thing at his command. Fa didn't want to give it a name – "You mustn't grow fond" – so Freddie only called him Wellington in private. He fed Wellington bits of bacon fat and sang songs to him.

> *The grand old Duke of York*
> *He had ten thousand men*
> *He marched them up to the top of the hill*
> *And he flew – exploded! – swept a black broom down*
> *the land and then…then…*

When Wellington died, Freddie wept. He cried so long, Fa went to Doctor Chalice for something to soothe him, but the doctor said he should be allowed to grieve. Fa gave Freddie some beer and disposed of the jackdaw in the hospital furnace. For weeks, Freddie dreamt of Wellington calling to him in the night, wanting more bacon, more songs. He took the empty cage down to Choke Wood and watched it sink in the old well.

He dusted up after the owl pellet and brushed off his trousers. Drummerboy would have said something if he was going for good. Freddie had been over his weather diaries with the utmost care. There was nothing – no sudden flare of rain or gales – to spook the bird. Nothing he could see suggested an omen. Drummerboy had simply gone.

That was the way of it now. Most of the orderlies were gone. Mister Daventry and Mister Rhodes went right at the start when it all felt like a big party. Doctor Chalice shook their hands and said he'd keep their white uniforms pressed and clean for their return. Clarence, the farrier's boy, was an inch too short but they let him go anyway. Freddie could hardly remember John Pollard who used to deliver the coal. And what about Scole? Scole had come back. And look at Scole.

But those were people. And people didn't work in the sensible circles animals did.

He set about checking the windows. It was mechanical up-down work that made stars glitter in his eyes, sweeping his hands over the outer sills searching for rotting patches, and when the last window was done, his heart was labouring as though he had never taken Doctor Chalice's healing water at all.

He rested against the sill. Fa was down on the driveway with the Albion van, craning his neck, waiting for Freddie to notice him. He was waving his cap, and not cheerfully. In his other hand, something dead.

"Here he comes. That's right, nice and leisurely."

If the pines of Edenwell could up roots and walk, they would strongly resemble James Ferry. At sixty-six, he was an old father to such a young son, but he carried out his duties with a glum humour which endeared him to everyone at the Hydropathic, his home for nearly thirty-five solid, careful years. Freddie had inherited his Fa's rather bashful, long-legged demeanour, but not much else. If any of the guests had seen the pair of them on the driveway that cold morning, they would have assumed this was a groundskeeper who would rather be alone, and an apprentice who felt similarly.

The squirrel dangled heavily in Fa's grip.

"It needs burning. But for now, we need traps."

Freddie tugged thoughtfully at his bottom lip. "I've never trapped a fox."

"A fox takes his leavings. Besides, they kill with a bite. Look at this." He pressed the limp animal into Freddie's hands.

The squirrel had been all but crushed. A motorcar would have left a clear track across the body, but the unfortunate creature was crumpled like a bullet. Freddie's sketching eye was drawn to the strange fall of light and shadow; a crater where the ribcage once swelled, broken angles interrupting soft fur. It was spongey to the touch, a cold bag of skin, and Freddie gave it back.

"I'll set a snare," he said.

"Snare won't do it. We need an ironmonger."

The weight of the metal settled into Freddie's core. He stole a look at the van.

"You has to learn," said Fa.

The Albion van was already loaded with shears and lawnmower blades for the knife sharpener. In Freddie's opinion, he had done enough learning. Learn to clean your boots of an evening, said Fa, learn to focus on the task at hand, learn to say good morning. And he had, but only when Fa was there to hear it, and sometimes in the afternoon.

Fa opened the driver's door. "Three or four traps, I reckon."

Freddie put his hands in his pockets. There were pencil stubs to fiddle with. "There's litter on the bowling green. While you're off, I can clear it."

"Can't lug four traps alone." Fa looked him over, and when the annoyance in his face passed, Freddie noted the drop of concern underneath. "You sickening for summat?"

He could say his heart was off. It had been hard to sleep lately with it thudding away like a drunken dancer. But he didn't want to worry Fa.

"Just hungry."

"We's all hungry," Fa grumbled, and gave him a gentle shove towards the van.

Freddie scrunched his long body into the passenger seat. With the window down he could hear the rooks calling. He looked to the trees. In town, there would be motorcars and horns and the clatter of horses and the squabbling of trade, all simmering around him until his head was boiling. He had tried to articulate the sensation to Fa, but the answer was always the same: he had to learn.

The van spluttered into life. When Doctor Chalice purchased the property, long before Freddie was born, he was struck, he said, by the aloof beauty of the breckland, with its mounds of bristling heather and spires of blue viper's bugloss. He put that in the brochure, a romantic quotation beside his serene portrait. A guest could take to the tennis courts and see almost all the way to Thetford, or walk through Choke Wood and emerge into the brecks where Freddie spent his boyhood searching for dinosaur bones in the sandy furrows. Guests came from smoky cities which teemed with motorcars; some had never encountered such peace. Freddie always wondered, why would anyone make the mistake of leaving?

When they came to the gates, Fa clambered out to open the latch, shooing away a pair of perching rooks. The gates of

Edenwell were another of Chalice's flourishes, a boundless ocean of winding iron. Freddie was too young to have ever seen the old gates before the rusted remnants were tossed away in Choke Wood, down in the well that swallowed everything offered to it with black indifference. The original gatehouse was long gone, but if Freddie were to believe the more ancient guests, it was a grim ecclesiastical thing, a relic of Edenwell's days as a site of pilgrimage. Better off demolished. "Monks are mawkish," Chalice said. "They had to go." Nowadays, instead of holy grace, a drink from the Edenwell springs brought clearer skin, stronger lungs and renewed husbandly potency. Respectable science, recommended by *Good Housekeeping*.

Freddie was jolted out of his reverie by Fa opening the passenger door. He nodded at the driver's seat. "Off you go, then."

Freddie's stomach rolled. "We could've had a horse."

"Who'd feed the horse?"

"You feed this."

Besides, you couldn't talk to a van the way you could to a horse. Couldn't get to know each other. Freddie wanted a giant plodding shire horse with feathered feet, but Doctor Chalice gave them a gleaming 1914 Albion van with the hotel's name emblazoned on the side, and Fa expected him to drive the thing.

Fa's grim old face was so hopeful, Freddie couldn't bring himself to refuse. He climbed over the gearstick and settled into the driver's seat, feeling the shape of his father's bony backside under him, stamped into the leather.

"There's a lad. Foot on the accelerator, gentle as a lamb. Ease up the clutch."

The van stalled immediately. Fa waited for him to try again. Key, clutch, gear, pedal, gentle as a lamb, *KRUMPH*. Freddie could feel his face turn red. On the third try, the van heard his prayers and sailed down the driveway. Automobile accidents were the worst, he reminded himself, second only to steam engines. When a train's boiler blew up in Cardiff, bodies were found strewn five hundred yards away. He traced the picture from the newspaper at the time, a spray of monstrous metal ribbons. The wrecked locomotive resembled the twisted winter hazels down in the woods.

In the rear mirror, he saw Fa watching him.

"Are you reet?" Fa said.

"You angry with me?"

"You're doing well. We'll park her up behind the munitions factory. When we've bought the traps, what say we have a pie from Henby's while we're waiting for the knife boy?"

There were no pies to be had, Missus Hardy said so. No pies anywhere. Still, eating together, even sharing an apple, sealed up inside the car down a quiet street… If Freddie could focus on that, he might ignore the spindles of electricity turning at the base of his spine. It might almost be possible to touch the other side, the creaky haven of his bed and books and pencils.

He was almost feeling better when a bird rocketed across their path. Freddie hit the brake so hard he and Fa were slammed back into their seats.

"Heart alive!" Fa cried. "What's the matter with you?"

Freddie swung out of the door, leaving Fa to pull up the handbrake. He looked up, spinning on his heel. A jackdaw, small for his age and uniquely half white, clattering joyfully across the sky and back towards the Hydropathic.

Freddie put his fingers to his lips and whistled.

"Drummerboy!"

White feathers sharp as lightning. His heart kicked against his ribs.

"Oi," said Fa. "Where you going?"

"He's back," Freddie cried. "It was him."

He heard Fa shout as he raced back towards Edenwell. "You see to them leaves in the fountain. Don't doss about." Then an afterthought, ringing out across the lawn: "I am not best pleased."

There was a chunk of potato peel bread in the larder, half of which was his by right. Who knew how Drummerboy had changed this past month? Perhaps he'd lost his taste for potato bread, found someone offering something finer. As a rumpled chick, Drummerboy had yelled for food. Freddie would smear fish paste on his finger and allow him to clamp down, squackering with happiness. Freddie wished he had a tin of the cream crackers the little jackdaw couldn't resist. He'd borrow the best hospital china to serve them on if it would tempt him home. And a napkin.

Freddie rushed to his room and threw open the window. All five of his hanging thermometers clattered like icicles against the casement. He hadn't seen the floor in years, cushioned by a layer of books and newspapers, and the pictures pasted to the walls shivered in the breeze. The ceiling was dark with silhouettes of rooks and crows, copied from life. Fa disapproved. A gypsy once told him if you looked up and saw through a hole in a passing bird's wing, you were born to hang.

24

Freddie sprinkled crumbs on the windowsill, trying not to dwell on the sad sight of Drummerboy's empty bed, an upturned cap trimmed with twigs of the bird's own choosing and a few fallen feathers. His food bowl was an ashtray purloined from somewhere – Freddie forgot. He snatched up Drummerboy's favourite toys from the floor and arranged them by the window to tempt him in. A spool of thread, good for rolling. A disc of mirrored glass for inspecting his handsome face.

It was a funny way for a young man to carry on, Fa always said. Before the war, when he and Fa still went to Saint Peter's church out in Thetford, Freddie listened with dread as the vicar spoke of casting off childish things. If Freddie were to cast off everything people wanted him to, there would be nothing left but bones. No Drummerboy, no paintboxes, no Martha Talbot picture books. Freddie knew every dog-eared page by heart. *The Heroics of Harold Hedgehog. Moon Over Toadstool Hill.* Those little books taught him to read and taught him to draw. Give a bird a crust, said Miss Talbot, and he'll fill your dreary life with magic. Why cast that away?

Come back, he willed the empty sky. Since Drummerboy disappeared, Freddie dreamt that he himself had died, his spirit hanging over the hospital. Whirling below him, the rooks and the crows left offerings to tempt their lost human back to the brecks. A bar of Fry's chocolate. Charcoals. Laundered socks.

But Drummerboy was not dead.

He went outside, watching the sky through his visible breath. He clicked his tongue, tossed chunks of bread, called the bird's name. But the thin clouds were the only things watching over him. Drummerboy, if it had been him, was nowhere to be seen.

25

Freddie took the last handful of potato bread and headed for the trees. The guests were still breakfasting, emptied out by the previous day's purging and massaging. No one would see him.

Freddie was privy to things not mentioned in the Edenwell brochure. Chiefly, he knew the four-tiered fountain on the front lawn was not the original holy well, as much as Chalice was happy to allow guests to believe it. The fountain, like the Gothic bandstand and the stone folly on the lawn, was a flourish of the Morton family's wealth. The true well did exist, but down an uneasy path, an incline of pines where no guest in their slippers would think of venturing. As a boy, Freddie had been free to play in the gullies of Choke Wood, spoiling his trousers in the loamy dirt. Lead soldiers, a stick for a hobby horse and a bulrush for a lance. A boy didn't need companions when he had such toys. Some of those soldiers were probably still waiting for him down there, reaching out from the bracken for their lost commander. But the well lay beyond, in the centre of things. It was never a place for playing.

He headed down through the frost-tipped bracken. Freddie always marvelled at how his cottage vanished when he stepped into the wood. Edenwell loomed – it could do nothing but loom – but his own little home could wink out of existence as quick as a sneeze. It was oddly comforting.

A few rooks clustered in the canopy, their bristly faces turned to Freddie as if he had intruded on a private conversation. As Freddie edged carefully down a rain channel, he spied one cracking a snail on a fallen log. A short black beak and strong talons made easy work of the shell. Somewhere, a pheasant shrieked for a mate.

The fountain on the lawn was a blousy affair of whorls

and trimmings, but the real holy well was far more beautiful to Freddie. The first one saw of it was a mossy stone easily mistaken for an oak split by a gale. It had once been a column, one of four, framing the circular pool. Freddie fancied there had originally been a golden cloth draped over the water, turning each ripple into a display of molten metal. Now leaves and algae made soup of the water, and the steps pilgrims had trodden for centuries were reduced to a shapeless slope of flint and mortar.

At the back of the well was an altar of sorts with an alcove where Fa said a Popish statue had once presided over the water. The nuggets of pork rind Freddie had laid out inside the alcove a week ago were gone, as he expected. The rooks knew what it meant to find Freddie down here, and they gathered above him, greeting and jeering.

"Have any of you seen Drummerboy?" he called out.

What's it worth to a knave?

"Traps are coming. But not for you." With chalk from his pocket, he sketched a jackdaw's stubby head on the altar. "My friend. If you see him—"

His audience snickered. A crack of twigs at the top of the gulley. Freddie stiffened, but it was nothing more than a hefty partridge grubbing about. He thought about the pork rind, how hungry he was. He should have brought his rifle.

"We're finding dead pigeons every day now," he said. "And hedgehogs, and squirrels. It's not eating them. And it's very nice for you, because it's easy meat, but it could be a wild cat, and they in't fussy."

The rooks laughed, and he reluctantly joined in. Nothing worried them. What was their trick?

27

He tore the bread into pieces and laid it out in a ring around the drawing of Drummerboy. As he withdrew to the edge of the well, the rooks swept down to claim the scraps. Feathers flashed blue in the morning light.

Watching them feast, Freddie dreamt of omelettes swimming in butter. Of plates of ham and cheese. He could open his ledgers at any page and see dashed-off drawings of pre-war teas with Fa, of toffees sucked in the street, Christmas dances at the Hydropathic with plates of sugared almonds. There was nothing in the shops these days, just women talking, women working, women where men once were. The town crier was a girl now, and Freddie had listened out for her shrill '*Oh yea!*' with uneasy fascination. Sixteen-year-old Florrie Clark with her long hair in ribbons, pasting up recruitment posters. *Men of Thetford, you are urgently wanted.*

His hands were covered in black potato rind and chalk, and he squatted by the water. He dipped his hands in up to the wrists, as pilgrims had for hundreds of years. The cold tremored in his pulse, clearing his mind of everything but how lonely he would be without the little jackdaw to come home to.

What more could he give?

The boyish figure of Lottie Mulgrave pushed through the dining room doors and out onto the veranda. She was rounding up the second chorus of 'A Little of What You Fancy Does You Good', her breath a white plume to match her Turkish cigarette. Lottie was Edenwell's resident celebrity, known better as Colonel Crumb of the vaudeville circuit. The laughing Irishwoman's morning performances had come to be part of the

Edenwell experience. At the fountain, scooping leaves, Freddie could hear the late breakfasters call for the Colonel's more ribald numbers. Lottie, her yellow braids bright against her paisley dressing gown, hailed Freddie with a salute of her fag.

"Morning! He'yer fa'got a dickey, bor? Come now, you know how it goes: 'Yis, an' he'll want a fool ter ride 'im, yew comin'?' We must work on your repartee, kid."

Lottie tipped her head, hearing something above. A second-floor window was thrown up, revealing half of Doctor Chalice, clapping with his usual happy sincerity.

"You're in fine voice, Miss Mulgrave," he called down. "I trust that's Edenwell water in that tumbler you have there?"

"Frightfully soothing, thank you, Doctor. Though one has to temper the taste with a little something stronger, I find."

"And you, Freddie-Fella. Caught any carp?"

Freddie shrank in the light of attention, but managed a grin. The skin of ice clinging to the fountain's rim took several hard thwacks to break.

"Come up here a minute," Chalice said.

Freddie held the net aloft. Busy.

"That's a shame. There's a small stipend in it for you."

Freddie didn't know what a stipend of any size was, but when Chalice mimed the opening of a book and the flourish of a pencil, he put down the net.

Matthew Chalice was handsome in the way any sixty-something man could be, given a sensitive barber. But his smile transformed him. One quirk of his sandy eyebrows made everyone he met feel included in an exclusive, clever joke. His accent had mellowed in the years spent in Norfolk, but there was still a trace of the Midwest in it, enough to make even the sternest

29

spinster turn buttery as she signed her name in the guest book.

Freddie enjoyed any moment spent in Doctor Chalice's company, but to be invited inside his princely den was a special treat. He could sketch it all from memory; the model cars, the crystal bowl of carnival-coloured candy shining on the wide, dark desk. Along the mantelpiece, a row of beer bottles paid homage to the Chalice family brewing empire, the fountain of his wealth. But it was the pictures Freddie liked, modern American cities with buildings so tall they could scratch the clouds and leave a scar. Framed photographs of film actresses, reed-waisted and dreamy. Freddie had never seen a film. When Freddie was small, Chalice permitted him to copy the pictures sometimes, crunching butterscotch while Chalice caught up on paperwork by the fire. Freddie was a man now, but that juvenile wonder came roaring back the moment his eyes fell upon on the gleaming telescope.

"My latest acquisition." Chalice grinned, patting the tripod.

All that glossy bronze. Freddie saw his face in it, the longing shape of his mouth.

"Want to see something remarkable?" Chalice coaxed him to the eyepiece and showed him where to point it.

At first all he saw was sky, the same empty space he'd watched for hours saying prayers for Drummerboy. Then, dancing on the horizon like a kite: an aeroplane. Forest green, with a red tail and target circles on the wing. It seemed to be flying for the joy of it, turning like a swallow.

Then he saw the guns.

"It's got teeth."

"Big ones. Lewis gun. You'd know about it if she bit you."

"What's it doing here?"

"There's an aerodrome out in Snarehill now, and Lakenheath. And what about you? Where's father Ferry this morning?"

"Town."

"Couldn't convince you to accompany him, I take it?"

Freddie said nothing. The aeroplane turned a slow arc as Chalice gently took Freddie's wrist, watching the clock over the fireplace.

Freddie took the focus off the aeroplane to scan the woods for Drummerboy. Beyond his cottage, Choke Wood was almost naked after the worst of winter, blotched with nests. In the tallest trees, the rooks gathered. A ripple went through the mass of black; they knew he was watching them. They no doubt wished they had a telescope of their own. Think of what a rook could do if he could see into every guest bedroom, spy every indiscretion and petty human embarrassment.

"You're not feeding them, I hope." Chalice released his wrist, satisfied with whatever data he had gathered. "Defence of the Realm Act, fella. You could be prosecuted."

"Why did you need to see me, sir?"

"I have business in Thetford. I need to pay an old colleague a visit, but then, more pleasingly, I have an order to pick up from the stationers. I could use the help. Paper is heavy. Of course, you wouldn't go home empty-handed, if you'd oblige me."

It was the one carrot guaranteed to tempt him. Freddie had only the most basic of schooling, so Chalice had taken his education into his own hands, providing composition books, pencils and instructional works of literature for Freddie to take to his little room in the groundskeeper's cottage and absorb. Freddie imagined it gave Chalice a pleasant, charitable feeling to think of him hunched by a candle long after bedtime,

31

attempting sums and letters with the materials he provided. Chalice might be less pleased to learn how Freddie filled those ledgers, or what happened to the books with pictures in them. He could feel the doctor's inquisitive gaze sometimes, cast down from his office where he sat up in the evenings, nursing a brandy while Freddie scribbled and daubed.

"Finished it," Freddie would say, a touch awkwardly, each time he visited Chalice to ask for a fresh ledger. Then, one day, sudden and unbidden as most of Freddie's communications were: "Colours. Are colours summat you can buy?"

Chalice was pleased to oblige. But what were Freddie's plans? Botanical sketches, perhaps? A budding naturalist? Colours? Certainly! All the colours of the imagination. But could Chalice see inside that ledger he was clutching? Could he take a peek? Freddie spooked easily. The thought of showing his drawings to anyone besides Drummerboy made his guts clench. Chalice didn't push the matter. That Christmas, a box of watercolours from Walker's Stationers, nicely wrapped. Nothing so extravagant as to embarrass the senior Mister Ferry, of course. He was perfectly content with a bottle of brown ale.

"Fa couldn't spare me, sir. He'll want help with the traps. He thinks it could be a wild cat." Freddie tugged on his lip, thinking about it. "Maybe a distempered dog."

"Fella…" Chalice gently took the telescope and replaced the lens cap. "If you don't get over it now, you never will."

> WHO *made these little islands the centre of the greatest and most powerful empire the world has ever seen? Our forefathers.*

WHO *ruled this Empire with such wisdom and sympathy that every part of it – of whatever race and origin – has rallied to it in our hour of need? Our forefathers.*

WHO *will stand up to preserve this great and glorious heritage? We will.* ENLIST TODAY.

Fa liked the poster outside the Tribunal, Freddie recalled. No pictures, no silliness. Plain talking.

When Freddie emerged from the Guildhall with a piece of paper in both hands, he watched as the lines of tension on Fa's face melted away. His father made a show of studying the poster, but Freddie had his exemption. It was safe to like things again.

"They measured me. Listened to my chest." Murmur, they called it. As if his heart were a dull child who needed to speak up. "Category E. Grade 4. One of them said maybe send me off as a cook. But the others were adamant."

They didn't embrace.

"Well, they know best," Fa said. "I reckon we can stretch to a quick half in the Red Lion before heading home."

Freddie didn't recognise the old woman watching them. She had stopped by the steps to open her umbrella, but he could feel her picking apart their conversation. He touched Fa's arm, silently agreed to a drink so that they could walk away from the crowded marketplace, but the woman took her opportunity.

"All smiles, are we?"

Fa pivoted. "Beg pardon?"

"Ought to be ashamed, parading about like that. A big lad like him. Shirker."

33

They could have walked away. Turning it over in his mind a thousand times since, Freddie could list as many methods of leading his father away. But her words lit a taper Freddie hadn't seen before or since.

"Shirker?"

"Fa—"

"Don't you turn away from me. *Shirker?* His mother died before his eyes were open. He nearly went with her, his heart was so weak, so keep your opinions to yourself, if you don't mind, madam. You join up if you're so keen."

He was shouting by the end. How people stared. Market grocers, bicycle repairmen, housekeepers with baskets on their arms. People who knew them. And it didn't take a tribunal panel to understand the looks on their faces, and where their sympathy lay when the woman stepped back, her lip flapping in distress. Freddie wanted to turn heel back to the Guildhall and beg them to give him any old uniform, any old post.

"Bitch."

It was the first and last time he heard such language from Fa. But it was that other word, spat out like gristle, that ran through Freddie's head at night and made his forehead prickle. He couldn't look into his shaving mirror. In his own eyes he saw those of the old woman, narrowed, disgusted; the eyes of the friends she surely told; the eyes of everyone who heard the tale, feeding it and breeding it until everyone in Norfolk knew there was a shirker in their midst.

Habit turned him to the comforting books of his boyhood, but even Martha Talbot had turned against him.

A coward isn't always plain to see. Like a chameleon, he changes his colours on a whim. Like a fox, he goes to ground. Like a cheetah, he

34

*will dash away in the blink of an eye. But unlike all these animals –
all God's dazzling furred and feathered creations – a coward comes
in but one form, and that is Man.*

Freddie tore out the page and with a pencil committed
his own form to it: a dishevelled dawdler, all legs and elbows,
frowning in ill-fitting clothes. He took it down to Choke Wood
and drowned it in the well.

Doctor Chalice brought him round with a pat on the back.
"Give me a couple of hours to prepare my things. I'll drive. Now
go and scoop those leaves. It's a good day, fella. We're taking off."

He scooped the leaves. He fed the chickens. He pulled the
milk thistles from the parsnip patch where Mister Tungate's
gardening hat hung mouldering on the hook. The gardener
left it there two full years ago, and now it had cultivated flora
of its own. Freddie stretched, looked back at the strip of sky
over the Hydropathic. Empty. He'd tossed his breakfast to the
birds, and now he was empty too.

With the guests' morning victuals over and the luncheon
broth simmering, Freddie could try his luck for leftovers down
in the kitchens. When he reached the bottom of the twisting
stone stairs, Missus Hardy was rolling out pastry perilously close
to Nick Scole's wooden leg, shiny and strangely massive on the
table. It made Freddie queasy that it wore a real shoe. Scole had
his trouser leg rolled up and was rubbing ointment into his stump,
and when Freddie noticed an unfamiliar girl skulking by the
pantry door he knew why. Squat little bruiser, with a long-skirted
Edenwell uniform and a mouth like a scar. She watched the
orderly, arms folded, as if to say he couldn't scare her.

"A lot of the lads likened it to Hell, but I've never seen Hell and I'm not one to draw false comparisons." Scole took a gobbet of ointment and warmed it in his palms. Freddie could see the pink tideline where a flap of skin had been folded over under the knee, packaging it up like a jam roly poly. "Still. I have seen France. And I'd forgive any fellow unable to tell it apart from the Book of Revelation."

Missus Hardy shielded her flour from Scole's bristled thigh. "Do you mind?"

The new girl spoke up. "I spent eleven months filling shells."

Scole didn't look at her. "I 'spect you stopped once your pretty hair started coming out, didn't you?"

The girl's cheeks coloured, and not charmingly. "My mum made me give it up." She rolled up her sleeve. Freddie was surprised to see a cross on her burly forearm, mortuary black, with a name underneath. *Thomas.*

Nick Scole saw. His face was unreadable, but he made an approving noise. So long, Thomas.

Missus Hardy paused rolling pastry to wipe her brow on her sleeve. "You sneaked in, Freddie. This is Tabitha Clarke. She'll be taking some of the strain for Annie and Maud in the guests' rooms and helping me down here from time to time."

Scole screwed the lid back on the grease and began the laborious task of reattaching his leg. Leather and laces and creaking callipers. It reminded Freddie of a suit of armour, only there was no flesh for it to cover and protect.

Will a knave ask where he left it? We are peckish boys and girls.

Scole's hands were too greasy to tighten his straps. "Freddie never served, Miss Clarke. The Home Office wouldn't let him go – thought they'd give the Boche a sporting chance."

36

"Lay off, Nick," Missus Hardy said. "There's a bun there for you, Freddie, you can share it with your father. I'm making stock from the ham, so keep your mitts off."

Freddie tugged at his lip and mumbled his thanks. Tabitha stared.

"How'd y'do?" she said tonelessly.

Good morning. That's what Fa would want him to say. The bun wouldn't quite fit into his pocket. "Don't go into the woods."

Nick Scole barked with surprise. "You what?"

"We're laying traps," he blurted. Everyone's eyes were on him. His face started to burn, so he focused on the bone bucket on the floor, a heap of used-up whiteish rock. "We think it's a dog. It could be foaming at the mouth and you shouldn't go wandering."

Missus Hardy was less inclined to amusement. She beat the flour from her hands. "Well, that's a fine welcome for Tabitha, isn't it?"

The new girl glanced at Scole, who was snickering still. Her hard mouth twisted, but then she was looking past them all, up at the window close to the ceiling where a dainty hand tapped on the panes.

Tabitha drew back in disbelief. A little princess in a blue gown bent down and waved.

Scole saw it. "Bugger off!" he yelled. He went to get up, forgetting his leg, and irritably hurried to reattach it. "You been feeding him again, Missus Hardy?"

The princess drew back, the tiny hand frozen mid-wave. Her sweet porcelain face was replaced by a flappy-soled boot, then a bent knee, followed by a dusky beard pressed to the window. Wearing a look of bovine confusion, the weathered complexion couldn't be more different to the sweet marionette's. Poor old

Mister Jenks, a creature of such grime and grit Freddie could have believed he had been born straight out of the earth if it weren't for his pristine puppets. People said he made them with his own crooked hands.

Scole bellowed up at the window. "I know you can hear me, you old goat. Clear off! I'll 'ave you."

"He only wants a cup of tea," said Missus Hardy.

"You bring him in here, we'll all be itching. You can make me a cup of tea, if you're desperate for something to do."

Tabitha was trying to get a better look at the princess. "Who is that?"

"The real reason you shouldn't go into the woods," said Scole.

It was as good a moment to flee as any. Freddie ignored their laughter as he slipped up the stairs.

When the war began, men queued to volunteer. They queued to have their measurements taken. They queued for khaki tunics.

If they were lucky lieutenants, their mothers went to department stores and bought them brown belts and swagger sticks. They had their pictures taken for the parlour wall. Freddie was not a lieutenant, nor a ten-a-penny Tommy Atkins, and he had no mother to frame his picture, so before the awful day of the tribunal he made do by standing in front of the mirror, posing with his chest puffed out and Drummerboy on his shoulder. Captain Ferry, Bane of The Kaiser.

But the Kaiser didn't hold his attention for long. As the months went by, Freddie was half convinced France was a place they'd concocted to hide where all the men were really going. Letters came, but they weren't written by anyone Freddie recognised. Postcards with pre-prepared statements, scribbled over in pencil where applicable. *I am well and happy [...] and am going on well [...] I have received your package [...] signature only on this line.*

Now he and Doctor Chalice drove past Dales, the butchers. Poultry hung in the window, three birds where twenty once dangled temptingly. Harold, the butcher's apprentice, was keen to go. People supposed he was, anyway, but Freddie thought his face said one thing and his mouth another. Harold and his nimble fingers joined the Navy. What went on at sea, Freddie didn't know, but he and everyone else prayed for Harold at midday chimes. Freddie could hardly recall the shape of Harold's face, let alone the boundaries of the ocean. Perhaps they were down a great black hole somewhere, a slave encampment, building pyramids all day. Freddie drew pyramids sometimes, great tricky tombs for him to hide in, his body safe beneath the deep cool stone.

He'd tried to draw Harold as he remembered him, doling out chops at the counter. A year later and he needed the paper, so now the butcher's boy dawdled alongside Saint George piercing the dragon, a page boy proffering a plate of serpent's meat.

Freddie remembered Thetford on market day as practically shoulder-to-shoulder – horrid thought – but Doctor Chalice had conjured up a fine rain to stop people milling about. Chalked outside Mitchell's Grocers: SOLD OUT BUTTER. All Freddie could think of then was buttered toast, buttered muffins, butter melting in his mouth like sunshine.

Chalice smoked as he drove, drumming a tune on the wheel. As they passed the meadows where the abbey ruins stood tall, he sighed with pleasure.

"I will never become accustomed to that sight. Living alongside the Middle Ages. When I come here, I feel like a noble knight."

A knight and his squire, riding out. Yes, Freddie liked that. Knights never ran out of butter.

"Doctor Ridley's office is near Burrell's factory," Chalice said. "I need to pay him a visit."

"Is the new girl from Burrell's?"

"You met Miss Clarke? Yes, a munitionette. Why? You like her?" Chalice made a naughty face.

"She made... bombs?"

"Big poisonous things, spoiled her skin. She was like a canary when I found her."

Chalice slowed, allowing a pair of women to trot across the road. Their skirts dark with rain.

"Do you remember what you said a few Christmases ago, about breeding birds for the guests?" Freddie ventured. "I was thinking, the old folly. We can sort out the draughts and make it nice. When we open up the North Wing again, we can bring in some pairs of canaries, and I can keep them happy."

"I suppose that leaves Ferry Senior to deal with the wild cats, doesn't it?"

Freddie stole a glance at Chalice, feeling he ought to elaborate, prove he wasn't making frivolous demands. "One of the lady guests said she wanted something to dote on. The lady with the stammer, you remember. I think it could have helped her, to have a friend."

Chalice looked ahead, a small smile on his handsome face. He breathed a long stream of smoke until Freddie couldn't see the American's eyes. "It'll all be different soon."

"Soon?"

"I believe it."

As the town swelled around them, the streets narrowing, Freddie could feel his heart protesting. "I'd like to look in Walker's."

"On a fine day like this? Only if you promise to take this and spend it on something frivolous."

Chalice tossed him a coin and dropped him off at the shop to save him getting wet. There was a new sandwich board outside the door:

The boys are doing splendidly in Egypt, Mesopotamia, France. Another Bahamas contingent will be sailing soon. Roll up, men! Make it the best. GOD SAVE THE KING!

Pyramids, Freddie quietened himself. *Deep in a black safe tomb.*

Much like a pyramid, Walker's was a gloomy cavern, one of the primary reasons Freddie liked the place. The windows were stuffed with prints and books, washed out by years of lacklustre Norfolk sunlight. There were two customers already inside: a woman buying baccy and a small boy waiting for an opportunity to pocket a bar of Fry's from the display on the counter. Pillowy Missus Walker was in charge these days. She had a bad hip, and it was an agony watching her laboriously fetch things for the more impatient customers, but Freddie felt comfortable around her. Mainly because she couldn't appear suddenly by his side, asking if he needed assistance. In addition to shelves of papers and sweets, her absent husband had amassed a wonderful collection of oddments. Freddie could happily root through the shelves and boxes for hours and never run out of artefacts to unearth. Postcards and watercolour tins and fat sticks of chalk. Penny mysteries and second-hand toys. Not everything good had passed away.

Towards the back of the shop, behind a stack of shelves, was a travellers' chest of disintegrated books. He spotted Martha Talbot and her forest creatures straight away, like old friends. The works of Dickens and Stevenson muddled alongside *Moon Over Toadstool Hill* and elephantine Bibles. He was drawn to a bundle of precious colour illustrations, loose pages of turtles and bobcats and fabulous birds. A vivid macaw caught his eye, flamboyant and grinning. Take a rook and wash him in a jungle waterfall and the dye of his feathers will wash away like so much soot, he thought. How to put that on paper? Indian ink? A few drops of water? And underneath, the fabulous macaw, laughing at his own magic.

The bell above the door tinkled. A woman and a man entered the shop. They were arguing in a friendly manner – chaffy talk, Fa would say resentfully. Young townies who wanted everyone to hear how clever they were. The woman wished Missus Walker a good morning, laughter in her voice.

"If only someone had told you to bring a scarf," she remarked to her companion. "If only someone – say myself – had informed you it's February."

"Look, I'm so used to filtering all the useless information you come out with…"

Behind the stacks, Freddie listened. The woman was young and petite, with a birdy jauntiness to her voice, but he couldn't fix the man. Mostly, he wanted to know if they were coming his way so he could pay for his macaw and go. Peeping out, Freddie could see the woman's red pigtails and a little of the man's back as they lingered around the newspaper racks. He was much taller than his companion, made more so by a long overcoat, but the lanky, insouciant way he moved told Freddie he was a lad of his own age or thereabouts. That was an unusual sight. A soldier on leave, perhaps, or a useless person like himself. Nothing appeared to be wrong with him, apart from refusing to take off his hat. Freddie watched the stranger's narrow back as he paid a ha'penny for the *Daily Mirror*.

"Lieutenant-Colonel Broadstair," the young man read aloud as the woman chose from a stack of postcards. "Yorkshire Light Infantry, brother of the Mayor of Sheffield, was killed in action last week at... I can't pronounce it. Malines?"

The woman dubiously compared two postcards of Marie Lloyd and her

toothsome smile. "Malines like marine, not malign."

"Turned out to be pretty malign for him."

"Would Mother like a local interest postcard, do you think, or something flowery?"

"There's an excellent picture of him. The Lieutenant-Colonel. Will you look?"

"We didn't know him."

"Look. I think he looks very fine."

"Jodhpurs make men look silly."

"Heaven forbid a man looks silly as he's slain by the Hun."

"Eustace."

Behind the counter, Missus Walker busied herself with a duster. Her husband was with the Royal Artillery and the words were hurtful. The boy – Eustace – ruffled the paper, turning to a depiction of a U-boat gliding like a shark underneath a supply ship. A black nest of hair peeked out from his cap. Freddie could still only see a slice of his profile through the shelves. He wondered how he would go about drawing him. The darkness of his complexion wasn't at all like a farm boy's tan. Taken with the strong, fine shape of his nose and brow, it said something different. Highborn. With his head tilted slightly to one side Freddie could picture him as a thief in a palace. No – a reedy prince, barefoot on Moroccan tiles, hand on his dagger, waiting for the thief to reveal himself.

He could sense Freddie looking at him.

Freddie crept to the right. Through a stack of parlour music, saw the Lieutenant-Colonel the boy was talking about on the newsstand. Broadstair was a bad name for a hero. Freddie would have named him Dash, or Hercules. It amazed Freddie to realise he wanted to tell the boy this. He could actually envision himself mumbling it to him as he walked by and left the shop. To speak his name. Eustace.

The impulse made his stomach feel strange, and he backed away to the safety of the animal prints.

The woman audibly sighed. "I'm not sure she'd like any of these."

"Phoebe, just pick one. She won't care."

"Are there any booksellers nearby? We could tell her we've seen her books for sale. That would be nice."

"Say it anyway. It will be true, and it'll save us the walk."

"Why must—" There was a terse pause. She took a postcard to the counter. "I'll take this one, please. I like a spot of medievalism."

"That's the old holy well," said Missus Walker. "Up at the Hydropathic, over the brecks."

"It's quite romantic. Does much remain of the original site after the Reformation?"

44

She said it as if Henry VIII had only recently decided to ransack the monasteries, as if the people of Norfolk were still tutting about it in their parlours.

"Oh, no," said Missus Walker. "No, I don't imagine it do. I remember my grandmother telling us not to go playing out there. Old wives' tales."

"We're actually heading there, to the Hydropathic. I suppose you can find out all about it, can't you, Eustace?"

Freddie's nails scored his palm.

Eustace was as interested as Freddie expected. He glowered at a poster of laughing soldiers over the till. *Somewhere the boys are drinking Baker's cocoa. Delicious dreams of home!*

Missus Walker counted Phoebe's change. "They say there's nothing better for a young lady than Edenwell water."

"Oh, it's not for me. No, my brother needs treatment, so we've driven up from Portsmouth. I was terribly impressed by the brochures, with the American doctor and the beautiful house, and…" Phoebe was running out of compliments, and ended rather feebly: "We find Norfolk charming."

Did Eustace snort, or did Freddie imagine it? He saw Missus Walker give a weak smile. "Well, that's very cheering to hear."

The small boy eyeing the chocolate still loitered in the background, listening to all this with a leaden expression. Eustace looked at him, then at the Fry's display on the counter. Freddie watched with tingling fascination as the lanky youth very slowly shifted to the left as if something uncomfortable was in his shoe. He caught the boy's eye and gestured with a tilt of his chin. *Over there, by the papers.* The boy went without question. As Phoebe and Missus Walker concluded their business, Eustace's long fingers flicked out, quick as a snake's tongue, so swift that Freddie could almost convince himself he had not seen the bar of Fry's vanish up his sleeve.

Eustace ran the same hand laconically through the tangle of black hair at the base of his neck. "I could demolish a cup of tea, Phoebe."

"There's Henderson's just a few doors down," said Missus Walker.

"Perfect. Oh, and why not?" Eustace took another bar of chocolate from the display. "And one for you, Phoebe?"

"We aren't made of money."

Eustace smacked the chocolate down on the counter and paid for it. As he held the door open for his sister, Freddie kept an eye on the other hand, the serpentine sleight of it, but saw nothing. Only the small boy, the dumb amazement on his face and a shape in his pocket where there was none before.

Then they were gone, bickering still. The slam of the door toppled a bottle of vegetable tonic from the window shelf. Green shards and brown liquid sprayed across the floor.

With quiet exasperation, Missus Walker shuffled with difficulty in the direction of her dustpan and brush.

Freddie emerged. "Let me."

On his knees, he held the green glass in his palm, transfixed by the glistening tonic in the drizzly light. Queer feeling. He turned the glass between his fingers and felt the rasp of the edge threaten his skin.

"Good of you, dear," said Missus Walker. "Take a paper."

TWO

'Malign'. Collage, mixed media on
cardstock. 24×16. C. February 1917.

One of the earliest examples of Ferry's adoption of collage.
Newspaper photograph found to be one Lieutenant-Colonel
Broadstair. To his flawless dress uniform, Ferry has added
fantastical elements – an aviator's scarf taken by the wind,
black hair in wild disarray. A Romantic vision. Slivers of silver
foil – sweet wrappers, precious treasure in a time of sugar
scarcity – protrude from every fold of his uniform. The man
is blasting open.

PHOEBE MONCRIEFF WAS an alarming sight at the
wheel of a car, not on account of her sex, but because
despite pushing twenty-six, her face and figure had barely
aged past fourteen. Eustace resented his sister's insistence on
wearing her red hair in two plaited pigtails; when they were
out together – she in one of her peppermint-pink shirt dresses
and he lanky and sullen in his overcoat – Eustace felt like a

stork being shepherded by a child. But Phoebe was confident in charge of a vehicle, and on the winding rural roads she was happy to go at a good clip while giving her usual running commentary on the scenery, so different to that of Portsmouth with its ramparts and gliding sails. Eustace disliked the air. Somehow less tangible without the presence of the sea.

"It's like a holiday, really," Phoebe remarked.

"Hm."

In the passenger seat, Eustace was making a square of chocolate last as long as possible. With the first threats of rationing, he had taken to fretting over sweets, hoarding them, sniffing the empty wrappers when no one could see. Phoebe stole a look at him, dabbing at crumbs with the tip of his tongue. His cap was in his lap, confronting his sister with the mess he had made of his hair. A clump here, a lock there, chopped with scissors, kitchen knives, tugged out by the roots. He had beautiful black hair, his mother used to say, fluffing and primping it for her guests when he was still small enough to collar. "With a few months of care and rest," she told him as Phoebe herded him into the car, "you'll be tossing the ringlets back from your eyes again." Appearances mattered to Mother.

"Chalice," Eustace mumbled, examining the wrapper. "Sacred chalice. The holy grail."

Phoebe slowed down to pass a horse and cart. He could feel her resisting the urge to baby him – *Look! A lovely horse*. He was a man now, for goodness' sakes, with a man's pressing concerns.

"You don't suppose he's one of the beer baron Chalices, do you?" she said, taking them down a sunken lane lined with stretching pines. "It's a big name in America."

48

"I've never been keen on beer."

"Mother hasn't said much."

"Why would she?"

"Well, she's working, isn't she? And between you and Harry, she has enough to worry about."

It may have been intended as an olive branch, but as always, her quick sharp voice turned it into something thorny.

Harry. Their elder brother's engagement to Marion Bachmann had always been tenuous, but the end of the affair – the circumstances – had sent their mother into a slump. Eustace couldn't see why. Even before the climax of their courtship, Harry complained that Marion was going to *meetings*. She had always been the type to go to meetings, but these were about the war, and there were men at these meetings who talked about conscience and God and all sorts of things Marion would parrot to him afterwards in tones of great reverence. And no, Harry didn't want to talk about it, except he did, constantly, until Eustace perfected his impression: *She thimply ithn't the gahl I thought she wath.* Phoebe had enjoyed that until Eustace's next trick went and spoiled it all. And now Harry was in Étaples chronicling the big camp there, writing articles about the bull ring where husbands and fathers were forged into warriors. It wasn't fair.

Phoebe listened to Eustace worrying his chocolate wrapper. "You could always say something conciliatory."

He shifted his long legs, put one foot on his knee and fiddled with his bootlaces. "Your driving is quite good."

At least her laugh was sincere. "You know I live for your approval."

The grudging crack in his mask seemed to soothe her. As Eustace turned back to his chocolate wrapper, Phoebe gave the wheel a yank. As the car swerved, he gave an unmanly squeak and grabbed the sides of his seat.

"The bloody— the trees! There are trees, Phoebe."

Mischief on her face. "Oh, you are paying attention?"

"I'll get out and walk."

"A five-mile constitutional, very commendable. Norfolk is doing wonders for you already."

He muttered something foul and turned his head to the window. In the glass, he saw Phoebe's smile. She made faces to catch his attention, snapped her fingers as he scrunched himself ever further into the corner. As children she would chase him around the kitchen table with a rolling pin like she was going to turn him into scones. Over now, of course. Though sometimes, in unguarded moments, he could put the recent past aside.

She tweaked the wheel again, and the car jerked across the road. Eustace jolted. "Phoebe!"

And he was almost laughing.

The windscreen shattered in a perfect ripple.

Phoebe stamped on the brake. They lurched in their seats as the tyres made an outraged noise in the scree, and Phoebe rolled the car to the side of the road, allowing brambles to score the paintwork. Only when they were still did she let go of the breath burning in her chest.

Eustace could have made some sardonic comment. Once, the temptation would have been unbearable. Instead, he opened the door and sauntered out to the road's edge, some way behind the car where wild horseradish sprouted in profusion.

"It's quite big, isn't it?" he called back after a moment.

Phoebe placed one shaky foot on the road, but went no further. "Is it an animal?"

Of course it was an animal. Even he would drop the nonchalance if they'd hit a child. The woods around the car stirred in the wind, and Eustace found himself looking about for witnesses. He could imagine men behind the trees, waiting and listening. Things the size of men.

"Eustace, get back in the car." Then: "Are *you* all right?"

"It's a bird."

The jackdaw turned cool much faster than he expected. The stony beak was open – pink strip of tongue, how queer! – nostrils leaking blood into his lap. A drop or two, no more. One white wing. Remarkable creature.

Phoebe drove the rest of the way with great care, craning her neck to see around the epicentre of the shattered windscreen. The Hydropathic was even more stubbornly isolated than the brochure had promised. As a place of asylum it was ideal, but Eustace couldn't imagine working and boarding there, looking out from one's window each morning to relentless nothingness. The Germans could march their way all over England and no one at Edenwell would be any the wiser until the Kaiser signed the guest book and asked for a glass of *das Wasser*.

"Isn't it pretty?" she said, somewhat weakly, as they passed through the iron gates. "Look at the big fountain."

He examined the dead bird and said nothing. He had always been a terrible believer in omens, like Mother. As they cruised down the drive, women in white played on the tennis courts, springing about in the cold like cheery ghosts.

51

There were funny little structures dotted about the lawn; a studded flint tower like a chess piece and a large, walled-off square of red brick – no doubt a kitchen garden. A shabby old cottage nestling up to the woods like something from one of Mother's stories. They curved around the fountain to the front door. Phoebe parked the car. The tennis players paused to look at them.

"Put it down," she said. "Come on."

"Just leave it here?"

"Yes, leave it here. In a bush. Don't *play* with it, Eustace. It'll have fleas."

"Your cat has fleas."

"Bernadette is alive. Put it— Good heavens, hello! You look just like your picture in the brochure. Phoebe Moncrieff. Gosh, it's been a journey."

A fair-haired old gentleman was skipping down the steps to greet them. Matthew Chalice truly did look like his studio portrait, friendly and serene, if a touch more lined around the eyes. When he saw the windscreen, the smile turned to concern.

"Are you all right? Was it a deer?"

"Just a bird. But that was quite enough."

While Phoebe shook hands with the doctor, Eustace hauled his suitcase from the back seat and got busy stuffing the bird inside. The same urge as picking up a penny from a gutter.

"And you'll be the trusted co-pilot." Chalice put his hand on the car roof and bent to smile at Eustace, who was hurriedly rearranging the contents of his luggage. "Mister Moncrieff, I'll send for someone to repair the windscreen. In the meantime, miss, I would be comforted if you would permit me to have a room made up for you. On the house, naturally."

52

"You're very kind, but I'm sure once I trundle back to Thetford, I can take up our old room in the Red Lion. Someone will be able to replace the glass there, I'm sure."

Chalice wouldn't hear of it. "Mister Scole here will park your vehicle in the old stables. Our facilities will be entirely at your disposal. Tell me, have you ever experienced a Turkish bath?"

"Why?" she said. "Is it delightful?"

Chalice gave a surprised laugh as Phoebe took his arm.

An orderly with a jerking gait stepped up to take Eustace's suitcase. With thick black hair combed at a harsh angle over his forehead, Eustace's eyes were drawn to the pockmarked plain of the stranger's cheeks. There were boys like that at school, though their scars were never so deep, like gravel dropped into raw dough.

The orderly caught his roaming eyes and pointedly held them. "If you'll follow me, sir…"

If Eustace were to deploy his imagination, he could pretend he was stepping into the reception of a grand hotel, but the drive had made him irritable and Phoebe's insistence on attaching herself to the American doctor instead of accompanying him inside put paid to any charitable feelings. A marble front desk, probably imitation, awaited like an altar, but the cobwebs threading the ceiling demolished any illusion of luxury. Harry had spoken of brothels in France with similar setups, ostentatious parlours laid out to make a guest feel important in spite of his grubby fingernails. A few of Eustace's fellow prisoners milled about, speaking of massages and the evening menu. Women of a matronly age eyed him as if he were the appetiser. They loitered in plush window seats sipping water from glass tumblers. An intricate lift sailed down to the ground floor, disgorging two elderly gentlemen. Their open curiosity made him stand straighter, look down his nose, eyes front.

Surely this wasn't the best Mother's money could buy?

The pockmarked orderly produced the ledger for registering newcomers. "My name is Mister Scole, sir. If you would oblige me with a few details…"

"Eustace George Moncrieff. Eighteen years of age. Profession none."

He made sure to amplify the last part for the ladies.

"And your nationality, sir?"

Eustace knew well enough what the question meant.

Scole's pen hovered over the page. "It's a matter of security, is why I ask, sir."

"What do you think I am?"

"Sir?"

"I'm adopted. Could I be a Chinaman? I don't think I am, honestly. People tell me I look like a Jew. I think it's supposed to upset me. Why don't you put me down as a Chinaman? Just for sport."

Scole's eyes narrowed. The hint of amusement that had been present a moment ago was gone. "You can be fined for that. In contempt of Defence of the Realm."

Knowing where to stop had always been his problem. Eustace caught the ladies in the window seat sharing a glance. He scuffed his boots against the faux-marble altar and looked over Scole's head at the languid cobwebs. The stairs coiled around the walls, and at their pinnacle was a sort of amateurish *trompe-l'oeil* of a blue sky and clouds fat with the false promise of rain.

The place was a slum. An absolute pig's ear. She'd done it on purpose, of course. All part of the punishment.

54

"Hampshire," he said sullenly. "Regular English Hampshire."

Scole came out from behind the desk and took Eustace's suitcase. "Open stay, Doctor Chalice says." He glanced back where the doctor was busy with Phoebe, demonstrating a tiled drinking fountain neatly operated by a golden button. "You're upstairs. A fair trot from the sun terrace, I'm afraid, but I think you can safely do without, eh? Follow me, sir."

With the two of them locked in the lift cage, there was little to look at but one another. The silver medal on Scole's chest begged for Eustace's attention.

"You served?"

"It didn't fall off by itself, sir."

Of course, his leg. And the mess of his face, all down one side as if Scole had turned away from a blast just in time. Eustace's eyes flicked over the orderly's stocky figure. There was a self-possession he hadn't noticed before, the insouciant air of a brave man.

"I'm waiting to join up," Eustace said, regretting his former attitude. "I ought to get my notice soon. I'm going to be a sniper."

Scole made a noise. Eustace couldn't interpret it, but the lift moved slowly, and he wanted every crumb of information the former soldier would give him.

"My mother has a study at home and she can't abide interruptions, so I've always been good at creeping around. Sometimes I can slow my heart down so much, all my toes go cold and I feel dizzy. But not too dizzy. I have good eyesight. I think they'll want people like me, won't they?"

"'Appen they do, sir."

The lift came to its shunting end and Scole held the gate.

55

Out in the corridor, Eustace found himself hurrying to keep up with the orderly, going *squeak-thump* past potted ferns and Classical portraits of bathing women.

"Do you have stories?"

Scole did not look back. "Apart from the peg leg?"

"It would be an honour to hear about it."

A grimace or a smirk crawled sideways across Scole's face. "Your room, sir. Breakfast is between seven and nine. Luncheon twelve and two. Dinner at eight, and the evening is very much your own, sir. Library, billiards, whatever you please. Doctor Chalice has provided a personal timetable of treatments, which you'll find on your writing desk. Avail yourself of the facilities and the grounds as you see fit, but we ask that you keep to the property and not stray into the woods over to the south. There's been landslides over the winter and we don't recommend the terrain."

Eustace looked around at the airy lightness of his new home, and the corresponding crispness of Scole's uniform.

"Feels a bit peculiar, doesn't it?" he said sheepishly. "You calling me 'sir'."

Scole laid the suitcase on the portmanteau stand. He stopped short of opening it, to Eustace's relief, remembering the jackdaw between layers of pyjamas. Did Mister Scole wear pyjama trousers, he wondered? Did he leave one leg flapping, or did he tie a knot in it? Maybe he kept a packet of Woodbines down there. Eustace admonished himself. Why was he always like this? He was in the presence of a courageous man.

"If you need anything, Mister Moncrieff, you come and seek me out." Scole stood in the doorway, a smile playing on his lips. "I've always had a soft spot for raw recruits."

The trap was a big one, and Freddie disliked it instantly. It opened out with an iron yawn, out in the dirt behind the cottage where no one would see what they were up to. Deep marks scored the earth where they had dragged all forty pounds of it from the van.

"Shield your eyes," Fa said.

He took a small log and dropped it on the centre plate. The trap awoke, sprang shut before Freddie could hear it move. Splinters peppered his trouser legs. He was thrilled and repelled.

"It wouldn't trap a bird, would it?"

"An albatross, maybe. This is for heavy things. And you're a heavy thing, so when we lay these out, I want you to take those spots and drill them so deep into your head, you'll see them in your dreams. What happens if you tread on one of these? I want you to say it."

"Splinters."

"Reet." He reopened the trap, showed Freddie how to set it, where to place his hands. "No dreaming. Dreaming gets you bit. We'll spread 'em out. We don't know his favourite places yet. He's roaming."

He. The cat or the dog or the abnormal fox. It seemed so unceremonious to Freddie. To be going about one's business, set on the single goal of sating one's hunger, to step right into your death.

Fa frowned as though he could hear his son's thoughts. "You can snare him nice and pretty if you like, Fred. We'll be shooting the bugger all the same. You take your rifle whenever you go down there, you hear? You see him, you kill him."

They laid the traps, all three, down in Choke Wood where the creature likely slept. A dead squirrel awaited them at the final site, draped across a fallen branch crusted yellow with winter lichen. Fa took it by the tail and shook it out like a duster. Like the others, the body was strangely jellified, broken inside.

"Wasteful bugger," he muttered.

While Fa searched for tracks through the mush underfoot, Freddie tucked the squirrel under his belt.

"I'll go back to the spring," he called out. "He could be rubbing his hide on the stone."

"Marking his scent, reet. Check for hairs. I'll see you back at home. You mind those traps, you hear?"

Freddie hurried back through the woods. A black mass of rooks and crows congregated over the stones of the holy well, bullying for space where the jackdaws hopped and cackled. He could sense their turbulent mood.

"Did you find Drummerboy?"

His question was met with laughter.

"You see this, don't you?" He held up the squirrel.

A knave can't see. Poor knavely knave.

They acted aloof, but when he took out his knife, they followed the flash of it with corvid hunger. He knew they liked their meat torn.

"I'll make the first cut," Freddie said. "If you tell."

We tell we saw a knave in the chariot with the Chalice. Poor Fa-fa-father's fa-fa-face.

He would go with the doctor and not with his father. Yes, he ought to have been more sensitive. But like all thieves and magicians, the rooks excelled at misdirection.

"Answer me."

58

We see all sorts abroad.

He placed the squirrel on the stone and began the long cut down the belly. They didn't usually bleed this much on skinning. The creature that killed it had crushed the insides, reminding Freddie unpleasantly of late summer strawberries.

"What did you see?"

Murder.

Freddie raised his head. "Murder?"

Snickering from the gallery. The speakers reconsidered their words.

Glorious death.

"Whose death?" Freddie strained his voice above the flapping commotion. "What did you see?"

The rooks kept their counsel. Meat beckoned. They could smell the rank tang of it, and Freddie was wasting time with his trifling questions. The few tuxedoed magpies, rankled by the tiresome company, went their separate clattering ways across the land. As for the jackdaws, their laughter was uncontained. Freddie couldn't make out a single sensible word from their breathless *chacka-chack*ing.

Freddie hadn't the stones to be jeered at. He closed his knife and shouldered his rifle. The rooks descended on the gift of squirrel meat without gratitude.

Dusk had drawn in without warning. As Freddie left the spring, he could see the nearest trap through the fog of his breath and gave it a wide berth. His trudge up the hill was slower than usual, relying on his ears for signs of the creature. He wanted to at least lay eyes on it. He imagined a beast with steaming nostrils rearing out from behind a tree, their eyes fixing each other to the spot. He would whip out his rifle and the creature would throw back its hoary head, dead, dead. He pictured Scole's face as he dragged the carcass down into the kitchen. A second of begrudged admiration before the sneer dropped again like a wrinkled curtain. He could have the hide treated. Hang it on his wall like an explorer would a bagged tiger.

But it wasn't a tiger. It was a wild cat or a sick dog, killing it would bring him to private tears, because he possessed about as much backbone as that squirrel.

Up at the Hydropathic, the windows were covered for blackout. Freddie could smell the guests' supper reaching out to tease him. Three courses of as little meat as possible, gritty bread with a scrape of margarine, fruit puddings crying out for sugar. Far more meagre fare than before the war, but still better than he could expect across the table from Fa. As he drew closer, he heard Lottie Mulgrave singing to herself on the veranda. Her cigarette glowed ghostly.

Freddie shyly pointed at the light. "Defence of the Realm, madam."

"Bugger the realm."

She offered Freddie a drag, and they sat together on the wall, watching the last of the daylight die over the pines.

"They won't bomb us out here," said Lottie. "The Kaiser's more artistic than that. Do you know, he killed eighteen Chelsea schoolchildren in one fell blow? The Gotha plane. It just sailed over London, crushing whatever was under it."

Freddie wasn't interested in the papers beyond the pictures. "Gotha..." he mumbled, testing the shape and colour of the word.

"Means 'skull', did you know that?" She studied the glowing tip of the cigarette before giving it to Freddie again. Lottie's hands defied her age. People said she started her career playing

60

piano in her father's pub. The usual tired ditties of girls pining for Johnny lost at sea, then cleverer songs of her own making. By the time she was twelve, she was singing on penny stages all over the East End. Sometimes, they even paid her. "They could stop it, of course, if they felt like it. But it's pride."

"Whose pride?"

"Wilhelm and George and all of them. One big royal family. A word from any of them – a Christmas card – would put an end to it." She turned a grin on him. "Do you know, in my former life, Prince Bertie came to my dressing room and offered me a hundred pounds to beat him bloody with my riding crop? I turned the swine down. Ask me why."

Freddie's cheeks prickled. "Why, madam?"

"'Madam'." Lottie snorted. "Because I thought of all the poor old soldiers up at Chelsea with their limps and their haunted faces, and I knew I wouldn't stop with the crop 'til they hanged me."

Choke Wood was nothing but an opaque mass now. Down at the spring, the rooks would be feasting in the dark, swallowing their secrets. Freddie tugged at his lip. "Lottie, I'm worried someone has died."

"Friend of yours?"

No use explaining. There was no use of reassurance either, but Lottie with her piano-playing hands was from another generation, one that still set store by such things.

"Sometimes there's no news," she said. "That's to be expected."

At the base of the distant trees where the lawn met the wild, Fa was coming up from the woods, and Freddie's mind again turned to supper. But his father's familiar dogged lope was somehow off. Too quick to be Fa, dashing across the open lawn with the efficient grace of someone accustomed to the dark.

Lottie followed the figure's progress with a frown. "Poacher. Leave him be."

Rifle in his hand, Freddie stood slowly, struggling to keep his eyes on the figure as it paused to crouch. His breath plumed out in front of his face until he was forced to hold it to see.

"Fa's alone out there," he said.

On all fours, the man was long-limbed and lean. With alarm, Freddie realised he couldn't be sure it was a man. It could even be an underfed stag, though he could see nothing of antlers at this distance. A startled buck, even an emaciated one, was capable of skewering a man as easy as a boiled potato.

Freddie was moving before he realised it, rifle tucked into his shoulder, keeping his barrel trained on the centre of the thing's narrow back where the white of its breath dissipated into the darkness. His nerves rose with his heartbeat. It was surely that apprehension that made the creature's long legs appear to bend at intolerable angles. As he drew closer, treading carefully across the stretch of lawn, he heard muffled huffing. It was eating, perhaps, or marking its scent, and seemed not to hear Freddie though he knew it must be able to smell him as strong as the meagre meat served up at the Hydropathic.

Meat – temptation moved his finger to the trigger. He could hear Fa now, telling the kitchen staff how his son had saved him from a dangerous animal and brought venison home with one bullet.

Step by silent step with the rifle at his shoulder. He'd shot rabbits before, punctured them like balloons, but something this size demanded the honour of acknowledgement. What would the rooks say?

A knave and his gun! A knave and his gun!

The man stood up.

The stock of the rifle fell from Freddie's shoulder. He watched with horror as the man went back towards the Hydropathic, heedless of Freddie or the gun trained on his back. In his shock he couldn't make out if it was someone he knew, a member of staff or one of the guests. The man skipped along the wood's edge and disappeared behind the huddling outhouses where the chargirls did the washing.

Freddie's heart was pounding. The pulse shuddered in his neck, his wrists, his finger on the trigger.

A man I nearly killed a god oh god.

He went to the spot where the man had squatted, down at the boundary between the lawn and Choke Wood. He needed to sit. The earth was cold. The mulchy smell of it started to bring him around. Feeling in the dark, Freddie could make out the print of the man's shoes. What the devil had the fool been up to? He traced the earth with his palms, raking through moss and twigs. Sparse winter grass. Sharp chips of flint. A mound of earth, freshly disturbed.

The shock was fading, leaving him cold and tearful. He *told* them it was unsafe. Lottie was right, it had to be a poacher using Edenwell land to hide his stolen loot. Or one of the crooked shopkeepers Fa complained about, keeping back salted beef and packets of tea for the highest bidder. He could almost hear the rooks cackling at his meagre supper when a feast lay under his feet. *Hungry knave, foolish knave.*

Freddie's fingers sank into the topsoil.

THREE

'Glorious Death'. Soil on a canvas of
Edenwell brochures, 1m×1m.

Frantic swipes of coarse domestic paint brushes are taken over by hand painting in this unusual piece. Thought to be a Modernistic meditation on the primitive nature of war and the waste of those Edenwell men who never returned, we feel the energy here, the purposeless grief, compounded by the fragments of optimistic advertising copy beneath the brush strokes.

FREDDIE'S HANDS REDDENED under the tap's frigid blast.

"It don't do to dwell on things," Fa liked to say. One of his old chestnuts. What did it really mean, Freddie wondered, scrubbing the soil from his fingernails over the kitchen sink, watching as the filmy skin of the cuticles scrolled and peeled. Was he expected to rid himself of an ugly or painful thought by depriving it of oxygen, letting it wither, or by dwelling on a memory was he turning it into fiction, polishing it up until he fooled himself into believing he held something profound? He'd seen such alchemy demonstrated by the rest of the staff; the past growing ever hazier and more holy as each year of war laboured past. Every spring bride had been the most radiant, every baby the bonniest, and every brother the strongest, the happiest, the gentlest of them all. Even the true bastards like Scole were given tin haloes in memory, whether they were dead or absent. *Remember when he used to blow smoke in Missus Hardy's eyes while she rolled pastry? Remember how he'd pinch your bottom and you'd shout? He was a laugh, Nick. Let's send him a package. Let's write him a card.* When Freddie heard the maids talking about drizzly seaside afternoons and disappointing dances with that wistful tone, he wondered if they knew how scared they sounded, scared that they never enjoyed those days when they had the chance, that the world was someone else's now, and all their chances gone.

A shred of black feather clung to Freddie's dirty wrist. *Glorious death*, the rooks had said, smug with secrecy. Dwell on something else, he ordered himself, as the water carried the feather away. Some other memory.

A knave remembers a grave.

"Stop it."

A knave remembers bone and beak.

He hadn't thought of that day in a long time. Three summers ago, rattling along in Chalice's car with the dust trailing behind them. The doctor had a surprise for Freddie, a discovery he wanted to share.

Chalice gave a hearty laugh. "It's not a grave," he said. "I should have made that clear. Of course you'd think that! Grimes Graves.

65

It's just a name, fella. Garbled Anglo Saxon. But this will please you, I promise. Our very own Tutankhamun. A Norfolk Valley of the Kings."

It looked no different to Freddie than the rest of the breckland. An expanse of stubborn scrub with insects flitting from clump to clump. It was high summer, and the swallows rolled above them in the blue. His bottle of ginger ale grew warm in his hands, and Chalice told him to finish it. He could feel the older man's excitement fizzing as he pulled up the handbrake with a crunch.

Men in stout boots milled about with tools. With their broad hats and dusty waistcoats, Freddie thought of the cowboys in The Boys' Realm. *A brisk fellow with a crescent moon moustache pumped Doctor Chalice's hand.*

"I'd hoped you make it down, Doctor. I see you've brought a budding archaeologist?"

"Freddie, this is Mister Peake. Did we choose appropriate footwear?"

Peake laughed. "I wouldn't recommend you follow us into the underworld. But you won't need to. We've brought some interesting pieces up today."

Looking out over the landscape, Freddie saw shallow craters between the trees, scores of them, wide enough to park Chalice's car in. Covered in parched grass, the field was an undulating sea. They picked their way over the uneven ground to a tent where a table was set up, piled with sketchbooks and rolled maps smeared with dirt. One of the craters was an open gash, the grass around it piled with sandy earth and winking chips of flint. The hole was surprisingly deep, with a set of wooden steps leading down inside and a pulley rigged to a frame overhead.

"Buried treasure," Chalice told Freddie. "They've opened up the

66

old flint mines again. Bronze Age, can you believe it? We drove here in a motorcar, and the people who dug these mines were the first to forge metal. Imagine what those poor fellows felt down there in the dark. Some of the passageways are so small, they'd have to drag themselves along on their elbows."

"Hands and knees with nothing but an antler to pick at the stone in front of you," Peake said, shaking his head at the thought. "We've counted twenty-five of these mines in this spot alone, but I'd bet my life there are far more. We're only just getting a sense of the scale of the operation."

Freddie peered over the edge. One of the workmen had left a lamp at the bottom, glowing like a coin in a well. "You're opening them up?"

"That's the idea. You probably think of our ancestors grubbing about in mud huts, don't you? It was far more sophisticated than that. You're a local boy, aren't you? These are your people."

Chalice beamed. "Mister Peake believes people have been living here for ten thousand years."

"See here," Peake led them into the tent and tapped a sketch. "At the bottom of the main shaft, smaller tunnels branch off for individual miners to work. We thought that was the extent of it, but some of those small passageways lead to chambers — barrows, we call them — deliberately sealed off before the abandonment of the mine."

Chalice lit a cigarette and extended the courtesy to Peake. As Peake cupped the flame, Freddie considered the hefting of earth and stone. All that painful labour. "Why go to the trouble?" he asked.

"Young men brought up the flint their families relied on for hunting, clothing themselves, lighting fires," Peake said. "It was a life-giving substance. But flint occurs naturally on the surface. In the topsoil, on the riverbeds, it's littered all over the place, no different *in quality to the stuff forty feet below. To our eyes, at least. But these people saw special value in all that work – that danger. The act of opening up the earth meant something to them, as did closing up shop behind them when they were through. But that isn't all. Look at this."*

Laid out on the table amongst the clods of dirt and chips of flint was an axe head made of stone the colour of sea foam. A pair of antler tips were arranged beneath it, crossbones style. Freddie was more interested in the skull of a small bird resting above the assembled treasures like a crown.

"This is how we found it all," Peake said. "Laid down deliberately. One might say artistically. That axe isn't local. Not by a long way. I'd say... Cornish? See the work put into making it smooth and tactile. And this bird – I'd wager it sang its last four thousand years ago."

Peake offered Freddie the skull to hold. A shore bird of some kind, he guessed, the sort found picking cockles from the mud. Impossibly delicate in his cupped hands. He looked into the filigree sockets of the eyes and imagined them staring into the mine's darkness while the world churned away above. Freddie turned his body, shielding the creature from the harsh light of the tent's lamp.

"A gift," he mumbled, stroking the slope of the bony brow.

Only Chalice heard him. "I prefer to show up with flowers."

"Mine isn't the first team down, of course," Peake went on. "Greenwell's men did some work in the sixties and found some peculiar articles. Chalk carvings, phalli, that sort of thing. There were hearths down the mines, and not the type for light or cooking. Threw up some heated discussion, I can tell you. Someone talked about a goddess statue, but everyone assumes Greenwell was spicing up his discoveries for the attention. The 'Grimes' of Grimes Graves was no goddess, of

68

course. He was a red-blooded Norse hand-me-down."

Freddie squinted into the bird's eye. "Grimes was a man?"

"Not so much a man as a residue," Peake said. "Odin, the father of the Viking gods, was said to wander the world in disguise, gathering hidden knowledge. One of his disguises was Grimnir, The Hooded One. Long before Christianity came to these shores, the people here listened to travellers from the North and adopted the name of Grimnir, let him melt into their own stories. These mines became known as The Hooded One's quarries – Grime's Graves in our local tongue. Of course, none of this was written down until as late as the tenth century, and after that much edited and suppressed. Who knows why these were The Hooded One's quarries, or what they were called before?" He spread his dirty hands. "Four thousand years ago, this place was an attraction, of that I am certain. And not for the flint. I'd love more time and more men, but I think we both know that isn't going to happen."

"Even if there is a war, it'll be a flash in the pan," Chalice ventured. "A Teutonic tantrum."

"I dearly want to agree, Doctor. Not just for my barrows."

The tent was hot and airless, and as the cigarette smoke thickened, Freddie silently excused himself and went to take a look at the nearest open mine. A damp, loamy smell emanated from the deep hole, touching his sweaty skin with wary fingers. He hadn't meant to take the skull there with him, but it felt good in his palm, smooth as a pebble, and the other men were so engrossed in conversation they didn't notice it had gone. Were they going to put it back at the end of the excavation? It was stealing, wasn't it, to just dig it up and take it away?

He stood at the edge of the pit. Beneath the trees, workmen were brewing tea over a fire, their backs to him. People didn't take notice of *a groundskeeper, not until something was broken. His arm hung over the hole, dangling the skull, white against the darkness. He imagined it falling, erupting into four thousand shards, one for each year it had lain there in the quiet barrow. His head felt light, the air outside almost as stifling as inside the tent. With his free hand, he reached for the ladder. He could clamber down quickly, put the skull back. He could have a look, at least, down in the cool. It was made for young men, Mister Peake had said so. Young things like him, born for work.*

"Oi!"

He was on his arse in the dirt and he couldn't feel his limbs. Rough hands on his shoulders. A man he didn't know was looking into his face, the sun behind him, obscuring his features.

The workman shook him. "You could've broken your neck."

"His heart is weak. Let me."

Chalice had rushed out of the tent. He was on his knees beside him, the worry in his eyes covered by one of his golden smiles. "Fella, fella, it's just a faint. Can you speak?"

His hand was numb. When he raised it to pluck at his lip, he felt the cold nudge of a beak against his chin.

"Look at the scrape on that. Thick as a duchess's finger." Fa held the plate of toast out temptingly. "Going for your bath?"

Morning, clogged with the grit of a sleepless night. At the cottage door, Freddie nodded at the floorboards.

"Take it with you. I've had mine," Fa lied. "Lovely it was, too."

Freddie put on his cap. Just something one did, wasn't it? Hat, coat. Without the appropriate layers, Missus Hardy might apprehend him in a corridor, or that new girl, Tabitha

70

Clarke. *You'll catch your death.* If he hadn't the heart to speak to anyone, he had to protect himself against their every opening. A mumble, a nod, a busy aspect, like the men unloading barrels of beer from lorries in the market square, or corralling bawling sheep to the auction pens. Useful people, not to be interrupted. Oh, but they'd always find something to gossip about, wouldn't they? *Did you see Freddie this morning? I think he'd been crying.*

Fa still held out the saucer. He must have used his own portion of margarine as well as Freddie's to make a great greasy layer like that. His grey eyebrows tweaked encouragingly. "Doctor Chalice said your treatments are best taken on a lined stomach."

"Later, Fa."

Four years ago, fresh paint on the cottage door, and Drummerboy was a nameless ball of spikes with a yellow sulking mouth. In Freddie's cupped hands he was warm and lizard-feeling, eyes squeezed shut. And when at last the eyes slit open, they were blue and knowing. Freddie said hello. The wide mouth stretched, and the baby bird said *Kyaaa!*

Fa stood at Freddie's shoulder. "Say 'Fred'."

"They can't make effs."

Fa was laughing, chucking the bird under his bald chin. "Gottle o' gear. Come on, say summat. You come down my chimney, you earn your keep."

"He's talking. In his own language."

"You've been reading too many of that Miss Talbot's books. Who's a pretty boy, then? Who's a pretty ugly wee fella? His mother's booted him out the nest, I shouldn't wonder. They do that when there's summat wrong."

71

Kyaaa! The bird fidgeted in Freddie's hands, bobbing the concertina of his neck until Freddie placed him gently down into a Tsarina cigar box lined with an old sock. The beak clonked against the Russian queen's impassive face.

"Your grandmother held table-turning sessions in her parlour, did I ever tell you that?" Fa tapped his knuckles on Freddie's back. "Knock once for nay, and twice for yea."

Freddie rested his head on the table, meeting the bird's blue eyes. "Would you like some fish paste?"

The bird tapped on the box without hesitation. *Tack tack.*

Fa asked, "Wouldn't you prefer a nice bit o' baccy?"

Tack.

"He says no!" Freddie grinned.

"Ugly bugger knows what he wants."

Freddie scooped some fish paste onto his finger and let the little bird gobble. *More*, he shrieked, tapping at the cigar box.

"A proper little drummer boy. He's taken a shine to you."

Four years ago. Nothing was left unchanged.

It wasn't fully light outside. The cold was insistent at the back of Freddie's neck where his hair needed trimming. Doctor Chalice said bad air allowed infection to saunter right through the lungs, like a quiet leak bringing down a grand old house. The steam cabinets would put you right on a morning like this, lockable boxes where old men would sit and turn the colour of corned beef. If Freddie showed his face in the Hydropathic that morning, that was likely where Chalice would send him.

He took the Tsarina cigar box from the woodshed and headed down to Choke Wood.

The well was still. He laid the box on the altar stone where his chalk drawing had faded to dust. Wash the body. Prepare the

72

coffin. It wasn't a good lining, the handkerchief, not like the satin in coffins for important men, but it was the best handkerchief in Freddie's possession. No flowers grew but the wood sorrel in the rotting branches. They would do for a pillow.

Freddie set about removing the dirt from Drummerboy's wings. His fingers slipped through the soft fan of feathers, watching the water bead and glitter. The white wing glowed as it had in life, that special part that marked him out to those who could only see birds, not know them.

Whoever had buried him hadn't bothered with a shroud, though Freddie noted they had folded him with care. They did not dump him, as they so easily could have. Freddie struggled to imagine who would have gone to the trouble. Scole certainly wouldn't bother himself with a bird, and Missus Hardy spent most of her free time snoring in her room. It made no sense for a guest to mess about with a dead animal; not when they had paid a great deal to improve their health. That left the new girl: Tabitha. Though why she would do such a thing, Freddie couldn't say.

At any rate, a man cannot bury a bird. A bird demands a sky burial.

A bent oak encroached upon the well. Freddie stuck his boot in the crook of the trunk and thrust himself up. The morning mist had left the branches slimy and hard to grip. A few yards up, with his breath coming harder than he would like, he straddled one of the thicker branches and got to work, laying out the death nest where it wouldn't be tossed down by wind.

Only then did he let himself truly look at Drummerboy. Curled amongst the flowers, his feathers had seldom been so oily bright. His talons were ridged black gauntlets. The clever face Freddie had drawn so many times was drained of expression. He didn't look asleep. Why did people say that when it wasn't true?

In the stillness, Freddie saw Drummerboy's cousins watching from the adjacent trees. The rooks stood guard.

"Why didn't you tell me?"

But the birds held their tongues.

He set about tying the coffin in place, gripping with his thighs to keep from slipping. In books, people wept at funerals. They held hands and sang songs and prayed. There was no such tender companionship at the funeral of a wild creature, though Freddie had heard of one dog buried with military honours. Freddie knew if he were to tell anyone, even Fa, how he had spent his morning and the depth of feeling attached to it, he would be met with laughter and, almost as horrible, concern. Was it safe to fully feel it himself? A great silent pit crumbled open inside him.

A shout below. Freddie stiffened.

"Bang!"

Freddie gripped the branches. The intruder stood at the top of the bank, a featureless figure from that distance. He had a rifle tucked into his shoulder that was pointed at Freddie.

"Got you," he said. He sounded like a man but laughed like a boy. The rifle was nothing but a stick.

Wind rustled the pines, and the birds kept quiet. Freddie's lips worried at words that wouldn't come. The thought of this stranger asking what he was up to paralysed him. He might come back when Freddie was gone, tamper with the grave. An unbearable thought. Freddie quickly set about untying the coffin, mentally calculating how many seconds he had to tuck it under his arm, clamber down, and run. But the intruder was already coming.

The trap. He had quite forgotten. From his vantage point he could see it in the bracken between the stranger and the well. He would walk right into it.

"Don't!" Freddie thrust out a hand and felt his body slide sideways. He witnessed his own fall with disbelief, barely registering the branches snagging his clothes and scoring his skin on the way down. They slowed his descent enough that when he hit the dirt he was merely bruised and winded. The stranger shouted something as he crashed down the hill, but Freddie could only stare dazedly at the holy well heaving beside him, and as the stars coursing through his vision faded he wondered what could have caused such a deep, beautiful ripple.

"No, no. Oh no, no—"

He struggled to the edge. On his knees, heedless of the stranger, Freddie stared into the inky water for some sign of the tiny coffin. With an anguished cry, he made out the colours of the Imperial Tsarina fading slowly from view.

The young stranger came to an unsteady halt, unsure of what he'd interrupted or what to do about it, and when he noticed the iron trap within biting distance of his shoes, he swore broadly.

"God," he laughed. "Nearly an amputation. Are you all right?"

Freddie's eyes stung. Fa would prompt him to say good morning, but he found he could do nothing but cough. The dark heroic countenance was just as striking as it was in Missus Walker's shop. They regarded each other quietly, Eustace lordly in his long overcoat and Freddie dressed in dead leaves, the spring rippling between them in ever diminishing rings. Freddie wanted more than anything to be alone.

Something whipped though the bracken, sweeping past Freddie's back. He had a second in which to recognise the sensation of bristles against his clothes – *through* the fibres, coarser, sharp and game-stinking – and with no chance to turn and look at whatever assailed him, he was shoved forward with surprising force. The air was forced from his lungs as the well's black surface and the stone beneath flew up and into his face.

The rooks chose that moment to sound their crude lament.

FOUR

*"For all things come of thee, and of
thine own have we given thee."*

Ponsonby's Folklorica, Dr Winston Ponsonby, 1910. Chapter VIII,
'Norfolk: County of Kings'.

*The Edenwell myth tells of a nameless servant boy who
spied an angel fleeing the crucifixion with a cup of Christ's
blood. As the angel passed over the natural spring, a single
drop fell into the water. Saxon chronicles tell of locals dipping
their clothes in the waters, washing infants, and tending
to wounds. The monks of Thetford took stewardship of the
shrine around 1180 AD, after which the baptismal rite was
performed at the water's edge. The first recorded buildings
were erected around the site: a small chapel, an altar, a place for
the storing of petitions and offerings. By the beginning of the
13th century, pilgrims flocked to Edenwell. In the beginning,
nursing mothers would wash their breasts to improve the flow
of milk, though this affection for pagan customs was frowned*

77

upon by the church. Ditto the floating of children's shirts to divine how long their lives would be. Archaeological digs of the area, as well as uncovering the Neolithic antler tools common to the brecklands, revealed offerings of food, coins, and even homemade effigies of bone and wood – poppets of afflicted parts or departed loved ones.

O N THE EVE of Eustace Moncrieff's sixteenth birthday, the boy in the next bed had his skull cracked.

It was unfair how he died, the other boys said, a sneaky trick. Had he spoken up at the time like a sensible chap, none of them would be in half the trouble they were in. "On my bloody birthday too," Eustace said, lining up for porridge with the rest of the boys; the bankers and colonels of tomorrow. "I hope we at least miss Latin Composition for the funeral." They grunted their agreement, and for that he was relieved. He was no longer obliged to comment.

A stretched sheet, a boy on each corner, and you had a method of flying. They played the game most nights, between cards and foraging for things to burn on the dorm fire. Books, sticks of furniture – it wasn't important so long as the masters weren't disturbed. The younger boys were expected to gather sweets and tea during the day for late night picking, but on the night of Parrish's death, Prefect Hartnoll's resourceful fingers had pilfered a bottle of whisky. Mister Lucas the Mathematics master had dozens of them stashed all over. He wouldn't dare report one missing, if he remembered it at all. By the time the sheet came out, Hartnoll had doled out drams to all his favourites – a group Eustace was unsurprised to find himself excluded from – and the boys were in a state of giddy excitement. Rawley, fifteen years old and almost as many stone in muscle, waved Eustace over.

"Cheer up, Aladdin. Have a ride on the magic carpet."

Eustace had seen bones broken in this game. Before Michaelmas break, one of the Harris twins went down awkwardly on his hand and hadn't felt his thumb since. He let them take turns hitting it with a book until it went white and wouldn't so much as flinch.

Eustace approached the sheet, stretched and waiting, when Lawrence Parrish pushed past. "Me! Do me."

"Don't." It was a foolish thing to say. He didn't care what Parrish did. He was a touchy little thing with a perpetually runny nose, and he sneered at Eustace as he passed.

"Too slow, Moncrieff." The other boys held the sheet tight as Parrish flopped into the middle. "I'll kick down the ceiling!"

Later, Eustace recalled the screams of delight. His own hair flying as the sheet billowed. He saw nothing, or told himself he didn't, but the thump and the crack and the cessation of laughter perched on his shoulder for many weeks after.

They got Parrish into bed. His eyes were bright and he was sniggering stupidly as they tucked him up, but that wasn't unusual. Hartnoll, Rawley and the rest left him there to finish the whisky around the dwindling fire.

An hour after cards and toffees, most were in bed. Eustace had never fared well with the unceasing noise of dormitory life. He woke, half dreaming to begin with, when he heard a voice close to him.

"Water."

It was Parrish, in the bed beside his.

79

Eustace grunted. His own tongue was parched. "Get your own."

"Wa–ter?"

"God's sake." Eustace had a cup, but Parrish couldn't seem to grip it. He went to sit the boy up, and Parrish gave a weird groan.

Across the room, Hartnoll called out. "Pack it in down there, will you?"

Parrish blinked widely in the dark. "Is someone here with us?"

Eustace didn't have time to feel the confusion he might. Someone threw a cup and it smashed a few feet away from him, dousing his bare feet in cold tea.

"Stop gassing," Hartnoll snarled.

Eustace silently returned to his bed, pulled the covers over himself and rolled away. His feet remained cold, and for that he bore Parrish a grudge.

It was only quiet for a moment. "Moncrieff?" came Parrish's nasal voice, childishly high. "Will you hold my hand?"

Someone laughed. "No, hold mine, Moncrieff."

Rawley joined in: "I've got something he can hold."

Eustace scrunched himself into the pillow. When morning chimes rang, all stirred except Parrish.

When term was over and the train brought Eustace home, Phoebe saw the death in him straight away, though it took many days to pry out the truth.

"Didn't the masters hear?" she asked, appalled.

"Probably. But it's not done, interfering."

"And this is why you can't sleep."

"When I try, he's there. Asking for water."

They sat in their old playroom with the door open, the way they would when they built cities of wooden blocks stretching all the way from the window seat into the hall, a trade route spanning continents. Phoebe rubbed his shoulder. "But what could you have done, really? What *would* you have done?"

"It's just the way things are. Once you're marked as prey, that's it. Hartnoll, he's a predator. Parrish too. That's why it was so revolting to see him so... *fragile* like that. If I were to get out of bed and offer him some comfort, my cards would be marked, and I couldn't allow that to happen, don't you see? I hate it there. I've always hated it there. I didn't know he was dying, but I did know he was suffering. I feel like I—" Eustace thought about it, his lips twisting, bloodless and hard. "I feel like I sacrificed Parrish. On some cowardly altar."

Before the words were fully said, Phoebe was stiff and still, looking at the doorway.

Their father never came up to the playroom. There was nothing he wouldn't buy for them, no string he wouldn't pull, but he was a man forged by the drawing room, by pipe smoke and whisky decanters and the admiration of other men who left their child-rearing to women in their employ. The idea of secrets existing in his own home was a grave insult to every material gesture of love he had ever made.

Eustace could smell Hartnoll's purloined whisky. His chest felt tight.

"What are you?" their father asked.

Eustace sat up straight. "An Englishman."

"And an Englishman does...?"

"His duty."

"Phoebe, leave us. Close the door."

81

Eustace sprang over the iron trap and down the bank, stumbling on rabbit holes and scratching his hands on tree trunks as he tried to stop himself from going headlong into the bracken. All he had was a stick, and he held it high, ready to defend himself however pathetically against the fast-moving shape that had disappeared into the thickest swell of the undergrowth.

The wood was so much larger than it seemed from the outside. The rooks clattered furiously. Perhaps the morbid creatures could see something he could not. The thing that attacked the scruffy boy had come and gone without warning, and could be crouching in the bushes still. The boy had fallen in the shallows, onto the flagstones, and his heavy woollens were holding him down, stunned and twitching and – Eustace realised with alarm as he heaved him up – trickling watery blood.

Something flashed past Eustace's head. He lost his grip on the boy's shoulders, and they both went toppling into the shallows.

"Get away." Eustace waved his stick uselessly as his assailant came back for another pass, shrieking and star-taloned. There was more than one, he realised. The water was freezing. "I'm trying to help!"

The rooks clattered through the trees. Eustace dropped his weapon as Freddie came up hacking, eyes rolling. He was alive, at least, though the thin stream of blood seeped through Eustace's trousers, as cold as the water he was kneeling in. As the birds swung in anxious circles around the pair of them, the boy tipped back into Eustace's lap.

Blue eyes, pale lashes clumped together in surprised spikes.

You could find all sorts down by the well. Coins bearing the faces of monarchs Freddie didn't recognise, shards of pottery or bone, points of flint. All the local farmers churned up blunted antler picks, though Freddie had only once seen a living stag, a vision panting fumes in the winter air, then gone. The monks of Thetford Abbey were said to have tossed their treasures into the black water when King Henry's thugs came for their share. Freddie once shone a lamp into the depths and swore he could see the wink of metal. *Don't go falling in*, said Fa. *It'll take your breath away. And won't gi' it back, neither.*

Freddie and Eustace made it up from the woods clasped to one another like drunks. Freddie could hardly protest, but he never expected this tall – startlingly strong – stranger to come all the way up to the cottage, let alone bang on the door with his shoe.

"I say! Anyone about?"

Without waiting for an answer, Eustace shouldered the door open and heaved Freddie inside.

It was a shock to see his little home play backdrop to someone new. Freddie noticed dirty cups he'd forgotten about, cobwebs on the windowpanes. His heart fluttered sorely when he thought what Fa would say if he came home suddenly, an embarrassment of fretting. *You're forever pranging yourself like this. I can't leave you for a moment.* Still, he was helpless to protest as he was half dragged to Fa's bed with its rumpled grey sheets.

"Your room, I take it?"

He thought of the alternative, plastered in children's drawings and fairy story nonsense. He nodded.

"Peel off. Do you have any more pillows? What about the fire?"

"Sorry for the trouble, sir."

Eustace was rummaging in the armoire, inspecting Fa's nightshirt. He didn't appear to understand that anyone lived there. It was as if, to him, the cottage was just a collection of objects to peruse and discard. It gave Freddie comfort to know he was surely just another, his shabbiness soon forgotten.

"What was it? I couldn't see. Some kind of boar?"

"There hasn't been boar in these parts for two hundred years... sir," he hastened to add.

"Well, if it was a stag, you're lucky to have lived." The excitement in Eustace's voice betrayed he knew nothing about such things. But he was right. An antler through the kidney and that was it.

Freddie removed his soaked shirt with a groan. His skin was hot where the beast's bristles had pierced his clothing. A rogue buck, perhaps, driven crazy with winter hunger. It had been tall. He felt the heat of it looming over him the second before everything went blank.

He could be down in the well, right now. Floating.

Eustace snatched the shirt from him and draped it over the fire guard. He'd already piled the grate with coal – far too much, Fa would go spare – and clumsily stuffed a lit newspaper into the gaps. It was entirely possible he had never lit a fire before. A life of servants and valets flashed before Freddie's eyes and he felt himself shrivel with mortification, standing there in his drawers.

Eustace was mercifully oblivious, stoking the fire. "What were you doing up that tree, anyway?"

Think of something. Blood dribbled down his chin as he clambered into bed. "B-birds."

"Ugh, don't. Birds are the reason my sister's still here. She hit a crow or something on the way and it took the car with it."

Pat-pat-pat against the coverlet, blood. Black epicentre, red areole, blooming out. If he stared hard enough, there would be no more room for anything else in his head.

His rescuer paced the room, touching the candlesticks and wiping dust off the furniture. He was especially interested in Fa's shotgun, hanging above the hearth.

"Look, do you have a mother or something to keep an eye on you?"

In Freddie's silence, Eustace read the truth. He dragged a chair over to the bed and sat down, back to front. Freddie had never seen such long legs.

"I don't have one either. Not truly. Adopted, see. My name's Moncrieff. Eustace."

A knave already knows.

"I'm Freddie."

"Why aren't you in khaki, Freddie?"

"My heart's wrong." He sat there in the blankets, blood drying sluggishly over his lips, braced for the backlash.

"Well, I bit my father, so that makes two of us."

Was he making fun? Dark ironic eyes, neat nose, a mouth that could belong to a child or a woman. Freddie's fingers cramped as if gripping a pencil. He was so cold.

He was amazed when Eustace took a folded handkerchief from his pocket and tossed it into his lap. Embroidery. A monogram almost royal. He didn't dare raise it to his face.

"He'll forgive me," he went on. "He usually does. And

besides, my Notice will arrive soon. I'm a decent shot, and if I make enough German widows, Daddy's bound to welcome me back with open arms."

Freddie had no idea what to say. Eustace stared for a moment, eyes large and, Freddie realised, brimming with unease.

"Sometimes I make jokes."

"Oh."

"Lucky I was there to pick you up. I wonder if you drowned down there, you'd fill up with all the holy water and just... get up."

Was that a joke too? He wasn't sure if he was expected to laugh. But Eustace was on his feet.

"Look, I have to go and sit in a steam box for twenty minutes. They lock you in with your head sticking out, and you have to try not to panic. Something about pores? Well, you know what they do up there. You'll be all right, won't you?"

"Yes, sir."

Eustace nodded briskly and made for the door. He was almost there when he noticed the bread and margarine Fa had left on the side that morning. He turned back to thrust the plate at Freddie.

"Do you good, probably. Cheerio."

Doctor Chalice had been quietly thoughtful in the car back from Thetford, but with the arrival of the Moncrieff siblings he was whistling again, striding through the corridors with a whisky tumbler of water. The morning after Drummerboy's failed funeral, Freddie went for his bath in the Solarium and found Chalice waiting for him, examining a fern overflowing from one of his Grecian urns.

"You're hurt," said the American.

Freddie, not the fern.

And he wasn't hurt so much as marked. The heat of the grazes had faded overnight, along with the solidity of the memories of the thing that had caused them. It was only waking up with the monogrammed handkerchief beside him that made Freddie trust his recollections, though they worried him in some indefinable way.

"Slipped on gravel, sir."

"Onto your face?" Chalice put down his glass and held Freddie's head gently, examining his swollen nose from all angles. "We must find you a helmet."

Freddie waited for the bath to fill, then eased his sore body down into the water. The familiar mineral steam was a comfort, even as it stung.

Chalice perched on the edge holding Freddie's wrist, and put a brass stethoscope to his chest. There was always something incorrect going on inside, even if Freddie couldn't feel it. Chalice had explained that sometimes the valves between the chambers in his heart – little frog's legs, kicking, he said – went too slowly, or too fast, or one leg knocked the other and whacked out the rhythm like a soldier spoiling parade. That was why Freddie was pale, he said, why he was tired some days for no respectable reason. It was why Scole called him lazy and threw wet plum stones at him, though Freddie suspected he could be fit as a flea and built like a docker and Scole would still find sport in him.

Chalice kept his findings to himself. "Are you dizzy today?"

"No, sir."

"Would you be up to a little job for me? Something different?"

He was busy enough with the North Wing, with the chickens, the daily chores. Mister Tungate's vegetable plot was his responsibility now, the weeding and the watering and picking out slugs, though he couldn't tell a potato from a turnip half the time. His face must have betrayed him, because Chalice chuckled.

"Remember what you said about the canaries, how you felt what some of the guests really needed was a friend? How would you like to be a friend to someone for me?"

A friend? His friend was in the well now, sinking. Was there an end to it, he wondered, some hidden riverbed beneath the earth? Or would Drummerboy drift downwards in the dark forever, dreaming of the sky?

"There's a young man," Chalice was saying. "A little younger than you. He could use a companion here at Edenwell. I don't expect you to go carousing or join a football team together, but... I feel you have the right sort of soul."

There were never any young men, not any more. Except one. Freddie felt the nervous tremor in his heart, and Chalice with his clever blue eyes saw it right away.

"Ah, you've met him already. Kismet, see?"

Did Chalice know about the well? His face said not. It was always so open. The water here was warm, fragrant, trustworthy, not at all like the frigid depths of Choke Wood. But then he thought of the handkerchief and was glad of the hot water masking the flush to his cheeks.

"Is he poorly?" Freddie asked.

"Oh, yes. A vulnerable young man. But he's safe here, and I know you will do your part. Particularly if he shows any desire to leave us, you know. Remember Mister Farrell who said he'd had his fill of douches and dressings?"

Freddie did remember. Doctor Chalice forbade the staff to serve Mister Farrell sherry, or whisky, or even a drop of stout. After storming out, he returned the following year, fatter, sicker and sadder, solemnly preparing to swear off all spirits. They performed that dance for three years until Missus Farrell wrote to thank Doctor Chalice for trying, but regrettably...

Freddie could imagine no such slow decline for Eustace Moncrieff, but if Doctor Chalice saw danger there, Freddie believed it.

Pleased, Chalice stood and dried his hands. "Say, when are you going to make me a nice fur stole out of that tiger you're hunting?"

Freddie smiled weakly. "Are you going to the opera, sir?"

"I know of a lady who may. But what time do I have for dalliances? I have to make you better. I have to make the whole world better!"

That afternoon, Fa asked Freddie to hold the ladder while he fixed the clogged guttering beside the portico. His thumbs traced the grain of the wood as clumps of dead leaves dropped from the gutter and pattered to the ground.

"Fa, do you have friends?"

"It's been a while since I've had time for friends, Fred."

"But do you have any?"

"School mates. Folk I grew up with. There's men in the Red Lion I'd count as friends. Your mother."

Freddie kept his doubts to himself. Fa rose of a morning, worked the day, and turned in at night, sometimes without saying a word to anyone but his son.

Fa tore up a sycamore sapling making a home where it didn't belong. The gutter was rusty, it would only get worse as the spring showers rolled in. Metal was increasingly hard to come by.

Freddie's mouth twisted. "What's the general... well, the method?"

"Just 'appens, lad. You can't make it pour, but rain 'appens all the same."

Freddie watched his father from below, the wiry stretch of him fighting with the ageing building. The only published technique of friend-making Freddie had ever seen was a recruitment poster – YOUR PALS IN THE ARMY ARE HAPPY AND SATISFIED. ARE YOU? Eustace Moncrieff was expecting his Notice. Plenty of friends awaited him. He hardly needed someone like Freddie.

"Hark at that. Some can't take a hint."

Freddie followed Fa's look. On the dining veranda, the dishevelled figure of Mister Jenks could be seen setting up for a marionette show. He was lucky Scole was indoors leading the gentlemen's water aerobics session. Jenks folded out a backdrop made from an old fire guard, a surprisingly well painted fairy-tale castle nestled in a forest of green and yellow trees. With his frazzled beard and bells on his ankles, Jenks was a clown born old. Freddie had seen him lumbering around with those dangling marionettes all his life but couldn't recall ever seeing him younger than he was then. It was no doubt the dirt on Jenks' face that gave him an immortal wizardly look, though once he overheard Missus Hardy saying he could well be smearing it on every morning for the sympathy.

Despite the cold, a crowd gathered. The musical box under his arm carried a tune across the grounds, and the rooks laughed to hear 'Clair de Lune' when the moon had gone in hours ago. It was only when Freddie settled himself at the back of the audience that he realised he never asked Fa's permission to leave.

Lottie Mulgrave lounged in slippers and dressing gown, garnering the usual stares. "Roll up, roll up, kid," she greeted him. The other lady guests were gathering as an alternative to the morning needle showers. Of the gentlemen, only Mister Harrington with the bad back and Mister O'Leary the melancholic were present, standing with arms folded as the dirty stranger unwrapped a pair of packages, little shrouds containing the bodies of his marionettes. First, the blue princess, pale as cream. Jenks wiped his hands on his thighs before lifting her to her feet. The second package he opened behind the screen, mumbling affectionately. "Tiddly-bom, rom-ti-pom."

Chief among the assembled women was Missus Bailey, the wife of a soap manufacturer and self-proclaimed expert on all things infectious. An annual guest, her business at Edenwell was a mystery to Freddie, though almost every time he saw the woman she was washing her hands or talking about doing so. She leaned towards a fellow guest and asked, a touch loudly: "Who is this vagrant?"

Lottie lit a cigarette and extinguished the match in a potted fir. "Mister Jenks was a sergeant under Wolseley in Egypt, madam. He'll oblige you with a look at his scars, if you ask, I'm sure."

"Tiddly-pom," Jenks muttered, oblivious to all but his marionettes. "Rum-ti-bum."

Satisfied with his preparations, he sketched an awkward bow to the crowd and scrunched his big body down behind the screen. 'Clair De lune' sang out, a little too fast. Freddie raised his hands to clap, not stopping until he realised he was the only one.

The second marionette turned out to be a bear. Waddling out on his hind legs, he examined the assembled guests with a curiosity so realistic some of the ladies laughed. Jenks' mastery of the puppet was impressive, and within seconds of the bear's debut, Freddie forgot there was a man controlling the strings at all.

The bear rubbed his bottom against a cardboard tree trunk. With a satisfied shake of the tail he put his paw to his ear. Something was coming. The tinkling of the music box heralded the arrival of the princess, swaying reedily in her blue gown. Her woollen hair glowed against the castle walls like a mass of sunflowers, and when she saw the bear she raised a hand in genteel shock. The bear bowed deeply, and with delicate precision, the pair began to dance.

More guests were drawn outside by the sound of applause. Two of the teenaged chargirls, Annie and Maud, always pleased to avoid work, paused on their way back from the coal shed. Habit forced Freddie to slide into the background, away from their catty glances. It was then he noticed Eustace Moncrieff. As a young man out of uniform, he garnered stares, and Missus Bailey turned her attention to him the moment he stepped onto the veranda.

"Have you seen the morning papers?" she remarked to a neighbour. "The scenes from France, my dear. Diabolical. An injured child was thrown to pigs. It's the German way. Their culture. I was relieved when the police rounded them up in London. All the horrid butchers and pawnbrokers, not a moment too soon."

Eustace showed no sign of hearing, though surely he had. He hung about with his hands in his coat pockets, nonchalant to all the world. Doctor Chalice had called him vulnerable, but Freddie couldn't begin to see why. He furtively examined the young man's black hair, sprouting at odd angles from under his cap. Guests recovering from the measles often turned up with haphazardly cropped hair, but Eustace showed no signs of protracted illness. If anything, he looked as if he might toss away his coat and go on a cross-country run.

Sensing he was being watched, Eustace turned his dark eyes in Freddie's direction. Freddie blanched and looked down.

Mister Jenks' marionettes turned and dipped like living things. The dance drew to a gentle close, with the pair going their separate ways into the forest. But as Freddie raised his hands to clap, the bear darted back from behind the backdrop clutching a tiny sword. On his head, a helmet topped with a spike.

How had Jenks managed that? Freddie wondered, reluctant to spoil the illusion. The audience booed like children at the sight of a German bear. The princess backed away, her gown rippling as she trembled. Even Missus Bailey jeered as the brute chased her around the forest.

The pursuit came to an end when the princess tripped and fell. On her knees, she stared up at the approaching bear beseechingly, and it laughed – Jenks' thunderous cackle came from behind the backdrop – only to spring back in amazement as the princess produced a sword of her own. As she skewered the bear through the chest, Eustace Moncrieff laughed like a boy.

Rain began spitting. Mister Jenks received a few small tips with thankful mutterings and packed up his things. The guests returned to their treatments. Freddie assumed Eustace

93

had gone with them until he spied a long figure in an overcoat bending down by the painted castle.

"It's such a shame Phoebe missed you. She's about the size of your princess, actually. But it's not her you need to meet, it's my brother. Harry's a journalist. He's all caught up in the war at present, but he writes stories for papers all over the place and I think he could get you some attention. You made all this yourself, yes? That Irish woman said you were in the desert with Sir Wolseley. You shouldn't be playing to paltry little crowds like this. Harry's always harping on about how we need uplifting stories."

He broke off when he noticed Freddie standing diffidently at his elbow. "Pardon me, sir. Mister Jenks don't really speak."

Freddie watched with regret as the excitement drained from Eustace's eyes. He dug in his pocket for a coin and left Mister Jenks to swaddle his princess.

Eustace called out to Freddie. "Don't run off. I was meaning to ask about your back."

"Sorry for putting you out like that, sir."

The rain was picking up. Eustace tipped back his head and stuck out his tongue.

"The only water treatment I'll accept without argument. Say, you're the groundskeeper's son. You must know all the good hiding places."

Knaves don't know everything.

"They put me under a scalding hot shower this morning and then marched me into a freezing plunge pool," he went on. "Positively Nordic. This afternoon they want to wrap me in wet sheets like a caterpillar. You must know somewhere I can hide until dinnertime."

94

"Don't you want to get better?"

"It's not going to make me better, is it? It's only water."

Up on the roof, the jackdaws screamed with laughter. Freddie was stunned mute, as if he had witnessed Eustace stroll into a church and spit.

"Besides," Eustace shrugged. "I'm not ill."

The dining room doors opened and the hoarse voice of Katie Healey the masseuse rang out. "Is that Mister Moncrieff with you, Freddie? He's running late for his treatment."

Before he could turn to reply, Eustace had a fistful of Freddie's coat and they were off. The folly couldn't be seen from the dining room, and that was where they ran, laughing as Katie bellowed out across the lawn that it was Eustace's own money he was wasting.

"Get the keys, get the keys," Eustace said, pushing him from behind as they struggled with the old door. "Do you think she'll come after us?"

"No, but I'll get a thick ear next time she catches me."

The folly was once a summer refreshment room, but in Edenwell's latter years it had become a store for all the patient activities scrapped through lack of staff. Guests used to look forward to the winter's day when they flooded the tennis courts to turn them into skating rinks. Now the skates dangled from a beam alongside string bags of footballs and croquet mallets, French boules and boxing gloves. Folded sun loungers leaned against the stone walls as if yearning for the warmth of the outside. Freddie put away his keys. Rushing across the lawn like that was hard on his heart, and he perched on a billiard table waiting for the pressure to fade from his chest.

Every cobweb seemed to charm Eustace. "This is fantastic. And you have the keys. Does anybody else?"

"Just my Fa."

"Your very own medieval turret. I'm still getting used to having my own room here. In school, everyone knew everything, not an inch of privacy. I could happily live here, though. Clear it out, put in a few radiators, and I'd live like a robber baron."

Freddie tugged on his lip. For an unnerving second he was close to telling Eustace all about the canaries. Aside from Fa and Doctor Chalice, he had never said anything about his plans to anyone at Edenwell. Besides, Eustace was frighteningly sharp. If Freddie let his mouth flap, he would surely divine the truth, that Chalice had tasked him with being his shadow. And what a terrible shadow he was, helping him bunk off treatments and not even daring to contradict the heresy that Edenwell water was just that – water.

A rushing noise in his ears. He closed his eyes and took a deep inhalation, just as Chalice told him to, and slowly felt the kicking of his heart slow to normal. When he opened his eyes, Eustace was there, still as one of Jenks' marionettes waiting to be brought to life. He was looking up at the conical roof where the sky showed through in a white slash. Rain dripped steadily.

On Eustace's arm was a bird.

The breath rushed out of Freddie, leaving him weightless. "Drummerboy?"

Eustace looked at Freddie with wide eyes. "It just made a beeline for me, can you believe it? God, it's so docile, it's— What's the matter?"

The jackdaw rocketed up into the rafters, a flurry of soot

and vitality. Water from his wings sprayed their upturned faces. Eustace was left wiping his eyes as Freddie clambered onto the billiard table, desperately reaching to see where the bird had gone. It was impossible, but that white stripe was unmistakable. The bird vanished out of the hole in the roof and Freddie burst outside after him.

The folly's door crashed against the wall. Overhead, that happy *chakka-chakka* he knew so intimately. He pushed against his body's protests, anxious not to lose sight of the familiar silhouette coursing over the lawn, over the walled vegetable garden, down the bank into Choke Wood. Waist deep in ferns, he could hear Eustace calling, but powered on after Drummerboy, who kept a teasing distance in front of him, weaving between trees, inviting him to follow.

When Freddie reached the crest of the hill, his lungs were full of fire. The wood seemed to teem with birds crowding in to see what the commotion was, and Freddie was half sure he had lost his mind. But there, down in the wood's centre, on the well's stone lip, legs apart, that funny indignant stance...

"You came back."

The rooks laughed to hear such scepticism, such human ingratitude. *A knave could shed a tear.*

He barely noticed Eustace clattering down through the thicket, so excited he was almost bouncing.

"Where did he come from? I blinked and he was just *on* my arm like he'd appeared out of the air."

"Drummerboy, would you like some fish paste?"

The beak against the stone: *Tack tack.*

How sweetly his heart hurt. "You miss your old bed?"

Tack tack.

"Will you ever leave me again?"

Tack.

His eyes stung. When he wiped them, Eustace was regarding him strangely.

"Do many of them have that white marking?" he said.

"He's special."

"Only, that is very like…"

Freddie laughed even as a tear rolled down his lip.

"No, you misunderstand me," Eustace said. "There was another, very much like this one. But that bird died when we hit it."

We. Hit. Freddie tasted salt.

"My sister was driving," Eustace went on. "We were both upset about it, and— well, I can't say why, but I went out that night and I dug a hole. I promise you, it was quite dead. I can take you to see the little grave—"

"I found it." It could have been Eustace Freddie saw darting across the lawn in the dark, racehorse lean and fleet. He brought about Drummerboy's death, but— "You were careful, folding him all nice." Freddie traced a fingertip down the bird's glossy beak. "Thank you."

"Pretty bird. It didn't feel right to just toss him away, after…" Eustace stared, a frown creased between his eyes. "He's a pet? You never said."

"Come here, boy. Let me see you."

Warm once more, talons grasping his arm like gentle thorns. Freddie could barely believe it. In his shock he stared at the leaf-clogged well, watching his wavering reflection as if the mouth might open of its own accord, offer up answers. All the promises of Chalice's beautiful brochures, he'd never doubted them, not truly, yet they sank like stones in the face of this stunning proof. As the midday chimes rang out from the Hydropathic, the daily call to prayer for all the boys overseas, he buried his face in Drummerboy's soft plumage.

And without hesitation, he told Eustace everything.

FIVE

March 1917. A change comes over Alfred Ferry, coinciding with the U-boat assault on British supply lines. Where the food supply dwindles, the luxuriance of Ferry's canvases increases. We see the start of his craze for enormous pennants of glued papers, some stretching eight feet long. It is as if he finally has a use for his collection of cuttings and scraps, pasting and tracing them with energy and enthusiasm to bring his private world into his physical reality. We see what may be comparable to Egyptian tomb paintings depicting the life and afterlife of a subject, a storyboard of events. Sweet wrappers, propaganda cuttings, fantastical animals, and fairy story accoutrements. A car, smashed to ribbons. A bird in flight, armoured, gargantuan. And on its back, a boy of dark beauty.

FREDDIE'S LEDGERS CAME alive with images of the coming spring; galleons tossed by fair winds, the Edenwell gates enveloped in sweet briars, the gossip of the charcoal rooks, building nests and alliances. The bite of winter was losing its vindictive force. In Mister Tungate's walled garden,

100

the broccoli plants were forming fat heads, and the wild garlic hummed deliciously. Feeding the chickens in the yard, Freddie lifted his cap and let the breeze play with his hair. Mornings were different now. A week ago, he would sneak in and out of the Hydropathic like a burglar, but now the guests greeted him cordially. Lottie Mulgrave gave him a salute as she went for her second coffee, and even Missus Bailey regarded him with grudging curiosity. People noticed him and they were pleased to, all because he was standing beside the intriguing newcomer, Eustace Moncrieff.

After a vigorous complaint from Katie Healey, Doctor Chalice explained to Freddie that Eustace was more likely to turn up for treatments if they took them together. That morning, Eustace was prescribed a stimulating compress of heavy linen applied to the crown of the head. Under the mound of fabric, he looked like a reclining pasha, and he grinned as Freddie joined him in the next tub.

"You're late."

"Drummerboy wanted toast."

"And you?"

"I had *some* toast."

"An egg might do you good."

The hens were hardly laying. Freddie tried bulking their morning oats with water to make them go further, but the chickens pecked and scratched each other over every last piece, and the stress was harming them.

"I mean it," Eustace said. "They give me poached eggs in butter and mustard for breakfast, with ham and muffins. I'm ashamed of myself. Tomorrow, I'll hold some back for you."

They lay side by side in companionable quiet.

"Phoebe's staying while the car's being fixed. I told her your bird was stronger than her windscreen."

Freddie's eyes opened. Should they be telling people?

"Did she say anything?"

"She thinks you're crackers. But she thinks I'm crackers anyway, so I wouldn't fret." He adjusted the compress on his head to get at an itch, revealing a patch of white, abused scalp. "Did you hear the great to-do last night? One of the girls who does the rooms thought she saw a zeppelin."

Freddie was never involved when something exciting happened. The rest of the staff lived upstairs together and guarded their gossip from him as if it were valuable. If Freddie had to bet, he'd say it was Annie. She was only fifteen, and Missus Hardy had clipped her round the freckly ears more than once for her hysterics.

"She went screeching down to the cellar," said Eustace. "I got up just as one of the old boys was turning on the lights and opening the curtains, the idiot. Turned out to be a cloud." He stared at the ceiling. "How is your, er...? Friend."

Freddie wore one of Drummerboy's piebald feathers tucked behind his ear. The strangeness of his reappearance was a spinning coin between them, one they were both reluctant to touch.

"Last night he chattered in his sleep. He does that."

"Do you think they dream?"

"They have more time for it than us."

Eustace stared at him, resting his cheek on the rim of the tub. Freddie resisted the urge to look back. He had a secret more valuable than anything the rest of the staff could boast, and if they thought he was crackers, all the better. His fingers ached to draw; he and Eustace, small and fleet as mice, in their folly fortress safe from detection.

Before long, he felt himself drifting off. Scole's voice jerked him awake. The orderly stood at the end of their bathtubs, hands clasped militarily behind his back.

"Your twenty minutes are up, gentlemen."

Eustace threw off his compress and hauled himself out. "I hate this part."

Scole smiled. "No prize-fighter would think of entering the arena without having his cold shower and rub down, sir."

"Do I look like a prize-fighter, Freddie?" He grinned, ribs heaving.

Freddie smiled at the floor before catching the look Scole sent him.

At the back of the Solarium was a metal contraption resembling a man-sized bird cage. A revolving shelf sat at the top, with a bucket fixed upright and a hanging chain. Scole had them both stand inside the cage while he wobbled up the steps to fill the bucket. The half-naked boys stood about awkwardly, on the brink of laughter, bouncing on their heels.

"And what's this called?" asked Eustace, a touch nervous.

"An affusion, sir. The Japanese swear by it for warding off infection. Hot bath, cold affusion. Never fails. Doctor Chalice once brought a man out of a coma with the affusion method, didn't he, Mister Ferry?"

"He did," said Freddie, though he couldn't recall any such miracle.

Scole stepped down and took the end of the chain. "All right, gentlemen. Three... two..."

Before Scole could finish the countdown, Eustace reached

103

over and yanked the cord. They both shrieked under a sheet of white-cold water.

Scole's pockmarked face stretched into a grim smile. "Glad to see you're taking an active part in your recovery, Mister Moncrieff," he said, wiping at his splashed trousers.

Later, burrowed deep into dressing gowns on Solarium loungers, they drank their dose of water.

"Did you see his medal?" Eustace asked. "That orderly. He's invited me up to his room. He has things from France to show me."

Freddie thought of the time in November when Scole tossed a bucket of bathwater over him from a first-floor window. He tried to imagine Eustace sitting with him, staring at his leg with worshipful wonder.

"How was he injured? Do you know?"

Freddie looked at his toes, splayed white on the tiles. His nails were yellow, he realised. He tucked his feet under the lounger. "I'll tell it wrong."

"Oh, tell me. I want to know so I don't act the fool in front of him."

It was rote by then, Scole told the story so often. "He was taking a machine-gun post from the Germans. Somewhere in France, I don't know. They killed his commanding officer, so he took charge, shot the two Germans behind the gun and turned it on the enemy. He didn't feel it at the time, but he'd been hit in the leg. They had to saw it off in a tent or summat."

Eustace shook his head slowly. "What a man."

"I can't imagine losing a leg," Freddie said. "Not the blood or the noise, but the bit where you wake up and for the first time it's… not there."

How do you picture something that isn't there? he wanted to say. Something that exists so loudly because it doesn't?

"But the stories you get in return," Eustace said, his eyes bright. "The glory."

"It chafes him."

Eustace was scandalised, but laughing nonetheless. "You can't talk like that. That's... reducing heroism to the mundane. You're supposed to do the opposite. Take my stupid brother. He spices up dispatch reports for newspapers, makes them readable for people like the guests here. He's not a proper correspondent, he doesn't have adventures, but it's still duty. And there's nothing more important than that. Our children will look back on our deeds. They'll question them."

Eustace towelled his hair, frowning as his fingers touched the bald spots. He didn't seem ashamed of them, nor had he explained when he caught Freddie looking. Freddie felt he ought to have said something kind or flattering because it was simply absurd that someone so handsome might go around thinking people were staring at him with anything other than admiration, but he couldn't get the word *plumage* off the tip of his tongue.

Up on the glass roof, the rooks scoffed.

"I'm going to have nine children," Eustace said, and drained his glass. "And none of them are ever setting foot in a school."

With the spring thaw came rabbits. And with rabbits came larger things.

The traps remained untouched, but the Big Bugger, as Fa had taken to calling it, had deposited more offerings across

105

the estate. Squirrels, hedgehogs, rabbits young and old. Even the rats were unwanted gifts, lying out in the open, shedding fur in clumps as their bodies swelled and shrank in the rising temperature. It was odd how no fox would deign to touch them. Odd and inconvenient. The bodies had to go somewhere, and Freddie studied the direction of the wind so he wouldn't bother the guests with the smell of roasted rodent. The fire pit behind the cottage was tantalisingly close to Choke Wood, and the smoke attracted some of the feathered residents to loiter in the pines, eyeing a limp squirrel as it crackled on the pyre.

Backbeforethewar, when a knave was smallish… currant buns.

"There's a law now," Freddie said. "I can't feed you."

Snickering. The law was nothing but men's words.

What had Eustace Moncrieff been like before the war? For all his careless attitude, the scraps he offered were strangely impersonal, painted set pieces like Mister Jenks' fairy castle. It was a rule of Edenwell never to pry into the guests' lives, even on the most trivial level, but something about Eustace made Freddie suspect he was being baited, invited to chase. Besides, if he didn't open up to Freddie, who would he turn to? Scole? A bone on the fire cracked as the marrow boiled.

Inquiries will be made, the rooks told him. *Pending buns.*

He threw them breadcrumbs left over from breakfast, such as they were. The chickens were grateful for their meagre seed but still only offered three eggs in return. He knew they needed green things, food with life inside. When he took a basket to the vegetable garden, he looked wistfully at Mister Tungate's pear trees trained up against the red brick, brown and congested with dead wood. He picked the slugs from the cabbages and took a basket to the kitchens. But even before he was through the tradesmen's door, he could hear the staff below coming to the boil.

"Mags, if you believe that, you'll believe anything. In France, you know what they'd call him? *Un charlatan.*"

Scole held court. Freddie heard a bark of Missus Hardy's most caustic laughter. He put the basket of cabbages down at the foot of the stairs and made to leave, only to find Tabitha Clarke had come in from outside. She was between him and the door, her chapped hands on her hips. "They told me you sneak about."

"They sound busy."

"I'm busy. They're gassing. But I've made coffee. It's stone cold now, and all chicory, but there's some left. You want it?" She turned her snub nose to the open door and made a face. "You smell summat?"

Singed squirrel hair was a particular aroma. "Coffee sounds grand," he said.

Sweltering in the kitchen, Missus Hardy prepared a pile of Cromer crabs for soup. The nutty, salty smell was somehow both tempting and sickly. Scole sat on the countertop, his dark hair swept across his forehead, his sleeves rolled up, proudly showing biceps smattered in pitted scars. "He'll come creeping along," he was saying, "cap in hand, and you and all them upstairs encourage him. Shuffling about in rags! He's got more money than us, I promise you that."

"Jenks can do as he pleases," Missus Hardy said, with a smart *crack* as she twisted a crab's claw from its body. "So can the doctor, and that's what worries me."

"It won't happen."

"Chalice is strutting around up there like cock of the walk."

"Won't happen, Mags. You think them upstairs will put up with an invasion like that? The noise? The smells? You might forget, but I've seen it. You think that heifer Missus Bailey and her lot will keep paying for that?"

Missus Hardy frowned at her hands, slipping through slivers of white meat parting like slick feathers. "Just think of all the extra work."

Scole laughed. "You like a bit of hard graft, don't you, Tabby? Come and show us your muscles."

Tabitha evaded his hands and poured the coffee. "I think it's a good thing the doctor's proposing. It shows he cares about our boys."

Freddie took the cabbages over to the pantry. "What's going on?" he asked.

Scole lit a Woodbine. "Maybe if you weren't away with the fairies all day, you'd've cottoned on, Ferry."

"Not in here, Nick," said Missus Hardy. "Nothing's happening, Freddie. Mister Scole will assure you of that."

"Here y'are." Tabitha handed Freddie his coffee. She was still slightly frightening with her hard mouth and her inked skin, but there was no mockery in her eyes. "Caught your monster yet?"

"Taking the waters alongside the guests now, isn't he?" Scole sent a plume of smoke out into the room. "It's all right for some. World-class treatment in exchange for what? Six cabbages? What can I get for six cabbages, Tabby?"

"A thick ear if you're not careful." Her voice was stern, but there was a slight smile playing on her lips.

Missus Hardy dropped a crab shell into a bucket of bones by her feet. "James, how do you feel about this arrangement?"

Freddie was surprised to see his father down in the kitchens. Then he remembered the coal scuttle he'd neglected to fill. It hung in Fa's hand, passively waiting for an apology. Mister Ferry removed his cap, revealing his shining bald pate, and nodded his good mornings to the ladies.

"The lad seems a decent sort. Bit of company..." He drifted off, not waiting to embarrass Freddie. Everyone knew a bit of company was a seismic shift in the world of the groundskeeper's son.

With the crab meat added to the pot, Missus Hardy stirred and sniffed, diluting her soup until it resembled little more than warm seawater. "Martha Talbot's son, though. First celebrity we've had since Lottie Mulgrave."

"Well, I never," said Fa, and he turned to Freddie with a surprised smile. "You like Martha Talbot, don't you, Fred? You have all her books."

The coffee stung as it went down the wrong way. The rooks cackled as he coughed. *Currant buns, knave. Deal's a deal.*

"We ought to see if he can get you his mum's signature." Fa wouldn't let it go, despite the low snickering coming from Scole's direction. For someone so keen for his son to act like a man, he was good at reducing him to a child in company.

But this was news, all right. Eustace Moncrieff – Martha Talbot's son.

I love your mother's books. I cut them up with a straight razor. No.

For the pictures. I use them.

It wouldn't do.

He made his excuses and went to his room, diving straight into the bookshelf, dragging piled books out of the way,

109

unfinished drawings, broken pencils, Drummerboy's sticks and thimbles. The jackdaw hopped around on the bed, babbling happily as Freddie retrieved the book he wanted.

The ubiquity of Martha Talbot's books in nurseries across the Empire had fed a great deal of speculation. Freddie recalled a letter in the papers claiming a clergyman from Bolton wrote the books, while a couple visiting Edenwell from Shropshire promised Miss Talbot made personal appearances at children's parties for a reasonable fee. Martha Talbot, her young readers all knew, was a modest young woman in a brambly cottage with a wardrobe full of sensible dresses she made herself. But when unauthorised autobiographies began to circulate, the modest young woman had to go. Martha Talbot, the flimsy ingénue, turned out to be forty-eight-year-old A—— M———, wife of a retired merchant of luxury goods somewhere on England's blustery South Coast. Missus M——— gave a number of press interviews through her publisher, revealing her many hitherto secret charitable works. She apologised for the continuing veil of secrecy, explaining that she only wished to protect her children until they were old enough to understand their mother's fame. Being adopted, all three could be particularly sensitive.

Freddie paid little attention to the interviews at the time – too few pictures – but he added Miss Talbot's next book to his collection. *Children of the World* wasn't her best. Fa bought it with tokens from packets of tea. With the aim of funding a new free school for underprivileged youth of Liverpool, the book was a tour of the planet via its smallest human residents. In Russia, Freddie and his fellow readers met Dmitri, drinking tea from something called a samovar. In Egypt, a carpet seller's son said that camels laugh when you tickle them. In Norway, yellow-haired Frida said she didn't like pickled herrings, but would hold her nose and eat them when her mother told her to, like a good girl.

The author, not blessed with children of her own, was moved to open her doors to little ones in desperate need of the love and constancy of a mother.

How many years had Freddie spent poring over those words, dreaming of Martha Talbot tapping softly at his door? *Constancy*, he would mumble to himself, not fully knowing what it meant. Soon the rooks learnt it, enjoying the three solid beats. *Constancy for the knave.*

He turned the page to the final colour plate. A redheaded girl and two boys were at play in a blooming English garden. They had a trunk of dressing-up clothes. The girl twirled joyfully in a cascading Pre-Raphaelite gown, while a boy in a clown's satin smock threw a ball into the air. The littlest child, a boy of less than six, had hoarded a mish-mash of clothes and trinkets around him where he sat on the grass. His black hair tumbled over a paper crown, and the telescope in his hand gleamed bright. The author's own children.

Eustace had been beside him all along.

Phoebe Moncrieff took a mineral seltzer with her luncheon, though Eustace knew she would gladly have polished boots for a port and lemon. As he noisily pulled up a chair, he caught his sister eyeing the more distinguished guests ordering wine with their meals, but the muttering of those at the lesser tables was deterrent enough. Indeed, when Eustace had come sauntering through the dining room, their looks followed him like searchlights. Phoebe wouldn't fancy giving them another reason to gossip.

"Do you have gills yet?" she said, turning the menu over to study the paltry selection of sweets.

"Push off."

"I quite like it, you know. Doctor Chalice put me down for a massage from this tremendous Norfolk lady in a white uniform. The hands on that woman! I thought she was going to fold me up like a napkin. But I felt revitalised afterwards. Slept like I hadn't a care in the world."

"There's a war on."

"Give over. What can I do about it?"

He picked up a knife and tapped a glass. "I saw the car yesterday. It's fixed."

"I just said, I like it here. Anyway, I've had my free sample, and I'm off. Especially if you insist on taking that tone."

He angled the knife and began cleaning his fingernails with it.

"Doctor Chalice is an interesting man," Phoebe ventured. "You ought to ask him about the history of this place. It's horrible, you'd enjoy it."

"What's that supposed to mean?"

"It's a sad story. They were a merchant family, the Mortons – just like Father. Did well on molasses and cotton, East India Company and all that. They owned a small fleet by the sounds of it. Built this house and brought up several generations in it. The last Lord Morton was something of an eccentric. He had six daughters and one son and was utterly convinced the boy would one day drown. Probably a culmination of all those seafaring yarns passed down by his grandfathers – men falling off rigging, that sort of thing. The boy swam perfectly fine, but Lord Morton was convinced he was doomed. So when the time came for the son to involve himself in the family business, Morton forbade him to go anywhere near the ships, let alone the colonies. Instead, he sent him up north to one of the family cotton mills."

"Let me guess…" Eustace twirled the knife. "He drowned in the river feeding the turbine."

Phoebe sipped her seltzer. "He did well. Made his fortune. Came home and was cudgelled to death like a badger in a sack, right here on the grounds. The assailant was never discovered. Lord Morton of course went wild. It's said his wife took the daughters and fled to relatives, all but divorcing him. That's how Chalice got the house so cheap. When Morton died, he'd let the place go to ruin. The surviving family didn't want to live here. They sold it for a song."

Eustace ran a finger around his glass, producing a thin whining sound. "It's boring here. Everyone is old. I've just been for a treatment where you drink until you practically burst, then walk around and around, swinging your arms. There were five other men in there with me, and they were so *slow*—"

"Your new friend isn't old."

Eustace had nothing to say.

"You ought to introduce us. He can bring his dead bird."

Eustace found it hard to form thoughts. It was as if a stone sat on his tongue, and he guarded it jealously. "Phoebe, can you at least understand this is all the most stupid waste of time?"

"It's only until you get better."

"From what?"

Her glass paused at her lips. She stared hard at the tablecloth, as if she was working out how to unpick the embroidered pattern

113

and redesign it. Her eyes flicked around the dining room, checking the other guests were engrossed in their meals before letting her voice drop: "Do you even recall what you did?"

In his mouth, the stone was hot and tasted of iron. Before he had the chance to do anything with the venom building inside him, the dark-eyed orderly with the limp entered the dining room, and Eustace seized the distraction. He got out of his seat, practically standing to attention. "Mister Scole!"

Scole sketched an indolent bow. "Afternoon, Mister Moncrieff. Madam. What can I do for you?"

"When do you leave off tonight?"

Phoebe groaned. "Please, Mister Scole, don't let him harangue you..."

"Not at all, madam. It's a pleasure to talk with a young patriot. Matter of fact, I have something that may be of interest, if your sister can spare you."

"By all means, take him off my hands. All I ask in return is a port and lemon."

"It's not strictly allowed, this," Scole told Eustace as they took the stairs. The Hydropathic's clean white walls and glossy tiles ended abruptly at the servants' quarters. Garish Victorian wallpaper peeled in dusty coils, and the darkness was muggy with camphor and cough medicine. It was a corridor crowded with ghosts, not that Eustace Moncrieff believed in such things. Except when they landed on his arm, feathers white and oily black, bristling with life.

"I'm good at keeping quiet," he said.

Having worked the early shift, Scole was walking slower

than his usual brisk thumping pace. Eustace could examine the smattering of pockmarks on the skin, on one side only, like a slap. It wasn't a heroic countenance. He tried to imagine it screwed up in pain, and to his faint disappointment realised it lacked the bone structure to look gallant or even likeable in such a state. Eustace packed down the urge to say again what a good sniper he intended to make. As they passed one of the bedrooms, a woman snored.

Scole's room was at the far end of the long hall. The walls were bare, bar a mottling of damp and a few French postcards of smiling girls with skin like cream poured over pudding. Blankets of rumpled wool and a rug with a touch of moth. Scole lived like a man in a cell. Eustace felt a rising anxiety that he was privy to something he would rather not be. The orderly shut the door behind them and thumped his way to the bed pushed against the wall, bending to fetch something underneath.

A tobacco tin. Silently, he bid Eustace sit with him on the musky blankets. Rolling around inside the tin were three crumpled bullets. Scole took one between thumb and forefinger.

"This what you want?"

Eustace took it with reverence. "Were these…the ones?"

Scole nodded, a half-smirk loitering on his dappled face. "Wash your hands after."

The orderly hadn't fully anticipated the effect the bullets would have on the boy, who sat there staring, a touch stupidly, turning the largest between his fingers as if it might bestow on him some saintly power. Pristine metal crushed against living flesh and bone.

"We were blowing up a bridge. Cutting the bastards off on the wrong side of the river. They didn't like that one bit, came at us blazing as we set up the dynamite. It was dead of night, and freezing. I was covering the explosives boys, buying them time, getting as many krauts back as I could with my pistol. Out in the open, nowhere to go but back, and we had to run for it, get a safe distance before blowing the thing. One fella goes down, hit in the thigh, and there's a choice – leave him there to get blown up with the bridge, or turn back and carry him. What would you have done?"

"You rescued him."

Scole nodded. "And he lived. Most of me did, too. You say you're raring to snipe?"

"Yes, sir."

"What's stopping you?"

"Well, I'm here. I mean— I'm in reserve. Too young." He paused, fearing his quick riposte would be mistaken for guilt. He added: "Only by a smidge."

"What do your folks say?"

The boy was silent. Scole's smirk turned wooden.

"You could be bundled up in cotton wool and your mother would still worry, lad. Even world-famous mothers never want us out of the nest."

At the mention of his mother, Eustace's square jaw clicked. Scole shrugged.

"A good soldier does his reconnaissance."

There wasn't anything she couldn't ruin, was there? Eustace fought to maintain his composure. "Look, I want to go and I will go."

Scole gave a long sniff. He was starting a cold, and when his face scrunched the pockmarks on his cheek rippled and stretched as if to emphasise Eustace's infantile smoothness.

"Could've stayed with the Colour for basic training, though, couldn't you? Plenty of the young ones do, until it's their time."

Eustace felt a fulminant blush work its way up his neck. "My lungs, they... there was an incident at school—"

Scole jabbed him in the ribs, laughing. "Just testing you, sir. I couldn't spend every morning in Ferry's company the way you do. I'd enlist just to get out of that."

Eustace handed the bullet back. Scole fetched them both a cigarette, and the room grew dim with smoke. Scole wanted to know more about Eustace, about all the mismatched Moncrieffs. What about the girl with him, the little gingernut? Chalice seemed to take to her, but then he would. He acted the gent, but Americans were savage in ways Eustace couldn't understand. It was in the soil. Scole looked Eustace over with a knowing glint.

"Here's a favour. If you ever want to get a girl, tell her you're shipping out. Then you show her these."

More treasures under the bed. A book was dropped in Eustace's lap, lumpen with pasted cuttings. He was about to open it when the older man swatted his hand away. There was something new in the orderly's face, hard and intense. Eustace drew back instinctively.

"You think you can kill a man from a cold distance? Wait it out, count the hairs in his nostrils, then blow him away?"

"A German, yes."

"You've got to mean it. They crucified a British soldier, did you know that? Nailed him to a church door. All your mates are in France, I take it?"

"Yes." The lie came in a smoky exhalation. "One died. Lawrence Parrish. Hit in the head."

"Lucky Lawrence. One of my lads was burned all the way from the waist up. Took him three days to die."

Eustace realised he was holding the book to his chest, shielding himself from the steel in Scole's eyes. "I'm not afraid to do my duty."

Scole snorted. "Duty's what you do because you've been told to. You have to want it. The way you grab a woman you want, you know, and shake her. Smash her. You let it go cold inside of you, so you can hold it. Bone deep. You think you have it in you? In your little bones?"

"I do."

"Well, good," he said. And he was laughing, a shift of tone that frightened Eustace more than his words, a current changing course, dragging him with it. "We have to make sure of that, don't we, before we send you off?"

The hot compresses steamed away, untouched, on the prepared tables. Had Eustace turned up for his afternoon treatment, his chest would be slathered in Vaseline and wound up tight in the hot linen. All that was left was to lie on a table and sweat for an hour. It wasn't the most pleasant treatment available at Edenwell, but neither was it the worst, and Freddie was quite looking forward to experiencing it for the first time.

Scole stood by in his whites, hands clasped behind his back. Katie Healey didn't hide her impatience.

"What's he paying us for if he's going to go swanning off like this every day?" she muttered.

"He's still in bed, most likely."

"How nice for him. I scalded my fingers getting those linens out of the steamer."

"Ferry, go and find him. He's your problem."

Freddie was already undressed and ready to be swaddled. As he padded to the changing room, he winced at the *crack* of a rolled-up towel against his bare legs. Scole's amusement rang down the tiled corridor.

As he emerged into the marble reception, buttoning his overalls, Freddie nearly collided with a wheelchair. It was pushed by a statuesque gentleman wearing a fine suit with a faint sheen on it, contrasting handsomely with the stranger's deep mahogany complexion. Freddie had never seen such flamboyant fabric, like a magpie's wings. Too rich for him. Too rich for anyone at Edenwell.

Freddie was mumbling his apologies when a voice came from inside the chair. He gave a start; he had taken the occupant for a bundle of laundry.

"Hiram?"

"A boy, Clarissa," the man said, with the dry resignation of one well accustomed to pointing out the obvious. He examined Freddie coolly, but without malice.

It was an old chair, surely not one of Edenwell's. Made of braided wicker, the high sides and back were hung with all manner of charms and knick-knacks. Rosaries and rabbit's feet dangled in tandem, while painted eyes of blue glass and an improbable number of four-leafed clovers caught the light in brass lockets. The chair's small inhabitant was more conservatively decked out, though the gold cross hanging heavily against her withered breast was almost the size of Freddie's splayed hand. The woman could have been a hundred years old, but her milky blue eyes were sharp behind her spectacles, and she squinted up at Freddie as if he might attempt to sell her something she didn't want.

"You work here."

It wasn't a question, but still Freddie mumbled in response.

"Young man, I noticed a squirrel this morning, in the gardens. Dead."

"I'm very sorry, ma'am."

"And a dear little hedgehog lay on the veranda. Quite deceased." The woman's gaze was hard, penetrating Freddie's diffident shell with ease. "Drive on, Hiram."

The pair jangled away without another word.

Freddie found Eustace out on the bandstand behind the hospital. He was like a stork felled by an arrow, flat on his back, knees up, arms stretched out over his head. When he saw Freddie he put his finger to his lips.

"Listen."

Bees hovered hazily over the forget-me-nots.

"Come here."

He lay down beside him on the boards. They hosted bands here, before the war. The guests sat in deckchairs and licked ices made with strawberries from Mister Tungate's garden. Now the paint was rolling up in dry spirals. Fa would have to strip the whole thing or no self-respecting band would play there again. Everyone kept saying it: soon.

"Close your eyes."

It was something you'd say before giving someone a present. But Eustace's face was sombre. Freddie heard bees bumping in the flowerbeds. The wind sighed in the pines. Eustace had been smoking. Freddie could smell it in his hair.

He slowed his breath to a halt; tuning in to Eustace's serious silence as the wind glanced off the Hydropathic windows in their too-old frames.

Underneath it all, stealing across the brecks: a low, unconscionable boom.

"The guns," Eustace whispered.

It shuddered on, a barely perceptible disturbance in the air. Faraway thunder as heard from deep underground. Scole said it was possible when the wind was in the right direction, but Freddie had never believed him. Were they English guns, or German? Like trying to match a face you'd never seen to a voice you'd never heard. Then the wind changed and the link was severed. Nothing but the indolent chirping of birds.

"I have something to show you, too," Freddie said.

That morning he had stuffed Martha Talbot's *Children of The World* into his pocket. It was meant as a surprise after their morning treatments, but why bother with them now, and break this weird intimacy; he, Eustace, and the far-off ghost of the guns?

"It's you, isn't it?" Freddie held out the book, open at the illustration of the three children romping around their dressing-up chest in a tidy English garden. Eustace and his boyhood likeness stared at each other as if through a fortune-teller's scrying glass.

Freddie was expecting recognition and laughter, but Eustace looked stiff and tired, and at the sight of the book he seemed to shrink. Freddie shut it immediately.

"You got me," Eustace said blandly.

A bone of panic caught in Freddie's throat. He hadn't prepared a plan for this scenario. Eustace turned his cheek, eyes downcast.

"Would you like to have a go with my rifle?"

Freddie blurted it, the first thing he could think of to please him. It had the desired effect. The dark eyes flicked up.

"Now? Yes! Shall we go looking for your big cat?"

"I was thinking we'd start with rabbits."

Eustace clutched him by the sleeve, his despondency forgotten. "Lead me to the enemy, Lieutenant."

They collected Freddie's rifle from the cottage and went together through Choke Wood, passing the yawning traps which were a familiar sight to them both now. Eustace walked at a pace hard to match.

"Do you think we can really bag a rabbit? I don't think I've ever *seen* a rabbit in Portsmouth."

Freddie followed him through the last of the pines and up into the sandy breckland. It was a troubled sort of land, rough and uncultivated, with mounds of brown heather and brawny grasses waiting to trip inattentive walkers. It felt as though there ought to be settlements there, little huts with smoke stacks and animal pens. Freddie remembered that hot day out at the ancient mines with Chalice, when he'd disgraced himself in front of all those men. They would have had to close up the mines again when the war came, leaving the field as featureless as this one. A land bereft. But the rabbits liked it.

He looked dubiously at Eustace's clothes, the brushed wool, the clean cotton. "You'll have to lie down."

Eustace was already settling onto his stomach in the brush. "Like this?"

"There'll be a fair bit of waiting. They're not daft."

"I insist you show me everything."

Into his shoulder, neck comfortable, feet braced. Eustace

let Freddie arrange him. It was a pleasant disturbance to discover Eustace smelled like sweet hot tea, a scent only one very close could discern. Eustace lay so still, Freddie suspected he had stopped breathing. His own heart was going like the clappers.

"The trigger," he said. "Squeeze it, see. It'll kick into your shoulder, but not much. Don't tense up."

Freddie could feel the cold of the earth creeping into his bones as the minutes dragged by, but Eustace never complained. When the rabbits came loping out from their warrens, he didn't get excited and scare them off as Freddie had feared. He silently picked a mark and let it walk into his path.

With a crack, the rabbit was sent into the air. Eustace was already up on his knees.

"Did you see it? I got him! Oh, don't look at me like that, you didn't think I could? I'm getting it before some fox does."

Eustace took off running. Freddie sat back on his heels, watching as the lanky silhouette in the field raised a limp rabbit over his head like a trophy. He had never seen Eustace so naturally, boyishly happy. He found his thoughts meandering towards a future of mornings together at the Hydropathic and afternoons out hunting. Yes, Freddie would like that very much indeed.

It was firm, the rabbit, nothing like the soft bags of skin left by the Big Bugger. Freddie realised he hadn't touched an ordinary dead animal for a good while. Nothing but gritty potato bread and undersized eggs.

Eustace said, "Can we build a fire?"

"Missus Hardy in the kitchens could do it up proper for you."

"But I want to do it here. So we can share."

Freddie cleared the ground, showed him how to build a fire of twigs and dry moss. With his pocket knife, he took him through the particulars of skinning a rabbit, how to remove the sack of organs without puncturing it. Eustace was clumsy with the knife at first, unsure of how much pressure to apply, but he worked diligently and didn't shy away from blood. It was nice to be listened to, Freddie mused. He had never thought of himself as someone with skills to teach.

The rabbit was bony and tasted of little, but Eustace sat licking his fingers with satisfaction after sucking on the hot white brain.

"This beast of yours," said Eustace, examining the rabbit's open skull. "It hunts, doesn't it?"

"After a fashion."

"Are you baiting the traps?" He indicated the mound of shining offal, sticky in the grass. "Why don't we try? Shin up a tree and wait for it."

Freddie thought about it. They would need to be upwind to even stand a chance of seeing it, but hiding up a tree was a decent idea. What was it Eustace said he wanted to be? A sniper? Killing like God, from some unseen place.

A sensation ran through him. Something like a thrill.

The offal glistened in the maw of the trap. They picked a suitable tree a short distance away and began the climb.

A rook laughed. *What does a knave think he's playing at?*

"Climbing," Freddie answered.

"What?"

"Nothing."

Freddie knew there was no chance of seeing anything. The creature wouldn't venture out with a fire recently extinguished nearby. But he felt buoyant nonetheless; Eustace's verve was infectious. With the rifle over his back, the younger boy swung his leg over a sturdy branch and straddled it, heaving Freddie up the rest of the way. Freddie settled in behind him, hanging on to a higher branch to steady himself.

"Eustace?"

It was the first time his name was in his mouth.

"All right back there?" came the answer.

"Yes, only..." A churning feeling, and something cold at his fingertips. "There's a nest. And there's..."

He gripped something, brought it down. It fitted in his palm, heavy metal, pointed.

Eustace craned to look. "What is it?"

"It's a star." He flipped it over. There was writing on the back, but the dusk was bearing down and it was hard to read. He ran his thumb over the ridged Gothic lettering. "For... K... U...?"

Before he could discern the next letter, Eustace snatched the star from him. In silence, he inspected the thing. With his back to Freddie it was impossible to see his expression, but his whole lanky body had seized with tension and the groundskeeper's son felt his own responding similarly.

"It was up here? Don't play tricks on me, Freddie."

"I never."

To Freddie's alarm, Eustace swung his leg over the branch and pivoted to face him. He waved the star in Freddie's face.

"*For Kultur.* That's what it says."

"Who's that?"

"Freddie! Christ, man. Do you not read the papers?"

He tugged at his lip sheepishly. "I look at the pictures."

"*Kultur* isn't a who – it's a what. *Kultur* is what this whole war is about. It's everything we're fighting against."

"I thought that was the Kaiser."

Eustace wore an expression of fervent excitement. "*Kultur* is the Kaiser's entire philosophy. The Knights of the Round Table, nowadays they'd all have the Victoria Cross. You see? Valour. Self-sacrifice. For the Germans, it's different. They have this – the Iron Cross. Instead of gallantry, cunning. Instead of justice, brutality. When the Kaiser was a child, he pulled the wings off sparrows. He's only ever wanted one thing, and that's this war, and to get it he's trained a whole generation of Germans who believe in nothing but destroying the balance of peace in Europe. Destroying *us*, because we won't let them get away with it."

Freddie couldn't get past the thought of those poor sparrows. "Where did you learn that?"

"Well, it's just... known, isn't it? Ask anyone. Freddie, where have you *been*?"

He turned his face to the ground, picking at the lichen clinging to the bark. If he told the truth, Eustace would walk away and never look back. After that terrible day at the recruiting tribunal, Freddie had taken the war and locked it in a chamber along with campfire tales of hikey sprites and newspaper reports of derailed locomotives. Even before that, the call for men was a game to be played, like the football matches Scole and Mister Tungate held on the lawn in the summer. He was never included in those, so why should a war be any different?

If Eustace divined any of this, he didn't let on. "I want to show you something."

They clambered down, their plans forgotten. Eustace delved into his big pockets and produced a book.

"Mister Scole's cuttings," he said. "He's been there. He knows."

At the mention of Scole, Freddie's stomach dropped, but the book nonetheless intrigued him. The orderly had pasted newspaper clippings and postcards into a cigarette card album. Freddie was confronted by a skeleton draped in a monk's black habit, grinning over the lifeless body of a British nurse. On the next page, the skeleton guzzled blood from a goblet inscribed 'Kultur'. Naked Huns with scarlet skin laughed over lists of casualties. *A good month's business!* Worst was the French postcard of a monstrous naked hag, all sagging flesh and lewdly snaking curls, a cannon under one arm and a barrel of beer under the other. *L'Allemagne dans tout sa beauté.* Satan, sporting a spiked helmet, shook the Kaiser's hand. *Let me congratulate you, your majesty. You have done more in three years than I have in three thousand.*

Freddie's head rang with monsters. Never in his life had he been tempted to draw anything so wicked. It would be like bringing them to life. His eyes fell on a gigantic ape grasping a club and a swooning damsel, mouth wide in a hellish roar. The club, like the skeleton's goblet of blood, was inscribed 'Kultur'.

He stole a glance at Eustace, the bones of his face gleaming in the dark. Freddie was beginning to understand. If he hadn't spent the last three years making every excuse to avoid the world outside the gates of Edenwell, he would have known all of this.

"There are more," Eustace said gravely. "When they sank the *Lusitania* in '15, there were some truly stupendous posters. Fire and towering waves. And this. Isn't this something?"

127

ENLIST. In the watery abyss, a woman in a white nightgown clasped a child to her breast. Bubbles, flying hair, the dark suggestion of circling fish.

"A thousand people died that day. I'm not going to let them get away with it, Freddie. Thank you for teaching me to shoot today. It's funny, isn't it, how you put the rifle in my hand and then we found the Iron Cross straight away? Don't you think it's strange? A blessing of some sort?"

The medal glinted, brutish and angular in Eustace's slender hand.

"Is it…" Freddie hesitated, feeling foolish. "Is it evil?"

Eustace's eyes were solemn. "Very much so. Even from here, so far from the fighting, you can feel it, can't you?"

With the medal in his palm, Eustace reached out and clasped Freddie's open hand. Cold metal, warm flesh. Freddie could feel something cascading through Eustace and into him, but it wasn't evil. Just brief.

"Will they come here, do you think?" he asked. Lottie Mulgrave said they flew over London. To Freddie, London had always seemed as remote as an outcropping of Australia, but Eustace's urgency made the world feel loud and encroaching.

"They may do. But you have guns. And we have this place. Windows looking out at all aspects. There are hiding places – the woods, the folly – but when they come sneaking out? *Bang.*"

Freddie's heart thrilled at the idea. Defending the castle.

"But what happens if they get inside?"

"We'll pounce and squeeze the life out of them. Bare hands."

And they shoved each other, laughing. Laughing that they could do it at all, just the two of them, and that it would be so easy against some lumbering, red-skinned Hun.

128

They enjoyed the quiet of the woods as the shadows grew long around them. When the temperature dropped low enough for Eustace to begin shivering, they ambled up the bank together. They were halfway to the lawn when they heard an unmistakable metallic *snap*. In unison they looked at each other, then went bolting back down, Freddie in front, clumsily reloading the rifle as he ran through the whipping fronds of bracken.

Eustace yelled, "What is it?"

"I can't see."

"Is it dead?"

"I don't know."

The trap was shut and the offal gone, but whatever had taken it had fled. Freddie examined the steel. He could see no blood, no scraps of fur; the thing had got away unscathed.

"Bad luck," said Eustace. "But it's like I said. He'll come sneaking out eventually. And then – *bang*."

The painted crows on the ceiling were dark constellations in the candlelight. Tucked up in bed, Freddie watched the illusion of them moving in slow orbits. When rooks made decisions, they did so as a clan. Every relationship, every newcomer, each old grudge was pecked clean for the good of the whole. It seemed more natural to Freddie than Doctor Chalice's proposition: watch Eustace, report back. But he did as he was told. The American's displeasure, as rare as he ever showed such a thing, was not something Freddie wished to earn.

That evening, as Freddie had traipsed up the kitchen stairs with a bucket of Missus Hardy's vegetable rinds for the chickens

– only the truly indigestible relics were left these days – Chalice appeared in the doorway and called him to his office.

"It may seem a natural thing for you, Freddie, to shoot a rabbit. But for one so fragile as our friend Mister Moncrieff... do you see? Can you understand why I need you to be your gentle self?"

But it made him happy, he wanted to say. You should have seen him.

Chalice wouldn't have been interested. Freddie sensed the invisible council of decision making. He sketched it later, when work was done, a dark cloud of bodies crowded around a bright spot. It didn't seem right to attempt a proper portrait of Eustace yet. He hadn't the skill. Instead he cut bodies from picture books. Aladdin's robe, Tom Sawyer's bare feet, the graceful hands of the wood sprites in fairy stories. When he put them all together, he had something approaching the long princely elegance of Eustace, but it was only when he added his own approximation of mad, uneven black hair that he felt a flutter in his gut. Drummerboy hopped across the coverlet to investigate.

"You recognise him?"

The bird gave an open-beaked grin. Down the hall, Fa was snoring. To him, Drummerboy's reappearance was just a matter of him turning up, as he knew he would. A sign that things could still turn out well.

"You like him?" Freddie stroked his head with a fingertip.

Tack tack.

"I do too. Our secret?"

Tack tack.

The crows on the plaster seemed to whirl in agreement.

130

Freddie's eyes ached – too much candlelight – and when he rubbed them sparks of colour exploded and faded, forcing to the surface the painful memory of the cigar box sinking into the spring. The Tsarina, Drummerboy's poor folded body. But he was here beside him now, bright-eyed in the semi-darkness. Fa didn't know how right he was. Whatever the nature of their secret workings, some things did still turn out well.

Freddie scooted over to pull his curtains. He shouldn't have had them open with the candle on; the whole Hydropathic was meant to be in blackout. With sleep weighing heavily on his eyelids, he rolled over to blow out the light.

His heart lurched. Eustace was with him, lying on his back in the creaky old bed with his arms rigid by his side. Drummerboy squawked and retreated to the headboard. The mattress sagged under their combined weight. He drew back, shaken and disorientated, but when Freddie put out his hand, the long figure was nothing but empty clothes. He always threw his trousers, shirt and waistcoat over the chair, even though Fa griped at him to hang them up. Scratchy, studded with metal buttons, these weren't his own clothes, he realised, but khaki wool, laid out as if on a stretcher. And *wet*. Freddie shivered at the state of them, stinking of coppery mud. The army sent personal effects home, didn't they, packaged up in lieu of bodies? Nick Scole said so. Filthy tunics and twisted collar badges to be treasured like holy relics. And where was Eustace? Freddie searched the bed for him, leaning over the edge to feel about on the floor. There was mud everywhere, he realised, a thick layer of it seeping into the bed linen. He shuddered as it leached into his pyjamas, and when he squirmed backwards against the wall, his hands sank into slick grit.

He was lying in the open somewhere, out in the brecks like a drunkard to be taken by the cold or the ague.

As he struggled into a crouch, Freddie heard his own shallow breath and knew he wasn't in the open at all, but somewhere coffin-tight and dark as water. He couldn't stand even if his shaking legs allowed him to. Dirt under his fingernails, sand in his eyes, his knees raw despite the pads of fur he'd tied with deer leather before his descent. They warned him the silence was the worst part, worse even than the hood over his face, but nothing could have prepared him for the slow climb down, the fading voices above, the loss of the birds, the light, nor the smoky, animal scent of home. They said it was another kingdom, the below, and he in his youthful arrogance had doubted them. He knew all about new worlds – the first hunt, the first rut. They'd laughed at him, and not kindly. Inching along, he clutched his pick with one hand and felt his way with the other, pausing every few feet to check on the gifts, bundled close to his chest as if the whole world above depended on them. Precious offerings: the rare axe head, the skull of the delicate bird, and the buck's antlers, sharp as teeth.

The barrow lay ahead. Old sweat in the stale air; miners' bodies come and gone. But he was alone now. As he crawled through the tight opening, he felt chips of flint enter the heels of his hands, splitting the skin. Wounds to match his father's, his brothers'. He would be the last to see this place, though his eyes were obscured by sackcloth. Respect demanded it, and tradition: arrange the gifts, say nothing. The sound of trickling earth in the tunnel behind made the hairs stand up on the back of his neck, and he wondered for an inexplicable moment if the elders had stealthily followed him down, waited for him to squeeze inside the chamber before—

No. They were his kin. And he, so much younger and stronger. They needed him.

Too much light. Fa was at the door with a candle.

Freddie woke so suddenly he caught the last of a dry, ragged moan slip from his slack mouth. His legs were knotted in tangled sheets. Drummerboy was shrieking and beating his wings.

"What's the matter with him?" Fa said. "He's screaming to bring the house down."

Freddie's heart shuddered. His hands grasped at something he should have been protecting. Gone.

"N— nightmare."

Already it drifted away.

"You sleep perfectly well when you've done an honest day's work," Fa grumbled, and he shuffled off, taking the candle with him down the short corridor. Watching the dying light, his pulse slowing, Freddie could not shake the inexplicable sensation of betrayal.

SIX

Page taken from the popular *Ponsonby's Folklorica* and subsequently 'illuminated' in proto-medieval style. Coloured pencil, watercolour and collage. Possibly March 1917. Ferry's magpie imagination is at work here, taking a scrap of writing that intrigues him and turning it into something holy.

The Great Sweat. The new acquaintance.
Stoop-knave-and-know-thy-master.

This contagious disease befell England in the period between the 1480s and the 1550s. Death came swiftly. Aches in the neck and back, and a rush of nausea followed by a thirst to rival Christ's in the desert. Wheezing like a dog, the sufferer would rarely see the sun rise the following day. A splash of cooling water must have felt like the briefest deliverance. Who knows what prayers were uttered or what promises were made at the edges of England's holy wells during those bleak years when monks who refused to give up their relics were strung up from the nearest tree?

134

AS MUCH AS staying still was one of Eustace's favourite talents and the one most likely to commend him to a recruiting officer, inaction made him uncomfortable. The niggling need to be occupied began on waking, and, according to his family, made him difficult to share a breakfast table with. His father suggested a brisk set of morning callisthenics, while Mother thought diary-writing might make him less prone to arranging his food into abstract structures. Harry thought he needed an apprenticeship with the sort of employer who met surliness and fidgeting with the swift discipline they deserved.

"The real world is going to come as a shock to you," Harry said, with no small measure of enjoyment. "Heroics are all well and good, but try walking to the office in the rain every day."

Eustace took another two slices of toast from the rack and stood them up on his plate, a steeple smeared in melting butter. "The day of my falling-out parade, I shall pretend not to know you. What brother? I don't have a brother. Especially not one who works in an office."

Mother cast a long-suffering look at Phoebe. "What are your plans for the day, darling?"

Phoebe was given no chance to respond. Eustace plunged his butter knife into the jam, contaminating it.

"I shan't come to your falling-out parade," said Harry, "because there won't be one. You won't hack it. You couldn't even withstand school."

Eustace set his jaw. "You do say some pointless things."

Mother gave him a warning look. "Eustace—"

"I agreed not to talk about it," he responded indignantly. "Spilt milk and all that. Though I don't think Parrish's mother would put it that way."

135

Phoebe attempted to steer the conversation back to herself. "I thought I'd nip into town for a new blouse to wear this evening. It's so nice to think we'll all be together for a change – and with guests. What do you plan to wear, Mother?"

"I think a visit from Mister Bachmann warrants a teensy bit of jewellery. Even Father's wearing his good suit."

Harry drained his coffee. "Has Eustace sworn to be on his best behaviour? I'm not having Marion believing she's marrying into a pack of wild animals."

Eustace regarded his toast steeple. Harry's fiancée was so far from his mind, she might as well be one of Mother's fictions. He knew well enough what Mister Bachmann's visit was about, and it wasn't to discuss a wedding. Eustace needed a trade. Mister Bachmann was a school friend of Father's, and his canning factories supplied food to the Admiralty. There were plenty of opportunities for enterprising young men whose mothers couldn't bear them joining the army.

"A bride for Harry and a paid position for me," Eustace muttered. "What a tactical stroke, Mother."

Phoebe pushed back her chair and stood to leave. "I'm not subjecting myself to this any longer. You don't need to join the army, Eustace. You create a battlefield wherever you go."

Eustace shook the memory away. Loitering in his room would only invite further recollections of that miserable day. A few early risers were about, heading downstairs for a pre-breakfast douche in one of the Hydropathic's tiled treatment rooms. The lift was commandeered by an elderly gentleman with a shuffling gait, so Eustace took the stairs. He was almost halfway down, frowning at the worn condition of the carpet, when it occurred to him now was the perfect time to explore. With few people around to stop him, he could claim to be lost if he rounded a corner and met someone of authority. He paused, thinking of cobweb-strewn boiler rooms and the illicit possibilities of the wine cellar, wherever it was. Both were intriguing, but the sniper in him craved a high vantage point. If he crept upstairs undetected, slipping by the maids in their sleeping quarters, it would be something to tell Mister Scole.

When he reached the first floor, he passed one of the chargirls, the freckly one – Annie? – who averted her eyes as she trotted by, pushing the laundry trolley. As he expected, she glanced back furtively, and he pretended to rummage for his door key until she passed. Eustace hurried on to the next flight of stairs, keeping close to the wall and out of sight of the long windows. The next floor, as far as he could see it from the landing, was quiet and still. He fancied he could smell Scole's cigarettes sneaking down the banister. He crept up the stairs, swift and silent on the toes of his boots. A cough made him pause, but it came from inside one of the staff bedrooms, and with the doors shut tight, he felt bold enough to slip by, tingling with the thrill of almost being caught. The staff quarters, even the landing, had smaller windows than the guest floors, and the comparative darkness gave him cover.

A door swung open with a peal of coughing. Eustace froze.

The stout cook came bustling out of her bedroom, wiping her hands on her apron. The busy wallpaper offered some cover, as did the lift shaft, though the lift itself remained downstairs; Eustace guessed staff were not permitted to use it for anything but large loads of washing. Long grass, rubble, even banks of snow: a good soldier could – and should – turn any environment to his advantage. The cage stood at more than six feet, just over his head. If he was lucky, the ornamented bars would turn his silhouette into something obscure. Sure enough, as he held his breath, the sniffling cook showed no sign of noticing him. She was so close he could almost have reached out to pluck the shell comb from her hair as she felt for the banister and began her descent.

When the cook was gone Eustace went to one of the windows, emboldened. They were the sash type found in cheap tenements, and he could pretend he had infiltrated a bombed-out town, picking off Germans lumbering through the streets like cattle. With a grunt, he forced up the sash and let the morning air wash over him. Between the arched gables, there was a section of flat roof outside, a little wider and longer than a coffin, skirted by iron railings. In his mind, he was already out there with his rifle cradled in his arms. Shooting the rabbit yesterday had been as easy as blinking, a test he'd passed with flying colours. He wasn't some lackadaisical conchie swooning at the sight of blood. He'd felt the animal go cold in his hands. The power of it, the elegant simplicity, sent a shiver through him.

A creak on the stairs broke him out of his reverie. A wet cough; the cook returning. Without another thought, he slipped out of the window, flopping on his belly on the cold, flat slate.

Lying below the windowsill, Eustace was perfectly positioned to hear the cook's tut of irritation as she walked to the window and pulled down the sash.

He could have laughed. This was the third storey; below

him was the gravel drive, a sure way to die if he tried to climb down. Wait, he told himself; stand at the window and attract the attention of the staff coming off their shifts. A humiliating course of action. He reached to see if he could prise open the window with his fingernails, but the wood was smooth and stubborn. Perhaps he could hail someone below. Freddie would surely be out working, soon, doing whatever it was he was paid to do. He rolled over, looking out across the wide lawn to the little groundskeeper's cottage nestled in the trees. With a sniper's rifle he could use the sights to watch Freddie's blond head shining in the dark windows. As it was, he could barely make out the little chicken coop. Thinking of eggs, his stomach rumbled.

A sniper must suffer privations.

The roof warmed slowly in the rising morning sun, and Eustace with it. Waiting for someone to walk by, head resting on his folded arms, he grew drowsy.

In the distance, the dark pines of Choke Wood shivered in the wind. Eustace relaxed his eyes, letting the mossy colours melt together and the details come to him subconsciously, the way soldiers claimed the battlefield communicated to them, outside of reason and time.

Four figures, drab brown. Floating, or appearing to, amid the trees. At first, Eustace only half registered them, thinking them part of the branches. Errant laundry, perhaps, carried away on the wind and snagged there in a row. His mind wandered to butchers' shop windows, to the stretched necks of quails hanging soft and cold against the glass.

But these hanging things had the faces of men.

"I say. It's not all that bad, is it?"

Eustace gave a start. The window behind him was open, and Scole's hand reached for him. To Eustace's confusion, he was no longer lying on his front. He looked at his boots, planted by the edge of the roof where the low railing separated him from the long drop. He did not recall standing up. A wave of dizziness took him, and he fumbled back towards Scole's reaching arms.

"It's— it's incredible up here. Strategically, it's—"

Scole's mouth was a hard line as he helped Eustace clamber back through the window. Only when he was inside did he realise how cold he was. Scole's hand against his brow burned like a brand.

"Scouting for the enemy, eh? Playing a little game?"

His dark eyes showed wary concern. Eustace blinked slowly, the sun still smarting in his vision. Figures in silhouette, dangling, swinging.

"Let's get you downstairs," Scole said. "Before you cost me my job."

It was unpatriotic to eat heartily in wartime, to dress extravagantly, to long for football matches or warm pubs open late. In the Edenwell dining room, most of these sins were committed at breakfast, along with a few lesser transgressions: laughter, gossip and petty complaint. The guests were unsure of themselves, checking their company before airing their grievances, relieved to find others still suffered small humiliations running parallel to the great events presented daily in the papers. The Kaiser danced on the bones of British nurses, but knees still ached and nerves still jangled.

None of this hesitation appeared to touch Doctor Chalice that morning. Freddie was crouched at the dining room door, attempting to fix the squeaky hinges, when he felt a tap on his shoulder. "Freddie, do you have a moment to spare? You'll love this, fella." Freddie wiped his oily hands on his trousers and trailed after Chalice. The American strode between the tables with a steaming cup of coffee, wishing the guests good morning, topping up their water glasses, and even snatching a cracker from Lottie Mulgrave's plate. Freddie tucked himself into a corner with the girls doing the serving. Tabitha, wheeling out the tea trolley, caught Freddie's eye.

"Who's tickled him?" she muttered.

Annie and Maud, the inseparable chargirls, cast her a unanimous look and collected the dirty plates as slowly as they could. Chalice was also taking his precious time, enjoying the curious glances as he dragged a chair to the centre of the room. He hopped up like he was thirty again and not pushing seventy.

"Ladies and gentlemen, if I might interrupt your victuals?"

"He's going to fall off that," Annie whispered.

Tabitha shot her a glare. "Shh!"

"I know many of you have heard rumours. I wanted to take this opportunity to be frank with you all. I recall the day war broke out – all the men in the market square signing up there and then. A stirring sight, I can tell you, all those friends and neighbours so keen to do their duty. That day, I imagined myself in such a position, knowing I must leave behind my family, my home, this hospital which I have made my life's work. Did I have the backbone? I asked myself. Despite the nation of my birth, I see my duty the same as yours, to this country I've made my home, and to the men and women I've lived alongside all these years. It is for this reason I will be opening up the spare beds of Edenwell Hydropathic Hotel to injured soldiers, and our grounds to the production of food for the people of Norfolk."

There was a murmur of shock. Annie looked as if she might cry. Maud glanced at Tabitha and mouthed an unbecoming word. Freddie's gaze drifted to the veranda. A crowd of rooks gathered up crumbs of gossip to take home to their nests.

Mister Harrington with the bad back raised his hand. "Are there no regular hospitals?"

"Overflowing, sir," said Chalice. "All across the country, institutions such as ours are volunteering to take the least injured."

All at once, the guests talked over each other. Missus Bailey had no trouble being heard. "Miss Mulgrave spoke of contagious men sleeping in corridors. On floors."

Up on his chair, Chalice gave a solemn nod. "Sadly, my friend Miss Mulgrave is correct. But no contagion will darken our doors, madam. These men are in convalescence, like yourself."

"Will these men be trustworthy?" asked a frail gentleman at another table. "Particularly in the presence of so many ladies."

A snort of derision caught Freddie's attention. The impolite sound came from a petite young woman with red hair dining alone over a newspaper. She caught Chalice's eye with a wry smile, and for a moment Chalice was utterly diverted from the gentleman's question. Close enough to stare without being spotted, Freddie recognised her as the girl from Walker's: Eustace's sister, Phoebe. Eustace had only ever described her in deprecating brotherly terms, but in the soft light of the

142

dining room, she was most pleasant to look at. Freddie could understand why Chalice was flustered.

Shiny things, see, said the rooks on the veranda. *See 'em catch 'em take 'em home.*

"I'm sure all they want is a dry bed and guaranteed meals, Mister Golding," Chalice said, gathering himself. "There will be no cavorting of any kind. These are hurt men. And there will be plenty to occupy them. In addition to rooms, we have a wealth of land. I see rows of potatoes, marrows, canes of beans…"

Mister Golding threw down his napkin. "Doctor Chalice, I'm sorry, but when I paid for four weeks of rest and recuperation I did not hand over my money to be billeted with soldiers."

A cry went up from the ladies. The man was shouted down.

Annie and Maud no longer bothered pretending to clear the plates. "What if the Germans hear there are soldiers here?" Annie whispered. "Won't they bomb us?"

"Your last zeppelin turned out to be a cloud," Maud said.

"There are spies!" People turned. Annie had managed to blurt it out just as a peculiar old woman entered the room, pushed in her bath chair by the regal footman everyone was talking about. Scole said he was a Moroccan mercenary, though Scole would say anything if it meant someone was paying him attention. The footman wore a sullen expression and a suit fit for a travelling dignitary, and as the pair sailed by, the momentary lull in conversation was filled with the jingling of the chair's outlandish decorations. While the rest of the guests gaped at the man in the fine suit, Chalice's eyes never left Phoebe Moncrieff as she smoothed her skirts and quietly took her leave.

The hubbub soon rose anew.

"Injured men..." Freddie echoed. He saw the Hydropathic heaving with soldiers, the floors slippery with copper-clotted mud, and him at the centre of it with his mop and bucket, contributing nothing. Understanding nothing.

At his side, Tabitha stood rigid. "That could mean anything. Missing in action, died of wounds, it's all just—" She sucked at her cheeks, turning her face into something ghoulish, aged. Through her sleeve he could see the dark outline of her tattoo, *Thomas* blurring under the cotton. "I feel sick," she said, and quickly left the room.

Eustace paid Tabitha no mind as she bustled past him. He hurried to Freddie. "I was looking for you. You hear that? We'll be overrun."

His face was radiant. Freddie felt a tug in his chest, like jealousy. "I already have so much to do."

"Buck up, it's exciting. Think of the stories they'll have."

Guests were leaving the dining room now. Missus Bailey was fretting about disease, specifically the French variety. Another woman vowed to knit socks during her treatments and advised her fellow patients to do the same: Kitchener stitch across the toes was best. Annie and Maud bundled crusts into their aprons and whispered their conspiracies.

When they were alone, Eustace pulled Freddie aside. "Have you checked the traps?"

"Nothing." Lying in wait in the sea of bracken, the metal teeth were adorned with snail trails, utterly undisturbed. He called to the rooks, but they had no fresh information. At least there were no new limp squirrels. Perhaps the increase in human traffic would make the Big Bugger shy.

"It's damned strange, isn't it?" Eustace said. "Do you think we'd do better with a cage of some sort?"

"It's not a pet."

"I've got you for that." Eustace laughed at his befuddled expression. "Come on. I've a bath to catch. Are you joining me today?"

"Yes. I mean, I want to. But I have my work. I'm leaving too much to Fa."

"We can go shooting afterwards," Eustace said hopefully.

Freddie couldn't bring himself to tell Eustace rifles and rabbits were now off limits. But then, the thought of all that khaki swarming into Edenwell eclipsed Chalice's gentle admonishment completely. After last night's fitful dreams, the thought of regulation wool and brass buttons clung to him, a stain he couldn't quite wipe away. How many men were coming? What would they say about him, the shirker with the coveted exemption? And underneath it all, the nightmare vision of Eustace's long body laid out stiff and dirty on the bed.

Eustace was waiting for a reply.

"You could die," he blurted.

Eustace laughed, surprised. "I'll try not to."

Freddie left him standing there, perplexed but unhurt, calling out a cheerio.

The North Wing hated him that day. It was chilly outside, but the sun was strong through the windows and he was sweaty and uncomfortable within minutes. Sweep the floor, check the windows, dust the fireplaces. The ivy was regenerating after the winter, creeping in at the sashes and peeling away the paint.

A spider scuttled through a crack. He needed to fix that before rot set in.

He leant on the window to catch his breath. Below, Phoebe Moncrieff was springing about the tennis court. On the other side of the net was Chalice, so much taller, leaping around with the same energy. The girl belied her size and whacked the ball straight past his outstretched racquet, and Chalice doubled up with good-natured defeat. *Enough!* Freddie saw him laugh. *I surrender!*

Soon, Chalice always said. Soon, Edenwell Hydropathic would rival the great Swiss resorts for luxury and expertise. And Freddie believed it. Yet now, soldiers. Eustace was right, soldiers would bring with them more than just noise and mess. These men would be fresh from the war, their stories of blood and valour more lurid and enticing than anything from Scole's scrapbook. And if Scole's clippings of monsters and devils hadn't been enough to ward Eustace away from enlisting, what chance did Freddie have? He had nothing to offer him. Even if Doctor Chalice had never charged him with Eustace's protection, Freddie knew the thought would still be clattering back and forth in his head like a rook guarding a nest: *Stay – with me – stay – with me – stay.*

Or disappear. The two of them. Let Edenwell crumble to powder. There must be somewhere left in the world where a young man could walk on the street without the fear of white feathers handed out by righteous women, a coward's badge.

A flurry of black shivered in the trees.

A favour? A knave is already in arrears.

"Vacant."

Freddie gave a start. Nick Scole had let himself into the

146

North Wing. Freddie must have left the door unlocked. He couldn't even complete the simplest of tasks.

"Nothing between your ears, is there, Ferry? I've been calling. Everyone's below stairs."

"What's happened?"

"'What's happened?'" Scole mimicked airily. "Nothing."

The kitchens were oppressively hot. Missus Hardy had been reducing stock, and a fatty poultry odour clung to the air. In the bucket where they tossed the bones, a fresh pile steamed. The cook had her sleeves rolled up, but she did no work, standing stoically behind a chair where Tabitha Clarke sat scrunched and fidgeting. Her face was red with furious embarrassment. Annie and Maud looked nervy and on the edge of laughter. Fa was there, and Katie Healey with her magnificent hands on her hips.

Tabitha turned her flushed face to Scole as he thumped down the stairs with Freddie in tow. "I thought it were you, trying to scare me."

"Why would I go to all that trouble and then not jump out and say 'boo!', eh?"

Fa gave Freddie a tight-lipped smile. "You reet, son?"

"He's reet," Scole said. "Tabby had a scare in the courtyard. She thinks it was your monster."

"It in't a monster," Fa interjected patiently.

"It felt like one," said Tabitha.

Missus Hardy patted her shoulder. "Why don't you tell them what happened?"

"I was hanging out the washing," she said. "Just the sheets from the staff beds, not the guests, so there weren't that many.

There was room on the lines, I could see—"

"You said you didn't see anything," Scole interrupted.

"Let me finish. I was pinning up the sheets, 'cause if I left it to Annie, they'd be black by the time they saw a bit of soap. It's a good morning for it, the wind's up a bit. It comes in from the two sides open to the brecks, doesn't it, so my hair was blowing about all over the show and it was taking longer than I'd like to get the sheets up, and then… I don't know how to say it."

Fa was patient, but Freddie knew he had work to be doing and Tabitha's hesitation was costing him. "Did you see something, love?"

"Yes. Well, not straight on. But you have to picture it, there's all these rows of whipping sheets, and my hair in my eyes, and I was just all of a sudden *knowing* someone was there."

Maud snorted.

"Oh, piss off," Tabitha hissed. "Someone was there. They kept a safe distance, but every time the wind picked up, it was like they were using it to sneak closer."

"It was likely one of the guests," Fa said, and instantly regretted the unsavoury implication. "Lost, probably."

Missus Hardy was sceptical. "They'd all run off to talk about Chalice, hadn't they? You could hear them in the drawing room."

Katie Healey was counting on her fingers. "I supervised the ladies in the gymnasium right after. Most of them were present. Nick, how many gentlemen were in the Turkish baths?"

"Can't say I noticed anyone missing," he said. "You got to the washing straight after Chalice's announcement, Tabby?"

"In a right state," Maud muttered. Freddie, listening in worried silence, had to agree. Tabitha had left the dining room so quickly, cheeks blotched red with an emotion he couldn't decipher.

"Some dirty old man, then," said Scole. "We're thinking it's the patients, but what about old Jenks? I've seen him eyeing up the girls after his puppet shows. And there's that fella pushing the wheelchair witch. Nice bit of white meat, all by herself…"

Tabitha rubbed her eyes angrily. "Are you laughing at me?"

Missus Hardy ran her hands over the girl's sweaty hair. "There, now. Chances are, it were nothing. Tired eyes playing tricks."

"I'm no more tired than any of you. There was someone there. I wanted to run away, but I knew if I ran it would come after me." Tabitha looked at Scole so seriously the mirth melted from his face. "It felt the way you said it does. The Germans, at night. You can't see them, you said. Can't hear them. But when one's got his binoculars on you, the hair on your neck stands up like he's breathing down it."

Scole turned on Freddie. "You need to do your bloody job."

"I was!"

"I know your idea of working, Ferry."

Fa shrugged. "T'be fair, Nick, there's me and the boy to cover the whole estate." He turned to Tabitha, smiling mildly. "Sorry you had a fright, lass."

"More traps," Scole said. "You don't have enough."

Missus Hardy sighed. All this talking wasn't getting luncheon prepared, or the crockery washed, or the ovens cleaned. "You still have your service revolver, Nick? Why don't you put it to use?"

Annie and Maud's giggles were cut short by Scole's venomous look.

"More traps. And when you get that thing, I want it stuffed and mounted right up there, above the ovens. And you, you cheeky mare," he said to Missus Hardy. "You can cut it into chops, whatever it is."

Fa nudged Freddie, and they left in guilty silence.

"James. Before you go."

Missus Hardy caught up with them in the stairwell and shut the kitchen door behind them. She pointedly said nothing until Mister Ferry shooed Freddie away. He waited at the top of the stairs, around the corner, listening.

"Not to put too fine a point on it. I wouldn't normally say nothing, but she's got herself in such a state."

"Soldiers, Mags. Here. No wonder she's—"

"It's not that. I wouldn't be saying it if I didn't think it important. You were a married man—"

What did that mean? Freddie jolted when Fa called his name. He shied away from the door, a blush creeping up his neck. Missus Hardy's voice dropped barely above a whisper. He heard *washing*, then *sheets*.

"Enough earwigging, you," Fa said loudly. "Get on. I'll be with you presently."

Blood.

SEVEN

'Landslides' – ink and pencil
on paper, March 1917.

A dizzying overlay of warning signs from the woodland around
Edenwell following the winter of 1916 and '17. WARNING
LANDSLIDES DO NOT ENTER. With a contrasting coppery
ink, Ferry modifies the plain script, beautifying ENTER until
it resembles something biological, architectural, even holy.
Enter, enter. A mantra.

"GOOD LAD, FREDDIE-FELLA. Don't lift anything more
than you feel comfortable with, you hear?"

The trucks arrived at daybreak. Chalice was on the drive
to greet the first nurses, shaking hands with each one as
they stepped down in their long dresses and tough shoes.
It seemed he had delayed his announcement until the last
possible moment. The Volunteer Aid Detachment arrived
before any of the Edenwell patients had a chance to lodge a
formal objection. Freddie had never seen Chalice as anything

but a learned man capable of near-miracles, but watching him surrounded by nurses who had seen – well, *action* – his chipper demeanour seemed to chime a dud note. He was a jovial uncle playing dress-up with his nieces who were all a little too old. Still, the greener volunteers warmed to him instantly, offering names that sounded wildly exotic to Freddie. He'd heard the volunteer nurses were posh girls looking for adventure, but never in his life had he encountered a Euphemia or a Vita.

"Doing our bit," Chalice beamed. "Glad to help. Welcome aboard."

"Don't touch that," snapped a woman in golden spectacles when Freddie put an inky hand on her luggage. He drew back, blinking, which seemed to please her.

"Calder. Matron." She pumped Chalice's hand. "This is our equipment, such as it is. Patients to follow. Look, I hope you know what you're volunteering for, Mister…"

"Doctor Chalice. Matthew, please. I hope I do. But suspect I do not."

"Where did you study medicine, Mister Chalice? Not to be rude, but hydrotherapy is a little old fashioned and I'm not a hundred per cent on the particulars."

The slight bounced off him with no visible damage. "Oh, we have all the modern conveniences here. I'd be more than happy to help you catch up. Have you ever experienced the soothing wonders of a Turkish bath?"

Freddie had to smile. Chalice and the ladies, even the frightening ones.

The VADs had brought a couple of local men with them to unload the heaviest equipment from the vans. Peculiar frame-like devices to hang over beds, crates of jangling bottles, wheelchairs piled with boxes of paperwork. It fell to Freddie to lead them up to the North Wing. Missus Bailey followed as far as the stairs before retiring with a sniff. With the keys jangling at his side, Freddie felt like a jailer leading the condemned. To his relief, Eustace was waiting at the banister.

He took him by the elbow. "Are they soldiers?" he whispered, indicating the men with the crates.

"Just men."

"What's through here?"

"Beds, bathrooms…" There was nothing interesting to show him, nothing worthy of his excitement. But the sight of men was enough to keep him there, curious and a little on edge.

"Any ghosts?"

"Just me." Freddie unlocked the door. "Oh, blow."

A fat wood pigeon had got in. It bumbled about the bare room, its yellow eyes blank with bewilderment. Streaks of white shit marred the floors Freddie had only just finished mopping.

"Pigeon pie for dinner, then," said one of the men, and put down his crate. He picked up a broom. "I'll deal with it."

"No, let Freddie do it. He's…" His look was unexpectedly tender, and when Eustace noticed the groundskeeper's son staring, he scratched at his uneven hair. "He's good with birds."

The men left them, because Eustace was princely, and men do what princes tell them. He flopped down onto one of the freshly made beds and put his feet up.

"Bad omen, isn't it? A bird trapped in the house."

"He's all right," Freddie said, and showed the pigeon his empty hands, the hands of a friend. "How'd you find your way in, mate?"

"My mother told us stories about it. A bird indoors means death."

Usually for the poor bird. Freddie set about opening all the windows fully, giving the pigeon the chance to free himself with as little stress as possible. "Drummerboy lives inside. He's never done anyone any harm."

"Except my sister's windscreen." Eustace watched from a pile of pillows as the pigeon blundered around the room, shedding downy feathers that hung in the air almost magically. "I wish she'd leave. I don't like her spending all this time with the doctor. You don't have siblings, you don't know what it's like."

"Your mum's books – the parts about the birds were always my favourites."

"*Ponsonby's Folklorica*, you know that? She lifts most of her stories from there. All her brilliant, original ideas. At school they ribbed me for being adopted, but she's the fraud in the family."

Freddie was embarrassed by the volume of his own disappointment. "*Ponsonby's Folklorica*. There's one in the library here. With the big laughing fairy on the cover."

"She dresses it up all sweetly. The gory stuff wouldn't make it past the publisher, but she loved to frighten us before bedtime, me and my siblings. Magpies have the devil's blood under their tongues, that was one of her favourite Ponsonby tidbits. When God flooded the world, they sat on the roof of Noah's ark and just laughed. Cut out a magpie's tongue, and the devil will speak through him in a man's voice. She told us that, whenever one of us was being too loud."

He stuck out his tongue and made a pair of scissors with his fingers. The pigeon hobbled across the floor towards Freddie, beating towards the ceiling the moment he moved to coax it to the window.

"Magpies have always been reet with me," he said.

"Have you ever cut out one's tongue?"

Freddie whirled. His stricken look made Eustace sit up.

"I'm sorry. I was joking. They're special to you, aren't they?"

Eustace held out his hands in supplication, and the pigeon made one last noisy circuit of the room before disappearing out of the window overlooking the folly. Freddie plucked at his lip.

"It's not like a man's voice at all," he said guardedly. "When they have summat to say it's like... it's just there, in your head. Like seeing a picture before you draw it."

Eustace knew, of course. Freddie had been as honest as he dared to be, more truthful than he ever had been with anyone bar Drummerboy. But putting it into words still felt dangerous, admitting to some obscure treason. The truth of Martha Talbot smarted; Freddie could hardly blame Eustace for assuming he, too, was telling colourful lies. He was too muddled to even look at Eustace as he swung his legs off the bed and came to him.

"I like it when you're standing at my elbow," Eustace said. A little smile. "Like a captain and his lieutenant."

How could such a large room feel so cramped? Freddie stepped away, closing all the windows until the sounds of the trees and the invading nurses were snuffed out.

The pigeon sailed out a short distance across the lawn, a touch tired but no worse off for its experience. It settled down by the folly where a couple sat on the steps, wreathed in the man's smoke.

Eustace leant beside Freddie on the window ledge. "Is that Mister Scole?"

"And Tabitha Clarke. He's stepping out with her."

"Practically skipping." Eustace paused. "I didn't... mean that disrespectfully."

Freddie snorted. "Hopping."

The couple were knee-to-knee. Tabitha laughed at something Scole said, and he flicked a speck of imaginary dirt from her collar, brushing her jaw with his fingers. He had a set of motions to go through, like drill. Nobody bothered to joke about wedding bells around Scole any more. It had become too comfortably rehearsed. Tabitha and her tattoo would go the way of all the others.

"I was thinking of taking the Iron Cross and showing it to him."

Freddie looked up. "Why?"

"I just can't imagine why it was in that nest. Don't you think it's strange? A German medal, here, miles from anywhere."

"He'll take it if he thinks it's valuable."

"Don't be like that. We're on the same side." Eustace looked around at the rows of beds. "Good God, Fred... any day now, this place will be full of soldiers. I can't wait."

Down by the folly, the pigeon pecked at the grass where Scole and Tabitha had been sharing a biscuit. Freddie watched as Scole threw a stone.

Eustace sensed the tension in the older boy's body. "He isn't trying to hit it."

The tired pigeon fluttered back down to the lawn, and Scole launched another stone. This time, the missile found its target. Freddie banged on the glass. When he tried to haul up the sash, he found it stuck fast. The pigeon spread its wings and retreated a few feet, only to be clipped by another flying stone. Freddie slammed his palms against the cold panes, hoping Tabitha might see him.

"They won't hear," said Eustace. "You'll hurt yourself."

"He'll kill it."

"Fred—"

"You don't know him."

He went tearing downstairs, past the men lugging crates, past the guests scrutinising the women of the Voluntary Aid Detachment from behind their newspapers. He could hear Eustace pursuing him, calling his name, but in the confusion Matron Calder was collaring any unoccupied men to help with the lifting, and Eustace was swiftly commandeered.

When Freddie reached the stone steps of the folly, only biscuit crumbs remained of Scole and Tabitha. The pigeon had flown, having shed a few feathers, but no blood. On the roof, Drummerboy blinked down at Freddie, breathless and feeling foolish. It was a comfort, at least, that Drummerboy hadn't been the target of Scole's ire. Fa had taken to leaving the cottage windows open, tickled by his unbreakable homing instinct. Freddie had no fear of allowing him to fly free, not any more.

"There's my boy." He held out his arm, but Drummerboy preferred to land on the faux-medieval shingles of the folly's roof.

Freddie would hide up there too, if he could. He looked to the Hydropathic, scanning the windows for Eustace's dark face. He hadn't stayed to watch. Why would he? Anyone with eyes could see Freddie was cracked. He wouldn't be surprised to find himself turning up in one of Martha Talbot's stories in a year or two; Fumbling Fred who spoke to birds but couldn't for the life of him make a human friend.

A sharp pain cut through his thoughts. Freddie hissed and clutched his temple. The stone clattered away, down the folly steps. He saw Scole sauntering back to the Hydropathic, looking back with a smirk.

Who needed the Hun?

Drummerboy made a merry noise. In the tentative morning sun, he was oily bright, watching the VADs come and go with interest.

"I never asked you. What was it like," Freddie said, "down in the water?"

Birds did not relish being quizzed. Drummerboy ruffled into an indignant ball and took off out towards the woods. That was how to do it, Freddie thought. Let the humans deal with their own nonsense.

Leaves crunched underfoot as he traipsed down into the cover of Choke Wood. The VADs could unload a few boxes without him, and the sound of Drummerboy laughing over the rush of wind rolling in from the brecks was the sound of another life, the one he had before nurses and trucks and expectations he couldn't possibly meet. He glanced back at the drive, thinking he heard the rumble of engines, but the vehicles were all tucked away in the old stables. The dim sound continued from no discernible direction, uncomfortably familiar, rushing like the blood in his ears as his heart laboured through the night. The wind had changed, Freddie realised. He felt it, iron-cold, raking through the scruffy hair at the back of his collar. And riding it, the guns.

"I'm actually very ill. Normally I'd leap up to help, but Doctor Chalice has been explicit."

A pair of VADs huffed their displeasure and continued lugging boxes of dressings through the tiled reception to the lift. Eustace lolled on a bench under the portico, watching the nurses tramp back and forth like ants transporting crumbs. He had hoped it would be more dramatic than this. Men on stretchers, bandaged and groaning. Perhaps a spot of heavy rain. The girls were disappointingly chipper and efficient. Harry had led him to believe the volunteer nurses were green and hysterical, as likely to kill a man as heal him, and that most only joined up to snare a husband. A blonde girl stumbled and almost dropped a bundle of clean sheets, and when she noticed Eustace, she smiled. Plenty of fellows would be charmed by that sort of thing. Perhaps Freddie Ferry would. His mouth twisted at the thought, and the girl went on her way.

Chalice didn't seem to mind his institution becoming a paddock for clumsy young ladies of marriageable age. Eustace spotted the doctor strolling through the avenue of lavender winding around the Hydropathic's lichen-stained walls, hands clasped behind his back. He was deep in conversation with a smaller person Eustace couldn't quite see past his shoulder. A glimpse of pink wool confirmed his suspicions as the pair turned the corner.

God, Phoebe. You'd better not be jawing about me.

When he finally caught sight of Freddie, off at the end of the drive, it was plain he wasn't taking notice of the nurses at all. Eustace could see his yellow hair billowing as he paced past the fountain, his fingers worrying at his lip in that childish way of his. At least Eustace could tell him the blasted pigeon was perfectly all right. He had gone searching for it when he couldn't find Freddie and found it bumbling around the trucks, attracted by the possibility of food. Like a complete buffoon he was relieved.

"Call off the search." His grin faltered as Freddie drew closer, walking too fast, his face drained of colour. "I say. What's the matter?"

Blue eyes like frosted glass. *Everything*, they said.

They went in silence down to the trees. The white flash of Drummerboy darted back and forth as if leading them. Freddie could barely speak more than a few disjointed words, his lips tasting of iron where he chewed at them.

"We should take your rifle," said Eustace. "The creature, you know."

"No time."

"Whyever not?"

"Can't leave him."

"Freddie, is your father down there? I can send for help."

A garland of warning signs strung from tree to tree read *Danger! Landslides!* in Freddie's artistic hand. Above, a host of rooks cried a greeting, though to Eustace it sounded outright hostile. The light was different through the branches, stippled and ever-changing. Thin shadows swayed all around them, and more than once he nearly lost his balance trying to focus on the winding roots and loose scree underfoot. Freddie went on ahead of him, more confident of his surroundings but simmering with worry.

"You haven't caught him, have you? Your Big Bugger?"

Eustace tried to hide his concern with a touch of levity: "It's not a tiger after all, is it?"

No. Not a tiger at all.

The man was face down. Abrupt, nothing to signal his presence. Leaves had blown over the filthy clothes, but it was unmistakably Jenks, the ancient puppet man. He looked to be in a drunken stupor, but the colour of his skin where it showed at the neck and hands made it impossible to mistake him for alive. When Eustace noticed the prongs of iron triggered by the poor old man's unwitting step, he took a step back, crunching over glinting slivers of black flint. The blood had been absorbed into the soil. They were standing in it.

"The trap. I'll hang," Freddie whispered, broken.

"He was trespassing."

"He's dead."

"Not your fault. There are signs, yes? All those warnings. He did so at his own risk."

"He's *dead*." His voice was stuck on that one solid, immutable phrase.

"He was a vagrant." Eustace stopped short of *just*.

"He was here. All the time. He was always... and now he's..."

Freddie hadn't realised he was shaking until Eustace took him by the shoulders.

"No one is going to care. Bar you, of course, bar us, and the people here who were fond of him... but legally, nothing is going to happen. Freddie, you will not hang."

He felt as if he was falling. How spectacularly he had let everyone down. Fa would be overwhelmed. And of course Chalice, and Eustace who needed gentility and calm, and poor Mister

161

Jenks who never meant anyone any harm, lying with his face in the mulch. So much flint; when the police came to move him, the slivers would scratch at his exposed skin, wound him even further. An image flashed across his brain, of Fa springing the trap and dropping the log, and how the splinters sprayed like—

Eustace's mouth was pressing against his.

He could almost deny it happening. The same as he could deny Jenks lying there, if he tried. The tickle of the younger boy's hair against his face and the bitter scent of too-strong tea on his breath. A hard, dry press of lips and then it was over. The shaking, too, was over. The woods were still.

"We're going to go up to see Doctor Chalice now," Eustace said. "And he's going to telephone the police, with a minimum of fuss. And they will send a coroner's car, sensible and unobtrusive, and that will be the end of the matter."

Freddie gave a mute nod. He could do nothing else.

"Did he usually go about barefoot?" Eustace was looking at the corpse's blue feet.

"No, he had… big boots…"

"If he fell facing that way, he will have come from this direction." Eustace was off, jogging over fallen trees. They walked for several minutes, past the well, almost to the far end of Choke Wood, where Eustace had bagged his first rabbit at the lip of the brecks. There they found a makeshift tent leaning drunk against a tree.

"Just as I thought. Poor fellow set up camp. Look, there are his boots. But if he was just getting up to relieve himself, why go so far?"

Freddie looked back in the direction of Jenks' body, hidden now in the undergrowth.

One peck, knave. Won't do any harm.

"Don't you dare!"

Eustace frowned. He rummaged inside the tent. The princess and the bear marionette had been carefully laid to rest in a tiny bed of their own beside Jenks' reeking pile of blankets. He had folded their little hands over the coverlet before turning himself in for the night. Seeing them, Freddie could almost hear Mister Jenks' muttered witterings, his harmless *tiddly-poms* and *tum-ti-tums*.

Puppet man, puppet man, ran ran ran.

"He was running from something," Freddie mumbled.

"Perhaps he encountered your creature."

"You think so?"

"That would do it, wouldn't it? God knows I worried about ghosts in the lavatories at school."

They looked about, conscious of every creak and rustle of the wood. The rooks refused further comment.

Drummerboy came to rest on the tent's sagging roof. Absently, Freddie ran his fingertips down his soft black head. He chewed at his ruined lips, thinking.

"We ought to go up now," Eustace said. "It's time to tell Chalice. The longer we stay..."

"Wait."

Freddie went off towards the well, Drummerboy in pursuit. Eustace watched him lean down and scoop a palm full of water. He went back to Jenks' body.

"No, Fred, we can't have them knowing we touched him—"

But Freddie was already sprinkling water all the way up the dead man, from his bare feet to his matted hair.

"You have to do it too." It was on his lips – *please* – ready for

163

the look of pity for Fumbling Fred and his foolish ideas. But he watched Eustace go down to the water without hesitation. He dipped his long fingers and came back with appropriate solemnity. With a flick of the wrist, he was baptising the corpse.

"Should we... say some words?"

Freddie shook his head ruefully. "I don't even know what we're doing."

"It's all right, Lieutenant. Trust Doctor Chalice to do what he must. And you trust me, too. Yes?"

"Yes. Yes."

"No one will hang."

The bread was gritty and glued Freddie's mouth shut. Missus Hardy was bulking it up with something new, making up the shortfall in flour with her endless creativity. Freddie wondered if she would stop at wood shavings and found he couldn't confidently rule it out.

No one would hang. No one, bar Chalice, passed comment to Freddie's face on the sad accident in Choke Wood. Even Fa was reluctant to speak about it directly, preferring to mull it over in passing mutterings over his bread and cheese rind as the foxes screeched in the twilight.

"Poison, per'aps. But what does he eat? Doesn't touch his squirrels. Can't poison a fella what doesn't eat."

Chalice had been kind.

"Freddie-fella. What a terrible, terrible day. Tell me, did Eustace see everything?"

Freddie couldn't compose his face to say otherwise.

"Well, can't be helped now. I'll speak to him privately in

due course, but it goes without saying, I hope, fella: this is not to be whispered about."

Not a word, barely even in his thoughts.

Fa glanced up from his cheese. "You reet?" The wrinkles around his mouth deepened. "Course you're not. It's a pity."

"He was running."

Fa carried on as though he had said nothing. "We leave the traps. I'll bait them. Bit of arsenic for good luck. You eating that?"

"My chest's funny."

Fa pushed back his chair. "Shall I fetch Chalice?"

"No, Fa."

"I'll save your supper. You get to bed."

Cold under the blankets. Frog's legs lurching in his ribcage. The kicks of blood in his head made it hard to think. Images, pulsing up and out. Jenks' feet. Leaves and steel. The soreness of his lips. The softness of those others.

When he did drift off, it was only to skim across the surface of a dream. Eustace was gone. Fa too. He called out for Chalice and received nothing but echoes. All the men had left Edenwell, the women too. Edenwell, Norfolk, the world. He stood, a speck amid crooked pines and sprawling oaks, doubling and tripling into infinity, muffling the sharp line of the horizon, diluting the daylight until there was nothing visible of the world but the sandy earth. And him, standing alone in the undulating brecks with an antler pick in his fist and a bundle of his useless little signs.

Landslide.

Landslide.

Landslide.

EIGHT

*Bones, studies in chalk and
charcoal. c. March 1917.*

Knucklebones of cows and pigs. Antlers in various states of
wear and tear. The skull of a small bird, perhaps a coastal
phalarope. An approximation of human bones seemingly traced
from picture books and extracted from imagination. These
studies take a surrealistic turn as Ferry creates hybrid skeletal
structures from his existing anatomical knowledge. An antler
sprouts a spray of toes. A stack of beef knucklebones becomes
an atrocious spine.

EUSTACE WORKED AT a worn hole in the damask arm
of the library chair, widening it with his finger. It was
better than going to bed. He had brought *Ponsonby's Folklorica*
down from the shelf, though he couldn't say why. Impossible
to read in anything but his mother's voice, lavishly illustrated
tidbits harvested to bolster her own twee literary emissions.
When Eustace first entered the library, an elderly gentleman

was smoking by the fire. He met Eustace's cordial 'good evening' with a rumble and soon left him with no companion but the ticking clock. Heavy in his lap, the book was dogeared at the chapter marked 'Norfolk'.

The Edenwell myth, sparsely documented, tells of a nameless servant boy...

There was a telephone in an alcove in the reception. He listened for the icicle vowels of the operator and asked her to put him through to Portsmouth.

"Moncrieff speaking."

There it was. A man's voice, marching testily down the line.

"Moncrieff speaking, who is this? Wretched machine. Hello?"

Eustace's breath tugged a sharp salute. It came out in a boy's croak: "Is Mother there?"

The clock in the Edenwell lobby had stopped. That or the night had gone without him, and the morning was here, sunless and silent as the poles, with only the regular suck and hiss of his father's breathing down the telephone to ground him. There was dust on the clock's hands. Dust on the top of the telephone. Did the staff here not have eyes, or...?

"That's all you have to say, is it?"

The receiver gave an accusing brass toll as he slammed it back onto its hook.

He would spend the whole night in the library. Under a table if he had to, walled in by books. The chair's faded damask invited him to pick at, ruin it, and he scrunched himself into a ball there with his mother's stupid book for a blanket.

Scole was turning down the lights when he found him.

"Can you not sleep, sir?"

Eustace jolted. *Ponsonby's Folklorica* slid off his lap. "Is it very late?"

"Most are abed," he said. There was pleased bafflement in his eyes at Eustace's compulsion to stand for him. "All the new girls are settled in. The kitchen staff too, but I'll gladly fetch you a drink if you'd like, sir."

Eustace smiled weakly. "I don't think that would help."

"How you getting on with that book of mine?"

"It's… stirring."

"You've been keeping up with the papers? The Kaiser's stepping up his raids on London. You can't wait to be at 'em, I expect."

Images tumbled as if blown by a strong wind. The rifle is tucked into his shoulder, the rabbit flies, the leaves crunch, the tramp is dead underfoot, and Freddie, Freddie is—

Scole jerked his chin. "Come with me."

Up in Scole's room, the girls with the satiny skin were still smiling on the wall. A jam jar lid held a mountain of cigarette ash. Leaving his private place in manly disarray was a way of saying he trusted Eustace, and Eustace told himself he ought to feel privileged. It wasn't as if he could go down to the billiards room and share a cigar with the old boys. This was so much more real.

Scole pulled a flask from a drawer and bid Eustace drink. Brandy, and not good brandy either. "For your health," he said, with a grin.

Eustace suppressed a grimace. "Such as it is."

"Nah, young fellow like you. Chalice knows you're sound."

"He does?"

"He's giving you what we call a baptism. Dunk 'em and send 'em home."

The brandy went straight to his head. He felt the heat rising in his cheeks. "I can leave? Now?"

"Not while you look like that. You're healthy enough, but if you stroll into basic training looking like that, they'll laugh you back out again."

"I thought they were grateful for men."

"*Men*, aye. Come here. Stand up straight. Know how to stand to attention?"

Eustace put his feet together, threw back his shoulders and raised his chin. Scole assessed his effort and snorted.

"Like a chorus girl. Look here. Don't lock those knees. You want to be the sort of man an officer will depend on?"

"Yes, sir."

"You're one man among thousands. No thoughts of your own. An officer has to look at you and know you'll be there for him, without hesitation."

Scole took a swig. With his greasy hair and his determined eyes, Eustace could see him in the field, taking charge when all others had fallen. He went thumping over to the wardrobe.

"Put it on."

The tunic smelled of drill hall grease and had hardly been worn, but Eustace supposed all soldiers had dress kit kept for formal occasions. It was rough to the touch, the colour of wet moss.

Scole turned him to the shaving mirror. They were small in the foggy glass, and Eustace noted with disappointment how the tunic's colour sapped the life from his complexion. But it was a beautiful thing. Like slipping on a fresh skin. For the first time in as long as he could remember he felt a man, or someone who might aspire to be one. A moment ago, he could not be certain if he was an Irishman by blood, a dark-skinned Russian, or a fisherman's bastard from the Mediterranean coasts. But this was the uniform of an Englishman, and Scole had draped it around his shoulders with his blessing.

Scole held him by the shoulders. "You want to do a little private parade, don't you?"

A flash of Freddie's face, his blue eyes alive with admiration. Eustace swallowed. "Oh, I… couldn't possibly…"

"Take it. It looks right on you. And you'll get a Sam Browne belt, and a swagger stick. When the girls clap eyes on you, you'll be swatting them off." Scole smoothed out the epaulettes over Eustace's narrow shoulders. His breath was a hot blast of brandy in Eustace's ear. "What did it feel like? When you found Jenks?"

Shock stiffened him. How could Scole know? And then there was the look on his face, the peppered grin, so casual.

"Buck up. This is your first." Scole slapped his arm in a comradely fashion. "You've got one over on the other recruits already. And the old man weren't going to live forever, was he? What was Ferry like? Did he lose his breakfast?"

A hot blush. *He was faultlessly brave and respectful and I think he'd make any officer proud if only he had the chance.* Of course, he said none of it. Somehow, around Scole, his own bravery crumbled as easily as the ash in that jar lid.

It was past midnight when Eustace slunk downstairs to the library again. He couldn't face the luxury of his own room after Scole's squalor. It felt as if the older man could see through his eyes, that he was hovering close by, measuring and appraising his every decision against a yardstick of soldierly virtue.

The front door was kept unlocked at night. Who was going to break in, all the way out here? When Eustace slipped out into the night, the cold enveloped him like a wave.

For the perfect night vision, Eustace knew he had to avoid any source of light, no matter how tempting. Just let the dark have you. It was one of the few useful facts his brother brought back from France, and Eustace had grasped it like a treasure ever since. He kept the moon at his back as he set out across the lawn. The nets on the tennis courts swayed gently, invisible players dashing about in the night.

A sniper wasn't afraid of ghosts; he *was* the ghost.

But the scene was undeniably eerie. In the wind, the trees swirled and buffeted like the sea back at home. He thought of Mother humming 'For those in peril' and cursed himself for ever picking up that telephone. He could imagine the anguish in her voice. *How can it be that everywhere you go—?*

Poor Mister Jenks. Poor snotty Lawrence Parrish. How could it be, indeed?

A few thin fruit trees dotted the approach to Freddie's cottage. There was the chicken coop, and a log pile, too, for the little kitchen hearth. Eustace felt a funny sort of affection for the place, like a tatty neighbour of one of Mother's fairy cottages. He made a circuit of the building. To his satisfaction, he could peep in at the window of the largest bedroom at the back. Under the gap in the curtain, he could barely make out the shape of a sleeping body. This was the room he deposited Freddie in after dragging him up from the well, but the figure looked more like his father. He returned to the little window facing the Hydropathic. Not too clean, he thought, knocking on the glass. The first he saw of Freddie was a white shape scrambling to put on a pyjama jacket.

The window opened with a groan. "You frightened the life out of me."

"I'm a sniper. Invisible. Can I come in?"

"Fa will hear."

"He's flat out. I did my reconnaissance."

Eustace clambered in, clattering against some hanging objects he couldn't see, and sank cross-legged on the little bed. It was warm where Freddie had been sleeping. As Freddie lit the stub of a candle, Eustace found himself considering the smattering of blond hair on the boy's chest where his pyjamas gaped.

Eustace pushed half a bar of Fry's across the coverlet. "My sister says I oughtn't eat chocolate when I'm upset. It becomes a crutch. You should have this." It was a poor excuse for practically breaking into someone's house in the dead of night. "I couldn't sleep," he added. That wasn't much better.

As his eyes adjusted to the candlelight, he looked around him.

"Good God. I knew you were up to something."

The walls were smothered with drawings and pasted cuttings. Posed between shining Egyptian pyramids, he recognised Tom Sawyer, Little Eva from *Uncle Tom's Cabin*, Tootles and Nibs the lost boys, and even some of Mother's creations, cut and spliced until they resembled creatures neither man nor animal. On the floor stacks of leather-bound ledgers teetered. Eustace bent to inspect the title of the tome on top. *Wevver Weather storms winds hot spells and other interesting things as well as Christmas snows and also temperatures and miles per hour of blizzards and summer tempests.* That explained the collision on his way in. Thermometers hung like icicles alongside a battered brass barometer like something from Captain Nemo's *Nautilus*. But it was the drawings that held his attention. Long, sagging canvases of butcher's paper stretched around the room's corners. He stood to inspect the details, stepping over discarded pencil stubs and feathers.

"It's like the bloody Bayeux Tapestry in here. Did you do all of these?"

Freddie didn't answer the question. He was fidgeting as if fighting an itch.

"This is us, isn't it!" Eustace lit up when he noticed two figures toasting golden goblets. Freddie had rendered suits of armour cascading smoothly over their long bodies like fish scales. The light around them shimmered somehow, sunset pink, as if the figures emanated some kind of barely perceptible power.

"It's very bad. I'm sorry."

"You do say some daft things. If I could draw like this, I'd be—"

"Please don't tell anyone."

Drummerboy, snuggled down in his nest on the bookshelf, gave a small *peep* in agreement. Eustace saw Freddie's seriousness.

"Very well," he said. "Our secret. Another one."

On the nightstand was a scrap of paper torn from a book. Freddie had worked to capture the woodland floor, repeating leaves and pine needles with patience Eustace could never muster. It was the wood as it ought to have been, he realised, undisturbed by tragedy.

"Have you ever seen a dead man before?" Freddie whispered. "I haven't."

"One of my father's associates almost died in our dining room."

He waited for the questions, but there were none from Freddie.

"Got through a fair bit of chocolate that week," he added with a weak laugh.

Outside, the birds were calling, announcing Eustace's intrusion. Freddie's blue eyes flicked to the dark window, then down.

"What are they saying?" Eustace asked.

"They're being impudent."

"Impudent?"

He tugged at his lip.

"What, another secret?"

"They're saying Doctor Chalice is in love with your sister."

Eustace blinked. Freddie was so shamefaced, he clearly believed the birds were speaking to him, but that wasn't what made Eustace uncomfortable; indeed, it was easy to accept it, even join in, submerging himself in Freddie's world as if he might drift away inside it. He had no proof, of course, but since arriving at Edenwell there had been the beginnings of suspicions, of nasty thoughts he didn't want to entertain. A little bird told me...

"That *is* impudent," he said carefully.

"You needn't listen to everything they say. They're like old maids sometimes." He added: "But Doctor Chalice is a good sort. Even they think so."

Eustace sensed it embarrassed him to speak of it, like discussing the romantic inclinations of a parent.

"Do they have opinions on everyone? Your birds?"

"Oh, yes. They're not shy in coming forward."

"What do they say about you?"

"Knave."

Knave? That could mean all manner of things. A peasant,

a rogue. Neither fitted the gentle young man on the bed before him. "Do they talk about me?"

Freddie paused, stymied. "They saw you take the rabbit."

"And?"

He looked down, considering it, unsure of how to translate. "Won't be the last."

"And the Kaiser?"

"Not their business. Their French cousins ain't too forthright."

Eustace covered his face. "I'm sorry, I'm not laughing at you. I mean, I ought to have known. I'm no good at French conjugal verbs either."

"And they want the medal back."

"The Iron Cross? What do they want with that?"

Drummerboy squawked.

"Oh, they're into all sorts. Interesting shapes. Things that make noise. They'll have a bash at the ladies' hatpins out on the sun terraces. You give Drummerboy a twig and he'll lever open the bread bin with it. He's magic, aren't you, boy?"

"Would they tell us how a German medal ended up in an English tree?"

"They're keeping schtum. It's all a big joke to them." After a moment's consideration, he opened his bedside drawer and showed Eustace a half-finished drawing. An opera box full of man-sized rooks, magpies and crows in top hats and cravats. He'd added a ribbon of speech: *We like a drop o' Kultur.*

It was faintly horrible.

"What are you wearing?"

Freddie was looking at the tunic. Eustace told Freddie all of it; the aborted telephone call, the smiling girls on Scole's wall, the kick of seeing his reflection transformed by the uniform.

He judiciously omitted the orderly's comments on Mister Jenks. Freddie agreed the tunic looked very fine, but his heart wasn't in it. It was his hair, Eustace thought. Scole was right; he looked like a madman.

"The police came after dark," Freddie said. "Fa had to go down and show them how to open the trap. It happens, they said. There's poachers all over. People are hungry."

"Did Chalice say anything when I'd gone?"

"He was sorry you'd seen... you know. Everything."

"I'm not a child," Eustace snapped. Freddie looked chastened, as if perhaps he were the one in need of shielding. Eustace added more carefully, "I mean you aren't my chaperone."

Freddie tugged on his lip. It took Eustace a moment to realise it was guilt he was looking at, as plain as pencil on paper.

"Oh, God." Old newspapers crunched underfoot. Eustace struggled to compose himself, knowing Freddie's father was asleep down the short corridor. "Has Phoebe spoken to you? Is that why she's still here?"

"Doctor Chalice only said to be friendly to you. Because everyone else is old, and—"

"And you like the old girl's books. You're perfect."

"It ain't like that."

"But Chalice has you shadowing me. Yes? Do you report back? Make sure I'm taking my medicine? Is he paying you to be my..." His voice was rising with emotion, and he caught himself, swallowed hard. "My lieutenant?"

"He may've asked me to do it, but I like it. It's probably as much for me as it is for you."

"So it's pity. Pity for me and pity for you. How lucky we are! My mother—"

Eustace's treacherous lip was wobbling. He tried to force his face into a mask of haughty indifference, but found he could only turn away. She had to banish him to the broom cupboard of the earth and then she had to taint Freddie too. She couldn't even let him have that. He felt an itching in his scalp, and his hand was tangled in his hair before he knew it, tug-tug-tugging for the familiar sting and sweet, smarting release as a fist full of strands came loose. As always, the second the pain faded to a dull red heat, it was disgrace he felt, and with Freddie's blue eyes on him, wide with saddened awe, Eustace knew no tunic or badge could turn him into an Englishman. Not with this kernel burning away inside him, this terrible bad luck.

"I should go. I have a six o'clock massage before breakfast and I wouldn't want to oversleep. You don't need to join me if you have work to do."

"I'm sorry."

"I know you're overstretched."

"But I *am*. I'm not a spy, Eustace—" Kneeling there, Freddie straightened, forcing a watery little smile like a biddable subaltern, or worse, a frightened new boy meeting his housemaster and hoping to make an ally. "Sir," he added, as if it might placate him.

Eustace made for the window. Freddie caught the hem of his tunic in his fist. Down the hall, the father's door bumped open. They jumped and pulled apart. Fa called out, hoarse with sleep. "Fred? What's all the noise?"

Eustace put his boot on the windowsill and hauled himself outside. In khaki he was indistinguishable from the earth, gone in a second.

"Just a—" he heard Freddie say. "Just a nightmare."

NINE

*Assorted sketches. Mixed media on
reused butcher's paper, 1910-17.*

Youthful experimentation with pencil: a summer afternoon so
scorching, blackbirds spread out on the Edenwell lawn like
ladies' fans. A drizzly Christmas Eve where the young artist
wished for snow so keenly, he burst a blood vessel in his eye:
the first touch of watercolour, bitter red.

"LAMP OR RIFLE?" Fa asked.

Freddie stared into the cup of weak tea cooling between
his hands. "I don't think we should."

"I can't speak for you, Fred, but I put a new hole in my belt
last night." Fa was polishing the lamp's glass and checking the
shade's hinge for squeaks.

"But after Mister Jenks..."

"When have you known an accident like that here?
Worrying won't put food on the table. God helps those...?"

"Who help themselves," he added sullenly. It dragged at his

insides, but the hunger had its uses. It took up space. If all he could feel was hunger, there was no room for the memory of that flare of hurt in Eustace's eyes. Last night's quarrel weighed heavily on Freddie. They were so obvious now; the blunders he didn't realise he'd made until it was too late. Irreversible now, like a trap snapping shut.

Only tinkers and gypsies indulged in lamping. If a boy admitted to it he could expect months of jokes at his expense. But it wasn't like before, not any more. Missus Hardy swore a woman in Thetford admitted to cooking her daughter's pet rabbit. Freddie had to admit, whatever his heart wanted, the rest of his body would crawl over a field of jagged bones for the chance of sucking their marrow.

The Albion van bumped across the black breckland tracks. Bare trees touched the sky in lightning formations; as Freddie relaxed his eyes they became cracks in an ancient rock face. Then he remembered the Germans up there, hanging invisibly in the sky. Monstrous balloons brimming with bombs. What were they thinking as they watched the tiny van?

"There," Fa said, pointing over the dashboard to a dismal stretch of land fringed by pines and clumps of yellow gorse. "We'll park up now and walk the rest of the way so they don't take fright at the engine."

Freddie took the rifle and Fa took the lamp. Now he was out, it didn't seem so shameful. No one would venture out this far, this late, and the thought of food waiting to be taken was too enticing to resist.

In the nearby trees, a nesting rook rasped:

A knave and his gun and his friend and his gun and a rabbit and a friend all gone but the gun ha ha—

"*Stop* it."

Fa glanced behind. "You trip?"

The sandy earth undulated beneath his boots, rooty with stubborn clumps of heather. He found himself tottering down slopes and back up again, as if carried by a wave. As his eyes adjusted under the moonlight he could see the rims of wide craters in every direction, dipping between the trees like sunken graves.

Just a name, Chalice had said. Not graves at all, but something deeper.

"Fa, I know this place."

Fa gave a grunt as he loped up another sandy incline. "The Devil's holes, we called them, when I was a boy. Hush now."

They headed for the patch of coniferous woodland at the site's edge. Pigeons were hopeless nest-builders. Freddie had spent every spring he could remember removing their ramshackle homes from window boxes and guttering. Even when the nest was successful, the birds squatted like admirals setting sail in a bathtub. In the dark they were easy to spot, blots in the shrubs and lowest limbs of the pines. Fa motioned to Freddie. They selected their mark, a nest balanced awkwardly on the very tip of a branch, something no rook would be foolish enough to do. The twigs bent under the weight of their occupant. Freddie tucked the rifle's butt into his shoulder and took aim.

Fa tore the shade from the lamp. Freddie saw the bird's eyes beam yellow. In the dazzling light, the lunar craters all around them yawned and bowed, and it was only the crack of the rifle that broke the illusion. The tree rocked as the pigeon plummeted, taking its slapdash nest with it.

"Strike a light!" cried Fa, and ventured out to collect their dinner. "We'll do one more for luck, shall we?"

Freddie's eyes smarted as the dark fell in on him once more. The heather beneath the tree rustled, Fa rummaging around beneath it. Freddie reloaded blind. The kill had returned a small sense of usefulness to him. He would eat the next day, and though he knew he would have to do it all again the following night, the satisfaction was uncomplicated. Looking around him at the ancient mines, he fancied this was what his ancestors felt when they had a little luck. Perhaps that was the purpose of those trinkets left behind in the barrows, he wondered, thinking of the axe head, the antlers, and that eggshell bird skull in Mister Peake's tent that scorching day before the war. Tokens of thanks lowered with care into the flinty depths for – what was the god's name? Where were they now? he wondered. Resting in a collector's cabinet somewhere, or reburied under his feet? Mister Peake could be buried, himself, now. It was easy to imagine it, like flipping a page in Scole's book and seeing him there. Mister Peake and all his men, Mister Tungate the gardener, Harold the butcher's boy, all tossed into a pit by slobbering Huns.

They'd take Eustace, too, given the opportunity.

If the swine were here now, he promised himself, he'd show Eustace the weight of his seriousness. Germans had brains and hearts and wet, heaving lungs, and as long as that were true, Freddie could put a hole in one as quick as blinking. What wouldn't he trade for such an opportunity?

Thoughts like cabbage moths, gnawing away at his core.

Thud.

Ten feet away, someone jumped out of a tree. Freddie felt as much as heard the body hit the scrub. Instinctively, Freddie backed up, stumbling on the uneven ground, but the figure had no such difficulty. He called out a weak "Oi!", scrambling backwards as the stranger advanced. Freddie saw no hint of the man's expression, but the angles and speed of his body turned his guts to water. A stalking, rickety-limbed poacher, most likely, enraged to have his patch invaded. Before the war, Freddie heard of a gang who left a rival hanging from a tree by his feet. His bloodless body was white as a fish when the gamekeeper found him.

Freddie's rifle found its mark with a resounding crack.

"Christ alive! What are you doing?"

Fa's cry rang out across the field.

"Is he down?" Freddie said.

His hands shook violently. Fa rushed over, the pigeon flopping in his hand.

"Is who down?"

"He's—" He pointed to the spot where his bullet met its target. "I hit him. A poacher."

"You don't *shoot* someone!" In the confusion, Fa had quite forgotten to use the lamp. He pulled open the shade, flooding the grass with yellow light. "There's no one, Fred. There's no one here."

"He's limped off." Freddie was trying to reload even as Fa took the rifle from him. "He was coming for me. Don't—"

"It was a squirrel, if it were anything," said Fa angrily. "I know you're upset about Jenks. But you're a fool. You could have shot me dead, Fred. And how would you manage then, with your head in the clouds?"

They drove home in silence. Someone was walking ahead of them, up the long road to Edenwell. In the shadows cast by their headlamps, Freddie couldn't tell if the man was extraordinarily tall or if they were simply gaining on him. A pedlar, probably, or a vagrant with a weary gait. Freddie glanced at Fa, who had placed the rifle on the back seat.

"I see him," Fa muttered.

They kept their distance. The stranger was laden down with a pack, and Freddie remembered the wandering workers who came to the Hydropathic last summer, asking for jobs in exchange for a meal. One of them was good with shoes, he said, there was no leather he couldn't make soft and fine. "Who here has corns?" He said. "There's always some poor bugger with corns. I have an ointment here, sucks the poison right out." No one at Edenwell had bad feet, or bad shoes. The man and his friends kept walking.

"If he stops, we keep going," Fa said. "He's not coming in with us."

The stranger was nearing the gates now, trudging along with his heavy load, refusing to glance behind at the van he could surely hear closing in on him.

"What if he's poorly?"

"Eh?"

"It's a hospital. He could be looking for help."

"You'd let the Kaiser in if he asked nicely." It wasn't said fondly. Freddie was glad of the darkness.

When the Albion reached the gate, the man had slipped away. Fa got out and lifted the lamp, shining it into the bushes either side of them. Moths and midges, spangles in the beam. Fa silently urged Freddie to open the gate while he cradled the rifle, displaying it with a studied coolness that made Freddie's heart race. Freddie's fingers trembled with the keys, but soon they were inside, locked into the familiar groomed gardens of Edenwell.

They were parked in the old stables before Freddie found his voice.

"I didn't imagine him, Fa."

James Ferry sighed. The wall of silence had always been his weapon of choice when faced with the prospect of an argument. But Freddie had no quarrel in mind. Only a little faith. After all, if he hadn't squeezed that trigger…

At the cottage, the chickens *chucked* crossly at the intrusion. Dawn wasn't far away, glittering in the dewy grass. There was almost no point falling into bed. Hunger and exhaustion swam circles in Freddie's head, and as he waited for Fa to work the cranky old latch, he pressed the heels of his hands to his eyes and let ink spots spread across his vision.

When he looked up, Fa's arms were slack at his sides. He was stock still, gaunt face turned to the lawn, the visible puff of his breath reduced to something shallow and tense.

"Go inside," Fa said shortly. "Stay there."

He was staring over Freddie's shoulder with a focus that woke Freddie up as quickly as a dose of ice water. Freddie's eyes smarted, blotches drifting across the lawn as he tried to follow Fa's gaze without success. Glistening grass and the eddying shadows of the trees in the last of the moonlight. No vagrant, no travelling pedlar. But the rooks, despite the approaching dawn, were markedly silent.

"I'll come with you," he said.

"I'm not having you shooting a guest."

Fa checked the rifle's hammer. Freddie watched him stride out into the Hydropathic grounds alone.

184

The dead pigeon filled the cottage with a gamey smell that attracted Drummerboy out from the bedroom. Freddie sat at the kitchen table, listening intently to the world outside while Drummerboy pranced about with a beak full of pigeon feathers. Twice he got up, thinking to go out and look for Fa. If the poacher had slunk around and through the woods there was every chance Fa would chase him back that way, right into a trap. His brain raced towards the grim possibilities of a confrontation. Hungry prowlers possessed a desperate strength.

"We shouldn't have gone out, Drummerboy. Every time we leave – for town, the brecks, it doesn't matter – something terrible happens."

He was dozing, head down on the table, when the door clonked against the wall. Fa was haggard but unharmed.

"Probably one of the new nurses out for a fag," he said. "God, my back. Freddie, come on now, look alive."

Freddie followed his pointing finger. On the table, the pigeon had leaked a long thread of blood.

"Sorry."

"It can wait. Get an hour's kip." Fa hung up the rifle and gave Drummerboy a quick pat. "And don't take things to heart, eh? We all get crabby."

Phoebe answered her door in her nightdress and pink quilted dressing gown. Her hair hung about her shoulders, frizzy, freshly brushed. Eustace could smell her rosewater cold cream, the same brand Mother favoured, and his stomach gave an unhappy clench.

"Good grief, it's still dark," she said. "What are you doing up so early?"

"Haven't been to bed."

A half-truth. Two nights in a row, he'd lain on the coverlet in his pleasantly furnished room, watching a harvestman creep across the ceiling. Eustace had plucked at his scalp until the urge to cry had lost its power. He felt foolish now, and sore, with a new bald patch the size of a coin just above his temple. Phoebe, of course, noticed it right away.

"Come inside," she said. "Show me."

He sat on the edge of the bed, bowing his head so she could see his scalp, pinkish where the roots had given up specks of blood. She pressed her warm fingertips against the spot, rubbing the pain away in soothing circles.

"You had the sweetest curls when you were small," she said.

"Think that's why Mother picked me? Like choosing a puppy from a litter. The pretty ones go first."

"That accounts for you and me, but what about Harry?"

He huffed. It was just past six, according to the carriage clock on the little mantelpiece. Phoebe's skirt and blouse were picked out for the day ahead, hanging on the wardrobe door. Her portmanteau was unfolded on its stand, he noticed. Her spare boots were already packed, along with some dresses. A limp pair of gloves hung from one of the compartments as if waving for his attention.

"I'm off," she said, following his gaze. "Tomorrow. I've already stayed too long. I can't sit around in the Turkish baths for another few weeks, as much as I might like to."

"What will you do instead?"

"Once I get home, I suppose I'll seek out employment.

It's not very becoming, is it, being a lady of leisure? There's a war on."

His jaw clicked, holding back a dozen sharp retorts as she tucked her hands into her lap, nervously fiddling with her dressing-gown belt. Freddie's flushed face came to him, wide eyed with embarrassment. *Doctor Chalice is in love with your sister.*

"You'll be looking for a husband," he said, a sulky child's mumble. He cleared his throat, threw one leg over the other. He oughtn't have knocked at her door. If she really was leaving tomorrow, he could have saved himself the anguish.

A smile tweaked at the corner of Phoebe's mouth. "I'm in no hurry in that regard," she said. "Eustace, whatever's the matter? You're never up this early, not willingly."

He dragged his palms across his face. He was nauseated with exhaustion and her great guileless eyes were needling at him, goading him, smelling of Mother's cold cream.

"Something must have happened," she insisted.

"He's so *old*, Phoebe."

She stilled. Her face showed no emotion, but her gaze slid away. The same guilty flinch he'd seen on Freddie the second he'd perceived the extent of Chalice's game.

"See?" he said, grimly triumphant. "You can't keep it from me."

Soberly, she began: "I don't know what you think you've heard—"

"What has he said? What promises has he made?"

"Doctor Chalice is kindly arranging for a specialist to examine your lungs." She spoke slowly, as if coaxing Eustace away from his lurid conclusions. "Remember those fearful colds you had

187

as a boy? You could have lasting damage, and this Doctor Ridley is making a special visit—"

He barked a laugh. "My lungs. Mother's idea, was it? So Mother's throwing her money at the Hydropathic in return for having me invalided out? And you, you're in—" He struggled. "In *cahoots* with Doctor Chalice while he pulls his little strings. It's disgusting. He's in his sixties. You're disgusting."

In her lap, her small hands twisted the belt. "Mother and Father have fourteen years between them. And pardon me, but what business do you have telling me what to do? You were a child not so long ago."

"At least you're not denying it."

"I have done nothing improper."

"Would Mother agree?"

She hurried to her portmanteau and began filling the compartments with jars from the vanity. A conspicuous excuse to turn her back on him. "I'm leaving. How far in *cahoots* can I possibly be? And who's been saying these things?" she asked, throwing a look over her shoulder. "You can't have come to your own conclusions, you're the most self-absorbed—"

He fingered the fresh bald patch on his scalp, puffy and raw. "A little bird told me."

Phoebe sighed, ramming her hand mirror into an inner pocket too narrow for the purpose. "Eustace, I didn't mind the fib about the magpie and the windscreen, but my God, Doctor Chalice is real, and I am real, and accusations like this have consequences. I would have thought you'd understand that by now."

She fell silent, her shoulders tense, Mother's pot of cold cream in her fist. Eustace couldn't stand the cloying rosewater any longer. He stood, surprised by the tremor in his legs.

On her knees, Phoebe's face was pinched with remorse. "Eustace—"

"Drive safely," he said, and left her there.

TEN

*Collage, spring 1917: pencil and assorted
newsprint on paper. John Bull, rotund
and accusing in his Union Jack waistcoat.
"Who's absent?"*

Overleaf: Corvus frugilegus, *taxidermy
rook mounted on a stoneware Chalice Beer
Co. bottle, c. 1900. Wellcome Collection.*

Still thought of as vermin by farmers today, rooks held special
significance for Ferry, being a constant presence in both his
art and his daily life. Observed to use tools and enjoy puzzles,
rooks recognise individual human faces and have been seen
to engage in grudges, even passing knowledge of dangerous or
useful humans down to their chicks.

*L*OOK AT A *knave, scribble–scribbling. Tucked up in his roost
with the tame one.*
   Freddie clipped the stout, scowling John Bull from yesterday's

Eastern Evening News and pasted him into the ledger. The bedroom was cold; he had started leaving the window open a crack at nights, even if it meant numb toes by morning. Just in case Eustace came by.

Tit for tat, butter for fat; If you kill my dog, I'll kill your cat. Shut that window. Turn that key.

A week since Eustace had clambered inside and cast his lordly eye over his drawings, his books, his collections; the sorry little museum of Freddie Ferry. A week since they'd fallen out. Freddie had kept a reluctant distance, making his rounds unnoticed amid the hubbub of the arriving VADs. It wasn't his place to accost a guest without invitation. Foolish how he had allowed himself to forget: Eustace was, in all things, his superior. For want of distraction, he'd turned to his weather diaries, plotting the winds and cloud formations as the long days passed. Once he'd searched for patterns and found satisfaction in them. Now he felt only an aching gulf.

Shut that window!

John Bull pointed his accusing finger as Freddie sat back to tickle the silky plumage at Drummerboy's throat. There had been no further sign of the vagrant after the night lamping at Grimes Graves. Still, Drummerboy nested on Freddie's bookshelf, ready to shriek if a stranger came sneaking, and for that he was glad.

Not listening, is he? A knave don't know what's good for him.

Open in his lap, the ledger awaited his attention. He'd worn his pencil down to a nub sketching the sandy undulations of the site, a moonscape of craters thronged with flowering gorse, like the crown of thorns on the big wooden Christ at Saint Peter's. Night after night, his overtired brain drew him back to those sealed pits, to the airless black barrows below. As he cast his eye over his own sketch, a queasiness shifted in the hollow of his gut. Barrel-chested John Bull with his Union Jack waistcoat, pasted over the pencil craters like a giant straddling a choppy sea, was preposterous in the face of something so ancient.

A knave should shut that—. Go give it a tap. Not listening, is he? Tame One, oi!

Drummerboy gave a restless *chack*. Freddie turned his face to the window, to the wide Edenwell lawn glistening in the lacklustre sunrise. Eustace would be asleep, still. Another hour until the morning baths were run, the hot compresses steamed, the Turkish baths opened. *Who's absent?* accused John Bull. *Is it* you?

Drummerboy tapped at Freddie's finger with one black talon.

"Reet. I should go and say sorry, really, shouldn't I? No use wallowing."

If Eustace was surprised when Freddie turned up for his morning bath, he refused to show it. As usual, he was the only bather in the Solarium at that rude hour, and the white tubs gleamed in the morning darkness, clean sarcophagi waiting to be filled. Eustace had chosen the centre tub where he could stare up through the mottled skylight, at once completely alone and at attention's hub.

"You look preoccupied," he said as the doors swung shut behind Freddie. The groundskeeper's son wasn't aware Eustace had even looked at him.

"Sleeping poorly."

Two hours of dim, dripping dreams last night, which was more than he could say for the rest of the week. When he'd stepped out for firewood that morning, the chickens were facing the walls of the coop. That usually meant they were preparing to die. He'd tried to coax them out with soft singing, but they refused to respond.

The tub was so warm, he was likely to sleep in it. But he couldn't rest while the Hydropathic was in flux. More trucks had rolled in at dawn, bearing wheelchairs and jangling crates of what must have been medicine. The workmen all wanted tea and tramped into the kitchen commanding Missus Hardy to make some. It was a conquest, and the soldiers hadn't even arrived yet.

When he opened his eyes, Eustace was staring at him.

"Phoebe left last week. I gave her a rollicking. Told her I knew all about Chalice." He grinned, though those moody eyes were unaffected. "Tell your friends thanks, spymaster."

I'm not a spy. But there was no use saying it. Eustace was beside him, speaking to him, and that was more than he had dared hope for.

"There was one parting shot," Eustace added. "Phoebe said a doctor called Ridley is coming to check me over. A lung specialist. Mother's idea, of course. If my lungs need a specialist, why not send me straight to him and skip all this water? She said something about Chalice arranging it all. You see?"

"He's very clever. He knows a lot of people."

"Freddie, come on. Isn't it obvious? Mother sent me here because Chalice knows a doctor – a real doctor, with clout – who will invalid me out when I receive Notice."

It wasn't obvious at all. The light creeping into Eustace's eyes was worrisome. "But you're unwell."

"Weak lungs! Look." He took a gulp of air and dived under the water. Freddie knelt nervously in his own tub, trying to see over. When Eustace eventually came up, his chest heaved for barely a moment. He pushed back the wet hanks of black hair, revealing the hard lines of his jaw and the incongruous moue Freddie had spent so long trying to capture in pencil. "Malingering, that's what it is. Imagine if this got out: Martha Talbot's son, spared by a lie. You know she wrote some doggerel for the papers? King Arthur calling brave men to rise. Imagine what the papers would say now. People would burn her books; she'd never set foot in a publisher's office again."

"I think…" Freddie said cautiously, "someone would only risk all that if they cared a great deal."

"You would think that, because you're not like my family. You're not… well, you're not…" He was splashing, gesticulating uselessly, and when he noticed the mess he was making, he stopped and sighed. "I *want* to fight, Freddie. Look, have breakfast with me today. As my guest. I was beastly to you last week, and you're the only one who ever listens to me. Thought you might never come back. Didn't like it, not one bit."

He reached out of the bath and offered his hand.

"You're supposed to shake it," he said with a wan smile.

Freddie gingerly stretched a finger and let it rest on Eustace's knuckle. They stayed like that, only breaking apart at the arrival of Scole, loping in to give them their cold showers. Eustace was silent around the orderly now, the watchful quiet that came over people in church. Freddie cleaved to his side, dripping and shivering.

"How's the terrible malady, Ferry?" Scole asked as he rigged up the buckets over the usual metal frame.

He knew better than to meet the orderly's eyes. "Reet," he muttered.

"*Tiddly-pom.*"

Scole laughed as Freddie flinched. He pulled the cord and a sheet of white water covered both youths, taking their breath and leaving them empty.

"We have toast, we have eggs… I was going to order fruit, but I don't especially like it, do you?"

Images of food cascaded through Freddie's head as Eustace led the way up to his room. Freddie rarely saw this side of Edenwell. Even riding the lift was an illicit thrill, and he gave a guilty start when Lottie Mulgrave shouted for them to hold the door.

"Hoist me up, gentlemen. I need my morning sunshine."

It would have been indecorous for any other woman to go about in slippers and dressing gown, but Lottie was from the stage, and her parameters for acceptable behaviour were wider than most. Even so, both boys politely overlooked the glass in her hand and the shape of the hipflask in her pocket.

Upstairs, the doors to the North Wing were obstructed by a barricade of boxes spilling their contents. The lift trundled slowly, affording them a long view of two VADs struggling to get past with a fold-out screen.

Eustace pressed against the lift gate. "Freddie, look. Films! Stop us here, I want to see."

Freddie did as he asked and the three of them filed out, Eustace first, heedless of the nurses who didn't appreciate him rooting through their equipment. Sure enough, one of the boxes was overflowing with canisters. Eustace read the labels excitedly, passing them to Freddie to look at.

"*The Vagabond, Bounce the Baby, Bombs and Brides...*"

"Films," Lottie scoffed, and sipped her drink. "It won't last."

"Have you ever seen one, Freddie?"

Freddie never had. Fa was dead against them. There was a fire out Suffolk way that killed three people, thanks to careless hosts packing people in. He made a watercolour at the time, a sunrise of flames against grim newsprint.

"I once saw a pantomime," he ventured.

Lottie made an approving noise. "Ancient, pantomime. Right back to the Greeks."

Standing close, they could all smell the gin on her. She twisted open a canister and held a reel up to the light. Inside a frame of celluloid the size of a man's thumb, they saw a tiny woman trapped, her shadows and highlights ghoulishly inverted. She was frozen in the act of waving and laughing, her hair gathered up by a playful breeze. Yes, Freddie could see how the soldiers would need this.

"You poor young things," Lottie drawled. She tossed the canister back into the box and rested her glass on a sideboard to top it up from her hipflask. "Starved, you are. Culturally impoverished." Replenished, she sauntered away in the direction of the sun terraces.

"She's left her healing water," Freddie remarked. A heartbeat: what was that cynical trace in his voice?

"Ours now. Come on," Eustace said, pocketing the flask. "Before she dries out."

Eustace's accommodation approached luxury, though the carpets could do with replacing. It was a shock to find himself

196

here, where Eustace slept and brooded. Freddie didn't know what to stare at first. He wanted to take up his pencils and fix it all to paper: the comb on the nightstand bearing a few loose black hairs; the tin of boot black left carelessly open. Scole's army tunic lay on the bed. He ought to hide the uniform, Freddie thought. Maud and Annie would make sport of it.

Breakfast waited on a silver tray. A silver pot gave off the syrupy steam of Camp Coffee, and the toast cut into triangles resembled actual bread. A boiled egg, one of the few Freddie collected from the coop that morning, was the brownest and most perfect he had ever seen.

Eustace clambered onto the bed. "Please," he gestured.

Freddie tore his eyes away from all that butter. "You mean it?"

But Eustace was busy drinking from Lottie Mulgrave's flask. His face screwed up in disgust and he passed it to Freddie. Sure enough, his cautious sip was met with a tongue-numbing jolt of gin.

"Crikey."

"You know she has a whole crate of champagne down in the larder. I heard the maids talking. We should liberate one." Eustace grinned. "Don't make that face. I do it all the time at home. Just fill it back up with lemonade and put it at the back of the cupboard. By the time they get to it, they'll think it's a bad cork and throw it down the sink."

They sat on the bed together and shared provisions. Freddie fairly crammed his mouth, chewing like a horse, pausing only to take his turn with Lottie Mulgrave's flask of fire. Soon Eustace was happily prattling, telling Freddie all about his life in Portsmouth. How his brother was a bore and his sister a scold; his father was a great mahogany cabinet of a man who made all his money while young and never learnt the knack of enjoying it. His mother, the celebrated Martha Talbot, was happy to personally reply to hundreds of letters from strangers' children, but reluctant to give her own an encouraging word.

"You know what Dickens said about Portsmouth? Mud, Jews, and sailors. That's all there is to the place. It's far better to live out here, with nothing to bother you. Though how you don't go crackers is a mystery. Are you enjoying that?"

Freddie was licking his fingers obsessively. "This is *butter*."

"Have another piece."

"No, you need to enjoy this, it's *butter*."

"That'll be Mother," he muttered, and took a swig. "Everyone else here gets marge. Not me, the golden son."

Eustace was beginning to sound drunk, Freddie thought. Come to think of it, he too was experiencing a certain unusual desire to talk. How typical of the urge to finally strike him when Fa wasn't around to see it. He tested it out in his head: *Good morning.* He could do it, right now, just stride out into the hall and *good morning* everyone in his path.

"Wait, wait…" There was a pencil stub in his pocket and a paper napkin on the breakfast tray. He set about sketching Eustace as he was, cross-legged on the rumpled sheets, all avian angles, tetchy and flushed. Freddie perched him on a gilded throne of buttered toast. When he showed Eustace, he was rewarded with a broad smile.

"Oh, I've missed you. Drink with me, Lieutenant Ferry. No silliness ever again."

Two sets of buttery fingerprints all over Scole's scrapbook, fetched from under the pillow. They flipped through the gruesome pages with mounting giddiness as they drained Lottie's flask.

IT IS MORE SERIOUS THAN YOU THINK
The Barbarian is almost at your door
He violates, plunders, murders
Don't let him get a footing on British soil
Repel the invasion – ENLIST TODAY!

Painted scenes of contorted bodies against luminous sundowns. Scole's postcards were so much worse against Eustace's clean white sheets. A thick-necked German lumbered away from a burning village, swinging a baby on the tip of his bayonet, so pink and raw that Freddie's stomach lurched. Tattered newsprint folded out into a list of atrocities which he and Eustace took turns to read, the fire of excitement catching and growing inside them.

"Germans have flung vitriol and blazing petrol over Allied troops."

"Germans have killed our fisherfolk and deserted the drowning."

"Germans have inflicted unspeakable torture by poison gases on our brave troops at Ypres."

"Well, I'm not afraid of the dogs," Eustace said. "That's what they want me to be."

"And me."

"They won't touch either of us. See that?" He spun the book and jabbed a greasy finger at Saint George rearing up on his white horse, piercing the dragon's heart. "That's you and I, Lieutenant."

Lieutenant. Freddie took a deep drink. The grin on Eustace's face shone beautifully, white and wide and a little mad. Or perhaps it was Freddie who was touched in the head. After all, this litany of horrors was being played out just across the Channel, and here he was, spending his days behind the Edenwell gates placidly tending to cabbages. He should have been panicking. Everyone should have been panicking.

"Take the day off," Eustace told him. "We'll go somewhere. Find a place showing films."

Go? A rush of anxiety came rolling through his besotted head. "I can't."

"What, work? Show me what you do, then. I can help, then we'll leave."

"It wouldn't be proper."

"I'll say I'm doing my bit. If little shop girls can drive trams…"

The toast was all gone, the egg too. If Eustace hadn't been there to see it, Freddie would have licked the plate.

"A lieutenant…" he said slowly, skating over the difficult shape of the word, "follows his captain's orders."

"I think you're drunk."

"I think *you're* drunk."

"Fresh air."

They went giggling down the stairs and into the gardens behind the Hydropathic. All around the bandstand were Norfolk lavenders, crisp and grey with the famine of winter, but under the haze of gin, they were purple and heady with scent. It was a clear, cold day, and Eustace's skin glowed.

"How long has Mister Scole been at Edenwell?" he asked Freddie.

"Long as I can remember. And I was born here."

"Right here? In your little cottage?"

Freddie nodded, watching Eustace's face. The thought seemed to please and sadden him in equal measure. Freddie supposed it was the novelty of knowing where one came from, of staying there, however small and dull.

"Where do you think you're really from?" he asked, feeling daring. "Can you feel it, like?"

"Mother says there's an agency that collects unwanted babies from all over the Empire. So somewhere on the map that's pink, presumably. But I don't know. P'raps we have the same mother, and she just keeps doing a runner."

Freddie had to laugh. Eustace linked his arm through his. "A couple of motherless knaves. Say – we should take flowers for Mister Jenks. No one else will."

Yes, flowers. There were always flowers in the ladies' day room. They were easy to steal, or it felt that way, none of the staring guests saying a word to stop them as they bumbled in, arm-in-arm. With bunches of heather and pink dried larkspur bobbing in front of them they stumbled out over the lawn, past the tennis courts to Freddie's cottage. There, to his dismay, one of the chickens had died.

Eustace got down on his haunches and peered into the wire coop. "I'm sorry. Did she have a name?"

"They don't tell us. I think they know we eat them."

"Can you still... make use of her, or...?"

Freddie shook his head, but he knew he would.

Eustace tucked a sprig of heather through the wire and straightened up. "Here's to you, dead hen."

Freddie ought to have removed the bird, but he didn't want to face the task just yet, or to think about what Fa would say in his doomy tone. Something he hadn't done, something he had: it would be his fault somehow. Let him be the one to find her.

Eustace pressed another drink on him. The flask was down to a dribble, and Freddie heard it drop into the dirt. They were both wobbly on their feet, and even pale Freddie had caught a blush. The repulsive reality of Mister Jenks' accident was softened into something sentimental, and with Eustace by his side, Freddie felt protected from the worst of it; somehow immune to the rules of the scene, like watching one of Mister Jenks' puppet shows. He felt like a puppet himself, bouncing down the bracken-strewn path to the well where dreadful things had happened, yes, but wonderful things too. Though he hardly dared bring those certain things to light, he felt them glowing within him, and kept them kindling in secret.

"No swimming this time," Eustace warned, nevertheless going straight to the edge of the well to gaze into the cold depths. With the shadows of the pines playing on the surface and the tremulous ripple coming from within, the water seemed to have expressions and gestures of its own, a language Freddie half understood.

"I feel a bit sick," he mumbled.

"Don't do it in the holy water, whatever you do." Eustace laughed. "I wonder how far down it goes…"

All the way, all the way, all the way down.

The rooks' laughter trickled through the trees.

Freddie swung the purloined bunch of flowers. He didn't especially want to tramp over to the spot where Mister Jenks died. He tried throwing a scrap of purple heather into the air, letting it land on the well's stone lip. He flung another and Eustace caught it, shredding the petals between his fingers, scattering them like confetti. Soon they were scampering about, hurling flowers at each other.

Knave?

For once, Freddie could ignore the rooks. He tossed a handful of petals at a magpie as it shot past, low under the canopy.

Knave?

"Aren't you supposed to say hello?" Eustace said, sprinkling heather into Freddie's blond hair. "For luck, isn't it, with magpies?"

"It's 'Morning, Mister Magpie, where's your wife?'"

"Cheerio, Mister Magpie!"

Eustace gave chase, bounding over the rooty undergrowth. Somewhere inside Freddie's gin-numb brain a voice reminded him they were nearing the spot where Mister Jenks had lain, so still and so quiet. But the racket Eustace was making smothered any bad thoughts. Gone was the long, sullen stork. He tripped along like a child, running his palms through the bracken fronds, and Freddie was taken back to that first breathless glimpse of him between the stacks in Missus Walker's shop. The radiant macaw glowing in the gloom.

Knave! the rooks insisted.

"Where you going?"

"*Waryewgowrn?* That's what you sound like."

"Do I?"

"I like it. It's appealing."

Like an orphaned chick? he wanted to ask. *Like something that fell down the chimney?* "Don't know what to say now."

"*Dunno whadda saynoo.*"

"You're a posh bleeder, yourself."

"Posh! I occupy the smallest bedroom in a very modest house—"

"How many bedrooms?"

"Just six."

Freddie snorted. He couldn't comprehend how the two of them were together like this. Nature had its rules: a crow would only roost among his own kin. Come to think of it, a macaw would never bring his colours to cloudy Norfolk, not without a heap of Martha Talbot's magic. And it did feel magical, as if someone had granted a wish he was unaware he'd even made.

The magpie was back, flashing in and out of the pines in a wide circle around them.

"Where are you going in such a hurry?" Freddie called to it.

"Nowhere! I'm—" Up ahead, Eustace froze. His wild hair bounced with the force of the sudden stop. He was staring past Freddie, where the magpie ducked and reeled high up into the canopy. Freddie heard it too.

Tum-ti-tum.

Petals fell from Eustace's shoulders. He scanned the trees, then looked to Freddie. "Did—"

"Shh!"

The rooks, to Freddie's discomfort, had stopped calling. Besides the nests and clumps of limp mistletoe, he couldn't make out a single black shape in the trees.

At once he was plunge-pool sober.

A *thump*. Freddie gave a start. He had once been sitting by the kitchen window when a pigeon flew into it, and the sound was the same, hard and unforgiving, shadowed by silence. Eustace was breathing visibly, his dark eyes flicking about.

"That was close," he said.

"Do you think the police have come back?"

What would they come back for? The body had been taken. More likely Scole had followed them down to play one of his tricks. Freddie looked around them through the knots of bracken and winter debris for signs of the white Edenwell uniform, but saw nothing.

Eustace was trying to climb a tree for a better view. "Give me a leg up."

"Mind out. The branches look rotten."

"That's the last thing I need, half a tree landing on—"

The noise came again and silenced them both. A subterranean *crunch*.

Freddie's voice dropped to a whisper. "Do you think we should go home?"

"I want to see."

Freddie couldn't hear anything, let alone see. Something had come between him and the habitual creak of the wood. Even the wood pigeons, usually so clumsy and crass, had disappeared entirely.

"The wind, it's…"

Eustace cocked his head. "Heavy."

Yes, there was weight to it. Whatever was passing over the wood, they were submerged in it. Freddie's body, slight as it was, felt too tight, shrunken somehow, as if he had aged. He itched to run – Eustace, too – but instead they stood facing each other, listening for sounds that didn't come. Eustace was touching his ears, covering and uncovering them, as if there lay the problem.

"Freddie, I don't—"

Eustace rounded off his sentence with a cry of surprise. A blur shot over the well. The resulting *thump* landed with sick intensity. Eustace scrambled to the source of the noise, slipping on the damp stones.

"A rabbit!"

He held it up for Freddie to see, its black eyes open in death. With its neck bent at a morbid angle, it looked like a child's toy with the stuffing taken out. When Freddie spotted a man standing motionless at the brow of the hill, his stomach lurched in relief. A poacher, of course it was. Some still hunted with slingshots, cheap and quiet. The rabbit had been sent flying by a stone, and the poacher was frozen in shock, knowing he could easily have felled either one of the two strangers hailing him below.

"I say," Eustace called out. "You want to watch where you're throwing your supper."

If the poacher meant to intimidate them, he knew precisely how. Stock still, swathed against the cold in overcoats, boots and gaiters, Freddie could not make out his expression at this distance. He could only see it was a gangling, knock-kneed man with a pugilist's stance. A fragment came to Freddie, a childhood memory of a travelling fair, of a bony man who could pinch the skin of his arms and stretch it out like thin dough. The performer tumbled about the stage, bending his angular body into insectile knots. Heels around his ears, elbows pinned to his spine like the wings of a plucked chicken, he grinned all the while at the crowd's hoots and jeers. Freddie felt that same catch in his throat now. He supposed it was the poacher's refusal to speak that bolstered his threatening appearance. He had a gun, or perhaps a staff, which he held in front of his face. In the woodland shade, it appeared he sported a horn.

Freddie touched Eustace's arm. "I've seen him before. Come on."

They took the long path back. The poacher didn't appear interested, remaining on the bank, staring down at his rabbit with indifference.

"He shouldn't be down there, with all the traps," Freddie said to himself as they emerged at the back of the cottage.

"He ignored the signs."

"Can he read?"

That hadn't occurred to Eustace. "If anyone knows how to spot traps, it's a poacher," he assured him. "Don't fret. Check the locks, though. I'll bet he's been skulking around."

Freddie tugged at his lip, thinking back to the man stealing across Grimes Graves in the night. He fought the urge to replay that desperate lolloping gait in his mind. Hunger, darkness, and an overactive imagination, that was all it was. But the man back in Choke Wood was real enough.

Poachers were organised. They had homes to go to, lookouts and cunning. They didn't wander where they could easily be discovered. The possibilities nagged at him. What if he was another Mister Jenks? One of the drifting men who took turnips from farmers' fields and chewed them on the roadside? Soft in the head?

"He could come to mischief."

Eustace sighed. "All right. But I don't trust the devil. We'll take your rifle."

With apprehension, they turned back. The sounds of the wood had returned, the creaking of the pines and the whispering of the needles. The legacy of the gin was a dry mouth and the threat of a headache. Freddie felt the need to be alert, but his brain and body refused to work in tandem, slogging slowly alongside Eustace as if through soup.

By the time they reached the well, the man was nowhere to be seen. The rabbit lay on the stones. Freddie was puzzled. A poacher or gypsy would never be so wasteful. It was some crank, then. All those blameless creatures and all those hours piling bonfires with their bodies. Freddie's chest tightened. This was his *home*. Printed words crowded behind his eyes, goading him for his inaction, his boyish timidity:

> *The Barbarian is almost at your door*
> *He violates, plunders, murders*
> *Don't let him get a footing*

He cradled his rifle where it might easily be seen. The swine couldn't have gone far.

Eustace strode around, hands on hips. "Bugger's gone to ground." He feigned an easy shrug, plainly uncomfortable with the situation. "Look, he could be in a blind. Let's go back. I bet the nurses have a projector out by now. Let me show you a film. Or better yet, let's make one up. You can draw it. You can draw me."

It was like a benediction. If Freddie could capture Eustace as he was, right at that second, his cheekbones and the tip of his nose flushed, he could happily give up paper and pencils for ever.

A sharp spray of bark. Eustace ducked, arms flung instinctively over his face. The man was back, pelting them from some unseen spot. A black shard of flint was embedded in the trunk nearest to them, as if shot with great force. Freddie grabbed

Eustace's coat and tugged him behind the tree and down into the dirt.

A shriek down by the spring. The panicked sounds of a rabbit, high and strangled like a baby's cry, followed by a dull *crack*.

Freddie's heart clamoured in his throat. "Don't," he hissed, but Eustace was already moving. Fallen trees offered cover as he crawled forwards for a better view. Freddie could do nothing but follow.

The stranger was standing with his back to them. He sidled up onto the stones of the well, though he was bundled up so bulkily it was a wonder he could move at all: layers of overcoats and fisherman's oilskins, hoods of leather and filthy wool, sagging and bunched until the shape of the man beneath was barely discernible. His over-large boots flapped at the soles, and the gaiters wrapping his scrawny calves might as well have been cobwebs, they were so holey and thin.

He moved with shambling indecisiveness, and Freddie felt a pang for old Mister Jenks, broad and bearded like a sea captain, always so careful in his ministrations. There was something crablike about the stranger; a scuttling, tetchy manner. As he turned and turned again, the glimpses of his face offered little more than smears of black Norfolk soil. But it was the man's headgear that held Freddie's attention. He wore a helmet. Snug to the crown of his head, it was black and of a bowl shape, beetle shiny, topped with a vicious spike.

"Don't move," Eustace hissed, barely above the volume of his breath. Excitement radiated from his body, flattened beside Freddie's in the fallen leaves. "It's a German."

Freddie stared at him, waiting for a sly grin to break, but Eustace's face was intensely serious.

"That's what they wear. You saw the pictures. That's why he wouldn't speak."

Freddie's mouth opened and shut uselessly. *Why would a German be here?* he wanted to ask, but of course, that was his naiveté on display. They were already flying over London; drowning fishermen just off the coast. The wide reach of Germany was the reason he went to bed hungry and woke up no different.

"The medal..." he whispered.

"He's looking for it," Eustace replied, his mouth a hard line. "Give me your rifle."

"What?"

"It's what they'll do anyway. Don't you see? Mister Jenks found him down here, so the swine killed him. I only need to clip him, stop him from running off."

"You can do that? Are you sure?" Freddie was dubious, but the exhilaration coming off Eustace's skin was like an electric discharge.

"We'll be heroes."

The German was pacing unsteady circles around the spring, his round dirty head rocking like a dropped cauldron. The more Freddie stared, the more he felt himself believing it. The brutish silhouette, the heap of rags, the ugly, creeping bearing. A German, at Edenwell. A shambling, bow-legged thing. Even from a distance Freddie could imagine him slopping blood from a goblet like the thugs lurching through Scole's book.

It would be a thrilling thing to see Eustace shoot him.

Sprawled on his stomach in the loamy dirt, Eustace cradled the rifle into his shoulder, rested the muzzle on the log. He let the German linger in his sights for a moment, gathering his courage, before pulling back the hammer with a click.

The German froze.

In the sickening silence, Freddie made the calculations: their narrow head-start, how many traps to dodge, how long the cottage door would hold if they barricaded it. But the German was training his senses on something else. Where before the wood had settled into unnerving silence, Freddie now heard the indistinct chatter of blackbirds and pigeons, of branches rustling in the wind. The animals were creeping back. A grey squirrel wound down one of the pines in a cautious spiral. The German still had his back to Eustace and Freddie, his round head absently wobbling. Perhaps he was nothing but a drunk, Freddie supposed. A gypsy after all.

He was about to whisper to Eustace when a squirrel skittered through a mound of fallen leaves. The stranger's head snapped in its direction, his body pivoting as if compelled, rags flapping.

Later, when Freddie put to paper what he saw – and he would, many times – the trapdoor of his memories would first drop him at Missus Hardy's feet, to the kitchen bucket piled high with steaming knuckle bones the size of his fist. No amount of careful study could replicate the shape of those bones. All shining bulges and pitted edges, lines where there should have been curves and shadows where definition belonged.

A jumble of shining bones in lieu of a face. Bones bitter for their lack of covering.

Eustace had forgotten all about the rifle. It lolled uselessly on the fallen tree. The German – the thing they took for a German, though there were no other words for it – had not seen them, and instead listened intently as the squirrel went about its business, scratching and snuffling in the mulch.

It stood so still, the animal clearly no longer regarded him as a threat. Perhaps, Freddie wondered, with the breath caught and burning in his chest, the scent of this German was unlike that of any other mammal. Unlike any other living thing at all.

Whatever the squirrel's thoughts, it did not live to regret them. The second it scurried into range, the German reached up for the spike on its helmet, grasped it tight and pulled.

The boys watched with nauseated horror as the spike slid from a dark dome of the German's head. At first, it appeared to be extending, like Chalice's telescope, yet the slide was seemingly endless. Longer and longer it grew, chased by a pulsing jet of black fluid, spurting and gushing until there was surely no liquid left in the German's body. It spattered against the flagstones and surrounding earth with a hard, tinkling sound as if the clouds had opened and the rain had turned to flint. At last the long spike shuddered free from the German's skull, a great knotted club the length of a man's spine. All this in barely a moment. With one hard swing the squirrel was rocketed across the clearing, smashing against a tree with the *crack* of an ensign snapping in the wind.

Tension left the strange body, and the great wobbling head bowed back into mottled shadow. The senseless death seemed to soothe the German. It was in those appalling silent seconds that Eustace gathered his courage. He righted the rifle, lowered his eye to the sight, and stared hard.

The German heard the look. The bone-jumbled face snapped up, the arm with the club raised in a scytheman's arc. As the German took his first rickety steps in their direction, the rifle gave out a deafening *crack*. Freddie's ears rang. His head reeled, but the German was unharmed. Heavily he trudged across the clearing, his raggedy clothes swinging with the weight of rain and grime. Eustace fumbled to reload, groping uselessly at the bolt, unable to tear his eyes away from that unbearable, impossible Hun face. Eyeless, it nonetheless appeared to see Freddie leaning over Eustace, feeding rounds into the chamber with shaking hands. "Give it to me," Freddie chanted, "give it to me," when Eustace again jerked hard on the trigger and sent another bullet spinning off at the German's feet.

Rotten boots slapped as they advanced. Through Freddie's terror, the words of the government poster came to Freddie in their absurd red capitals: *To dress extravagantly in war time is worse than bad form, it is unpatriotic.* Boot leather sagged around emaciated ankles, stick legs, brown shins from the bone bucket, traipsing up the bank as strings of moss swung from the upraised club like black spittle.

Over the clamour of Freddie's breath and Eustace's fumbling, a voice slipped through the wood like a wind:

"*Tum-ti-tum.*"

The German lurched to a halt as a magpie flashed across his path, so close they almost collided. From the magpie's beak came a stream of Mister Jenks' customary bimblings, as clear as if the old man were with them under the pines. The bird bothered the German in a way the shots had not. He swung blindly with his hideous club, the smooth confidence of his earlier kills lost entirely. Chips of that gleaming black substance sprayed the clearing as the weapon crashed into tree trunks and tore up bracken, each blow nimbly avoided by the feathered meddler, calling gaily all the while: "*Rum-ti-bum, tiddly-pom.*"

Eustace grabbed Freddie by the collar. "Run."

They went scrambling through the woods as fast as the terrain would allow, all the while expecting the *slap-slap* of decaying boots behind them.

Freddie's heart was too large in his chest. Cold panic cascaded up his neck and across his shoulders and only stopped where he felt Eustace's hands fisted in his clothes, hauling him out into the relative light of the Edenwell lawn.

The noon bell was ringing out for prayers. When Freddie fell, he didn't hear Eustace call for help.

ELEVEN

Prose Poem No. 14.
c. April 1917.

One of dozens of prose poems put down by Ferry in his naïve handwriting. Though the poems are unreadable, being little more than streams of ploughman's patois, or possibly recorded fragments of fairy tales passed down in the oral tradition, some researchers – notably Howard and Campbell – insist there is some code at work, though the poems can be enjoyed on a purely aesthetic level.

When a man is hanged dead for doing wrong they put him in a dangling cage and the man is dipped in sticky-black to keep him from falling to bits, but that don't stop us, we are tenacious people, and as he hangs there we clings and pecks and works our will while the knaves watch him swing.

Gifts! For their kings.

We feasted well at these hanging places, but the knaves
called them cursed and built walls to keep the living from
the dangling and in the days of our forefathers' forefathers
they called these hanging places Nomansland.

THE CHARGIRLS TWITTERED like little starlings. Eustace fidgeted in the waiting chair outside Chalice's office. His fingernails were lined with the soil of Choke Wood. He had neither slept nor washed since yesterday. Halfway up the twisting stairs of Edenwell Hydropathic, just out of his sight, Annie and Maud worked together to tamp down the carpet rods. He had no intention of paying their gossip any heed, but they broadcasted at an insistent pitch. Both girls were beginning to sweat. Eustace could smell it: high and unladylike, and almost as bad as himself. The younger girl, Annie, had sneaked a look at the morning papers as she laid them out in the dining room. She'd been unable to talk about anything else since.

"It was all the guests talked about at breakfast. I'm surprised they ate anything. A newspaper man in Belgium, he come across a pit full of children with roasted feet. The Germans hung them over a fire and watched them kick."

"Surely you don't believe that," Maud said. Eustace heard her push hard on one of the carpet rods with both hands. It locked into place with a snap. "Ugh, my knees. If I have to darn these stockings one more time they'll be more darn than sock."

"They bombed Scarborough, didn't they?" Annie said after a thoughtful pause.

"And Folkestone. You keep saying."

"Put a shell right through one end of a terrace and it come out the other side, four houses deep."

"I remember."

"And the U-boats, blowing up ships whenever they please, even hospital ships."

Eustace winced as Maud slammed the tender heel of her hand down onto a rod. "You ought to go easy on the papers, duck," she said. "They're doing you no good."

As they worked their way up to the landing, the girls noticed Eustace and fell into mortified silence. Annie's great brown eyes flickered over the windblown mass of his hair until Maud gave Annie a look she couldn't misconstrue.

When Doctor Chalice emerged from his office, his smile was as bright as ever despite the haggard appearance of his patient.

"There's the look of a man who needs a strong glass of water. So sorry to keep you waiting. I had a telephone call. My colleague knows how to hold up a conversation."

Eustace stood. "Will he be all right?"

"Freddie? Over-exertion, and hunger too, I shouldn't wonder. Nothing more serious. But I'm very glad you were there. Please, come in."

Doctor Chalice had quite literally come running. He saw them, he said, through the telescope in his office window. Out on the grass, he listened to Freddie's chest, holding his wrist. Eustace had watched so intently, Chalice offered him a try. The earpieces were cold, but Freddie's heart spoke warmly. A flag in the wind.

When Freddie's eyes fluttered open, they fixed on Eustace. "What happened?"

"I don't know."

That much was true.

Equally true was that he should have shot the thing.

Chalice's office was warm. The groundskeeper's cottage trapped the cold like an ice house, and he hadn't wanted to leave Freddie there, bundled up in scratchy blankets in that filthy bedroom with feathers all over the place. Chalice had taken Eustace by the shoulders and steered him out of the house. When he looked back, Mister Ferry was rubbing his forehead, his face creased with worry and embarrassment.

Eustace sank into the great riveted leather chair designated for visitors. Chalice poured him a glass of water from a crystal jug.

"The thing is, Mister Moncrieff, we can't have you roaming about willy-nilly. There are landslides to consider, but something you may not encounter at home is the phenomenon of the rural drifter. Broken-down farm boys, men with nothing left to lose. Poor souls think they'll get a better reception here than in the cities."

The doctor pushed the glass across his desk. Eustace regarded it with sleep-deprived eyes. His throat was dry, but he couldn't muster the desire to drink.

"I know about the intruder."

Chalice met his eyes gravely, but without surprise. "Freddie told you, I take it?"

He only said it to prove he wasn't as ignorant as the doctor assumed. Now he wanted to take it back. "Just someone at the gates, wasn't it? And he wandered off."

"Perhaps."

"Was Mister Jenks… very attached to this place?"

218

"We often encountered him, yes," the American said sadly. "If it comforts you, Mister Ferry said our intruder was a long-legged kind of gentleman. Mister Jenks was quite the opposite."

Long legs. Wrapped up in fraying linen. Reaching out for the glass of water, Eustace's hand trembled, though strangely he felt nothing.

"I'm sorry," he said as his brain caught up with Chalice's words. "I don't understand."

"Mister Scole says you were reading bogie tales in the library. We don't believe in ghosts here, Eustace. Stories are fine for the fireside, but tragic accidents are more than stories. It isn't healthy to combine the two."

Ponsonby's Folklorica. They really were keeping tabs on him. But there were no fairy-tale words for the incident down at the well. He imagined Chalice reporting back to his mother, those ghastly images set down with the strict click of a typewriter. *Your son tells me that if you cut out a magpie's tongue, the devil will speak through him...*

When he spoke again, his voice was an adolescent croak. "What did Doctor Ridley say about Freddie?"

"Hm?"

"Your telephone call. Doctor Ridley." Eustace shrugged. "I eavesdropped."

The admission provoked nothing but another smile. "Doctor Ridley was rather more interested in you. You come from Portsmouth, don't you? Yet the sea air has done very little for your constitution. Doctor Ridley studies the dry air of this county, the pines, how the combination may have restorative properties. If he were to drop by, how would you feel about him giving your lungs a quick listen?"

"Only if he'll listen to Freddie's."

"Young Ferry's *heart* is the problem, always has been."

Chalice's dismissive tone surprised him. *I know what you're doing*, Eustace wanted to say. *This Ridley character, crooked old sawbones*—

And there the thought went black. No talk of bones today. A tap at the door. Tabitha Clarke had brought coffee.

Eustace watched as Doctor Chalice poured them both a cup and took a thoughtful sip. In the quiet, Eustace wondered if the American was given to pondering the insurmountable barrier between medical science and the watery arts he practised. Eustace thought of his mother at home, with her tinctures and breathing exercises. She liked Chalice from the moment she read about him. *This is a man who understands*, she said, though understanding *what* was left to interpretation. So much was.

Coffee was costly, hard to obtain. On the surface of his cup, bubbles winked and vanished.

"If someone fails at their duty..." Eustace began. "But tried, actually tried to do it... does it still count?"

"In my day, an eighteen-year-old's duty was to be surly to his parents and pine over girls." When Chalice saw the look on Eustace's face, he sobered. "But I know. It's different now, isn't it?"

He hadn't even mentioned the war, but there it was, the uniform between them. Eustace held a hot stone of rage in his mouth. If Chalice didn't write to Eustace's mother today and tell her he was strong as an ox and on his way home, he would write a letter of his own. A few indelicate truths. An American doctor seducing an unchaperoned girl – all right, a grown woman, but one who looked so shockingly childlike – while his staff were away at the Front. He'd bring down the full wrath of their father and the papers, too. Why not? What was one more scandal?

But a bomb like that would have shrapnel. He pushed away the image of Phoebe, her face red with betrayal. Worse was the real memory of Freddie, long and limp on his bed, sweating and mumbling: *It's not safe here, we'ave to go.* And his father, the groundskeeper, his equally lanky body bent over the bed: *Y'are safe, lad. Tha's talking rubbish.*

But he wasn't talking rubbish. Eustace was the only one who knew that.

When he took his leave of Edenwell, he realised, it couldn't be alone.

Doctor Chalice heaped sugar into Eustace's coffee. Expense, doled out by the spoonful. "Your sister said much the same about duty. She's heading for the VADs, I understand?"

"She *what*?"

"We talked. She was interested in the possibilities of rehabilitative therapy. She's intelligent, clearly. Resilient too, I feel. Just the kind of girl a man needs to see in his hour of need."

Phoebe, all five foot of her, trotting about in a pinny amongst wounded men. The image ought to have been comical, but all Eustace felt was a fresh twist of treachery. "She never said a word."

"I have an older sister myself. They don't like to worry us. I'm certain mine sees me as a child, still."

And how did Phoebe see this doctor? Eustace took the coffee, if only to cover his face. Cloyingly sweet. Something you'd give a child to fool them into taking their medicine. He put the cup down in disgust and it tipped, flooding Chalice's desk. Eustace jumped to his feet, but the doctor bid him stay.

"Not to worry. I'll see if Tabitha's still about." Chalice shifted the least-damaged papers out of harm's way and went to the door. Eustace was left with his foolishness, a fulminant blush reaching the tips of his ears, when a tap at the window startled him.

One of Freddie's black birds tottered casually along Chalice's window ledge. In the scruff of its face, its eyes shone with beastly intelligence, surveying the shining trinkets of Chalice's office with a bailiff's cool. The shelf of gleaming bottles, the telescope, the crystal candy dish – none of these things were as intriguing to the rook as Eustace. *Tap*. Beak on glass. *Tap*.

He couldn't stand it. Eustace got up, shooing the creature.

As he turned, he noticed an envelope bearing a familiar hand. It lay on Chalice's chair with the rest of the salvaged documents. Eustace snatched it up, the letter paper inside wet but legible.

My dear Doctor,
As promised, proof that I am home. A less eventful journey than the last, you'll be pleased to hear.

My brother Harry is back from France. He arrived shortly before I did, with much melodrama, having brought with him a whole ship's worth of fleas and a bad cold. The fever is making him talk, and Mother hates to play nursemaid so it falls to muggins here to mop his brow.

How many more times can I hear 'It is so much worse than you know' without breaking down entirely? Mother is very quiet. Father furious. Harry doesn't know what he's saying, of course he doesn't, but some of this information is tantamount to treason. You must destroy this letter.

My mind is made up. I believe I can cadge a post in Norfolk, perhaps even with you. Would that be stupid of me? You must be honest, Matthew. I need honesty more than ever.

Take good care of Eustace. He'll understand when he has children of his own. The Martha Talbot Wing. I can see her cutting the ribbon now.

Yours, etc.

Phoebe

By the time Chalice returned with Tabitha and a dishcloth, Eustace had read the letter three times as the ink spread and the words blurred to watercolour nothings. Destroyed, as per his sister's wishes. He tucked it back amongst Chalice's other sodden papers.

When the coffee was mopped up and apologies brushed off, Eustace took himself down the stairs to where the two chargirls worked on their knees, griping about the VADs and their clattering shoes.

He hung on the banister, letting their conversation fizzle out as they noticed him. He swung back and forth under their wary stares, letting them gawp their fill at his wild hair and sleepless eyes.

"It is so much worse than you know," he said.

Maud gave him a look that could draw blood.

The yolk plopped into the glass, jelloid and specked with blood.

"Outdoor living and six raw eggs a day," said Doctor

Chalice, smiling down at Drummerboy as he treated the jackdaw to the gentlest of scratches. "That's the Trudeau system. He made consumptives in the States sleep on verandas bundled up like this, no matter the season."

The exposed oval of Freddie's face stung with cold. Following his collapse, he was under orders to spend his days wrapped in blankets on the sun terrace until full strength returned, whatever that truly meant. A week had ground tediously by and he was sick of being a spectacle. Tabitha had brought him so many glasses of milk she grumbled she ought to just lug a cow up there and let him get on with it.

Through layers of wool, he tried to feel his heartbeat. They said people died of fright, didn't they? *I nearly had kittens*, Missus Hardy was always saying. Everyone knew the story of the expectant mother terrified by a toad in her shoe, then delivering a monstrous baby, reptilian, ruined. Fear sneaked inside through the skin. Freddie couldn't bear to think what might be coiling inside him now, waiting to be born.

On the lounger next to him, Eustace took the waters. He refused to wrap up quite so thoroughly as Freddie, and his hair ruffled in the cold breeze, hanging in hanks where he had tugged on it, waking himself up whenever his eyes threatened to drift shut.

When Chalice went on his way, Eustace found his voice. "We'd had so much to drink…"

Freddie hesitated. *Strictly no excitement*, Chalice had said, listening to Freddie's tremulous pulse. Excitement was hardly the word.

"Could do with some now." Eustace's laughter came out weak, thin as hair.

"I can offer you some milk."

"Is it helping, at least?"

"I don't know what it's s'posed to be helping."

From the terrace they could see all the way to the groundskeeper's cottage clinging to the skirts of Choke Wood. In the wake of Freddie's collapse, Fa had aimed all his anguished energy at the dead chicken. Never enough eggs, he grumbled, and then the ungrateful things went and died. They could offer up their own potato bread in the hope of keeping the flock going, but what short-sighted mathematics was that? They ate the chicken that night. Whatever killed it would likely be roasted out. Freddie licked the grease from his fingers as he lay in bed trying not to think about the German, that un-man, lurching about with his vicious club like a cave-squatting revenant.

Fa didn't comment on the chair wedged under front door's handle.

"I should have let you take the shot."

Eustace's voice was dull with shame. Freddie looked at him, the fullness of his lips tamped down into a bloodless line.

"I can admit it. I missed, and it nearly got you killed."

"You did more than I could've. I could never… shoot a man."

"Is that what we're calling it?"

They fell silent as Scole came lurching out of the veranda door to collect the empty tumblers. He noted their guilty stillness with a smirk. "Conspiring, are we?"

Freddie stole a glance at Eustace. Their looks agreed. They would say nothing, no matter how tempting. The one physical proof they had, that inexplicable Iron Cross, hung heavily in Eustace's dressing-gown pocket.

225

Down at the drive, some of the guests had come out to look at the trucks arriving in convoy.

"My God," said Eustace and stood up. "Are those men?'

Scole frowned. "They're not due 'til Thursday."

Figures in blue flannel uniforms were clambering down from the vehicles, some helped by VADs. Others refused feminine aid and took time to steady themselves on crutches and the shoulders of their fellows. Eustace left his blanket on the floor and stood at the rail with Scole, his dark eyes alight with wonder at the display of shuffling and coughing. Men in wheelchairs, left lopsided by the surgeon's saw. One man's eyes were bandaged, his mouth wide, as if hoping to take in the new scene by taste alone.

"I thought they were expected to dig potatoes," Eustace said. It had been little over a month since Chalice made his speech about the healing properties of cultivating beans. Seeing the men, it seemed to Freddie the doctor had made promises far beyond his capabilities.

"They'll be glad of the opportunity," said Scole. "We all want to contribute, don't we?" He looked back at Freddie with a frigid smile. Eustace was preoccupied by a man with a black moustache set against a face so pale it was practically blue. In the chilly sunshine, the contours of his cheeks stood out like barren terrain as a nurse tucked his scarf more snugly around his throat.

"Why would that one be such a frightful colour?" Eustace wondered aloud.

"Gas," Scole said. "Or frostbite. Sometimes, my lads found themselves—"

The orderly took a moment to see which man Eustace meant, talking all the while. When he stopped mid-sentence,

Eustace glanced at him. The pale man, despite his cadaverous condition, flashed a nurse a smile so broad and true he might as well have been strolling into a ballroom.

Eustace nudged Scole. "Do you think they'd like us to go down and say hello?"

Scole had straightened up, blinking rapidly. "Bloody— ! Questions." He thumped away, the tray of empty glasses jingling bitterly in his hands. "Get under them blankets, both of you."

Eustace grinned sheepishly. "Well, that's me in my place."

"Chafing, see?" muttered Freddie. Puffed up in a merry ball, Drummerboy laughed.

"You're appalling." Eustace flopped down onto the lounger, pulling the blanket around his shoulders. "Does this mean you're on the mend, Lieutenant Knave?"

Better for his proximity. Doctor Chalice assured Fa it was perfectly normal for a patient to be jumpy after a collapse, piecing together fragmented recollections and measuring lost time. Fa didn't ask for Freddie's memories, and for that he was glad.

He took a folded paper from his pocket and pressed it into Eustace's hand. He'd done the best he could with haste and a blunt pencil, long drags of the lead to extend the crustaceous hinges of the figure's limbs. He hadn't the skill for it, scrubbing away his mistakes, beginning afresh, wasting more paper than he would ever usually dare, because *surely* his memory had misled him. If the Hydropathic library had stocked books of natural history, Freddie could have taken scissors and snipped out a grasshopper's legs and a bullock's boulder of a skull, to at least begin to piece together a likeness.

Starting points only, but proof – flimsy, but proof nonetheless – that he wasn't deluded, that these shapes did exist in nature alongside the sorts of men who crept through private woods to subsist on stolen game. Since boyhood he'd sketched the desiccated carapaces of stag beetles, the empty skeletons of foxes, dappled with clumps of fur, all from sight, but nothing had prepared him—

Together they looked at the dark figure in silence.

"That's the fellow," Eustace said flatly. As he slowly reacquainted himself with the spindly legs and the bundled rags, his hand unconsciously reached up to the crown of his own head. "I like what you've done with the, er…"

"It was an antler. I was wondering why it shook me up. It's an antler, the long kind from a red deer. We're always digging them up round here."

"So he filed down an antler and strapped it to his back. Then there's the matter of the…" His lips twisted, searching for a polite term for what had, in person, been so obscene. "Discharge. The spray of flint. A bit of theatre know-how would do it. A squeeze pump hidden under his arm. I don't see why he'd go to the trouble, but it was terribly impressive, wasn't it?"

He was putting on a brave face, showing too many teeth.

"Parlour tricks?"

"No," Eustace said, his faint bravado spent. "No, I saw it – same as you."

"Saw what, you little tinker?"

Lottie Mulgrave slammed the veranda doors behind her with her hip, busy with one of her aromatic Turkish cigarettes. "Thought you were looking at mucky French prints, the way you're whispering."

Freddie went to snatch the drawing from Eustace, only Lottie was faster.

"Suffering Christ," she muttered. "Looks like a man I saw dragged from the river at Wapping. Barely a man at all by that point."

The boys looked at each other in silent agreement. It was no man.

"A word to the wise, lads. Don't go scribbling where anyone can see you. Defence of The Realm. Police will confiscate anything sketched too close to the coast."

Eustace was indignant. "Well, that's preposterous. We aren't anywhere near the coast."

"No, but we're within spitting distance of an airfield, and wouldn't the Hun dearly love to know that? Fine. Have it back. I only came up to say I know what happened to my flask. And I'm not angry. I could be. But that lot down there are going to need a proper welcome, and Lord knows we have nothing to feed them, so I was thinking of wheeling the piano into the North Wing and doing a few numbers tonight. Opinions?"

"That sounds very nice," Freddie said dubiously.

"I need help pushing the thing – not you, kid – and I want you both to come and clap, because these poor bastards only have three and a half arms between them."

When she left, promises given, Eustace had regained some of his exuberance. "I feel as if I've been waiting for this my whole life."

"I can't."

"Blow work. It's just one night."

"I mean I don't think I can."

"But I have so many questions."

"What if they ask *us* questions?"

It took a moment for Eustace to understand. "You're not shy about it, are you? You're unwell. You were assessed."

He chewed at his lip. "You have… feelings… too."

"Me? If some woman strolled up to me with a white feather I'd slap her silly." Eustace flashed a grin. "I don't mean that, for the avoidance of doubt. Look, why should they be funny about you being invalided out, when that's precisely what's happened to them?"

Freddie hadn't thought of it that way. But still, those men had uniforms. Scole had the silver Wound Badge. That was valour that could never be disputed. Freddie wished he had never touched the Iron Cross. In some perverse way, it felt as if that was his medal now. A token of appreciation from the Kaiser for not causing him any bother.

"We don't have to go," Eustace said softly.

"No, you should. You'll enjoy it."

"Not if I'm worried about you." He jerked his chin towards the woods. To Freddie, the thought of spending the evening in his cottage kitchen, listening to the reptilian shuffle of the trees, was no more appealing than the prospect of taking his pillow and bedding down at the well.

In Freddie's lap, Drummerboy burrowed down into the blankets.

"Might be nice," Freddie said. "To hear music again."

The housewives of Thetford donated what measly spare sugar and flour they had to the Edenwell kitchens. Whatever therapeutic treatments the men would receive at the Hydropathic, it was agreed that currant buns would speed along the healing process. After pushing Lottie Mulgrave's piano up to the North Wing, Eustace and Freddie had been seized by Missus Hardy to take the gleaming silver tea urn and the rest of the victuals. They waited in the kitchen's stone doorway, politely pretending not to hear the cook's grousing as Maud piled fist-sized buns onto a plate.

"If those ruddy nurses think I'm chasing after them, they've got another think coming," Missus Hardy said, scrubbing a pan as if it had done her personal harm. "The *lip* on those women. Never in all my years—"

Maud wiped her hands on her apron, a grin on her face. "I don't mind taking the tea up, Missus Hardy."

"You're having a laugh. Two minutes alone with all those scallies and you and Annie'll both be in the family way."

At that moment, Tabitha came struggling in with a tray heaped with dishes. Catching the end of their conversation, her face turned an unlovely shade of red.

Laden with rattling cups and a great steel urn of tea, Freddie and Eustace wheeled the trolley to the lift and waited for it to come ticking down. Freddie breathed in the smell of fresh baking. "Do you think they'd notice if I walked in with crumbs around my mouth?"

"Take one."

"They can probably shoot you for that," he grinned. "Stealing from the army."

Eustace broke a piece off a bun speckled with currants and put it to Freddie's lips. "Can't have my lieutenant going hungry."

Lottie Mulgrave had been a beauty in her day. She never married – not for want of offers – preferring to court her audience with a boldness bordering on indecency. At fifty-five she had lost very little of her looks and none of her zest, tossing her head so her thick braids flew out like golden bullwhips as she struck up a marching beat on the piano.

"I long ago gave up searching for the right man," she said. "I'd rather have a wrong'un. And I have the pick of them tonight, haven't I, lads?"

Pausing with the trolley at the North Wing doors, Eustace shot Freddie an excited glance. The soldiers gathered on their new beds, in easy chairs and on windowsills, more interested in their Woodbines than anything else. The men sat in three clear camps: the ones with no interest in being there, a few who weren't sure where they were, and the majority, so relieved to be safe they wouldn't do anything to jeopardise their luck. A round of polite applause followed each ditty, and a few weak laughs. Lottie had avoided war songs, sticking instead to the safer music hall favourites. "Not so much as a *whisper* of Ivor Novello," she had promised as Freddie shunted the piano into place for her. She was convinced that if the nurses would just let the men get a little drunk, they'd make an easy crowd. But a considerable percentage of the VADs were Temperance Society sorts. Good girls, Fa said. Now Freddie eyed them furtively; tense young women in spotless uniforms. Judging by their expressions, Lottie with her smoking jacket and raucous laugh was about as popular with them as a dose of clap.

Matron Calder stood close to the piano, a spectacled chaperone with the bearing of a headmistress wielding the nit comb.

"A rousing hymn wouldn't go amiss, Miss Mulgrave. Do you have 'Onward Christian Soldiers' in Ireland?"

"Sure, ma'am, we do. The orders at Waterloo were given in Gaelic."

This elicited the first proper snigger from her audience. The men had evidently received the sharp end of Matron, too. Lottie didn't hesitate. She plunged into a song.

> *Though I'm wheezy across the chest*
> *And gouty about the knees*
> *I'm learning to shoulder arms*
> *But I'd rather be standing at ease...*

Lottie felt a crack in the ice. Matron Calder's beleaguered expression gave the men something to warm to.

> *Forty-nine and in the army*
> *And soon I will be in the fighting line*
> *If somebody holds me rifle*
> *While I borrow a pair of steps*
> *I'll be over the top and at 'em at forty-nine.*

Lottie's nimble fingers skipped along the keys. "I reckon we'd do well to introduce ourselves, seeing as we'll be living in each other's pockets for the foreseeable. You there, with the headgear. What's your name?"

The man had lost most of his hair – a burn, Freddie guessed – and a poultice was strapped over one eye with white bandages. "Thorpe," he answered.

"Do you have a first name, Thorpe?"

"Corporal."

The automatic response made the rest of the men laugh.

Lottie dived in with a rousing vaudeville tune.

> *Oh, his name was Corporal Thorpe*
> *At the girls he liked to gawp*
> *Belgian, French, Australian*
> *He'd watch them like a hawk*
> *When he wasn't dodging shells,*
> *He was chasing mademoiselles,*
> *Till it made him quite unwell*
> *Corporal Thorpe!*

Thorpe was pleased to have so amused his mates. "Don't ask how I put my eye out."

"How about you, longshanks?" said Lottie. "Got a name?"

The legless boy flushed as everyone turned to look at him. His voice was little more than a croak. "Private Fry."

> *Private Fry caught my eye*
> *A handsome fella passing by*
> *What's a girl to do, says I?*
> *He's got no knees, so I'll straddle his—*

Matron Calder crossed her arms. "Miss Mulgrave, I won't have this."

Lottie sustained the marching beat and caught the eye of another soldier. "And you, fatty? What do they call you?"

The man was shockingly attenuated, pale as bacon rind. "Butler," he grinned. "But I doubt you'll find anything to rhyme with dysentery."

Poor Mister Butler, he's in quite a to-do
He only went out to the oyster bar
And now he lives in the loo

Butler slapped his twiggy knees with delight.

"That's him," whispered Eustace. "The man from the drive. Look at the colour of him."

Freddie's heart gave a nervous kick. There were so many men; more than he had braced himself for. When Eustace pushed the trolley through the double doors, dozens of faces turned to look at them. It was only for Eustace's sake that he didn't duck his head and retreat.

Lottie Mulgrave called from the piano. "Ah, victuals! Fatty here needs double rations, lads."

"In and out in eighteen seconds," said Butler gaily. "Who has a watch?"

The men's curiosity didn't last long in the face of solid food. Soon the soldiers were talking amongst themselves against the backdrop of Lottie's merry piano, smearing margarine on their ill-fitting hospital blues. Freddie and Eustace soaked up their idle chat as they doled out cups of tea.

"First chance I get," said Corporal Thorpe around a mouthful of bun, "I'm on the train to give my landlord a kicking. Caroline wrote me. The littlest has stopped growing, all 'cause our pay's going straight into his pockets. He's been having a lovely time of it these past three years."

An older man with a turban and a great scrolling moustache chimed in. "When all this is over, you'll see. They'll need us."

"They're saying our jobs aren't waiting." Thorpe fretted

with his bandage, angling to scratch an itch he could never quite reach.

"I can't drive a train now anyway," said Private Fry.

"That's hardly the point," said the man with the turban. "They made a promise."

"Pie crust, Sandhar," Thorpe shrugged. "Made to be broken."

Whey-faced Butler nibbled his bun with caution and evident pleasure. "I had a good look on the way here," he remarked. "All that land and no men to work it. I'm looking forward to this. I am, no joke. It's a job. And I reckon we'll make a better go of it than they expect us to."

Sandhar nodded soberly. "Better than making toys, like that sad lot in Lord Roberts' workshops."

There was a general grumble of agreement. The notion of maimed men painting baby dolls with brushes gripped between their teeth both an insult and a threat.

Thorpe's face was a mess of crumbs and scorn. "Eh, Butler— if we're good little farmers, do you suppose they'll let us have a bit of land in the end? Something to own?"

Butler snorted. "I'm not daft. I'm looking forward to getting out there, that's all."

Sandhar licked the margarine from his fingers. "Personally, I could become accustomed to idleness. Any surplus buns, friend?"

Passing by with the tea trolley, Freddie felt an elbow bump his ribs. He followed Eustace's look, spotting the silver Wound Badge on the Sikh soldier's tunic.

"One of the orderlies has one of those," Eustace said eagerly. "He lost his leg, but you'd never know. For King and Empire."

236

Clinging to his side, Freddie dared the tiniest cough. Scole would want to make the big reveal himself. But Eustace kept talking, heedless of the men's looks, half suspicious, half entertained. "He was wounded in France. As were most of you, I imagine."

Sandhar accepted a cup of strong tea from Freddie. "Palestine."

"Fromelles, me," said Thorpe.

"He tripped over an Australian," Fry quipped. There was no humour in it. They had all heard the shocking Antipodean casualties.

Butler took no tea and gave the remaining two thirds of his bun to Sandhar. "What are you lads doing out here in the sticks, then?"

"Waiting to be called up," Eustace said. "I'm learning to use a rifle."

At this, they all laughed.

"I'm almost nineteen," Eustace added, a touch self-consciously.

"And you. You're older, aren't you?" Butler said to Freddie.

This was the moment he dreaded more than anything – the judging looks of strangers, their distrust and distaste – yet now it had come he was blank inside, as if he had slipped into a plunge pool and let the water fill his ears and mouth.

Sandhar eyed him coolly. "The man asked a question, friend."

"Category E," he said flatly. "Grade Four."

"Someone has to keep all these females in line."

Freddie blushed to hear Eustace take such a tone. But the men were easy to placate. The atmosphere had melted into warm conviviality and Lottie Mulgrave was singing in her Turkish tobacco voice:

I didn't care what happened to me, so I went and joined the infantry...

The act of eating a bird-like portion of bun had used up Butler's scant reserve of energy. The light in his eyes faded with startling speed, and he waved weakly to Freddie. "Help me into bed, will you?"

With great care, they flanked Butler through his geriatric shuffle to his designated bed, framed by clean white curtains. They peeled back the bedclothes and helped Butler orientate himself, lifting his legs for him when he grunted with effort. His ankles were knots of gristle barely capable of supporting a man, and Freddie wondered how full the other hospitals must have been to send a specimen like this away.

Given a little distance from the other soldiers, Eustace's enthusiasm was free to return. He perched on the next bed with Freddie close beside him, trapping his hands between his knees to stop them fluttering.

"Can we do anything more for you, sir?"

"Oh, don't 'sir' me, please." Butler swallowed with effort, giving them a full demonstration of the sinews of his throat. "But thank you. I do apologise, I didn't catch your names."

"I'm Eustace. This is my best friend, Freddie."

Inside his boots, Freddie's toes curled with pleasure.

"Butler. Christopher. Help yourself to a cig. I find it actually taxes me these days, the smoking."

"Were you very badly wounded?"

At this, Butler chuckled as if at some private joke. "You

don't want to hear about all that, surely. Not after those lovely scones."

"We love stories, don't we, Fred? I mean," Eustace added quickly, "we're always eager to hear the latest from the Front."

Freddie offered an unconvincing nod.

Butler didn't mind the interrogation. To Freddie, his expression was fondly accommodating, and when the soldier caught his eye he felt no shame. "What would you like to know?"

Freddie was surprised to find himself speaking. "What are the birds like? In France?"

Butler's thin lips quirked in a smile of surprise. "Birds? No, no birds. No trees, you see. Not any more. Come to think of it, yes, I did see one or two. Great black things. Always busy after a skirmish, that sort of bird."

Parly voo froglay, Knave? We was at the Somme and Agincourt both. Picky-nick.

The jeering of the rooks was unbearable with Butler lying there, so frail and beaten down. Freddie bit his lip and looked away. Beside him, Eustace was practically bouncing, imagining blasted fields and gaping craters.

"Can you begin to describe it?"

"Don't have to."

Butler reached into his breast pocket and produced a black slab the size of his hand. With a few clicks, the device unfolded into a small set of bellows with a lens at the front, winking black and glossy.

"It's a tiny little camera!" Eustace exclaimed, captivated.

"My mother bought it for me. They're not allowed at the Front, but you can get some pretty fine shots if you're clever

239

about it. Plenty of fellows have them. I'm hoping to take some pictures of the work here, and the men. And of this beautiful house. Jane Austen would have written about this house if she'd seen it."

"Freddie was born here."

"Were you? It's a wonder you're not a Romantic poet by now, surrounded by *Ye Presences of Nature*."

Freddie examined his boots. "I'm not... that sort of person."

"Neither am I. Though I think the portrait I just took of the two of you is halfway decent."

Freddie looked up. "You took our picture?"

Butler's pointed shoulders bobbed. "The enthusiast magazines publish articles on how to avoid detection. I think of it as a game."

"Do you have pictures with you?" Eustace asked. "Of the Front?"

"I do. Though I'm more of a naturalist than a journalist. No paper would pay to print my pictures of Belgian poppies."

They heard the voice of Corporal Thorpe, who had listened to the whole exchange with disapproval. "Then there's the small detail 'bout it being illegal."

"I've done no one any harm." Butler wound in the concertina with the little silver handle. "With this, at least."

"Can we see it? The one you took of us?" Freddie was stuck on the idea; a portrait made without the sitter's knowledge, secretive, silent and clean, with none of the faults or prejudices an artist brought to a sketch.

"Only when it's developed. I have my things with me, but I need a dark room, a cupboard or something where I won't be disturbed."

Eustace looked at Freddie, wide-eyed. "You can help you with that."

Butler raised an eyebrow. "He can?"

"A dark room..." Freddie wondered. "Is that really all you need?"

Butler's parched lips stretched in a disarming grin. "Magic is surprisingly mundane."

The invaders had stuffed every available corner with their crates and trolleys. As Freddie and Eustace escorted Butler through the reception, pushing him along in one of the shiny new army wheelchairs, they interrupted Missus Bailey taking it upon herself to inspect a trunk of corned beef with dainty disapproval.

"Is this *all* food?" Freddie asked. To his shame, he imagined his pockets heavy with tins.

"Nothing you'll enjoy," said Butler. "Apple and plum jam, army's finest. I've heard it's been hard here, with the blockade."

"There are soup kitchens," Eustace said. "My brother works for the papers and he says—"

Butler made a dismissive noise. "The papers. My mother wrote me from Newcastle, they're burying more babies than men. But they can't print that, can they? More dangerous than my photographs."

For all the soldier's genial tone, Eustace still looked chastened.

There was one place in Edenwell darker than any other, and that was the service tunnel between the hospital and the laundry house. It was a serious excursion for Butler, who weighed little more than a boy but laughed all the way. They entered through a swing door marked 'Staff Only' around the back of the lift, where the turquoise tiles dwindled away to bare brick and the faint smell of boot polish and rust. The tunnel rumbled with the labour of the pumps that kept the Hydropathic going. There was a boiler room somewhere, Freddie knew, but the thought of the place had frightened him since boyhood. The antithesis of the silent pyramid vaults of his imagination, a hot and noisy Hell waiting below the calm waters of Edenwell. When Freddie showed Butler into the disused broom cupboard with its sagging garlands of cobwebs, the thin man looked as though he had been ushered into Paradise.

"I've been using a cardboard box and a prayer for months! You have my gratitude, Freddie. And you, Eustace, for helping me down here. You know, I feel like walking back. I do. I'm going to do it."

He would accept no help from either of them, but they walked with him, prepared to catch him if those frail ankles crumpled. Freddie promised to take his equipment down as soon as he wanted it.

Butler chuckled at the grandiose implications. "A billy can, a cloak, and some choice poisons."

Their new companion safely delivered back to Matron Calder, Freddie felt ready to roll over and sleep until further notice. His knees were still bruised from last week's meeting with the hard, rooty earth, but the idea of complaining about it was absurd after meeting the North Wing's new residents.

Eustace took the stairs two at a time. In the marble reception, he paused for a drink from the fountain. "He's so *thin*, Fred," he said, water dripping from his chin. "You should draw him. Do it in your style, like some pyjama-wearing arachnid. You ought to show him some of your pictures if he's going to show us his."

Freddie tugged at his lip. No, that wouldn't do at all.

"Besides *that* one, obviously," Eustace agreed. He walked with Freddie across the lawn to the cottage. With the blackout curtains drawn and the trees moaning in the wind, the Hydropathic seemed to drift away on a secret tide. Freddie wondered if the conditions were right to hear the guns over the sea or if the persistent low hum was the product of his overburdened brain.

"It feels safer with all of them around, doesn't it?" Eustace said.

"The men? I don't know. A bit like it used to, before, maybe." The cold was beginning to creep into Freddie's clothes, sliding past his collar and teasing the hairs on the back of his neck. "What should we do? Really?"

"We can go up to Doctor Chalice's office, right now, and tell him we saw a man in the woods battering squirrels, and his face was... the way it was. And I was so scared I was almost sick."

"I know. We can't."

"I mean it."

"People will think we're pretending to be mad."

"It's not even a very good impression of madness, is it? They'll think I'm a coward and you're just going along with whatever I say."

They stopped. For a second, Eustace looked at Freddie like he was preparing to apologise. But honestly, the thought of tagging along beside Eustace, doing whatever he said, was a perfectly comfortable idea.

They could do it. Knock on the door right now and watch Chalice's smile liquefy into concern. It was a powerful thing, holding a secret. Freddie wasn't sure his hands were big enough.

"They wouldn't print news of a downed plane, would they?" Eustace mused. "Not if there was a Boche pilot on the loose."

"Wouldn't they want everyone looking for him?"

"I don't think so. It's a failure, isn't it? There's an airfield right there, and they still couldn't kill one German. I think they'd be embarrassed."

It was perfectly plausible. In the papers, German planes had the lightweight, spiteful look of wasps. Freddie could easily imagine one silently dropping out of the broad Norfolk sky, coming to rest in a gulley somewhere, out of sight. He had no idea if those small craft had the power to creep over the Channel, but if what Lottie Mulgrave said was true, the Kaiser was sending giant bombers over London, smashing and splintering everything in its path. How you'd bring one of those monsters down was a mystery to Freddie, but his mind's eye traced the shape of the flames and the great ploughed scar of earth behind the felled beast. A lone figure staggering from the wreckage. Yes, that breath-taking face down in Choke Wood could have been the result of burning. But the German looked so strong, so fast. One of Scole's favourite stories was of a dairy lad on the farm he worked on as a boy; the careless youngster caught himself with an oil lamp. He was shaking and frothing in bed for days before he died.

At the cottage door, they paused, unsure of what to say or do. Inside, Fa could be heard rattling around the kitchen, and

Drummerboy was with him, alerting him of Freddie's return with happy chattering.

"You shouldn't have come," said Freddie quietly. They made such an odd pair, opposite in looks and rank; surely everything they did was noted. They couldn't go on hoarding secrets for ever. Given enough time, all things would be dug up. "You have to walk back now. You should take summat. A knife."

"I'm not afraid of him."

Freddie ventured a small smile. Of Fa or the German? Eustace was fidgeting on his feet, his sniper's eyes darting about. When Fa dropped a spoon, he stifled a flinch.

"I believe you," Freddie said wryly.

A grin flashed across Eustace's face, vulpine bright in the darkness. Freddie watched as he turned on a heel and ventured back out into the night, strolling despite the proximity of the woods and the possibilities within. When at last Freddie lost sight of him, he heard his voice ringing out, clear and defiant.

"I'm not afraid of you, Fritz. Or Wilhelm, or Klaus, whatever you're calling yourself. I am not afraid of you!"

TWELVE

He's My Companion. *Pencil and
watercolour on paper. April 1917.*

Reminiscent of Victorian fairy painter Richard Dadd in
both composition and colour, here Ferry takes familiar East
Anglian fauna – bees, bats, dragonflies – and swaps their
wings for flapping human lungs. The insects are lifting a
funeral bier to the heavens, a stretched sheet bearing the body
of a human child.

"AND ONE MORE, Mister Moncrieff, arms extended,
don't lock those elbows. Three, two, one... one and three
quarters... and release."

The medicine ball came down with a leathery thump
against the tiles. Eustace doubled up, hands bracing against
his knees as his chest heaved against the cotton of his vest.
In the weeks since his sister left Edenwell, he had been
determined to whip himself into shape, and spite was proving
to be powerful fuel.

Scole gave a slow round of applause. "A sweat to be proud of, that. Now drink."

"I think my arms are going to drop off."

"When you're sniping, you'll spend hours in one position. Lying on rubble, up trees, in rain and snow and mud. It's going to hurt. Still, what do you do?"

"My duty," he wheezed. He had it down pat now, like a groom-to-be practising his *I-do*s.

"Good lad. Get under that shower and soak in the pool. Minerals for your muscles."

Freddie floated on his back in the gentlemen's pool, his head inclined to one side so he might keep an eye on Scole for any tricks he tried to play. Eustace's look was worshipful as usual. He couldn't make sense of his friend's devotion to the orderly. His entire purpose was to keep him away from such malign influences, but Nick Scole was no bad sketch that could be rubbed away with stale bread and determination. Besides, it was a sin to wish ill upon people. Think how sad everyone would be if Scole had never come home, Freddie told himself. How, without a doubt, they would spend every Christmas, every New Year, every May Day, wistfully toasting his memory. Would they extend that courtesy to Freddie, had he gone, he wondered? Not bloody likely.

The right and the wrong of things. What a tangle, he mused, letting his body drift across the surface of the pool. How was it you could shoot an animal deemed a pest, but to do so to a man, with so much more power and imagination at his cruel disposal, was murder?

"If I caught a fish as ugly as you, I'd throw it back."

Startled, Freddie splashed. He had taken his eyes off Scole

for a moment, in which time the orderly had sneaked around the pool to stand behind his floating body. Freddie's eyes darted to the needle showers off in the corner where Eustace washed, oblivious. That was enough time for the boot to come down on his head, thrusting him under. Water flooded painfully up his nose. When the pressure was released, he bobbed up, gasping and thrashing. Scole was ambling back to the showers to pass Eustace his next glass of water.

When Eustace clambered down into the warm, mineral-smelling pool, he was pink and gleaming, and the look on his face was brighter than Freddie had seen him in a long time.

"I think I'm getting stronger, I really do," Eustace said. "I couldn't have lifted that medicine ball once when I arrived here."

"Don't see the point, myself."

"I'm going to punch our German's head clean off." Eustace made a playful jab at Freddie, who countered with a splash and dived away. Now that Scole was out of the way, they made a game of it; Freddie a monstrous fish and Eustace trying to wrestle him back to the ship alive to exhibit him in a tank at the fair. Scole left to lead the ladies' morning walk, though the presence of Tabitha Clarke at the door with a face like a wet funeral suggested he had other business to attend to.

Freddie came up laughing and splashed someone's shoes. He blinked up at a short-legged old gentleman with a neat, peppered beard.

Freddie knew the intruder. Everyone could recount the story of the time Doctor Ridley came upon a man crushed by a cart on market day. He sawed off the trapped arm so quick the poor fellow never had the chance to squeal. It was said Ridley kept the arm, boiled down to the bone and knitted together with wires, and it hung in his office with a ring on the finger. Maud the chargirl swore she had seen it. Then again, she also said she saw it twitch.

The visitor regarded them with begrudging amusement, as if they were rambunctious farm animals who had somehow got into the parlour.

"I'm glad someone is enjoying this miserable morning," Ridley said. "Mister Moncrieff, I presume?"

Eustace trod water at the far end of the pool. "You're Doctor Ridley," he said evenly. "You're here to listen to Freddie's heart."

"I'm more interested in your condition, as it happens."

Eustace shimmied to the edge where the doctor waited. He folded his long arms on the tiles and flicked water from his hair. "I've just been tossing around the old medicine ball. After a swim, Freddie and I thought we might wander out to the tennis courts. Didn't we?"

They had planned nothing of the sort. Doctor Ridley plainly understood as much. Eustace hauled himself out of the pool, giving Ridley an extended exhibition of his long, lean body. Ridley stood by, the picture of impassivity, and waited until the young man was on his feet.

"A touch out of breath, I see," the doctor said, ignoring the hint of challenge between them. "Do you often find yourself wheezing?"

Eustace enjoyed the advantage of height. "Not really."

Without doing Freddie the courtesy of eye contact, Ridley shot a glance at the pool. "Young man, would you mind affording us some privacy? I'm sure you have plenty to be getting on with, with the shortage of men."

"I'm his work," Eustace said steadily. "He's my companion."

A hot blush prickled at Freddie's neck, hidden by the waterline.

"Mister Chalice did mention it," Ridley said. "I think it best—"

"We're busy."

Ridley met Eustace's obstinacy with a cool smile. "I am here as a favour to my colleague, and also to you, Mister Moncrieff. No one in the Eastern counties knows as much about the human lung as I."

"That's wonderful news," said Eustace, all innocence. "There's a lot of men upstairs who've suffered gas attacks and I think they'll be terribly glad of your input."

He was magnificent when he was stubborn, Freddie thought. An immovable, infuriating rock. Eustace stared down at the doctor, lordly even in his dripping trunks and vest. Ridley removed his spectacles to wipe them on his lapel. He was keeping his growing tetchiness well hidden, but fine cracks were beginning to show.

"You could come back later," Eustace suggested. "Or just put up with my assistant here."

Ridley stifled a sigh. For the first time, he took a proper look at Freddie, who trod water quietly. The doctor's eyes rested on him for a long heartbeat. He tried searching the doctor's face for whatever he was trying to communicate, but the moment had passed.

"Very well," Ridley said to Eustace. "Give me your wrist."

They sat on a lounge chair while Ridley listened to Eustace's pulse, keeping time on his wristwatch.

"Your hair. What happened to it?"

"Nothing. Just ugly."

"I read of a young patient from Zurich who experienced hair loss as a result of a chronic lung infection," Ridley said, with the utmost seriousness. "Indeed, she died of it."

Eustace's lips hardened into a thin line. "I do it to myself, Doctor. Do you mind if I continue my exercise? The soldiers will want the pool soon and I hate to share."

The examination was far from over. Ridley checked Eustace's fingernails for colour and quality, tested his reflexes with the tap of a small hammer, and had him cough while he held a stethoscope to his back, tapping with a finger in various places, making a hollow sound. Finally, he checked the straightness of Eustace's spine.

"No." Ridley began packing away his instruments. "This place won't do at all. I shall write a full report. With adequate care, you may yet make a full recovery, but if I were your mother, I'd find you a good climate and a clean sanatorium."

Eustace twisted to face him. "I know a lot more about my mother than you think, Doctor."

Ridley made a great show of locking away his silver hammers in their case.

"There's the blockade to be considered, so I would recommend Cornwall. Perhaps South Wales for the summer months, until Switzerland is feasible..."

"I'm fine where I am."

"Many of my younger patients feel similarly in the face of a stark diagnosis. If denial is of some psychological utility to you, by all means, be *fine* somewhere else."

Down in the pool, Freddie's skin prickled, despite the water's warmth. "But here's a good climate. Here's clean."

Ridley raised a finger towards the ceiling where the paint peeled like pencil shavings. "Damp. Where there's damp there's mould. Fenland miasmas drift in from the Little Ouse, of that I have no doubt. Winter has passed, the frost no longer protects us from last year's rotting vegetation and animal matter. It's very simple. You must leave."

All possible retorts wilted on his tongue. Doctor Chalice had so often praised the Hydropathic for its uniquely healthy position in the landscape, its distance from the fens with their unclean vapours and bloodsucking insects. In the Edenwell brochures, nymphs in billowing gowns promised healthy air infused with the scent of the pines. People came from across the country. They always had, for hundreds of years. Surely Ridley knew that?

And what did he mean, *leave*?

Eustace's fists were balled at his sides. "She can't stop me, you know. She can pay you all she likes, but I'm practically nineteen and when I receive Notice, I bloody well intend to make a go of it. Like everyone else."

Ridley absorbed his passion with flat disinterest. "I will write a full report. The army will not accept you on account of your lungs, Mister Moncrieff. To say nothing of your past... paroxysms."

Ridley turned his bland look on Freddie, who listened with innocent puzzlement. He had never heard the term, and the wintergreen odour of it filled him with discomfort. A paroxysm? Some rupture, surely. A spittle-flecked fit. It occurred to him with more than a touch of disappointment that Eustace had chosen not to tell him about this paroxysm. But when he noticed the younger boy glance back at him with something

252

like shame, he forced a reassuring smile. *It be reet.* Improbably, it made him feel like Fa.

"Shall we discuss it?" said Ridley mildly.

Eustace looked away. "That won't be necessary."

"You fail to understand the value of the gift being offered to you, Mister Moncrieff."

Glowering at the tiles, Eustace scoffed. "No one is offering me anything. All they do is take."

Ridley hefted his bag and made for the door. He paused, turned. "It may be of small comfort to know that I have been offered every inducement imaginable, these past few years. Handsome cars, pockets of land, even bags of boiled sweets... but I must confess, in all this time, I have never once encountered a coward. I leave you to your swim, gentlemen."

The doors swung behind him. Eustace stood dripping, and Freddie watched as his right hand shakily rose to his scalp. He held a hank of hair in his fist, staring hard at the floor as Freddie climbed out of the pool and came to him. The fist turned a slow twist. White scalp under a tangled black nest.

"Don't get too close," he said morosely. "I'm contagious."

At last the hand dropped. His ribs rose and fell, the wet vest clinging. *I'll draw this*, Freddie decided. *And do away with it.* Take this weakened, shaking sight and drown it so Eustace could be strong and brave, the way he ached to be.

Just thinking it had an effect. The younger boy's eyes flicked up. The brown irises were dappled with a deeper, flintier grey. Always new treasures to unearth.

"Do you want to hear something ridiculous?"

———

The story of Lawrence Parrish's death came out in a cold flood as they huddled together inside the safety of the folly. Freddie sat quietly on the billiards table, watching Drummerboy hop across the stacks of chairs, disrupting their cobweb veils. A boy begging for water as he died. He could see how Eustace bitterly regretted ignoring Parrish, but it wouldn't have helped. A crack on the head did for a boy the same as it did for a cow in a shambles.

"That was the end of my education," Eustace said, his knees drawn up to his chin. "When the new term began, the bed beside mine was empty – of course it was, but I was so sure everything would be back to normal. Our dormitory was a long room with wood panels – we called it The Coffin. The noise at night could be inhuman if the weather was rough. That winter, it was gales and sleet practically every day. A tree came down in the grounds and took one of the chimneys with it, and the whistling… I was afraid to go to bed in case I heard— stupid of me. I'd lie there listening to the rain on the windows, and half expect to hear Parrish asking for water again. But the funny thing is, I never did."

"Fa said after my mother died, he'd hear her calling."

"Did he say what it was like?"

"No. He'd had a few one Christmas when he told me. That was the only time."

He remembered the brown ale. The sliver of Christmas cake with nuts and apricot jam. Half an orange.

Eustace stretched out his hand for Drummerboy to nuzzle. "I didn't hear Parrish. But I did hear something. It could have been one of the other boys; they laughed all the time. Broken bones on the rugby field. Dead fathers. If you ever heard of a master messing around with a boy, you laughed about it, that was the game. The noise I heard was a cheerful one, I'm sure of that. But it didn't sound like Parrish, or any actual voice at all. More like…" He shrugged, the barest wrinkle of a frown between his eyes. He looked to Freddie like a man trying to remember a dream. "Have you ever been set lines as punishment? 'Thank you,' it said. Row upon row of 'thank you' running through my head. Except I hadn't put it there and I couldn't make it go away. But not 'thank you' as I'd say it to you. Rather… from a high place. As a king might accept tribute, you know. 'Thank you for giving me what I'm due.' Yes. That was the tone of it." He gave a deep sigh. "Look, I've never said a word of this to anyone, and I'm not— well, I'm not enjoying it."

"But you didn't give Parrish the water."

"It wasn't Parrish saying 'thank you'. It wasn't anchored to anything. No personality, no body. I couldn't be sure it was even talking to me. If I'd ever dared to answer, it would have been like talking to an echo. Do you see? I sound like a lunatic now, but you should have seen me back then. I tried keeping myself awake." He gave his hair a gentle tug to illustrate. "After nearly a week, you start to go potty. Stumbling over nothing, seeing shadows behind every door. And knowing all I'd do that night is lie there and listen to it, rolling over and over, 'thank you' in that entitled voice. Thank you for *what*?"

Freddie licked his dry lips. "Was that when you had your… para… roxy…?"

"No." The hole in the roof had his attention, offering a spot of bright light in the otherwise dark building.

"When the rooks talk," Freddie began hesitantly, "it's like when you go to the churchyard on St Mark's Eve. You ever try that? Folk say they see the spirits of all those destined to die the next year. It's like it's all decided. That's what the rooks say, anyway. When they die, they just pop straight back into an egg. All their ancestors and all their babies, they're all here. It's all happening at once, in a muddle, like a ball of string. Sometimes the likes of you and me might just catch a glimpse, that's all."

Eustace inclined his head, letting the light cascade down his face. "I much prefer that idea to a ghost."

"You ought to see Annie and Maud, calling up their future husbands with mirrors and candles."

Drummerboy burbled, hopping onto Freddie's lap and rolling over, puppy-like, to demand affection. His talons grabbed at Freddie's tickling fingers. Eustace stretched his aching arms and lay back to look up at the hole in the roof.

"There must be scores of men who want an exemption letter," he said. "Just not me."

"You said you weren't going anywhere."

"I'm not going away from *you*," he said, as if there were an obvious distinction. "But I've had it with them. Mother thinks because she bought me as a baby, she owns me. Chalice is just as bad. When the war's over, we should ditch the lot of them. You heard the men upstairs, they aren't content to go back to their old lives. Everything will change."

Freddie's heart tripped. "Doctor Ridley said you should leave."

"You have all those pictures of the pyramids. Don't you want to see Egypt?"

"I have seen it. I seen pictures."

Eustace shifted to face him, his eyes bright with possibilities. "But wouldn't you like to feel the sand under your boots? Or a studio, then. For drawing. A great big room all to yourself with no one to bust in and tell you to sweep up or scoop leaves. I'll have money by then; when I'm twenty-one there's a trust, Mother's doing. You can save some, too. And if that's not enough, we'll bump off my father and make it look like Mother did it."

Drummerboy's cackle bounced off the rafters.

"We could buy this whole place, then," Eustace added. "Boot everyone out. And if Ridley comes crawling up the drive, we can just—"

"Shoot him."

Eustace laughed to hear such an unexpected thirst for blood.

"If you go anywhere without me," Freddie said, "I think I might die."

It was no threat, no ultimatum. There was nothing but the soft pad of Eustace's thumb skimming over Freddie's bitten lips.

"It's you and me now, Lieutenant. Whatever happens."

THIRTEEN

Who Is The Boy Down In The Mines?

In the unusually warm winter of 1869, men digging in the Grimes Graves barrows discovered the skeleton of a young man forty feet beneath the surface. Thought to be around eighteen to twenty-five years of age, the youth was arranged carefully, tucked up as if sleeping; in his arms, the tool of his daily life – the ubiquitous antler pick, honed for chipping hard flint. How this individual met his end is impossible to say, but his fellows packaged him up inside the barrow and sealed him there with apparent deliberation. It is tempting to surmise our young friend was sacrificed in some atrocious pagan ritual, his youthful blood offered up to the community's heathen gods. As precious few human remains have been discovered in similar circumstances in these isles, we can guess that such a burial was considered a rare honour, or perhaps a lonely curse.

Ponsonby's Folklorica, Dr Winston Ponsonby, 1910. Chapter VIII, 'Norfolk: County of Kings'.

THE MORNING SKY was clear as a Nordic plunge pool when Doctor Chalice addressed the soldiers on the front lawn. Already sectioned out with chalk, the pristine grass of Edenwell Hydropathic was to be torn up and put to practical use for the first time in hundreds of years. Hardy root vegetables, potatoes, fruit bushes. Freddie thought of the sweat and devotion Mister Tungate once put into the little vegetable garden and how trivial it was by comparison. And then there was his own aching back as he pushed the lawnmower up and down, up and down, like a sinner in purgatory, knowing as soon as the task was complete it would need starting again.

But it wasn't the lawn that held his attention. Doctor Chalice had hopped up onto the tallest available structure, which happened to be a brand new motorised tractor with magnificent red spiked wheels. The doctor looked like a Roman in his battle chariot as he hailed the assembled crowd.

"I don't enjoy making speeches…"

"Or telling lies," said Eustace under his breath.

"How fine you all look this morning. What a privilege to be your host. What does he want, this old Yankee? Up there like a monkey? Gentlemen – ladies – my country has only lately joined the war effort, and for all the manpower and guns America has to offer, I believe it's these beauties that'll snatch victory from the jaws of the Kaiser."

Freddie couldn't take his eyes off the gleaming tractor. "How much did that cost?"

Eustace's look was sullen. "Bet you ten bob you can thank Martha Talbot for it."

"Allow me to introduce The Titan," said Chalice. "She's

simple to drive, and never tires. I can't wait to see what you can accomplish with her. And tonight, when you're weary, the gentlemen's baths will be open to you and your sore muscles. We'll create a new Eden here, of that I have no doubt."

Most of the men were relieved to have a task to focus on. They applauded Chalice, much to his pleasure, and set about dividing tasks immediately, deferring both to rank and experience. Plenty were former farm boys eager to take a turn on the Titan, and soon the engine could be heard growling into life.

Freddie and Eustace ambled up to the veranda where Missus Bailey and one of her usual accomplices watched the soldiers with a mixture of suspicion and interest.

"Saddens me to think of this beautiful lawn torn to smithereens," Missus Bailey remarked.

"It's all for the best," said a woman with her, unhappily twirling her parasol.

"Just the spectacle of it all coming here, to our doorstep. I never dreamed it possible."

They fell into an abrupt silence when Mister Butler approached, his camera in his spindly hands. "Excuse me, ladies. Might I trouble you for a picture?"

Missus Bailey raised her pointed chin. "What do you mean by that?"

"I'm documenting the work here, madam."

Missus Bailey was more interested in Butler's dishevelment, his blue dressing gown tied tight to defend against the light breeze. There had been muscle there once, a sturdy young man eager to work and explore and taste life. That young man could still be glimpsed in Butler's open, friendly expression, the way he held his camera as if offering a gift.

Inspection complete, Missus Bailey warmed a fraction. "How long does one need to stand still?"

"Seconds. If you could just stand where you are, with the tractor and the men off over your shoulders. Parasol down a touch. That's lovely. Thank you for your time, ladies."

Butler slid a tiny stylus from the sheath within the camera's bellows and wrote something in a window on the back of the device where the film sat in its compartment. He paused, looked about him.

"Ah! It's you two. Do you have the time? I like to record it all."

"Five past ten, Mister Butler." Eustace stopped short of 'sir', though his feet had snapped together, Freddie noticed, and he stood tall and straight, very nearly to attention. "How are you today?"

"Better all the time. What excellent beds you have here. And the dawn chorus is really something, isn't it? There must be scores of species here. Might spend an hour in the library tonight and see what I can find out."

Just then, the broad figure of Katie Healey, the masseuse, came out of the dining room doors, wiping her hands on her apron.

"Mister Moncrieff. What might you have forgotten?"

He winced. "Oh. That." Eustace gave Freddie an apologetic shrug. "See you in the aftermath?"

Freddie watched him go. While Eustace had his muscles wrenched, Freddie would work on his own, chopping firewood and hefting baskets to the kitchen. His recuperation couldn't go on for ever. Fa looked haggard, and there he was, a strapping young thing hiding under a blanket with a glass of milk.

The ladies cleared off the veranda. As Freddie walked away to his duties, he glanced back at Butler, standing alone, a little lost, fiddling with his camera. He wasn't at all how Freddie had imagined a soldier. Perhaps he could draw him, as Eustace suggested. There was endurance there, pale but undeniable.

"Are you making a nuisance of yourself?"

A hand gripped Freddie's shoulder. He found himself hauled around the corner where the wisteria wound its way up the wall. The wood twisted into his cheek as he was slammed into it, his arm wrenched behind his back.

Freddie could smell the grease Scole rubbed on his stump.

"They don't want you staring like that."

"I weren't staring."

Freddie winced as his arm was released. Scole spun him so they were eye to eye and affected a girlish whine: "*I weren't staring.* That's what you sound like to them. They're fed up with it. A couple of them had a word with me. You and that Moncrieff boy, gawping. What are you like?"

"They seemed all right at the party."

"It wasn't a *party*, you idiot. A party, looking the way they do? And you, rubbernecking. Like animals in a zoo. Their words."

He couldn't understand it. He might have made a fool of himself alone, but Eustace's manners were pristine. Surely he wouldn't have allowed Freddie to make any blunders. Scole's pockmarked face was livid. He gave Freddie a hard shake, rattling the wisteria.

"You want a look at a war wound?"

"No."

"Eh?" His hands were at his belt. "You want a good look?"

262

White drawers. Bristled thigh.

"No, sir."

"Come on, now. You're game, get cosy with it." He had Freddie's wrist in his grip, pulling on him painfully until his fingers brushed the place where stump met prosthetic, hairless and sticky with perspiration like a gobbet of warm dough. Freddie cringed back into the wall, letting the vines sink their spurs through his clothes, reminding him of that cold morning down at the spring, of bristles burning his back; something too fast to catch, too strong to fight.

"You work here," Scole breathed into his face, belt buckle jangling as he dressed himself. "All the time you attach yourself to them, you're leaving the slog for everyone else, and I'm not putting up with it. Pissing about with that Moncrieff fanny is one thing, but the men? You stay away from them. All right?"

Scole released him with a shove and went back to his work, flicking his dark hair out of his eyes. Freddie's heart juddered in his throat. He was thankful that no crowd had gathered, at least. He picked scraps of blue wisteria from his jacket. It was baffling. He was sure Butler and the rest were comfortable, but Scole's eyes were alight with the sort of fury reserved for the worst *faux pas*. It was like the Albion van again; Fa could teach and coax until he was blue in the face, but Freddie could never catch the knack of making it go without a jolt.

He trudged inside, his head full of wool, and immediately regretted it. The Hydropathic was busy with VADs finding their way and guests curious to watch them. Freddie had to flatten himself against the wall to keep from bumping into soldiers carrying spades and rolls of twine. There was a brief commotion as a uniformed girl almost collided with a guest; a clattering of rabbit's feet and glass clovers as the footman pushing the wheelchair halted abruptly.

The shrunken woman in the chair cried out: "I don't like it. I don't *like* it, Hiram. Get them all out. Get Mother. Get Mother down here, this instant."

Freddie was almost at the safety of the kitchen corridor, the old woman's shrieks echoing behind him, before he heard Butler's gentle call.

"Freddie, isn't it? Don't make me run."

Freddie found he couldn't look the man in the face, let alone answer, but he waited while Butler caught up with him, labouring under a thin sweat.

"Here's me yelling and hollering. You move like a sleepwalker. Look, I've just finished a roll of film and it's a perfect opportunity to show you how it's developed."

There was a window beside them, casting Butler's cheekbones in watery light. Freddie stole a glance to check if Scole was in sight.

"If you're busy..." began Butler.

"I don't— know— what I am," he stuttered. He wiped his palm on his trousers but the heat of Scole's flesh refused to leave him alone.

"Me neither," Butler grinned. "God, me neither. They think I might be up to some light weeding in four weeks or so, but for now I'm free to dawdle. Join me?"

With the exception of Scole, Freddie realised Butler was the first man he'd truly spoken to who'd been out and come back. If he had Eustace's courage, he'd wait for the right moment to spread out Scole's scrapbook in front of him. *Is this how their faces are? Would you believe me if—*

264

It was out of the question.

But for all his cloth-eared ineptitude, Freddie could see it without trying: Butler was desperate for a distraction.

"Lead the way, sir."

Butler visibly relaxed. "I took a few snaps on the way here," he said as they walked. "Have you ever seen a photograph of Thetford before? It's funny how your own town ceases to look familiar."

They took the lift to the top of the North Wing. The beds were packaged in white linen crisper than anything Annie and Maud could be bothered to attempt. Freddie thought back to those mornings clearing the chimneys and checking the windows; the great empty space of the place. And now the war was here, or at least the store-cupboard dregs of it. It had crept into Edenwell and set up home, and as he listened to the rumble of the tractor outside Freddie knew it wouldn't be leaving any time soon.

Butler went ahead of him to his bedside locker, his shoulder blades bobbing through his dressing gown, and handed Freddie a box. The contents shifted heavily, suggesting an apothecary's assortment of bottles. "Powder at the ready. Now if you'd be so kind as to lead me down to your dark room again?"

He was able to walk, albeit slowly, with frequent pauses to perch and flex his ankles, peeking out white and bristly from the hem of his blue suit. Down in the service tunnels, the Hydropathic's innermost workings grumbled around them and the ceiling dripped mineral-smelling water down their collars.

"Fred, you have no idea," Butler grinned. "Darkness and privacy. And it's warm! The cold can stop the chemical process altogether. The times I wanted to hurl the whole kit in a crater..."

The broom cupboard offered space enough for the both of them. Butler arranged his powders and bottles on a dusty shelf, disturbing a white spider that danced away at his touch.

"Pass me that string there. We'll rig up a drying line. Now it's of utmost importance we don't allow in any light but this red one. And be warned, it's going to get rather pungent in here. Put this rag over your mouth and nose. I haven't christened it, you'll be pleased to hear."

"Sir?"

"That's what they had us do in the beginning. Gas attacks. Drop everything and piss on the nearest rag to cover your face. It didn't work, anyway. Not unless you submerged your whole head. Now then, I am an amateur, please do remember that. I won't have done justice to all this sweeping breckland of yours, not on a two-inch contact print…"

Butler commenced his strange alchemy. In the lantern's red shade, he doled out spoonfuls of chemicals that stung Freddie's eyes.

"To develop…" Butler said, adding liquid to the first tray. The second contained a shallow layer of something caustic, like the stuff Missus Hardy rubbed on Freddie's grazed knees when he was a boy. "Then to fix. And finally, we wash."

Once the trays were prepared, Butler produced a sheet of plain card from a thoroughly sealed package. He blew away any dust before laying it flat on the shelf beside the lamp. Deftly dismantling the little camera, he retrieved the roll of film, laying out a selection of cells on the card and holding them there under a glass sheet.

"Exposure." Butler reached for the lamp. Counting under his breath, Butler swiped aside the red lens, bathing the negatives in light. *Like lamping*, Freddie almost said, but stopped himself. Seconds, and it was done.

The images – each smaller than a pack of Woodbines – came like a rumour as the soldier slowly dragged the card through the first pungent solution, unhurried at first, gathering momentum as barely perceptible outlines evolved into things Freddie half recognised; cobblestones like a crocodile's back, weeds sprouting from a pavement, a familiar shop sign. Dales, the butchers, only not as Freddie knew it. The windows were boarded up. As the image sharpened, he saw shards of glass sparkling on the pavement.

"What happened?"

"I spoke to the owner's wife," Butler said, lowering the print into the second solution. "Someone got it into their head she was keeping back meat, so when she shut up shop, they thought they'd check. Of course, there was nothing to be had. Silly buggers."

"Poor Missus Dale."

In the red gloom, he watched as Butler pulled card after card out of the darkness. Soon, a garland of them hung above: a mug on a windowsill, men in discussion over a chess board, nurses laughing as they stripped a bed. Freddie had seen these faces in motion, tried without success to put them to paper. Seeing them staring down at him, frozen but so alive, in perfect duplicate, the hair on his arms pricked up.

"Have a try," said Butler, handing him a card.

He swept it through the solution.

"Recognise anyone?" Butler said, his eyes smiling above the rag.

A miniature Eustace looked directly into the lens. Butler had fixed him in that characteristic motion Freddie had noticed so many times, his animal way of tensing before blooming into excitement, one shoulder up, one long leg over the other.

"He's like a statue."

Butler's eyes smiled. "He is a bit."

Freddie barely glanced at his own snub-nosed likeness, perched on the bed beside Eustace. All he wanted was to take the photograph and tuck it inside his waistcoat so his heart could beat against it all day long.

Butler pinned it to the line with the others. Reluctant to let it go just yet, Freddie watched with dismay as a black smudge crept over the corner of the image, a watercolour darkness feathering over the end of the bed, leaking onto Freddie's clothing.

"Ah, what a shame," Butler said. "That can happen. I'll do you a better one another time."

The discolouration hadn't touched Eustace, though Freddie's own shape was less distinct than before, like a man underwater. Freddie brushed at his sleeve, an instinctive twitch, as if his hand might come away gritty with soil. He couldn't have heard the rooks from here, not so far under earth and concrete, yet their laughter was palpable.

Three men on the bed. Eustace, Freddie, and the smeared impression of a third.

No peeking, knave.

Eyes down. In the dark, Butler's soft chatter was a welcome distraction.

"It's nice to have a fellow enthusiast around," he said as they waited for the prints to dry. "While I'm here, I'd like to spend more time on compositions. It was always so rushed at the front. Court martial if you're caught, you know. I got it down to ten seconds: notice a decent scene, check for officers, whip out the Kodak, and Bob's your uncle. After a time, I worked out who I could trust. Got some funny little domestic snaps of my mates shaving under the 'keep down' signs, that sort of thing. Haven't got around to developing those films. I don't know. I'd like to hand some over to their families. When I'm able."

"Do you think you can teach me?" Freddie asked. "To take pictures, I mean. D'you think I'll understand?"

"You can use a rifle and keep it clean? You can manage this." Butler swept the rag down from his mouth and regarded him. "Son, you're not a simpleton. Keep the picture, please. But I mean it – iron your Sunday best. I'll do you a proper portrait."

Complaining of an oncoming headache, Butler put his equipment in order and let Freddie lead the way back to the North Wing. Seeing Freddie helping Butler into bed, one of the VADs hurried over.

"Do you think you might be sick?" She was one of the upper-class girls, fresh out of school, and spoke as if she had never seen vomit and didn't wish to start now.

"No, no." Butler was sanguine, but that thin sweat had broken out again, all over his narrow body. "Stand down, sister."

"Mister Butler's been very poorly," the VAD told Freddie.

Butler sank heavily into the pillows, eyes shut in relief. "Touch of the collywobbles, that's all."

Relieved there was no need to fetch a bucket, the nurse fluffed the pillows behind Butler's back. "Well, don't let it put you off French cuisine for life."

At this, a smile broke out across Butler's shining face. He laughed as heartily as his sunken chest would allow. When the VAD left them, somewhat puzzled, Butler patted Freddie's arm.

"There was never enough water, you see. We used to put our tongues out when it rained. We'd scoop billy cans from flooded shell holes to boil for tea. Only this one trench we took over was French. And we brewed up, as we always did, with the water from the ground, and it was only when we all started heaving that we realised the bloody French—" He wheezed, his shoulders shaking with laughter. "The bloody French had only been burying their dead, hadn't they? In the walls of the trench. French cuisine!"

Through the open windows, the rooks guffawed.

When Butler had exhausted himself, he let Freddie pour him a glass of water and support him as he leaned forward for a sip.

"Your friend's keen, isn't he?" he asked, wiping droplets from his moustache.

"He wants to be a sniper."

"There's an ambition." Butler's tone was mild, but as he sat back his expression was distant. He looked out across the ward at the empty beds, waiting for their occupants to return from their labours. "You can't stop him. I know you want to. Everyone on the line has a little brother or someone training at Salisbury. But if you stop him, someone else will fill those boots. He knows that. If he lives to a hundred and two having never fired a shot in his life, he'll still be thinking about it, and that's not your fault. They've set the thing in motion now. Nothing's going to slow it down."

"But the Germans have done terrible things."

"Undoubtedly. But we had prisoners. Usually just waved them on if they had their hands up – no one wanted the bother of feeding them – but one or two carried our stretchers, slept beside us, chatted away in English. They seemed as sick of it as we were. A tenacious lot, though, especially the Saxonites. Now, the Prussians, on the other hand... even the prisoners told us to give them what for. Vicious buggers, the Prussians."

Freddie stared at his boots. The levity of the dark room had quite evaporated, leaving him with nothing but the thought of Eustace's lanky frame draped in Scole's khaki tunic.

He stood to leave. "Thank you for talking to me, Mister Butler."

"I'm glad of the company."

"Sorry to have bothered you before."

"Eh?"

Freddie tugged at his lip. "Some of the men were cross that me and Eustace came and pestered you the other night."

Butler was surprised. "What silly bugger said that? It was a pleasant evening. Are we not allowed those?"

"Mister Scole said— he's one of the orderlies here. I don't wish to be a nuisance, sir."

"Less of the 'sir'. Tell me something. This Scole. Mardy sort of fellow? Nick Scole?"

"That's him."

"I spotted him yesterday. Said to myself, don't be daft." He gave a little snort, as if finally understanding a private joke. "Gratifying to know I'm not potty on top of everything else."

Freddie was stunned. "You know Mister Scole?"

Butler smiled and said nothing.

"You didn't make a complaint?"

Butler dabbed his brow with a clean handkerchief and settled down into the crisply laundered blankets. "Is this the face of a man with something to complain about? Comfy bed, new mate, lovely darkroom. Edenwell is paradise."

The grass – what remained of it – was crisp in the April sun. Wild violets were trampled by workmen's boots, and when Freddie sketched the footprint left by a soldier in his hospital blues, it came out misshapen and crude. Nothing could capture the truth like a photograph.

Away from the smell of tractor fuel and turned dirt, he retreated to the back of the Hydropathic. Out on the bandstand amongst the lavender bushes, he could be alone.

On the back of yesterday's menu, he drew from memory. A rook's wing at full spread, the feathers fanned like fingers. In the spaces between: an axe, the seashell intricacies of a tiny skull, a pair of antler picks. *Gifts*, he named it, and paused, wondering if he ought to add his name to the drawing, like the men who painted the bathing ladies framed on the Hydropathic walls. Butler couldn't sign his pictures, not for fear of court martial. Freddie asked himself what reprisal he was afraid of, out here in the brecks where no one cared what he drew, or said, or did, so long as the Hydropathic didn't topple over for want of repairs.

"You have a keen eye."

Freddie dropped his pencil. This voice wasn't one he knew, and through the pale April sun behind the man, he saw a woollen sleeve the colour of a magpie's sheen.

Freddie heard the jingle-jangle of the decorated wheelchair before he saw the old woman.

272

She called out: "Hiram. That boy—"

"I've got him." The footman didn't take his eyes off Freddie. "Please step down where we may speak freely."

With reluctance, Freddie pocketed his sketch and accompanied Hiram down to where his companion waited, bright-eyed and serious in her white blouse and summer hat. The golden cross weighed heavily against her ruffled breast, and as Hiram came to her side, she placed her wizened hand on his with unexpected tenderness. For Freddie, she reserved a look of cool authority, despite her size and fragility.

"Young man, you are the groundskeeper here, are you not? How would you like to earn a shilling?"

"Madam?"

Freddie's lack of enthusiasm displeased her. She tapped Hiram's hand. "Hiram, tell him. Tell him I can't walk."

"Miss Clarissa would like to know if there is a clear path down into the woods over to the east," he supplied.

Freddie looked from Hiram's face to Clarissa's, both of them quite sober and – he realised with a gnawing in his stomach – not prepared to be denied. "I'm sorry, madam," he began, "but there's landslides—"

"Hiram, tell the boy I'm hard of hearing."

The footman's dark, impassive gaze held Freddie. "Miss Clarissa would very much appreciate if you would escort us."

"As I say, madam, Doctor Chalice has been very clear—"

"Hiram, tell him two shillings."

"Miss Clarissa is fully aware there *are* no landslides," Hiram told Freddie. "If there is no path available, perhaps you would be so kind as to help me carry Miss Clarissa down to the ruins of the holy well."

273

She wanted healing. Someone must have filled her head with stories of monks and fortune tellers, and now a hip bath and a doing-over by Katie Healey wasn't authentic enough. Freddie sighed. Saying no to a guest was not something he had the authority to do.

"I can bring up some water in a jug, if you think she'd—"

Miss Clarissa's ancient face creased into a scowl. "This is *my* house. I will roam it as I please."

Freddie looked at Hiram dubiously. He waited for a sign on the footman's face, some hint of an acknowledgement that yes, his mistress was raving mad, but Hiram's expression remained imperiously blank. Finally, the footman opened his fine blue jacket. Strapped over his waistcoat was a long knife, curved and clean as a serpent's tooth.

"No padfoot has ever tangled with me and left smiling, I assure you." Hiram's lips twitched in the briefest of expressions, though Freddie couldn't say which. "Freddie, isn't it? Alfred Ferry, son of James Ferry. I've seen you maintaining the North Wing in the mornings, before all this chaos descended. You always dust the Morton coat of arms. Such attention to detail deserves a shilling."

Something like fear tightened around Freddie's lungs. He glanced about for signs of Fa, of Eustace, even of Doctor Chalice. The old woman's low laughter cut through his thoughts.

"Magnificent, isn't he?" Clarissa said. "My lucky star."

A look passed between the pair, truly fond. However mismatched they were, whatever Clarissa saw in Hiram, he saw something of equal virtue in her.

A scream rang out over the gardens. Freddie jolted. Hiram's hand darted to his knife.

"A woman's cry, Clarissa."

"Well then, go," she said. "Go!"

They left Clarissa where she sat. The cry came from the courtyard under the North Wing, and as they rushed over Freddie heard a clattering bucket and the scuffle of boots on cobblestones. Pegs were scattered and the washing basket had spilled its contents. Tabitha Clarke. At her feet was Annie the chargirl, covering her head with her arms.

"Thought you'd have a giggle, did you?" Tabitha drew back her foot and kicked Annie with the full weight of her body behind it. The chargirl wailed.

"It weren't me! I swear."

"You pig. You *pig*."

With a fist full of Annie's hair, she dragged the girl over to the washing basket and made to rub her nose in it.

"Where's that cow Maud? Run off and left you to take the rap, did she? You think I'll bow my head and take it, 'cause I'm new and I'm—" Her tirade broke off as she noticed Freddie and Hiram, standing immobile under the washing lines in shock. "Don't you interfere!" she shouted. Tears streaked down her cheeks.

Freddie stepped back to show he meant no harm. Hiram's hand had dropped from his concealed knife.

From the ground, Annie beseeched them. "She's lost her mind."

"You'll see," Tabitha said. "Come and look what she did."

Tabitha tipped the laundry basket up. Piles of clean, soap-smelling sheets were speckled with dirt. When she pulled aside the first layer of cotton, Hiram's face contorted. Freddie looked to Annie, who shook her head.

"You think I'd do that?" she sniffled.

Hiram shook out a fresh handkerchief and held it over his mouth as he bent to inspect the high-smelling tableau.

A chicken, most assuredly dead, was dressed with the greatest care in a white christening gown and linen bonnet, framed in frills. A feathered infant, eyes cloudy in death.

A fresh tear ran down Tabitha's nose. "Waiting for me as I hung out the sheets. What a jolly joke, eh?"

Hiram let his handkerchief drop. "I'll give you the pleasure of handling this," he told Freddie. "I have my duties. Do not forget what we discussed."

The footman turned smartly and left.

Annie gathered her cumbersome skirts in shaking hands, trying to right herself. "I don't know anything about it. Tell her, Freddie."

"Maybe one of the soldiers…" he started dubiously.

"No *man* has the imagination for something like this," Tabitha snapped. "And don't you play the innocent, Annie. I've heard you and Maud spreading muck. Missus Hardy's husband likes a drink, does he? And Lottie Mulgrave's funny lady friends from the theatre? Got to keep an eye on them. You should hear what they have to say about you, Freddie. Why don't you tell us, Annie? Explain your prank so we can all have a good laugh."

Freddie flinched as Tabitha booted Annie, once again knocking her to her knees.

"Tell us!"

Whimpering, Annie covered her face with her arms. "Maud said… she said Chalice only brought you here because he felt sorry for you. We're all meant to think you left your position at the factory 'cause your hair fell out, but— We didn't put the bird there. It's horrid. *Horrid.*"

"And why did I leave the factory, Annie?" Tabitha asked evenly. "Go on."

A miserable bubble of snot blossomed from Annie's nostril. "Because— you were in the family way."

Tabitha leaned down until her ruddy nose was almost touching the chargirl's. "If you go poking about in my business again," she said, "I'll break every finger you've got."

In a flurry of tears and muddied Edenwell skirts, Annie fled.

Freddie squatted to inspect the strange bundle. The chicken wore a ribbon in its bonnet, lovingly tucked under its avian chin. Someone had taken great delight in creating this scene. It wasn't self-pity or even grief burning on Tabitha's face, but rage, he realised. Rage that in such a world of cruel misfortune someone still found mirth in causing pain.

She stood by his side, her breathing slowly returning to a natural pace. "We were promised to each other, me and my Thomas. If both my boys had lived, they'd be nice as pie to me, those girls."

Freddie was slow to understand. Burrell's would never have an unwed mother on their payroll, he knew that much of the world.

"Miss…" Freddie ventured. "I don't think this is Annie's work. And Maud's gruff, but I've never seen her go to trouble like this for a lark."

"You think this is Nick's doing."

He was surprised she could so easily divine his thoughts. "I couldn't know for sure, miss. Only…" He faltered. *I don't think you know him like we do.*

She wiped her face roughly. "He's a tinker, but he's not a monster. Get rid of it, please. I don't care how."

Freddie took the bird from the basket. As the head flopped backwards, he felt the individual nodes of broken backbone shift between his fingers. That uncanny jellied consistency, horribly familiar. He stole a look at the trees beyond the courtyard, sighing in the breeze.

Tabitha set about picking up the strewn sheets. She would have to wash half of them again to get the smell out, and the dirt would set if she didn't get them back to the copper quickly.

"I called him Timothy. My son."

She threw the words away. With difficulty, Freddie met her eyes.

"I'm very sorry, miss. For all of it."

He headed back to the cottage, careful to avoid the men cutting up furrows in the lawn. The air was wholesome with dirt and cut grass, despite the dead chicken warming under Freddie's arm. Someone had the tractor going and was making slow progress. The spiked wheels churned up the black earth with ease, and the driver laughed, waving his cap at his mates.

A less pleasing sight had Freddie's attention. Amongst the furrows, live chickens went bumbling about. The men swatted at them with their tools.

"Oi. That's my tea, that is," laughed a florid Welshman as Freddie darted past, just managing to snatch up a chicken before it could blunder under the tractor's wheels. "Someone must've left the coop open. I counted four."

Under his breath, Freddie swore. Sure enough, Fa was coming up from the cottage with consternation on his face. He bent his long body to scoop up one of the loose fowls.

"You didn't fancy checking the latch, then?"

"Sure," Freddie answered. "When I fed them."

"You didn't feed them. Bucket's on the hook, and Mags says you've been nowhere near the kitchen all day. I can't believe this, Fred. You used to be a grafter. If we lose one chicken, think of the eggs. We're already one bird down. What the devil do you have there?"

"Someone played a trick on Tabitha Clarke."

Fa's expression twisted. "They're valuable, boy! You take care of that jackdaw more than anything, and he in't feeding us, is he?"

Fa's voice was rising. Freddie caught the Welsh soldier glancing up from his work and felt a blush flood across his cheeks. He could have sworn he had been out to the coop. He could remember the bucket in his hand, the smell of the morning's meagre peelings. Or perhaps that was the day before. "Fa—"

"It's that Moncrieff boy. You aren't paid to run after him, Fred. You're mooning. There's work to do. It needs doing now, and it'll still need doing when he's gone."

Gone! The rooks caught the word and tossed it about. *Gone gone!*

"I in't mooning," he said weakly.

Fa corralled him back to the cottage. "They're making comments, the staff. And I wished that Missus Bailey a good morning only the other day, and she said it must be tiring doing the work of two men. With that grin of hers."

"Missus Bailey's like that to everyone."

"You're not a bairn any more. It's my own fault for letting you carry on like one."

They stopped at the coop and Fa deposited the escaped bird inside with a grunt. Freddie could hear Drummerboy inside the cottage, chirping his greetings. If he fled to his room, Fa would only follow him. Eustace's studio idea sprung to mind, cavernous and secure and all his to fill with private pictures, private thoughts. Out on the lawn, the soldiers barked with laughter at some exclusive joke. The blush on Freddie's face was back like a slap.

What must they think of him?

"I've been lazy this week," he admitted. "Doctor Chalice had me put my feet up, and I s'pose I liked it."

"This week? It's been a damn sight longer than that in my book."

Freddie took the kicking chicken from under his arm and returned her safely to the coop, shielding her as best he could from the sight of her dead comrade. Despite his excuses, Freddie knew he'd shown himself up. And worse, there were things Fa wasn't saying, things simmering away that Freddie could sense but not see. When he closed the coop door – fixing the latch with care – Fa was standing where he left him, staring at the grass, his lips pressed into pallor.

"You're sentimental lately, Fred. I can't say it pleases me."

When the last chicken was safely back in the coop – just the one loss this time, thank God – Freddie made a point of scooping the leaves in the fountain and checking Mister Tungate's garden for slugs. The lawn was loud with men's voices and the tractor's engine, and his worries droned distractingly.

A knave is in arrears!

For the first time in his life, Freddie wished other people could hear the ringing laughter of the rooks as clearly as he could, their prophesying and jeering misdirection. If only he could block up his ears, unlearn their language, be free to be an ordinary, useful young man.

He paused in the walled garden. The weeds were springing up with gusto, and in some beds the vegetables were indistinguishable from the milk thistles. Freddie felt in his pocket for Butler's photograph. He could feel it; that was comfort enough.

Over the garden wall, a couple of soldiers stopped for a cigarette. Freddie felt exposed again, despite the brick barrier, and slunk through the gate. His first impulse was to creep back to his bedroom, shelter awhile, let the feel of Drummerboy's feathers soothe him. He felt a pang. Fa wouldn't shoo Drummerboy out, would he? Teach him a lesson by scaring him away? No. Fa was Fa; harried sometimes, taciturn, but he had never once shown his son an ounce of cruelty. Still, Freddie's heart was tripping.

There was one place he could go where no one would look at him.

With most of the soldiers outside, the majority of the VADs were standing by for medical emergencies, blowing on their cold hands and offering lukewarm encouragement. The few young women still indoors were preoccupied with cleaning and keeping the place in order. Freddie kept out of their way, cleaving to the tiled walls of the corridor leading down to the service tunnel. As the noise died away, he felt his insides unbuckle a little.

Someone had let the chickens out on purpose. He could almost blame it on a soldier giddy to be safe and amongst friends – a mindless prank – but the dead bird in the christening gown loomed large in his mind's eye and the poultry reek of it caught in the back of his throat. The devastation in Tabitha's eyes. Then there was the matter of all those lost eggs. His stomach gurgled pitifully, anticipating cold mornings with nothing but black tea for comfort.

"What did I say?"

A hand in his hair. Freddie yelped as he was spun around. The door to the main corridor swung shut behind them and he was dragged into the darkness of the service tunnel.

Freddie scratched at the hand in his hair. "Let go!"

Scole thudded him against the wall. "I *told* you not to talk to him."

"Butler?"

Hearing the soldier's name took some of the wind from the orderly's sails. Scole's face faltered. The fist in Freddie's hair loosened, leaving his scalp burning.

"I don't know, do I? Any of that lot. I tell you to do summat, you do it."

In this small space, Freddie realised for the first time that Scole was shorter than him. But the older man was broad, breathing noisily from the nostrils like a horse agitated in his stall. Freddie didn't fancy his chances.

"You're needed with Tabitha," Freddie said. "You should see what she did to Annie."

"Annie's convinced she's dying when she stubs her toe.

What do I care about Annie? And Tabby's my business. Who are you, telling me what to do with my girl, you little—"

Scole's fist caught the light, raised and ready. It would only have taken a second to smash Freddie's face and walk away, but something made Scole still. At least he hadn't flinched, Freddie told himself. He'd denied him that satisfaction.

Before Freddie could offer any placating words, the older man hauled him off again, further down the corridor, stumbling to the cupboard where Butler had shared his photographic magic. The trays of chemicals tickled his throat with potent grey tendrils as Scole yanked open the door.

Freddie saw Scole's plans clearly then. He kicked and thrashed, but Scole's wooden leg felt no pain.

A shelf slammed into the small of his back, sending a spark of pain through his kidneys that took his breath away as the darkness closed in on him. Freddie heard Scole's boots fading down the corridor.

Freddie's hands fluttered over the dusty surfaces, discerning Butler's bottles of developing powder. His nostrils were already stinging in protest at the overpowering apothecary odour. Something was dripping. His trouser leg was wet. A developing dish had toppled in the scuffle and his boots slipped in the spirit spreading across the floor. Fumbling, he found Butler's lamp, only to send it crashing to the floor.

Freddie tried the door, knowing it was futile. He sank his teeth into his lip to crush his rising panic. Someone would come by. The service tunnels of Edenwell were nothing compared to the burial chambers he'd seen in books. *The Boy's Own Paper* printed thrilling stories of the discoveries of the Egyptian desert; of ancient priests who traversed the darkness of the pyramids, mutilating the dead for the pleasure of their strange gods. Explorers had discovered the bones of those priests, walled in with their royal masters. Done their part, seen too much. Pyramids were mazes of winding avenues, sending thieves to dead ends and cursed chambers, but at Edenwell a new batch of towels needed laundering every hour.

He waited. Freddie had only the increasing disgust at the fumes from Butler's equipment to measure the passing time. A dim throb was setting up home behind his eyes. He pushed on the door, put his back against it and used his weight, but it wouldn't budge. Scole must have wedged something against the handle. Freddie slid to the floor and put his mouth to the crack for air. Maud would come by soon, or Annie if she'd stopped crying.

The heels of his hands stung. He was kneeling in the acrid puddle. He could taste it deep in his throat, and that ache behind his eyes had grown a thorny pelt.

Boys carrying gifts.

Freddie shook himself. He couldn't hear the rooks, not down here. Still their knowing cackles filled the cramped space. His chest felt heavy, as if a swaddling cloth were wrapped tightly around it. His body curled in on itself, back hunched. He couldn't be allowed to drop the— to break the— precious—

What?

A trolley was rattling. One of the washing carts, with Maud or Annie at the helm. Freddie struggled to his knees and took in a breath to shout, but the fumes caught in his throat, needle sharp, and a frenzy of coughing took him. When the spasm passed, the trundling wheels were distant and fading. Yes, he realised dizzily, he heard the heavy clunk of the door at the far end of the tunnel. He was dwindling in and out of consciousness.

"I— can't— breathe."

He almost cried when he heard the scrape of a broom being removed outside the door. The reprieve of cold air. Scole, smiling fondly.

"Lesson learned?"

He nodded mutely.

"Not convinced."

And as the world went dark once more, Freddie heard the turning of a key.

FOURTEEN

Things Shown Me In The Pit. I.
Pencil on butcher's paper. April 1917.

A crowd cheers as a column of uniformed men march by. Cowled monks shuffle among them. A stocky girl holds a newborn baby, lavender blue. James Ferry, tall and thin, holds up the rear, his distant look impossible to read.

"WHO'S THAT KNOCKING at the door? Could it be... big sister?"

Phoebe Moncrieff's coppery hair was bound up in a bun. With the white cap framing her face and the apron tied tight beneath her breast, she might almost have resembled an adult were it not for her impish smile as she peeked around the door.

Eustace glanced up from the book he was tolerating. Sprawled on the bed, his hair damp from his afternoon steam bath, the first sight of his sister in more than a month only deepened the bad mood that had simmered away since Freddie had failed to meet him for lunch. "A new outfit."

Phoebe's face fell. "Are you not surprised?"

"Had a feeling you'd be back, that's all."

"You're looking well."

He shot her a withering look. She, by contrast, looked wan despite her cheerful entrance. Her nose was pink at the tip. A touch of cold.

She ventured inside. He had barely unpacked, she noted, darting a look at his washstand and writing desk. "Are you genuinely not surprised to see me?"

"I heard a rumour you'd joined the VADs. You must have told someone with a big mouth." He shut the book with a snap. "What's it like?"

She grinned, flopping down into his untouched desk chair. "Hard work."

"I meant the uniform."

"On the large side. But that's that way of it, they say — always too small or too big. You remember Fat Hannah I was at school with? She's a higher-up. Got me sent here straight away when I wrote to her. I'm learning on my feet, but so is everyone. Some of these girls have never made their own breakfast."

"You've come to keep an eye on me, then."

"Not everything is about you." She shot him a scowl, but it quickly paled into concern. "How *are* you? Where's your little friend?"

"I was hoping you were him when you knocked."

"You'll have to bring him home to meet Mother."

Eustace stilled. They were in on it together, of course. He could see them in the drawing room even now, Mother and Father and Harry and Phoebe, the whole committee gathering to dissect Eustace's latest crazes, his boyish attachments. Some families played whist.

Phoebe sensed the weight of his silence. "It's what people do, darling," she added gently. "They have friends. Share meals."

She looked sweet in her uniform, he had to admit. Natty and elfin. The men would take to her. And she could handle herself, he had no doubt of that. She always did have a brain in her head. Seeing her again, Eustace ached. It was impossible to deny. He felt it physically: envy, ugly and bulbous, for her new position, her freedom to choose. Growing up, he had always seen Phoebe's future mapped out in flat domestic colours, a natural contrast to his own impending adventures. It was thoughtless of him, expecting his sister to wait at home for him. Something a child would believe.

"Did anyone tell you about the woods?" he asked.

"The landslides? I expect I'll be far too busy to go exploring."

"Stay close to the Hydropathic. A man died down there. Freddie found him."

Her face creased in sympathy. Genuine, as far as Eustace could tell, but he reminded himself of that coffee-drenched letter, of her half-truths and hidden schedules. He pressed on: "Promise me."

"You weren't there, were you?"

He nodded, tight-lipped. Phoebe gave a long sigh.

"I knew something was wrong. I meant to write, but Harry came back from France with some sort of ague. Good God, nursing him was exhausting. He's a horrible patient. I slept on the floor in his room. The dreams I was having…" She shook her head. "I'd wake up shouting."

"How is the eldest?"

"Hollowed out. Goodness only knows what it was. Mother hired a nurse in the end, my nightmares were depriving him of rest. He's strong, though. When I left, he was just about walking again."

Eustace tried to imagine Harry 'just about' doing anything. What humiliation his brother must feel, having to submit to a nurse's care. The thought gave Eustace no pleasure. Perhaps it ought to.

"You will promise, won't you?"

"What?"

"Don't go into the woods."

She got up and sat with him on the narrow white bed, laid her small hand on his. "It must have been terrible, for Freddie and for you. If you ever want to talk about things, I'll only be sleeping a few minutes down the hall. Though Matron probably won't be happy if you come knocking in the wee hours."

He stared. "Talk about what things?"

Phoebe's small hand retracted as if stung. "The Parrish boy. Come off it, Eustace, you were devastated. This surely must have brought back memories."

"Can't say it did."

"Of course not." She pursed her lips, holding back a sharper retort. "Well, I've offered."

They sat in silence, listening to the work outside. He wondered if she had duties to attend to, assuming Mother hadn't slipped Matron a little something to sweeten her experience. All the bribes in the world wouldn't help her if she strayed too close to Choke Wood.

"You need to promise."

"I won't go near the woods."

"Don't say it like that! You need to mean it."

"Are you *crying*?"

With his sleeve, he wiped angrily at his eyes. "Don't change the subject."

Phoebe stood up, compelled to have her own space. His eyes followed her with febrile intensity.

"He's covered in rags," he said. "Tall, even taller than me. He walks like a drunken sailor until he notices you, and then he's fast. If you see him, no matter how far away he is, you get away. Promise me. Promise now."

"Eustace, who are you talking about?"

"He carries a— it's a staff. An enormous antler filed down. And he swings it. I don't think he can see, Phoebe, but he is so strong—"

Her brows knitted together as she tried to understand the joke. "This is a man in the woods?"

"He's not just a man—"

"Eustace."

"Don't *look* at me like that."

"Well, how would you like me to look at you? You aren't making any sense."

She was laughing. Innocently, nervously, but it set something off in him. At once, he was on his feet. She stepped back, her regulation shoes stuttering on the floorboards.

"You expect me to believe you just felt like volunteering here?" he said. "Of all the places in the world?"

"I wanted to be near you."

"Me? Or Chalice?"

They fell into an uneasy silence. Outside, there was a faint commotion of men and machines. Eustace stared at his sister, watching her face move from anger to hurt, eyes closed in defeat. As her mouth twisted, trying to find the right words, the fuss from outside intensified. Phoebe's eyes flicked open. A man was shouting. Others joined in. A scuffle, perhaps. It was only when the VADs started calling for help that Phoebe broke out of her trance and rushed to the window.

He heard her intake of breath.

Crows and rooks and jackdaws and magpies and jays.

He couldn't breathe.

Foxes and badgers and pine martens and field mice.

He couldn't breathe.

Slow worms and adders and sowpigs and bishy-barney-bees.

He couldn't.

Marshflies and cave spiders and colourless crawling mites.

Breathe.

Tabitha Clarke's face was mapped with tiny red veins the colour of beetroot juice running through the cracks in a chopping board. Freddie's vision throbbed and pumped to a staccato beat; Tabitha's flushed face juddered in and out of the too-bright light. Her shriek jabbed through his head like a knitting needle.

The next face was more welcome.

Eustace fell on his knees, hands fluttering over Freddie's prone body. "Get Doctor Chalice. Freddie? Good God, get out of there. Get some air."

They slumped together on the flagstones. Eustace wrapped

his arms around Freddie, tugging with all his strength until they lay in the cold corridor under the flickering electric lamps. Freddie fought the impulse to vomit in front of Eustace. Such a thing would be impolite.

"You've been gone so long. You're a bit poisoned, I expect. It was locked from the outside. What happened, Fred?"

"Tabitha... she'd been crying."

Eustace nodded. He thought for a moment, his face serious, and touched Freddie's forehead. Not hot with fever, thank God, but Freddie's colour was something frightful.

"There's a little time yet," he said softly.

Freddie's eyes flickered open. Time? He must have been inside the cupboard for hours. He tried to grasp the lost time. Dreams and memories poured through him in disturbing earthen colours.

He had to take the— had to place the—

Eustace brushed the sweaty hair from Freddie's eyes. "You're always falling on me, have you noticed that?"

Freddie chuckled. The effort almost made him sick.

"Your heart is strong, isn't it? Even if it wobbles a little. How is it now? Ticking away. Oh Freddie, I was looking for you all over. We set up such a hue and cry."

"For me?" he croaked.

"It's late. I wanted to be the one to find you." Eustace swallowed hard, grimacing against the stink of the developing liquid on Freddie's clothes. His dark eyes were wide with worry. "You look like hell."

"Feel it."

"Freddie, the others will come in a moment, and I need to tell you something."

Could it not wait? Swimming there in the half-light with Eustace's arms around him. Good. Yes. Nothing more important. The elders had done the same for the boy in the mines. Slowly taken their hands from his throat when he finally stilled. Held him a while. A beautiful gift, the best there was: young and strong. If he had known, he would have understood. A moment of violence for a great spell of peace. Laid out beside the bird skull, the axe and the antler picks, he was a breathless bride with a fabulous dowry.

Freddie lay there, eyes revolving sluggishly with confusion. Eustace waited until he held his gaze.

"Freddie, there was an accident on the lawn. Your father was killed, Freddie. He died."

The boundaries of the corridor seemed to melt and stretch.

"He in't working on the lawn," Freddie said after a long silence.

"I wasn't there when it happened. But I have seen him, and he did die, Freddie. I'm so sorry. One of the soldiers was driving the big American tractor. He clipped a trench. The whole thing went over. The VADs did everything they could."

Dimly, Freddie registered Eustace's long hand resting over his heart, feeling it lurch and drop, squeeze and struggle.

Eustace said something else, something consoling, but he didn't hear it. He was the pains inside his head, the chaos of his pulse, the cold invading his joints. Fa was dead. Fa was dead.

And Eustace was holding his still-living, still-aching body, murmuring tender promises that at any other time would have him singing to himself like a jackdaw laughing over the pines.

Fa was dead.

Eustace, calling down to him through forty feet of soil:

"I'm your family now."

FIFTEEN

BUTLER'S THIN FINGERS raked gently through the white streak in Drummerboy's plumage.

"He's a fine fellow. And you raised him from a chick?"

Drummerboy looked from Butler to Freddie, compressed uncomfortably in a chair he had pulled into the corner of Eustace's room where they had spent the last twenty-four sleepless hours. The jackdaw gave a soft *chack*.

"He likes fish paste," Freddie said dully.

"If he stays still like a good boy, he shall have some." Butler backed off to the bed. He had his camera cupped between both hands. Drummerboy was happy to remain perched on the back of the chair, arched and preening in the light of attention.

"It isn't like the bad old days," Butler explained. "Staying still for sixty seconds. No puff of smoke and a man hiding under a sheet. You still have a set of bellows, see, and there's still this window to look through, but it's all in beautiful, portable miniature. We're free to go out into the world and document it as it is."

"Like an eye."

Butler held Drummerboy in his sights. "And like an eye, it carries the viewer's prejudices, his choices, his way of seeing..."

Butler handed the camera to Freddie. It was heavier than he expected. It took a moment for his vision to adjust to the warped window of the viewfinder. Drummerboy's familiar shape, upside down. He scanned the whole room. Eustace's bed, not slept in; the curtains, pulled so he wouldn't see the lawn. Edenwell was quiet. The soldiers had withdrawn to the North Wing. Their blue uniforms could be glimpsed through closing doors, at a distance, each man nothing more than a glance and a hasty exit. Freddie was ushered places. Up from the tunnels. Through to Matron Calder. Doctor Chalice, white as plaster, moved back and forth while she pulled at Freddie's eyelids and listened to his lungs. Ushered to bed, practically marched, though he couldn't bear to go back to the cottage. The little house might as well have been ablaze.

They took him to see Fa. He had to ask. With one of Tabitha Clarke's freshly laundered sheets up to his chin, he looked like a picture from a book. Freddie tilted his head, studying the lines on his father's face. Someone had washed him, he realised dimly. A bead of water rested in Fa's left eyebrow, magnifying the bristly hairs. Chalice mumbled something in the Matron's ear, to which she responded at full volume:

"I don't approve of sedatives. Besides, we must account for everything in our inventory. He isn't one of mine."

Freddie ran his fingers down the edges of Butler's camera, the rough case, the stiff leather strap.

"Can a photograph tell a lie?"

"Outright?" said Butler. "Actresses have their waists taken in. But a trained eye can spot it, most of the time. Are you hoping to play some tricks?"

Drummerboy spread his wings, shook them out.

"Hope to be believed," Freddie said.

"Then never shoot into the sun. Watch where the shadows are. Take the time to rest your camera somewhere stable. Even if you don't move, your heart does."

"Snipers say that."

It was Eustace. The door bumped open and he wobbled in with a tray of tea and undersized currant buns. Since finding Freddie in the cupboard, he was unwilling to sit passively and wait for anything. Blankets, tea, fresh clothes from his own luggage. An endless night in his room, scrunched up in chairs with the windows open, listening to the owls. At dawn, the rooks rose to gossip, but if they had a message for Freddie he kept it to himself.

"They fire between beats, you're right." Butler took one of the sad little buns. "Cor, these are ever so nice. You should try a bite, Fred."

The camera clicked. Drummerboy was in mid-preen, one wing up, beak shining obsidian.

"Did I do it?" Freddie said. "Is that right?"

"Now wind on. Turn the key. And there you have it. That's yours now, you captured it."

Eustace leaned over Freddie's shoulder, hoping to see something, he wasn't sure what. "And then we just... fish out the film and dip it in the smelly stuff?"

"It is a touch more complicated than that, but I'm told I'm a decent teacher." Butler watched as Freddie raised the camera

296

in Eustace's direction, holding it still, testing the frame around the subject. Butler smiled. "Have it, then. Just don't use all my film on him."

Freddie unfurled himself from the chair and went to the door. "Are you coming?" he said to Eustace, who had settled himself on the bed, letting the teacup warm his hands. The younger boy was exhausted, whereas Freddie felt himself taken by some unseemly energy, driving him on without fuel.

"Your oppo looks worse than I do, Fred," Butler said, stifling a yawn. "I think you and I ought to keep an eye on him, don't you? In case I fall asleep. Which I might, honestly. What time is it anyway?"

Eustace yawned. "Missus Hardy said it was nearly six."

"I need to feed the chickens," said Freddie. He still held the camera. In the viewfinder he watched as Eustace put down his cup and rested his head against the piled pillows, his uneven black hair spreading out like a bleed of ink. Butler, too, was on the brink of sleep.

"Do your duty, then, son," the soldier said. "But come back and get some rest."

Nobody spoke to Freddie on his way out of the Hydropathic. It was too early for guests to be up and about, but Annie and Maud were taking fresh towels to the treatment rooms and Katie Healey was out in the laundry yard smoking a cigarette. They saw him but had no words to offer. He possessed an aura now, the poison colours of one touched by tragedy.

The front lawn was a stark mess of churned earth. Some part of Freddie knew he shouldn't look. But he knew that if anyone should look it was him. If he didn't look now, it would be lost, and that meant that somehow Fa would be lost. In the numb pool of his brain, that obligation was his.

The tractor had been removed from the scene. Freddie felt the slow, uneven beat of his heart as he picked his way over the dark lawn towards the score in the earth where Fa had surely died.

He got down onto his haunches and touched the earth, feeling its cold, soft reality. There had been rain overnight and the soil was saturated. He let his hands sink. Buried up to the knuckle, he touched a hard mass. He pulled, but the object was stuck. He never knew Edenwell water rushed so close to the surface. Coursing, like blood beneath skin. Freddie found himself splashed.

He tugged at the thing inside the trench, wrenching with all his strength until it slid free, long and large and heavy as iron. He stumbled backwards with the thing weighing down on his chest. A set of antlers, spread magnificently wide, pinning him. The crown of the skull was still attached, drilled with two distinct eyeholes, blankly staring. Hanging from the cap of the skull, the dripping remnants of a leather hood.

It was hideous. Freddie struggled to shove the antlers away, but a sound coming in off the brecks caught his attention. He turned his head to try and catch the direction, but it eluded him. Not the distant rumbling guns at all, but a sound imbued with feeling, like a man's far-off yell. Over near the driveway, the gates were indistinct in the morning gloom. Freddie could easily imagine the old gatehouse standing firm, though he had never seen it himself. Lord Morton, mad with grief, had taken a hammer and obliterated his family crest there and everywhere else on the estate.

He understood it now. He never had before.

Freddie's eyes were weak, his eyelashes tacky. The tyre tracks travelled in the direction of the gates. A straight line punctuated by a sudden jolt to the right, sending the vehicle over the lip of the nearby trench. The driver had swerved – but why? He struggled to stand, slipping in the mud. That noise hummed on, a pressure in the chilly air, and as his breath came before him in clouds Freddie watched it shudder with the intensity of that wavering, unseemly drone.

He took up the antlers' iron weight. The holes aligned to his eyes, the stag's skullcap resting over his face as if the animal had grown it just for him.

The rooks cried out, and Freddie howled with them.

"Freddie! Freddie, it's all right. I'm here."

Eustace caught his flailing wrists. His eyes cracked open, gummy, sore. His shirt stuck to him with cooling sweat and his neck ached as if he had laid down a great load.

Eustace squatted beside his chair. "You've been sleeping all day. It's just me and you, Butler's gone for his dinner." Eustace was smiling, then appeared to realise he ought not to, given the context of their proximity. "Doctor Chalice came by. He said he's taking care of everything. You needn't worry."

"Worry?" Freddie whispered.

"Planning and… and such." He looked away, embarrassed. He meant the funeral. There was a funeral to think of, of course there was. "You just rest."

"Is it night?"

"It is."

He swore softly. The haze of the dream, uneasy as it was, faded into shadow. All but the clinging damp of his clothes.

Eustace reassured him: "You don't need to be anywhere. One of the men showed me how to feed the chickens. Old farm hand, lovely fellow. Anything else will wait."

"The driver saw something."

"Birds tell you that?"

No mockery. Eustace held his gaze like an equal.

"They're quiet." He tugged at his lip with damp fingers. "It's all quiet now."

Eustace felt as if he had aged ten years in the past day. So much to do, so much to shoulder. It threw the indolence of his former life into stark relief. Most importantly, there was so much to shield Freddie from. An inquest! Once upon a time, Eustace would have been thrilled by such a thing. Poor Mister Ferry, taken on a stretcher to his little cottage and laid out on his own rumpled bed. The coroner blandly reporting the cause of death as 'fairly clear for all to see, I'd say'. Eustace hadn't gone. Maud and Annie were twittering about it in the kitchen when he went down to fetch tea.

"Did they question the driver?" he asked, and they looked up, startled to find a guest in their domain.

"They tried, sir," Maud said. "The poor man's neither use nor ornament now – bumped his head good and proper."

"Was he drinking?"

"We all thought the same, sir, but he only turned out to be a Methodist, didn't he? Teetotal. 'No one to blame,' the coroner said. These things are sent to try us."

What a way of looking at it, Eustace thought. Freddie hardly deserved to be tried. The undertaker took the body away that afternoon, while Freddie slept. What had Chalice been thinking, showing off with that big tractor, handing it over to depleted men? And of course, the papers would print the details. That was another thing to shield Freddie from, Eustace reminded himself as he made his way back downstairs to the kitchens with the tray of empty cups.

"Young man. A word, if you have the time."

Eustace paused at the landing. An ageing couple hailed him. Despite it being past nine at night, the old woman was dressed for the sun terraces in a cream bonnet, and the man with her – a husband? A good deal younger, but grey about the temples – was resplendent in a blue-black suit with accents of silk. The woman's wheelchair jingled merrily, but as it drew closer Eustace frowned at the morbid trinkets making the sound. The rabbits' feet pitter-pattered uselessly, going nowhere.

"You wanted to speak to me?"

"Privately," said the man.

Eustace kept his feet planted where they were. There was something about the man's look he didn't take to. Sharp, like a fishhook. He was angling for something.

The old woman spoke up. "You're chummy with the son, Hiram tells me."

"We know him," added her impassive companion. "Miss Clarissa and I wish to offer our condolences."

Eustace was doubtful that Freddie knew such a pair. Never mind mentioning them, Freddie would without a doubt have drawn them if what they said was true. All those hanging treasures – antlers of coral, miniature horseshoes – swinging

301

together against the wicker chair. The effect was like one of his strange pictures.

"He isn't seeing anyone," Eustace said. "But I'll pass on your message."

"A tragedy," said the old woman, grasping the cross around her neck. "Unspeakable."

"Yes. But I daresay you don't need to speak to Freddie about it directly."

Hiram met his scepticism with grave eyes. "On the contrary, Mister Moncrieff, we must speak with him about a great many things."

Eustace let his polite façade drop. Rubberneckers, Harry called this sort. Always the first on the scene at an automobile accident or factory fire, gobbling the gruesome details like barley sugars. Perhaps Hiram and Clarissa were the religious type, hoping to bring Freddie into the fold in his time of terrible uncertainty. But, looking again at the wheelchair with its assembly of amulets, Eustace felt the pair were something altogether more difficult to define.

Clarissa, annoyed to find her fishing was yielding no results, jabbed a thin finger. "You can wipe that surly look off your face, young man. Hiram, tell him. Tell him this is no mere *hotel*."

The surly look, Eustace decided, would stay. But he would not. As he moved to step around them, he felt Hiram's large hand close around his bicep.

"Miss Clarissa takes great interest in all the comings-and-goings," Hiram said evenly. "She has a keen eye."

"Let go of me."

"You like to lie on the bandstand," Clarissa said airily. "It hasn't always been there, of course. I recall Mother had a divan brought out on that spot in the summer. Good light for reading. She had the time for it then."

Eustace could feel the final dregs of his patience turning to dust. "Right. Well. Things to do."

"You aren't coming to the concert?" Clarissa asked.

Eustace shrugged off Hiram's hand. "Concert?"

"That raucous theatre woman will be playing in the dining room. Doctor Chalice thought an evening of Chopin was what we all needed."

Eustace pictured everyone together in the mirrored lounge, gossiping, speculating. A hot stab of disgust went through his guts. The soldiers, at least, were only minimally interested. A dead body was no novelty to them. He tried to take comfort from that, the possibility that it wouldn't always feel this bad. After all, in his uniformed future there would be a next time, and a next…

Eustace straightened up, shoulders back, just as Mister Scole had taught him. He looked Hiram in the eye, then the old woman. "Freddie is my friend," he said. "Not yours. Nor anybody else's here, as far as I can tell. And I won't have him disturbed."

To his surprise, Clarissa nodded. "You care about him. It is important to care for one another. To watch over each other. And that, you see, is why we must speak with him. Now. Today."

"Enjoy your concert."

Eustace left them at the lift and headed down to the kitchen. A concert. And dinner as usual, he could smell it. What must Butler and the others think of them, these feckless civilians? And of course, he was one of them. All he could do was avoid blending into their decadent ranks as best he could. No tattling, no brooding, and certainly no public displays of anguish. Phoebe, of course, had never seen a dead man before, but she conducted herself sensibly amongst her new colleagues. The same couldn't be said of many of the girls. Despite his hard feelings, Eustace was proud of her, proud of their shared upbringing. All Father's drilling about duty had finally served a purpose.

As he suspected, the dining room was full. Lottie Mulgrave played a doleful tune with surprising tenderness and skill, not that her talkative audience appreciated it. Eustace hung around at the door. As usual, Missus Bailey held court.

"This is what happens, don't you know, when a military organisation collides with a leisure facility." She paused, allowing the assembled women to murmur their agreement. "I said it from the start. Disaster was simply inevitable."

It occurred to Eustace that nothing was stopping him from striding over, picking up Missus Bailey's butter knife, and plunging it into her eye. He saw himself do so, as if in some serene dream. His hand gripping her soft, unblemished chin. One decisive thrust.

It came and it went, the vision, leaving an odd satisfaction glowing heavily in his limbs. Nothing to stop him.

The air was cooler in the reception, but his face was uncomfortably hot. The lights were dimmed for bedtime. Doctor Chalice was a great believer in daylight rhythms and their effect on health. With no one around, he could stand in the tiled gloom waiting for that obscene urge to pass. He placed the tray of cups on the faux-marble front desk. Too easy to drop it, to spray the floor with shards of pottery, tempting palm-sized slivers...

He had to get back to Freddie. The stairs coiled above him, two storeys of gleaming tiles and the faint mineral smell that permeated every cranny of the Hydropathic. And at the very top, faint in the low light, was that tacky painted ceiling: phoney clouds with their empty promise of cooling rain. As he neared the first landing, he realised the breeze against his skin was not an imaginary one, and he followed it eagerly until he found the open window on the servants' floor. The blackout curtains waved lazily, defying their purpose, and Eustace strode across the dark landing to shut the sash. He paused, letting the cold air wash over him. For the first time that awful day, he allowed himself a minute of rest with his head against the frame, remembering that morning weeks ago when he crawled out onto the roof. Juvenile stupidity. Accidents happened, he knew that now. But the temptation niggled at him still, to swing his legs over the sill and get out into the frigid night.

Unsettling compulsion. Like the voice inside his head when a train passed through a station. Nothing to stop him from jumping. From offering himself.

A shadow and the thump of a boot. Eustace froze, feeling movement behind him where the stairs hugged the peeling wall. All the guests were at the concert, and the soldiers were shut up in the North Wing. A figure was moving slowly up the final steps to the landing where he stood. Eustace stepped back, slipping behind the blackout curtain, praying that the lift cage offered enough cover.

A man sneezed. In the darkness, Eustace saw thin wrists protruding from an ill-fitting suit as the man fumbled for a handkerchief. What was Butler doing in the servants' quarters?

He was about to announce himself as gracefully as he could when one of the bedroom doors opened.

"Someone there?" came a rough voice.

"Some say 'bless you'."

Eustace stayed quiet, peeping out from the curtain at the dim shape of Butler. Of Scole he saw nothing, but his voice was clipped with tension.

"Wrong floor, sir. You want the next one down."

"Do you not know me, Nick? I'm know I'm much changed. I said to myself, what are the chances? Nick Scole, as I live and breathe. And I do – just about."

A silence of several heartbeats. Eustace firmly regretted not making an exit when he had the opportunity, and as he tried to formulate a plan – the roof? God, no – he saw Nick Scole come slowly out onto the landing in his Edenwell whites like some broad, hesitant spectre.

"I've nothing to say to you."

The smile in Butler's voice showed no sign of flagging. "Nick, it's me. Christopher Butler. You owe me about a hundred cigs."

"I know who you are."

Scole regarded Butler, as if unsure whether to attack or retreat. Butler leaned on the lift cage, worn out from the exertion of the stairs.

"You look well. Better than me, at any rate." He looked down bashfully. "I… heard. I was already in France by then, so I had to assume…"

"Whatever you heard, it was wrong."

"Well," Butler said brightly, "I'm glad you're here to put me right."

"As I said, sir, you'll be wanting the floor below."

Butler held up his hands. "I understand. But if you ever change your mind—"

The thin man was backing away when Scole took a lurching step, jabbing at Butler's chest.

"You came here on purpose."

"If you think we're permitted to make decisions, Old Nick..."

"Don't *call* me that."

Again, the baleful silence. Eustace hoped that was an end to it, that whatever had been hanging in the air between the two men was spent with a few terse words. Freddie was alone down in his room. He needed to extract himself.

"Why don't we get a pint?" Butler suggested. "Not here, somewhere in town."

"The pubs close early now. It's not the same as before, nothing is."

"A drive, then. Is there a hospital van? Or we can jump on the back of a hay cart, if you give me a boost up." Butler chuckled weakly, hinting at past adventures. Scole met his smile with a glower.

"I'm not going nowhere with you."

Butler sighed. "Very well. I'll go. I just wanted to say I'm glad we're both still trundling along. You've a fine job here and a lovely girl—"

Even in the dark, Eustace saw how the mention of Tabitha twisted Scole's face. "I don't want to *trundle* with you," he hissed. "I don't want you talking to my girl. I don't want you following me around and I don't want to relive *nothing*. All right?"

The sharp arches of Butler's shoulders slumped. "You haven't changed, have you?" he said. "You know, when I spotted you,

I thought I'd have to work on you, show some patience, but you're the same old Nick Scole, the absolute martyr. No such thing as a scratch you couldn't turn into a gouge, was there?"

"You've always had a mouth on you."

"And you'd rather I didn't go flapping it. What's it been all this time, eh? Did you throw yourself on a grenade to save your captain? Did you take down a battalion all by yourself?" Butler's eyes opened wide as an idea came to him. "Perhaps a bear!"

The punch lifted Butler off his feet. Scole swung around, following the arc of his fist, the weight of his false leg sending him off balance. Then the both of them were on the floor, grunting and swearing. Butler was laughing, though his bony body was by far the worse off.

"You bastard," he wheezed. "Overreacting swine."

Scole was struggling to stand, hauling himself up by the lift door. It swung, opening wide, and Butler cackled as Scole was almost sent over backwards.

"Look what you've done to us. Nick, you silly ass, it was in all the papers. I don't know what you're thinking, but people were sympathetic. Something like that is a tragedy of war whether it happens at the Front or... what was it, Folkestone? You were shipping out, weren't you? Bloody hell, you've done my shoulder a buggery..."

Scole, panting, watched Butler struggling to right himself, but offered no hand.

"I don't give a damn," Butler insisted. "I don't know why you think I do. I practically shat out my own kidneys, how's that for a war wound?"

"It weren't my fault."

"Of course it wasn't. Let me up. If there's no pub, there has to be a bottle of something on the premises. Let's get tight and forget all about it."

The gate squealed as Scole swung on it. Down in the dining room, Eustace heard applause; the first bars of a song.

"Some stupid bugger lit a fag." Scole's face was drained of all expression. He appeared exhausted, like a man pausing to rest, knowing he still had miles to go. "Warning signs all over the hangar, engine oil all over the place, but he still says to himself 'I need this'. I never even saw France. He took that from me. Worse than the bloody leg."

Butler's nose was running, but not bleeding. The shock of the blow was wearing off, giving way to pain.

"Take me back to bed, Nick. I'm shattered. We'll talk tomorrow."

"We will not."

"So you lost a leg! You lived. Patterson didn't. Little Rowley. That long McShane fellow with the teeth, he's missing. All those other lads you owe cigarettes. If you want to play the hero, you go ahead. You surely aren't the first. I won't *say* anything, if that's what you're afraid of."

It was the closest Butler came to sneering. Eustace held his breath for Scole's retort. Downstairs the diners were joining in a chorus, one of Matron Calder's hymns. The sweet sound of untrained voices. On the carpet, Butler hissed and touched the reddening place where Scole had hit him. He was incapable of standing under his own steam, Eustace realised. He wanted to break cover and offer assistance, but how could he now? Scole's pitted face was creased with emotion. He'd seen a look like it many times, back at school. Boys fresh from a beating, hiding their shame. Boys with bright eyes, eager to join in a fight, to be the victor for once, no matter how unfairly. Seeing that look on a grown man filled him with alarm. It was a relief to see Scole offer Butler a hand, for the thin man to take it gratefully, groaning as he was hauled to his feet, the lift gate swinging behind him. Butler's sheepish grin, an acknowledgement of the absurdity of it all.

When Scole pushed, Eustace thought it was in jest. A boxer's feint. A matey shove, not even a hard one.

But Butler was gone.

His footsteps slapped down the empty hall. Sound carried at night, all the worse when the sky was clear and cold. Eustace had slipped from his bed, resisting the urge to breathe in case Prefect Hartnoll and his cohorts stirred. The older boy snored as Eustace tiptoed past.

The school chapel was meant to be locked at night, but the custodian had been known to ask if anyone had seen the spectacles sitting plainly on his face, and sure enough the arched door opened without incident when Eustace tried it. The windows were high and wide, and a thin sheen of moonlight allowed him to see his way into the arched space, somehow even colder than the rest of the building. He knew that climate well; Sunday mornings spent studying his own blueish fingernails, wondering just how hard David hurled that rock to split Goliath's skull.

There was no sign of company. Eustace let the door shut with an ancient clunk, careful not to spill the cargo he clutched to his chest.

Pennants hung from the walls, the colours of regiments and battalions muted by decades of dust. Even in the barely perceptible draught of his entrance, they swayed as if beckoning him. Old boys

310

had fought at Waterloo and the siege of Sevastopol; they would have been at Agincourt had the school existed then. A school for the victors, they were so often told; a place where heirs to the Empire were forged into its masters.

Lawrence Parrish wouldn't be forged into anything now.

The pitcher was heavy in his arms. He had filled it higher than he needed to and was beginning to regret the decision. The weight of it made his mission all too real, and to think on the particulars made his cheeks burn.

He would be quick.

Parrish's funeral was held at home, a private affair. Where "home" was, Eustace did not know and hadn't felt like making himself conspicuous by asking. The boys attended a service in Parrish's memory the first Sunday after his death. Such things happened, said the Headmaster. One summer, not so long ago, ten boys were carried off by typhus in as many days. Such is the way in a community of living, breathing young men, he said. Tragedy, sooner or later, will take a seat at the table.

And all the while, Eustace sat studying his blueish fingernails, in sure and certain terror that every eye was on him.

He headed down the aisle, feeling the stale air against his prickling neck like an unwanted touch. In an alcove to one side of the chapel, partially hidden by a spray of lilies dropping their curling petals, was a wrought iron rack with sconces for candles and a locked box for offerings of coin.

He set down the pitcher, feeling a splash as it wobbled unsteadily on the dimpled flagstones. He had no coins, but he could make it up later. One debt at a time.

His hands almost shook as he struck a match. The small flame caught the wick with a thin stream of tallow smoke, the smell of

311

nights in the nursery telling bogie tales with Phoebe, frightening each other in whispers. He set the candle down in its iron cavity, the small light taking away his invisibility, again making this whole charade all too real. Aware that the light could be noticed from outside, even at this dead hour, he made haste.

He cleared his dry throat. It made an unseemly sound, like a shout in the cold chapel, and he glanced over his shoulder reflexively. He half expected to hear that wretched litany of his dreams, the thank-you-thank-you-thank-you, *mocking and lordly, impossible to shake.*

A glass of water wouldn't have saved Parrish, he reminded himself. It wasn't as if Eustace had murdered him. It wasn't as if he had picked him out, marked him up, given him up to—

Who?

He hadn't slept a full night in months.

Mother would call this indecent. Pagan. Something a Roman might do to atone for all his wickedness. Eustace swallowed that thought and picked up the heavy pitcher, sloshing in his grip.

With a dry mouth, he spoke:

"You needed water. I've brought you some."

A thin, keening noise brought Eustace to his senses. By the time he realised it was coming from himself, so had Scole. The orderly made a drunkard's stumble towards the window, and, seeing Eustace cowering there, gave a despairing sound of his own.

Butler had gone down the lift shaft.

When Scole hoisted him by his collar, Eustace thought he was about to die too.

"You helped," Scole hissed, hot against his face.

"He's—"

"How long have you been there?"

"He's—"

Scole backhanded him across the face so hard the landing turned white. When his face swam back into view, it was almost touching Eustace's.

"Word gets out your mother sent you here to save your neck, she's through. You'll have to move. Change your name. They'll use her books for kindling."

"He's hurt."

"He's dead. And you're in on it. Do you hear me?"

"I didn't—"

"Stop your whining. Do you want to hang? You sat there on your arse and did nothing. What's your pretty sister going to say about that? What's Ferry going to say, eh? Not just a lily boy but a coward too."

Eustace blinked hard, his ears ringing.

"You heard," Scole hissed. "And if you don't do exactly what I say now, everyone's going to know. When I'm done singing, the whole country'll know your names. Won't be spending many cosy evenings together then, will you?"

Eustace had never been so cold in his life. "I'll do whatever you want," he whispered.

"So you do have stones."

Eustace dared a glance at the lift door. He had a queer feeling that Butler might climb out, limbs bent at violent angles. Scole smacked his arm.

"Pull yourself together. You'll see worse when you're sniping."

But how would Scole know? He'd never been to the Front. He'd probably never been out of the country. But duty was true, as unchanging as stone, and as if it were his father in front of him now, Eustace stood at his full height and nodded with as much firmness as he could muster.

"Good," said Scole. He pushed the lift's call button with a trembling hand. "We'll fix this. There's a well down in the woods."

"I know," Eustace said miserably.

"You're going to help me get him down there."

Eustace stared, aghast. Freddie's secret place, so horribly contaminated. Butler, poor Butler. He was going to take Freddie's picture...

"We need stones. Weight. They float, bodies."

"There's an iron in the kitchen," he mumbled.

"No. Nothing to link staff to him. That's what they look for."

They. Detectives. Newspaper men. Butler's body slowly ticked into view. Eustace devoted himself to studying the carpet.

"Steady," Scole told him, stopping the lift so Butler's body was level with the floor. He took his splayed ankles and dragged. "You're no good to me here, Moncrieff. Get me a wheelchair. I want a clear path through the back way. You come across anyone and you tell 'em someone's done a shit in the Turkish baths."

Eustace did his best not to run. Nonetheless, sweat soaked through his shirt. Nothing on God's green earth would get him into that lift ever again. In the time it took to descend the stairs, Butler's fall had become like an over-dramatic dream, something he would wake from in the school dormitories with a shout and a sheepish laugh. But of course, he reminded himself, some boys in those dorms didn't wake up at all.

The entrance hall was clear. The drinking fountain tinkled prettily and the sounds of evening drinks in the dining room wafted up in honeyed draughts. Two VADs struggled with a laundry trolley by the front desk. The girls were exhausted, coming to the end of their shifts. The taller one kicked back her heel and pulled it up behind her, groaning at the ache.

Eustace wondered what to do. Scole's line about the Turkish baths rang loud as the lie it was.

He could cut himself. It came to him in a flash: cut his arm, drip on the floor. *Ladies, I'm sorry to interrupt, but one of your patients has had a nosebleed. He was so embarrassed, he took himself off, but if you could just fetch me a towel…*

Blood on the floor. Christ, what was he thinking? The VAD called the lift and went to rest against the marble desk, rubbing at her sore calves. When Matron Calder came bustling down the corridor, both girls sprang up guiltily.

"Perry, have you taken tonight's inventory?" said Matron. "And McDowell, what's all this huffing? Your shift isn't over."

"I was just heading upstairs, Matron," said the nurse.

"A nice, slow meander, was it? McDowell, when you volunteered, it was amply explained to you that this was work, and hard work, and no special dispensations would be made for any girls unused to such a thing."

Eustace was poised at the foot of the stairs, panic building in his chest. When Matron Calder marched Perry and McDowell towards him, he was certain they would see the guilt in his face. He stuttered, looked around him for some prop, anything to stop the women supernaturally divining the events of the past five minutes.

"Good heavens."

Perry froze. McDowell put her hand to her mouth and stepped back. They were looking over Eustace's head, to the half-moon window above the grand front door. Matron Calder seemed on the verge of explosion.

"Young man," she said, her bespectacled gaze trained on the window. "Is this your idea of a joke?"

Eustace only half heard the accusation. His eyes were on the tableau played out against the blackout curtain. Someone had strung up a hare, quite lifeless, one long paw outstretched with the graceful deference of a courtier mid-bow. Eustace immediately thought of Mister Jenks and his marionettes. But Jenks had been a gentle soul. Everyone said it. This, by comparison, was perverse.

Perry stepped up to examine the creature. She was made of sterner stuff than her friend, peering into the hare's citrine eyes with fascination. "Why would someone do this?"

Matron Calder fixed Eustace with a look. "This may not be a hospital in the traditional sense, but there are vulnerable patients here, and if, as I suspect, you are amusing yourself—"

"I am as mystified as you," Eustace said, mouth dry. His dazed stare convinced the matron, though it did little to reassure her. She turned to her nurses, clapped her chapped hands together.

"McDowell, I want this curtain replaced and this floor clean. Hot water, disinfectant. I'll dispose of the hare, as you're such a delicate flower. I'll need a ladder. Perry, why are you still here? Inventory, girl. Good God, do you want instructions in writing?"

As soon as the three women had clattered away, Eustace heaved the contents of his stomach into a potted fern. With no time to find a wheelchair, he settled instead for the abandoned laundry trolley. The lift had come all the way down, so he shoved the trolley inside and closed the gate behind him, doing everything in his power not to look up at the lift's ceiling and think about the frail figure that had recently sprawled above it. Mercifully, it was all but impossible to think at all.

When the lift reached the servants' floor, Scole was pacing, red in the face. "Good lad. Good thinking. With me, now."

The orderly shoved Eustace and the cart towards his bedroom where he proceeded to drag Butler's body out from under the bed where it had been stashed, rolled up in blankets. As they bundled the body into the trolley and covered it with Scole's bedsheets, Eustace marvelled at the older man's composure. Eustace had overheard the soldiers telling stories of the Front. Sometimes there was so little time to bury the dead, they covered the faces with dirt and left them where they fell.

He swallowed a sour mouthful of bile.

"From now on," said Scole, "whatever I do, you do."

And like a broken-down mutt, he found himself following.

The blackout curtains were pulled, Eustace told himself as the lift ticked down to the ground floor; all he had to do was escort Scole outside and they would be as good as invisible. Matron Calder and Nurse McDowell were occupied with the hare hanging in the window. Eustace had to glance back to be sure he truly had seen it. The creature's yellow eyes stared down, sharp with accusation, as Calder struggled with the strings lashed to its limbs.

Scole backed out of the lift, the trolley between them heavier now, though not by much. The women were too busy to pay them any mind.

"We can't take this outside," Scole muttered as Eustace held the utility tunnel door open for him. "It'll leave tracks."

"What about the traps in the woods?"

Scole looked at him sharply. "You know where they are?"

"I… I think so."

"Then we'll manage."

Annie was in the laundry room. She looked up when they entered, surprised to see Eustace. Her pale face was bruised, he noticed. When she saw the trolley, her shoulders slumped.

"Not more washing?"

"One of the old boys had a few too many brandies," Scole said, avuncular as ever. "I'll deal with it, duck. Don't you worry."

"One more won't make a difference. Give it here."

She held out her hand. Eustace's heart hammered in his throat. He looked from Scole to the girl. If Annie were to glimpse the contents of the trolley, there was no telling what Scole might do.

The orderly glanced back at Eustace. As he swept his hair from his eyes, his smile was sly. "Would you give us a moment, sir?"

Eustace did as he was told, moving with a steadiness that amazed and frightened him in equal measure, back into the tunnel to wait behind the door. The urge to pull his hair passed through him like physical pain. A dark strand between his fingers, that bee-sting satisfaction. Soon he held out his palm, scattered with hairs, each one a fragment of himself to dispose of, to destroy.

In the laundry room, he heard Scole's low voice:

"It's hard finding privacy, ain't it?"

"Can be trying, for sure."

"I've been trying to get you alone for weeks."

318

"Me?"

"It's like that, is it?" Scole chuckled. A human enough sound. "She don't need to know. I'm through with her anyway."

"Nick—"

"Had my eye on someone special, see..."

Annie's voice was rising in shrillness. "Give me those sheets, silly."

"I'll give you the sheets when you give me a kiss."

Boot leather on tiles. He was chasing her. Eustace nearly fell forward as the door was yanked open from the other side. Annie went tearing past him without looking back.

Moments later, Scole came sauntering out. "Won't tell a soul. She's terrified of Tabby. Come on."

The laundry trolley juddered over the flagstones. Scole unlocked the back door. In the thin moonlight, Eustace recognised the old stables where Freddie's father kept their van. They would have to carry Butler over the gravel path, across the lawn and down the incline into Choke Wood. With his eyes adjusting to the darkness, the weight of what they were doing pressed down on Eustace, along with more practical considerations.

"We should have brought a gun."

"Don't be daft."

Eustace felt his breath hitch. "No, if we're going into Choke Wood, we *need* a gun."

"For a cat? A fox?" Scole busied himself pulling the piled sheets off Butler's swaddled body, dumping them on the floor. "You really are a coward, aren't you?"

"It isn't an animal."

Scole looked up sharply. "A man?"

No. But what other word was there? "He's the one killing the animals. We've seen him."

"You and Ferry?"

"We should have said something, but you don't believe us – why would anyone else? *I* wouldn't—"

"No," Scole cut him off. His tongue slid across his lower lip, his thoughts racing. "No, this is good. And you think he's living down there, in the wood?"

"We've never seen him at rest." Eustace swallowed hard. Scole wasn't taking this as seriously as he should. If he could only get Freddie, make him show Scole that cadaverous drawing… but no. A hideous thought. He couldn't be dragged into this nightmare. "He's terribly strong," he added, sounding to himself like a schoolboy telling a tall tale.

Scole nodded slowly, turning something over in his brain. "He probably did for old Jenks too."

"Too?"

Scole slapped Eustace's arm. Full of renewed energy, he scooped up Butler's body in his arms and kicked away the trolley. "We drop this one off in the well as planned. We wait. There'll be a search. They won't find nothing. But we will."

Eustace's stomach cramped. He kept his eyes on the floor, afraid to catch even a glimpse of that blue uniform through the blankets. "You don't understand. He's not that sort of man."

"Doesn't matter," Scole said, his face unreadable in the dark. "Now take his legs. Let's find out what sort of a man you are."

320

SIXTEEN

Things Shown Me In The Pit. II.
Ink on black-edged cardstock. May 1917.

James Ferry's funeral order of service. A modest coffin sinks into a weed-choked lake. A wish, perhaps, for the restorative powers of Edenwell water, or a washing-away of grief. The accompanying fragments of dialogue offer little in the way of explanation:

> *He was so awfully pleased*
> *Happy as pig in muck awfully*
> *A pig accepts all offerings gladly*
> *Wouldn't let him hear that*
> *Need a gun need a gun hahahaha*
> *Not if he's so awfully terribly pleased*

THE BUNCHES OF lavender in reception had dried to little more than paper, and in the watery light of dawn they looked to Eustace somehow synthetic. Annie and Maud

321

had found black crepe in the back of the linen closet and were draping the mirrors. The old ways were fitting for Edenwell, far past its prime. Freddie watched them from the first-floor landing. He was dressed for the funeral and cradled a glass of water in both hands.

"It's strange," Annie reflected. "I keep thinking I'll see Mister Ferry out on the drive. I'm so used to him plodding along with his rifle."

"It's a terrible thing," Maud agreed. "Poor Freddie. Shame he isn't more outgoing. If he just tidied himself up a bit..."

Annie snorted. "Then what?"

"I don't know. Someone's got to want a nice quiet husband, haven't they?"

While Annie removed the faded flowers, Maud buffed the sideboards. Annie complained of hunger. Her hands hurt, she said. Her nails kept tearing, the skin peeling away from the sides like loose threads.

"My brother used to call me Atora," she said, "like the suet. I could probably run him through with my elbow now, look at it."

"You've worried yourself thin," Maud said. "Look at Missus Hardy, she's built like a sow. She don't sit around fretting. It's been a bad winter, that's all."

That was a lie; Eustace knew it and so did the girls. Annie swept fallen lavender petals into her palm. "There's Germans all over the sea from here to America," she said. "All our food, at the bottom of the ocean. There's not enough growing, we need help from... Australia or summat. I heard the soldiers."

"I daresay they're right," said Maud flatly.

"He wants us on our knees." Her voice wavered, as if reciting some wicked prayer. "The Kaiser, he wants us to beg."

Maud, who was on her knees, summoned her last grain of patience. "He wants you to get yourself in a tizzy."

Annie took a cloth and worked on scooping up the scraps of lavender from the floor. As she planted her palm on the sideboard to help herself stand, she tugged the black crepe draping one of the mirrors, sending it sliding to the floor.

Maud turned at Annie's half-shriek. Seeing the leggy reflection of Eustace Moncrieff, she stifled a grimace. "Oh, sir. What are you doing there in the dark?"

He drifted down the last few stairs. In his funeral black, he knew what a ghastly picture he made. "She's right," he said quietly.

"I am?" said Annie, eyes wide in her bruised face.

"My brother's been out there. We're surrounded."

Harry's fevered rantings served up with lashings of spite. Annie bit her ragged thumbnail. She looked into his dusky face, saw the stark look there and was convinced.

Eustace took a long draught from his glass. "He isn't allowed to talk about it, of course."

They couldn't contradict or question him. It wasn't in their power. Maud doggedly continued sweeping, glancing at Annie in the hope she would do the same, but the younger girl had frozen, awaiting Eustace's next revelation.

"It won't do to worry," he said, and to Annie it sounded almost kind. "You must have noticed we're next door to an airfield. All the big guns are guarding the ports, so if I were the Kaiser, I'd blanket this place in bombs. Just sink us like a tanker full of bread." He wiped his nose. "A damn sight faster than starving."

Annie felt her lip wobble. She stared up into his face with weak defiance. "You're having a laugh at me."

"Can't think of many reasons to laugh, miss."

They buried Fa on a steely afternoon with a wind that nipped at every bit of Freddie's exposed skin. *Bit parky*, he could hear Fa say. *Wind gets up yer*. He heard it in Chalice's car all the way to Saint Peter's, through the desolate breckland and the thatched streets of Thetford. He ought to have brought a scarf.

Doctor Chalice wore a good suit with his fair hair neatly parted. Eustace sat behind him, his long legs cramped like an insect's. He, too, looked fine in his dark wool.

"I'll sit with you, if you want," he'd said as they walked to the car. "In church."

It was then that Freddie realised he was the only family member present. The front pew was his alone.

"If you would."

"That be reet," Eustace ventured a joyless smile. "I'm picking up your language. Going native."

He helped Freddie neaten his tie. Pallor showed as a grey wash under the rich tone of the younger boy's skin, and if Freddie were capable of feeling anything, it would be concern. He was glad he had the shadow of that feeling to distract him as they drew into Thetford, with its motorcars and horses and muttering women like flies buzzing around his head. He shoved his hands in his pockets and fiddled with the pencil stubs inside.

The church was even colder than the street. It had been many months since Freddie last attended a service, but the faded flags hanging from the rafters and the marble monuments lining the walls remained unchanged, as if preserved by the pervasive chill. The staff of Edenwell filled the pews, along with men from town whom Freddie recognised as tradesmen Fa sometimes dealt with. He so frequently made his excuses when it was time to go to town, they probably didn't remember him.

Doctor Chalice had paid for a good coffin and flowers, but the vicar spoke a language Freddie could only half follow. The hymns, too, were distant, as if broadcast on the wind from some far-off isle. Nothing was real but the press of Eustace's long thigh against his. When they left the graveside, he heard Missus Hardy remark that she had always loved 'Jesu, Joy of Man's Desiring'. He wondered numbly if the cook had been to another service before Fa's.

As the mourners dispersed, Chalice walked with Freddie. "A few of the gentlemen here would like to take you down to the Red Lion. Your father's friends."

He blinked slowly. "Will you be there?"

"I will. And we can leave whenever you please."

"Will Eustace be there?"

Chalice glanced at the lychgate. Scole had come, bundled into a suit that strained across his expansive chest. The orderly stood in conversation with Eustace, who picked at the soft wood of the arch, avoiding his eyes.

Chalice said, "We'll invite Mister Moncrieff. He's been good to you today."

"He seems…"

Just then the rag-and-bone man rattled by with his pony and trap, calling out in his sing-song voice: "Any rags, any bones, any raaaags?" The trap hit a bump in the road and the sacks of bones in the back gave a hilarity of clattering. Freddie flinched.

Chalice said quietly, "We don't have to go."

Bones angry to no longer be clothed.

There was no use explaining.

The Red Lion had always been the hearth of the town, welcoming locals and travellers long into the night with a friendly fog of pipe smoke and ale. Fa had learned to play backgammon in the pub when he was small. As a man he played darts – poorly – and discussed shotguns and horseshoes while the small Freddie sat with his back to the wall, surreptitiously sketching the patrons with their knotty knuckles and weather-beaten cheeks.

As he shuffled in behind Chalice, Freddie vaguely recognised two old men hailing them from a table by the fire. Farm boys from Fa's days working the fields. Mister Larwood with his sun-browned hide, and Mister... Miles? A bent-over fellow with long whiskers the colour of wet straw. Freddie felt the dim stirring of a memory of the old man conjuring a penny from his ear, of shrinking back from the sensation of coarse fingers.

There was Chalice leading the way, Eustace quietly at his side, and, uncomfortably, Scole, who wished to pay his respects to his old colleague. Freddie couldn't think why. He could barely bring to mind more than a handful of dry pleasantries between the orderly and his father.

"Same again, gentlemen?" asked Chalice. Freddie hoped he wasn't expected to buy everyone drinks. All there was in his pockets was pencils and string.

Say hello, then. That's what Fa would tell him. Freddie ventured a nod, and to his relief the men responded in kind.

As Chalice went to the bar, Scole manoeuvred himself between Freddie and Eustace. The orderly eased himself down onto a stool as the old men regarded them over their empty pints. Mister Larwood glanced at Mister Miles, who found something amusing.

"Someone watching your horses?" Miles asked, his lips tight in his tanned face. He was looking at Eustace. They both were. Eustace stared back with cool indifference.

"He means you a gypsy, bor?" Larwood said evenly.

From the bar, Doctor Chalice admonished them gently. "Come now, Mister Miles…"

"Lad's got the look, you can't deny it. I don't mean no harm by it."

Freddie glanced nervously at Eustace, but he was laconic about the insult, picking at an old penknife carving in the table.

"A lot of people say that," he said quietly. "The gypsy thing."

Tiredness added years to his voice. Freddie wished Scole hadn't barged between them like that. His heart might stop its clamouring if only he could feel Eustace's proximity.

"Horse thieves," said Miles. "Reckon they had a hand in the old Jenks business, too."

Scole nodded. "Thought the same myself. A gypsy'd kill you for the boots on your feet."

Smirking, Mister Larwood indicated Eustace's feet. "Check 'is boots."

Scole's laugh was a touch too loud. He gave Eustace an affectionate slap on the back. "No, if this one had his way, he'd be killing for the king, isn't that right, Mister Moncrieff?"

"Soon," Eustace mumbled.

Chalice was back with the drinks.

"Much obliged, Doctor," said Larwood. "Cheers to old Ferry, God rest his soul. And to you, son."

The barmaid, whose name Freddie did not know, came around with a small funeral cake cut into dry slices. He had no idea his father was so well liked by so many.

"You mind you keep a piece for the bees," she said, her hand resting on Freddie's shoulder for just a moment. He fought the urge to brush it off.

"What did she say?" Eustace asked, when the girl was gone.

Mister Miles licked the beery foam from his moustache. "Did you not tell the bees, bor?"

Freddie shrugged. "The bees were always Mister Tungate's responsibility."

"He'll be dead in France now, and I'll bet you ain't told his bees that neither. Terrible bad luck not to invite the bees to the funeral. And if there in't no funeral, they still like to know. Stick a bit of crepe up over the hive."

"Your grandmother was a great one for that, Fred," Larwood said. "All the old ways."

"Fa said she did the table turning."

"Ah, a game. But she was a good woman, a laugh. Us littl'uns would tell her we were going to dip her in the witch pool, and she'd pull faces. There's one up at Waveney, Harlestone way. Proper witch pool, not like yours up the Hydropathic."

"The cold water cure, they called it," Miles added, and they huffed at the irony.

Chalice listened with grave interest. "If the lady lives, she is condemned to death. But if she drowns she is innocent. Our spring was never a torture implement, though. Ours is well documented, a holy place. The monks—"

"The monks only writ what they liked about the place is how I see it," Larwood said. "And look how it turned out for them." With a jerk of his bristled chin, he mimed the tightening of a noose.

Freddie looked at Eustace, jammed in tight with Scole. His dark eyes were clouded with boredom or exhaustion. Either way, he evidently wished to leave.

"It amazes me, the history surrounding us," said Chalice. "We're not far from Grimes Graves. An ancient mining operation! But what I don't understand is how men so primitive went so deep. There's plenty of flint close to the surface. What were folks looking for down there all those millennia ago?"

"They weren't looking for nothing," said Miles. He took a long drag from his pint and smacked his thin lips. "They were putting summat down there."

Chalice was charmed. "A woolly mammoth, perhaps! Prehistoric hunters luring their prey over cliffs. I've read there's evidence for such practices."

Freddie was trying to catch Eustace's gaze, seeking out reassurance, but Scole was determined to remain in the way.

Just then, Mister Miles's rheumy eyes travelled over to the window. "Eh, look out."

They all looked up. Peering in at the dimpled glass were a familiar pair of faces. One, a good deal lower than the other, framed by a wide white bonnet.

Larwood frowned. "She one of yours, Doctor?"

"That she is," said Chalice, and waved as the couple continued to stare. "I didn't think she was at the funeral, though. I'll ask if she needs assistance."

Chalice went outside to check which direction they had gone in. Scole chuckled darkly and finished his drink.

"We have been known to attract the occasional eccentric up at the Hydropathic," he said.

"You want to mind yourself, bor," said Miles. "That's Clarissa Morton."

"You're having a laugh," said Scole. "Morton? They're all dead."

Larwood shook his head. "Not that one. She and her *companion*" – he sneered the word – "have been skulking about, asking all sorts of questions. Putting people's noses out of joint. I reckon she's after buying the place up."

"Good luck to her," Scole said. "How much of the Morton money is left, anyway?"

Miles tugged absently at his whiskers. "There's no telling. When Lord Morton went mad, his wife legged it. Took the daughters. But it's her ancestral home. Why else would she be sticking her oar in?"

Eustace drained his pint rather too quickly. His eyes shone, but his expression, at least, was more animated. "My sister told me the son died young."

Miles shrugged. "They never did find out who did for him."

"Gypsies," muttered Larwood.

Freddie tugged at his lip. The Morton tragedy had always been little more than a bogie tale, the finer points altering with each telling. Having left Edenwell to make his name, young Morton was cut down in an alley or some desolate highway, Freddie couldn't recall which. Now he found he hadn't the stomach for it. "She wanted to speak to me. The old woman."

"And me," Eustace said. Their eyes met, both sensing

something just beyond their understanding. To Freddie's astonishment, Scole gave Eustace a nudge, and not a gentle one.

"Well don't."

The bees were not visibly offended when Freddie and Eustace approached the hives offering funeral cake and belated news.

Eustace dug the shining toe of his boot into the cabbage patch. He didn't recognise half the vegetables growing in the walled garden. A few limp leeks spilled over onto the brick path, punctured and silver-slicked by slugs.

"Do you think Mister Tungate really is dead?" Freddie asked.

"It's a safe bet, I'd say."

"Let's not tell them. It might make it true."

Eustace smiled wanly. Yes, he liked that.

It was a cold afternoon; only a few bees hummed lazily, turning their satellite circuits around the row of hives. Freddie took the key to his cottage from his waistcoat and held it up for Eustace to see.

"Telling the bees. You take the housekey and knock on the hive three times, like this. Then I s'pose..." He rested the heel of his hand on the droning wood. "Bees. Fa's dead. Fa's dead, bees."

And because nothing happened the first time, Freddie was compelled to lean in and whisper it like a secret, feeling the warmth of the hidden swarm against his cold face.

The statement felt no more true than it had that morning. He left the sliver of cake on the roof and backed away while a few dusty drones ventured out to inspect the offering.

Freddie turned on his heel, eager to take off his uncomfortable shoes. Eustace didn't follow. Freddie looked over his shoulder and was surprised to see him bending over the hive. Freddie could see his lips moving, and when Eustace righted himself he seemed unsteady on his feet, keen to get away.

Freddie looked to the woods. "I must check the traps."

"Not yet," Eustace said. "Come with me. I'm due a treatment in the steam room."

But there was the cabbage patch to check for bugs, the leaves in the fountain and the gravel to sweep. The tasks crowded around him as he numbered them, all Fa's daily drudgeries, the work he mulled over in silence while he slopped soup from the cracked bowl he always preferred, or tamped down tobacco in his old cherry wood pipe with his little finger, the one with the nail forever stained yellow, or, or, or...

It would be like this for ever, he realised. These sharp little rememberings, these tasks never completed. Overgrown lawns, rats in the cellars, hungry chickens, rotting decks, peeling paint. In the pines, the newly hatched rook chicks were honking for food.

He wouldn't have to worry about the lawn. Somehow, in the days following the accident, a farm had erupted, fully formed. Regimental furrows and irrigation trenches rippled all the way from the walled garden to the folly. A new scarecrow stood in their midst, wearing someone's old pyjamas. Something hung from its cruciform arms, a pendulum in the breeze. A hare, glittering with flies. They stood there, watching the bloated body sway.

"Did they shoot it?" Freddie asked.

"I found it, like the others. It was inside. I think... I know it will sound stupid..."

"He's taunting us."

There was no use denying it. Since that terrible night, Eustace had harboured a queasy expectant feeling, like sensing the arrival of a caller who preferred to show up unannounced.

Freddie approached the hare and flicked open his pocket knife. The rooks would use the meat, at least, if he made the first cut the way they liked. He gripped the velvet ears, pulling the body taut to better slice the swollen undercarriage. Fur and skin parted under his blade, the shining giblets slid free and hit the tilled earth with a *thud* that surprised him.

Eustace bent to look, even as he covered his nose against the iron stink. "Jesus, that can't be—"

Freddie nudged the hare's viscera with his toe. Eustace was right, it couldn't be, yet the hard, tumescent organs made a sound he'd known since he was a boy, digging forts for tin soldiers down in Choke Wood. Freddie squatted, slit the hare's stomach and a green section of intestine.

Shining shards of flint. Packed in tight like grave dirt.

Eustace turned on his heel. "Oh, God. He is. He's taunting us." He coughed as the stench reached him. "Come away. Don't touch it, please."

Freddie stood, wiping his hands on his thighs. Distantly, he noticed them trembling. "You can't go leaving," he said.

"I have to."

Freddie said nothing, thought nothing.

"But then we'll go west," said Eustace. "Far west, where they've never even heard of the war. We'll live in a tent by a river and we'll mine gold, and when we have enough gold we'll make a pyramid of it."

Freddie's mouth tweaked. He might once have believed it.

"And we'll hide in it, deep down, away from—" He glanced

333

back at the spilled contents of the hare, wicked-sharp. "All this. You can draw, and I can shoot rabbits…"

Eustace was smaller, Freddie realised. Folded in on himself.

"Something's happened. Talk to me."

"I can't."

"Then help me find the man who drove the tractor."

As Phoebe Moncrieff hurried down the corridor, she looked like a girl late for school. A hikey sprite in crisp nursing whites.

To Freddie's amazement, she reached up and embraced him. "You're Mister Ferry. My brother speaks highly of you. You know, in his way." She mimicked Eustace's surly face with surprising accuracy, considering their vast physical differences. The sympathy in her eyes was genuine. "I really am terribly sorry for your loss."

The Hydropathic was appropriately quiet following the funeral. Having been served their dinner and encouraged to rest, most of the men had gone downstairs to the gentlemen's pool to soak their aching muscles and gossip somewhere the nurses wouldn't follow them. The civilian guests had almost all retired to their rooms, their evening plans spoiled by the sombre mood. Earlier, Doctor Chalice extended an invitation to Freddie to dine with him in his rooms, but he declined. The grinding burn of hunger was somehow preferable.

"The man who was driving," Eustace asked her. "Do you know him?"

Phoebe inclined her head dubiously. "Private Price has been taken to a private room. He's in a bad way. My god, Eustace, you look dreadful yourself."

"Haven't slept," he muttered. He was swaying a little, as though he might faint. "Freddie was hoping to see him, to say a kind word. We heard how distressed he is. It might help."

"I absolutely understand, but Private Price won't be answering any of your questions." She drew a finger across her lips. "It can happen that way – shock."

Freddie sank under a wave of disappointment. Price might not even remember the accident. "Has he said anything? Anything at all?"

"I'm sorry, I've not been with him. You can ask some of the other VADs, but we're somewhat distracted this afternoon." She looked over her shoulder, checking none of her colleagues were around to eavesdrop. "Someone's done a runner."

Freddie glanced at Eustace. "Who?"

"One of the soldiers. We're supposed to take a register each morning, but the girl in charge has a disgusting head cold and forgot. She fudged it. He's been gone four *days*. I can't think what he'd be running away *to*."

Eustace fidgeted. "We should do this another time."

"If you want to see Private Price, now's your opportunity. Matron's busy organising the search. Much longer and they have to inform the army. You know they shoot men who run away?"

"You know gossip aids the enemy?" Eustace retorted.

Phoebe's eyes were wide, only serving to magnify her youthful look. "No, they have military police. I'm learning all the time. I think the poor man was just startled by… everything that's happened. Some of them are quite delicate, underneath the bravado. I'm sure he'll turn up. He's too weak to get far."

A suspicion was growing in the back of Freddie's mind. "Is he a very thin man?"

335

"Lance Corporal Butler," Phoebe nodded. "Please do keep it to yourself."

Freddie darted a look at Eustace, stricken by the possibilities, but his friend was rubbing his dry eyes, longing for the haven of his bed.

"But I have his camera," Freddie said. "He wouldn't run away without his camera."

"I'm sorry, Mister Ferry. You could help with the search, if it would put your mind at ease."

"Phoebe, for goodness sakes," Eustace said. "Not when Freddie's in mourning. It's inappropriate."

Phoebe offered Freddie a rueful smile. "See what I have to put up with? Give me a moment to check on Private Price. If there's no one around, I'll let you in."

As soon as she was out of earshot, Freddie turned to Eustace, whose hands were busy separating individual strands of his black hair, straightening the curls until Freddie could see the roots straining at the pale scalp beneath.

"They won't really shoot Mister Butler... will they?"

"Of course they won't. He'll get a prison sentence, I expect, if he has run away, which I'm sure he hasn't. Oi. Where are you going? Don't you want to—?" He gestured weakly, but Freddie was striding off towards the double doors of the North Wing.

Butler's bedside cabinet was just as he had left it. His shaving kit and comb were inside, along with envelopes of photographs and an open carton of Woodbines. When Eustace caught up, he found Freddie flipping through the soldier's pocketbook for railway timetables, addresses, any signs of a plan.

"His pyjamas are still here," Freddie said, without looking up.

"He's hardly going to run away in his pyjamas."

Freddie spun around, riled by Eustace's attitude. But when he faced him, the younger man's body was taught with stress. Freddie softened. "What is it?"

"I just don't think this is good for you. Let them flap around. You've barely eaten today."

A flock of VADs clattered in, arguing over whose turn it was to administer the evening medicines. Jumbled together in their white uniforms, they resembled a flock of gulls, and Freddie was reminded that his own feathered companions had said almost nothing to him since the loss of Fa, no words of comfort or the usual teasing provocations. Drummerboy waited in Eustace's room, enjoying the novelty of fine drapes to climb and a clean mirror to preen in. He would enjoy Butler's shining pistol, he thought, quickly packing the soldier's bedside cabinet back as he had found it. His fingers lingered on the gun's textured stock. Surely Butler shouldn't still have his weapon. And at any rate, if he had fled the Hydropathic, would he not have wanted it with him?

"Are you gentlemen lost?"

One of the VADs had noticed them. Eustace calmly stepped up, smiling earnestly in the face of her displeasure.

"Ah, sister. Matron Calder asked us to fetch you. One of the men has – shall we say – befouled the baths."

The girl's cheeks blanched. "I beg your—"

Eustace shrugged. "I'm sorry, sister, I don't know how else to put it."

The distraction gave Freddie the opportunity to tuck Butler's service revolver into his trousers, under his shirt. Even Eustace didn't see him. The barrel was cold against his skin, and he disliked the feeling. But it was a tool like any other, and when the thought of what the gun had no doubt seen and done came niggling at him, he found he could push it aside. His newfound numbness had its uses.

The diminutive figure of Phoebe was at the double doors, beckoning urgently.

It was a small guest room, reserved for single men on a tight budget. Inside, the nurses had locked the shutters, and the shaded lamp gave the man in the bed a reptilian look. Billiard-eyed and clammy, Private Price was sitting up, knees hugged to his chest. A long bruise spread across his face from under a fresh bandage. Freddie remembered the man from Lottie Mulgrave's concert that first night, clapping along in his blue uniform. Now he stared over Freddie's shoulder at the corridor beyond with unsettling vigilance.

Phoebe bent to meet his eyes, speaking softly: "Hello again, Private Price. I have some visitors for you."

Freddie had half expected the man to recoil or throw some kind of fit – *paroxysm*, echoed a voice in the back of his mind – but Price knew Freddie right away. The soldier reached for him wordlessly, not touching, not quite daring. With a look of immense remorse in his bulging eyes, he placed the hand on his own heart.

"I've not come to shout at you, Private Price," Freddie said.

"Freddie wants you to know he doesn't blame you for what happened," offered Eustace, looking to him for agreement.

"He was all I had," said Freddie, to no one in particular.

Price's hand, on his heart still, drooped. Eustace and his

sister looked similarly chastened. Big families easily forgot what they couldn't understand.

Freddie crouched down. He didn't want to sit on the bed's edge and crowd the man. "Private Price, they're saying you had a funny turn. I think there's more to it than that, isn't there?"

Eustace's breath against his ear: "I don't think he's taking it in."

Private Price's bloodshot eyes blinked slowly, mired in thought.

"Look at me. I think you saw something from up there on the tractor. You remember, don't you? At the edge of the trees. Something like a tramp. All bony and musty, bundled up in old clothes."

Eustace's eyes darted to Phoebe. "Fred…"

"You remember. With a helmet like a cauldron and a spike coming out the top."

Price's tongue twitched in his open mouth, dry and too red.

Freddie's heart ached, willing the man to speak. "You weren't imagining him, Private Price."

Eustace took him by the arm, urging him away, but Freddie resisted.

"You're not the only one, Private Price."

Phoebe spoke up, discomfort in her voice. "I think Private Price is tired now, Mister Ferry. Perhaps we ought to let him sleep."

Freddie surrendered to Eustace's hands. Eustace was right; Price was broken, and leading questions would help no one. But as he turned disconsolately to leave, a groan from the bed made him turn.

"Buh. Luh."

Eustace's fingers tightened around Freddie's bicep. Freddie broke away.

"Yes, Private Price? I'm listening."

"Eyesore. Bu'luh." The soldier swallowed hard, the bruise on his face contorting. He grasped a handful of Freddie's shirt, dampening the cotton with sweat. "Ammer."

"Nonsense," said Eustace.

"You saw Mister Butler?"

The soldier screwed up his eyes as if wrestling with a pressing equation. "Ammer," came his pained voice. He raised his arm and brought it down, stopping at eye level as if striking a nail in a wall. "Like this."

"Brandishing a hammer?" Eustace echoed flatly. "Mister Price, everyone was digging. That'll be what you saw. Mister Butler was too weak to join in, besides."

Price's eyes flashed with anger. His raised arm swung, though it clearly pained him. "Smashin'. Sprayin'. Flint." He sniffed, his swollen nose flaring as tears filled his eyes. "Horrible."

The door flew open. Matron Calder took in their guilty faces one by one.

"Out! All of you." She swatted Phoebe's arm as the young woman scurried guiltily past. "You are on probation, Moncrieff, don't forget."

Retreating to the privacy of Eustace's room, Eustace turned to Freddie.

"I'm sorry. He really was cracked, wasn't he?"

"Maybe. But he did see something. He saw Mister Butler."

"That's what he thinks. Who knows what the man's been through?" Eustace said. "And then he comes here and listens to your chargirls telling bogie stories about mad lords smashing the place to smithereens." Eustace's cheeks were a high colour, chasing away the funereal pallor of the day. "It was his imagination, Fred. A patchwork of nightmares."

"And the hare?" Freddie said. His trouser legs were smeared with the creature's blood, horribly pungent in the neat and airy room.

Eustace's mouth worked around words that wouldn't come. "There are things…" He sniffed, holding back a bitter little laugh. "*Evidently*. Things neither of us understand."

The rooks outside cried out in grim accord. Butler's revolver was warm against Freddie's skin.

SEVENTEEN

'Grime', *pencil on paper, May 1917.*

Following the death of his father, Alfred Ferry's creative output took an understandably macabre turn. In 'Grime', Ferry confronts us with an emaciated British soldier, slumped like a discarded puppet. On his shoulders, candles ooze, trailing tallow smoke. The viewer cannot say where the candles end and the man begins. This startling drawing was likely inspired by the rumours spread by the British press of the 'Kadaververwertungsanstalt', German factories where the dead were rendered into fuel to further the war effort. In a typically Ferrian flourish, the soldier sports a pair of stag's antlers, flaming at each pointed tip.

WORK DOESN'T STOP for death, Freddie reflected as he dragged the paint scraper along the windowsill for a second pass. As he crouched in a flowerbed, flecks of old paint caught under his nails and snagged on his overalls. The Hydropathic was rotting by degrees. If Fa were here, he would know how to fix it. Then again, Freddie thought with a drop of self-reproach, if he had ever listened to Fa, he would already know how. The best he could do was cut away the rot and paint over it, a hack job that would have made his father wince.

One day, there would be nothing left to cut away.

"Don't make me scoop you up in a net this time, young man."

Freddie jolted, sending up a small spray of paint chips. Clarissa Morton and her well-dressed companion had rolled up behind him, hemming him against the wall. The old woman smiled from under her wide-brimmed hat, brown-toothed and wry. Freddie's legs were dead from squatting. She could easily have caught him in a net if she wished.

"What do you want? Ma'am," he hastily added.

"To feed you, as it happens," said Clarissa.

Hiram fixed Freddie with one of his implacable serene looks. "Please join us for lunch. No need to change."

"That's kind of you, sir, but—"

"Miss Clarissa isn't asking, Mister Ferry."

He downed his tools like a good little tradesman and traipsed behind them into the Hydropathic. Locked in the lift together, he felt even more like a filthy navvy than usual. Clarissa made no attempt to reassure Freddie, looking placidly past him at the passing scenery with her milky eyes, keeping her secrets.

The couple's room was one of Edenwell's finest, once reserved for distinguished guests who came from the cities with mountainous luggage and unfamiliar accents. Clarissa's own portmanteau, buffed to a chestnut shine, was open to reveal her many outfits and cosmetics, along with strings of globular pearls that would have Drummerboy cackling with want. The room was divided by a folding Oriental screen and lunch was waiting for them on the table. Three places set, Freddie noted. Never any question of him not coming.

"My mother always said the surest cure for an aching heart was sweet tea and a brisk walk," Clarissa said, allowing Hiram to wheel her to the table. "She was always a great one for platitudes. Please, Mister Ferry, sit."

He looked dubiously at the cream upholstery, then at his overalls.

"Stop fussing. How many sugars?"

Against his will, his eyes flicked up. "You have sugar?"

"I am a woman of means."

The chair creaked under Freddie's weight, and he looked about him, embarrassed by the treasures spread out for his arrival. There was indeed a bowl of clean white sugar lumps, and sandwiches cut into triangles like folded handkerchiefs. Real bread, white and soft as eiderdown. He wanted to touch as much as taste.

Clarissa maintained a magnanimous smile. "I refuse to spend my last months on this earth eating hard tack. It's expensive and not at all virtuous, but there we are. Take one. Take two. And take some for your handsome friend. So terribly drawn of late, isn't he?"

Hiram poured him a cup of tea and plopped in a lump of sugar. There was jam in the sandwiches. Copious and sweet, gooseberry. Freddie was dizzy with pleasure.

"There, now," Clarissa said, watching him stuff his cheeks. "We forget the good things, don't we? All too easy to grow accustomed to privations."

"Is this…? What do they call it?"

Hiram, pouring the milk, smiled tightly. "A bribe?"

"What would you give for such enticements?" Clarissa asked. There was a playful light in her eyes. Freddie chewed in silence, if only to finish the sandwich before they could snatch it from him.

"We want very little," said Hiram.

"So little," Clarissa agreed. "Would you listen a moment? To an old woman. Would you suspend your disbelief?"

"Try this." Hiram offered him a trinket from his waistcoat pocket, a cross of olive wood. "Hold it. If you feel alarmed, it will keep you safe."

Freddie blinked. For a strange second he felt like the only adult in the room. "No one's *safe*."

"Out here?" Clarissa said, unoffended. "Safer than the coast, or the cities. The thought of those monstrous German cannons chills me."

Hiram watched him. "I don't think Mister Ferry means the guns."

Her shrewd eyes narrowed. "I don't think so either. You understand more than you think you do, young man."

Freddie licked jam from his fingers, feeling the grit of Norfolk soil through the sweetness. "You want to buy up Edenwell."

Clarissa gave a husky laugh. "What would I want with the place? After everything that's happened here. Take the cross, hold it. I don't care about your objections."

Freddie had a trinket of his own: the German medal, cold in his pocket. He was reluctant to give it up to these interfering strangers. He had a feeling that if he were to reveal it, they would set something in motion he could not control.

Clarissa went on: "It was the chicken that made up my mind. The bird dressed up and left for the poor girl. Hiram told me everything."

"A nasty joke," Freddie mumbled.

"You don't believe that. Will you believe this, I wonder?" She took the bulky cross from around her neck. The thing unhinged, revealing a locket lined in faded velvet. In its small compartments Freddie saw a wisp of dark hair, a cutting of fabric frayed to little more than dandelion fluff, and a painted portrait of a small boy, barely larger than a fingernail. The child stared, jaw pugnaciously set. "My brother," said Clarissa. "You will have heard of him: Jonah Morton."

The Morton name came chained to madness and the spray of shattered plaster. Freddie kept his thoughts to himself, but the trip of his heart gave him away. He shied away from Hiram's steady gaze.

Clarissa closed the locket. "My brother was a little boy once. He was not a monster, but like many children he did monstrous things. And then something monstrous was done to him. But he was my brother – and I loved him."

"Why are you showing me this?"

"Because the gravest mistake we can make is believing that we – here, now – are somehow unconnected to all that came before." She patted her lips with a napkin. With a glance to Hiram, who nodded shortly, she began: "My mother had a succession of girls. The youngest was carried off by diphtheria aged three. My brother Jonah – barely more than eight – thought to dress a doll up in her clothes and leave it for Mother to find in the nursery. He thought it would be a comfort, but my mother, in her grief, took her riding crop to him. A ghastly episode.

346

You might well expect that to be an end to it. But Jonah was never one to forget a bad turn. He persisted in positioning the doll around the house, leaving it upright in my sister's favourite chair, on the stairs, in the gardens… It afforded him a special glee, that game, until Mother had the doll destroyed.

"On my fourth birthday, he took me down to the well in the woods and told me we were going to play baptism. For at a baptism, the baby gets gifts, does she not? All she must do is withstand a little water." She stared at the tablecloth. "He held my head under until I almost stopped thrashing. When he hauled me out and slapped me back to life he gave me a handful of sharp flint and said I'd been a good girl. For years after that, all he had to do was leave a flint on my pillow and I would wet the bed like an infant.

"That was all before Reverend Greenwell came. An old man, with a white beard. Jolly, like Father Christmas. I remember laughter in the house. I believe, had Greenwell not come, Jonah might have grown into an ordinary man."

Freddie studied the dregs of his tea. Black specks bunching together in meaningless patterns, like birds in a greying sky.

"You've seen my father's folly out on the lawn? The little gothic tower? All covered in flint from Reverend Greenwell's mines. He was always a curious man, my father, eager to learn. My family has a long history of voyages to distant lands. I know you think him the madman with the sledgehammer, but to us he was wonderful. Always a story to tell, always a question to be answered. So when an educated man wanted to excavate the ancient mines over the brecks, Father did everything he could to be involved. We hosted parties for investors, celebrated his finds. My sisters and I put on our best dresses and lined up to greet the professors like sweet little maids. I was almost fifteen and quite appealing in my way." She glanced at Hiram and they shared a grin.

"It was August when Father put on a dinner to showcase Greenwell's discoveries. Mother had Cook turn out a lovely lemon punch, I recall, and the brandy only added to the excitement. Everyone was speculating. Someone said Greenwell's men had found something *utterly inappropriate*, which set our brains spinning. But the good Reverend was never one for mere spectacle. He took us children aside and lectured us on the mountains of flint he and his men had to dig through. Ancient, unimaginably old. 'And three thousand years on, the men of England still source their gun flints from Norfolk'. I remember his look of satisfaction. He brought with him other treasures: small cups carved from chalk, pieces of glittering quartz, antlers from long-extinct deer. But there was one thing I especially liked. An axe, a little hatchet of stone. Rare, he said, for East Anglia. Basalt, smooth and dark as water. I wanted more than anything to place my hand upon it.

"But Reverend Greenwell was a man of a time, and a girl in a party frock eager to hold a weapon was a hilarious anomaly, so he called up Jonah instead. The old man handed him the axe with both hands, like some sacred honour. Of course, the handle had rotted away long ago, leaving only the sharpened head, but seeing it in Jonah's hand, so pale and untouched by work of any kind, was… well, I didn't like it. The way he gripped it, blade turned outwards. A wanting thing.

"He had a few years left, after that, our Jonah. Danger became a joy for him, not just mean-spirited pranks. When my sisters told Mother he was diving into the holy well and running off to the excavation site at night, she wouldn't believe us. But then she found him on the roof, up there, where the servants' quarters are. He'd clamber out of the window with one of Father's guns, and stand on the gables, shooting at rooks. She said each time he fired, the gun kicked and he slid about as if on ice. It's a miracle he didn't fall. Laughing all the while. Laughing."

At the thought of violence towards the rooks, Freddie's stomach turned a sickly somersault. Clarissa took a sip of tea.

"The night swims and the treks out to the dig continued. He wanted to help, he said. To understand. And when you asked him what that meant, he was full of scorn. *We* hadn't the slightest idea, he said. He could swim and he could climb and shoot and what were we? Clothes horses. Mannequins. And did we know Greenwell found a big clay cockstand down in the mines? A man's pizzle the width of your arm? No, because a man wouldn't tell a bunch of trivial little girls that, would he?"

Freddie felt his cheeks colour. Clarissa gave a dry huff.

"From then on, Jonah seemed to hate us, and everyone. A stray look, a misheard word, anything would set him off. If the farm boys failed to treat him with due reverence in Thetford, he'd thrash them. And when he came home satisfied, caked in dirt and bleeding, he'd have the servants bring his bath out onto the veranda and he'd wallow out there as naked as the day he was born, in full view of anyone who came by. Once, he stood up, declared the water was 'warm as blood, like something you'd give an invalid', and he strode out across the lawn without a scrap of clothing, down into the woods to bathe in the spring. We thought he was insane. Father was distraught. 'He'll drown down there', he kept saying. It was so cold, that water. I knew it.

"So Father sent Jonah away. He had outgrown his childhood home, he said. Needed a man's challenges in life. Make some money. Make his name. I see now it was implicit he find a wife, an outlet for all those unwholesome energies. I am grateful he never found one."

Freddie listened, watching as Hiram's dark fingers played along the olivewood cross he had declined to hold. He swallowed; his mouth was dry despite the tea. "The story goes, he died young."

"Died?" Clarissa echoed. "Oh, not yet. He spent a month in the north learning how to run the mills with father's associates. We received letters – from them, not Jonah. His conduct among the noisy machines. His... unusual responses to the accidents inevitable in such surroundings. And then he took off. For two years we wrung our hands and prayed for his safe return. Despite everything, we missed him. It was quiet without him. No gunshots in the night." Clarissa paused, the crepe of her eyelids creasing as she frowned. "For all our hopes, I think we each privately knew we would never see our brother again."

She took up her teacup, only to find it empty.

"We think..." She paused, gathered herself. "We *presume* he intended to announce himself at the house. But, for whatever reason, when he returned, it was the well he was drawn to. That was where he was found."

"He came back?" Freddie said, shocked. "I heard he was beaten in a back alley somewhere."

"Father paid off the newspaper men. And who would believe

the truth? My brother returned brown as a nut, his hair stiff with salt, his pockets heavy with currency I had never heard of. The coroner reported scars in every quadrant of his body. Even a healed gunshot wound in the left thigh, inexpertly tended to. No one would have taken that weathered stranger for young Jonah Morton were it not for the tattoo of the family coat of arms across his heart. I know well why Father destroyed every crest in the house.

"Judging by the contents of Jonah's knapsack, he abandoned the mills and took up the old family business. Jamaica. Tortuga. American slave money, deeds to properties no doubt won at cards. Because, you see, his killer didn't rob him. Neither did he work in haste. The coroner had never seen the like. Indeed, he prayed he never would again.

"And the rest, you know. No killer was ever apprehended. No weapon was discovered, and certainly no witnesses. My brother was laid to rest and my mother took my sisters and I to live on our uncle's estate in Somerset. My father's condition swiftly deteriorated, as you know. That much is true. To stay in this house, overlooking those woods…" She shook her head. "I thought I would never see the place again. Yet we come to the end of our lives and we see the chance for resolution dwindling away. The search for answers coming to a close."

With that, she gave the cross a kiss and carefully hung it around her neck once more. With the miniature of young Jonah Morton hidden, Freddie found it impossible to reconcile that downy-cheeked boy with Clarissa's description of the man found battered in Choke Wood. It was too obscene a transformation. But he could feel it in the echo of the rooks' laughter, their knowing chatter. They always did say they had seen it all.

Clarissa went on: "My dear Mister Ferry, you recognise people, even when you're as old as I, and they long gone. You see them everywhere. A stranger's glance. The first bars of a song. You are little more than a child, and I mean that with no disrespect. You cannot understand the haunted nature of growing old. The echoes crowding in around you." She looked away for a brief moment, her narrow chest rising with a deep, disconsolate sigh. "That girl in the courtyard. The bird in baby's clothes. The calculating nature of it... Mister Ferry, you may dismiss what I am about to say as the delusions of a dying woman, but I ask that you listen. I felt my brother then as surely as that night when he stood on the roof shooting rooks. I felt him so strongly, I fought the urge to leave Edenwell and never return."

Freddie looked from Clarissa to Hiram, both utterly unreadable. "I don't understand."

Clarissa inclined her silvery head. "I respect your honesty. Jonah could be a cruel little boy, and he grew into a troubled young man, but he is dead, and the dead seldom trouble us. Hiram, if you please..."

He went to the writing desk and retrieved a book. Freddie recognised the dancing fairy on the cover of *Ponsonby's Folklorica*. The man carefully cleared Clarissa's cup and plate and placed the book in front of her, opening it on a ribbon-marked page. Freddie saw it upside down, the illustrations unfamiliar at that angle. A grassy landscape like the face of the moon.

"A violent change came over Jonah from the day he touched the axe brought up from the mines at Grimes Graves. But that wasn't all they discovered there. Reverend Greenwell's excavations uncovered the body of a young male deep in those mines. There was no sign of an accidental mining death, as one might expect. He was placed down there, deliberately, and sealed up in the barrow. We will never know for certain, but we may safely assume the boy was placed there in an act of offering."

An uneasy memory of Mister Miles in the Red Lion, his grin wet with beery foam. *They were putting summat down there.* Freddie bit the inside of his cheek. "What does that have to do with Jonah?"

"The tramp in Choke Wood," Clarissa said. "Caught in a trap, I understand? Bled to death."

"Mister Jenks." He had a name. Why did no one care to discover his name?

"When I was growing up here, the kitchen women always told me to beware the hikey sprites. 'Say your prayers before bed, Miss Clarissa, and always blow out your candle.' Mischievous creatures, the little people, elementals bound to the land." She looked at him with a touch of humour. "Now, I expect you to say, 'But hikey sprites aren't real, madam'. But you can't, can you? It's been drummed into you, hasn't it, Mister Ferry? Like arithmetic. My sisters and I used to leave out saucers of milk for the hikey sprites until Mother reprimanded us. Unchristian, you see. And here we were, living on a holy site… Though that didn't stop the king's men hanging all those monks from the trees when they refused to hand over their treasures." Clarissa examined her softly wrinkled hands. "It's in the chronicles, if you care to dig deep enough. When the king's men ransacked the monasteries in the 1530s, the Thetford monks hid their valuables out in the breckland, digging a pit where the earth undulated like the sea. When they returned to the shrine at the holy well, the soldiers were waiting. That's how it got its name, of course: Choke Wood. Violence, Mister Ferry. Act upon act, building like a stain. It needs it, you see. Like a spoiled child comes to crave gifts."

It.

She held his gaze. Freddie could feel a pressure building in the pit of his gut, the razor-edges of a hundred shards of flint. "There's a man," he blurted. "Me and Eustace—"

To his astonishment, Hiram cut him off. "It is no man, Mister Ferry."

Clarissa was impassive. "How does he appear to you? I see my brother in him. Oh, yes – I have seen him. Wearing my brother's tanned skin, his restless look. When I was a girl, our old cook claimed to see the ghost of a monk; a weighty sort of ghost, made of flesh and bone. He gathers these impressions, I believe, like a chameleon feeding on light, stealing its colours. They nourish him, give him form."

Freddie took the folded drawing from his pocket. Feeling incredibly foolish, but sick, too, he slid it across the table. As Clarissa studied it, his nerves were alight with dread.

"A German," she sighed. "Of course. What fresh horrors each generation brings him." She bid Hiram pour more tea, her hand only shaking very slightly. The casual nature of the gesture ignited something in Freddie. He delved deeper into his pocket, slapping the German medal down on the clean tablecloth.

"Then explain that," he said, "if it's a… *ghost,* as you say. That's solid. That's real. Eustace thinks a plane came down. A German could easily hide out in the brecks—"

Hiram interrupted him, speaking slowly, as if explaining a simple concept to a simple person. "Mister Ferry, this is no Iron Cross."

"But—"

"Any reader of the *Daily Mirror* can send a donation for one of these trifles. It's a joke, you see? The Kaiser gives out medals so freely, everyone possesses one, even his enemies. Do you not read the papers?"

Freddie's breath hitched miserably. "I look at the pictures."

"It is a trickster, my dear," Clarissa sympathised. "It knows just how to wind us up and watch us go."

"If it's not a man... what is it?"

"It is my belief that the ancient people who dug for flint established a relationship with the mines. After all, flint was essential to survival. Grimes, they called it. It's Old Norse, but the mines are far older. They gave the place a name, a character. If you like, a soul. The ancient Romans would call it *genius loci*. Whether that spirit existed before they began to dig or if their faith willed it into being, we cannot know. I kept abreast of research over the decades following Reverend Greenwell's excavations. When Mister Peake reopened the mines in 1913, he discovered more offerings inside the sealed chambers. Antlers, crystals, valuable weapons from distant places..."

"A skull," Freddie said, his mind drifting unwillingly back to that hot day out on the brecks. "A bird's skull. Tiny, it was. Like china."

"Delicate things," she nodded. "Beautiful things. Perhaps they weren't enough to satisfy Grimes' spirit. Young men often fail to see their own fragility. I imagine that is why it was so easy to lure that prehistoric boy down there and murder him. A man does not ravish a woman because he is overcome by desire, Mister Ferry, he ravishes her because he enjoys inflicting pain."

"What me and Eustace saw weren't no spirit."

"We said it was no man, Mister Ferry. Plenty of hard, solid things are not men. In the Middle Ages, a ghost was a tangible, fleshly thing. Not a wraith of smoke. It crawled its way out from the earth and physically attacked the living. This thing roaming the breckland is no will-o'-the-wisp. It walks and it wants and it plays its tricks. It murdered my brother, it drove my father to his death, it killed your vagrant puppet man, and it has no concept of satiety. Tell me this, Mister Ferry: how many of your colleagues have gone to fight?"

The sugar on his tongue turned sour. So many. So, so many. They rose up in Freddie's memory, crowding on the lawn. Harold, the butcher's apprentice. Mister Walker from the little paper shop. Mister Tungate, his hat mouldering on a hook in the walled garden. Every man who sprang to mind, shovelled like coal into a great furnace. And the animals, the limp squirrels and rabbits and hedgehogs. Their senseless deaths. He sensed the acrid pyre in his nostrils and fought down a wave of nausea. Freddie grimaced against that grating, uncanny sensation in his gut. If he could hear the guns, he thought, so could It.

Clarissa closed her eyes, as if listening to his thoughts. "A war on this scale, to him – to *it* – must be ecstasy."

"Eustace wants to go."

Hiram nodded gravely. "I'm sure he will."

"No." Freddie stood. The chair wobbled and nearly fell. He felt giddy, furious. The sugar spun through his bloodstream like an electrical current, and he snatched the drawing away from the old woman, crumpling it in his pocket. "He's not going. Not letting him."

Clarissa watched him with pity. When Hiram placed his

large hand on hers, she blinked away tears. As Freddie lurched from the room, he heard Clarissa calling after him.

"It won't like that, dear. It hates to be denied."

Three shirts, one best, hardly worn. Two pairs of mended trousers. Socks, surprisingly numerous, stiff with darning, and a wad of handkerchiefs that stunned Freddie with their familiar scent, magnified in the cotton folds. Fa's possessions were strangely anonymous without him there to claim them, and yet his absence set each item of clothing alight with meaning and importance. The shabby little cottage overflowed with holy remnants.

Freddie considered torching the place.

Eustace slouched on one of the kitchen chairs, one knee drawn up to his chest, twitching along to a brisk rhythm only he could hear.

"You don't have to go through it all now. My mother has all her parents' old things. She says it's family history, but I mean, whose family? I didn't know them. She can't expect me and Phoebe and Harry to want any of it."

A reel of paper stretched down the hall, hoarded scraps pasted together. Freddie lay on his stomach. No one had swept since Fa died, and there were crumbs of sandy earth all over the floor. He was drawing each item of his father's clothing. Each cracked and weathered shoe. Each limp glove. Between every other sketch, small dashed-off figures appeared: a lanky youth on a rickety kitchen chair, hair standing up in black tufts; and another man, a stranger, his hard gaze blue as the West Indian sea.

That morning they watched a biplane make a lazy circuit of the breckland. The craft was little more than a dot in the cloudy sky as they stood shielding their eyes from the sun. When Freddie sneaked a look at Eustace, the younger boy's face was sallow.

I let Fa down, Freddie thought, *but I shan't do the same to you.*

Together, they took coloured pencils from the chaos of Freddie's room and drew the biplane, its forest-green wings and red tail, a waspish warning. Eustace struggled to portray the spindly trees.

"I never really tried to draw before. I should have." He sounded wistful, as if his time was up. Outside, another party set out in search of Butler. They no longer bothered to call the soldier's name. Each day that passed was another day closer to the involvement of the military police. Butler's disappearance, as worrisome as it was, seemed to Freddie only to prove his old theory that men were vanishing into the earth somehow, one after another, as if their time had simply come. No battalion of investigators could stand up against such a strange, irresistible force.

Freddie pencilled in the Hydropathic, the surrounding pines, the brecks and the moonscape of the mines. It all looked so trivial on paper, as if the smallest crack in the crust of the earth could erase Freddie's whole world in the blink of an eye.

Freddie sketched himself and Eustace laying in the dirt of Choke Wood, guns drawn and waiting. *No man*, he wrote. *No man's land.*

"He wasn't a happy person, was he?"

Butler's camera lay on the kitchen table, a blunt reminder

of the soldier's absence. Eustace fiddled anxiously with the leather strap.

Freddie shrugged. "Seemed cheerful to me."

"But we can't truly know what he was feeling. Can we? After everything he went through." His finger was tapping unconsciously, and the sound was beginning to grate on Freddie. "You shouldn't have spoken to that Clarissa woman. She's a busybody."

Freddie said nothing. His pencil skirted across the page, ghosting gangly limbs and a faceless head.

"She's a crank," Eustace grumbled on. "All those crosses and rabbits' feet. You don't seriously believe she is who she says she is?"

Freddie tried to reproduce that bludgeoning antler, its jagged heft. "You're angry at me."

"No! I just hate the idea of our private—" The train of thought dropped off, as if abruptly running out of fuel. Drummerboy hopped onto the table, nudging Eustace's long fingers for a scratch. "It's dangerous when people talk about you, Fred. I know."

Freddie stood and stretched out the kink in his neck. Looking at Eustace, some hot and fetid voice urged him to split him in two and crawl inside. Whatever it was men did together. So little of what he recognised as himself or his life was left. Just Eustace.

The younger boy wrapped an overlong hank of hair around his finger, tweaking it to the point of what surely must have been pain. "We could get in your van and never look back," he said. "Why stay here? What's left?"

"Duty."

"Please don't use that word."

On the table, Drummerboy beat his wings. Fa's rifle was smooth and cool in Freddie's arms. He had to keep it clean, ready.

"All right," Eustace relented. "Assuming Clarissa is who she says she is, and not completely cracked. If what she says is true… It's a *thing*. How do you kill a *thing*?"

"But to try. That's all we have."

Eustace taught him that. The look on his face said he knew it. And worse, he understood.

"Stay where you are." Eustace took up the camera. With some fiddling, he unfolded the bellows and looked through the sights. A frown creased between his eyes. Freddie knew what he saw: an upside-down vision, standing long and narrow and peculiarly self-possessed with the rifle in his arms. He must look like a stranger. His body felt like a stranger's, weary and easily broken, despite the mask of confidence afforded by the gun. Before the shutter could click, Drummerboy shot past him to the kitchen window, a bright *chakka-chakka* bursting through the quiet.

"I've never told you why they sent me here," Eustace said.

But Drummerboy's cries were too insistent to ignore. Freddie hurried to the window, stepping over piles of Fa's clothes.

"Miss Clarke?"

The chargirl was on her hands and knees in the dirt. At first, Freddie thought she had tripped, but when she raised her head her face was a ghastly colour.

She saw him at the window and grimaced. "You forgot to bring in the eggs, you lazy beggar."

They went out to pick her up. "Allow me," Eustace said,

offering his arm. She wouldn't take it, struggling to her feet by herself. "Miss Clarke, forgive me, but you don't look well."

"I'm always running after someone or other, that's why." The wind had whipped her hair free from her cap, and when she pushed it from her eyes she winced at the sight of him. "Sir," she added.

They half carried her into the kitchen and set her down by the meagre fire on Fa's old chair. For all her protests, the momentary rest was appreciated. Her hands, Freddie noted, were even more careworn than his own, scrubbed pink with strong carbolic.

Eustace put on his coat. "I'll take the eggs to Missus Hardy, how about that? Put you both to shame. Freddie, make the lady a cup of tea, like a civilised chap."

"Don't tell her I'm loafing, sir," pleaded Tabitha.

Eustace sketched a small bow. A look went between the two boys – *Keep mum* – and Eustace left.

"Right. Tea."

"Don't go to the trouble." Tabitha gave the glowing coals a lacklustre nudge with the poker. Drummerboy hopped down onto the hearth, watching the young woman with interest. "They told me you had a pet bird. I didn't believe them."

Her cheeks had a bloodless cast. She sat motionless, the poker swinging from side to side like the rods old men used to find water under the earth. Freddie was no doctor, but she looked incapable of carrying out her duties.

"Something to eat, then?" he ventured.

"There is nothing to eat. That's the trouble." She looked at him seriously. "You will not go tattling to Missus Hardy, you hear? I need this position."

"What's he done?"

Tabitha's silence deepened. Freddie had never been direct with her, never with any of the staff, and she stared at him as if someone new had materialised before her eyes. Despite the heat of the Hydropathic kitchen, she had pulled down her sleeves to work, covering up poor dead Thomas. Her cuffs were dark with sweat.

"You can tell me," he said. "I'll believe you."

"You're a man."

A knave cannot smell the blood.

"You won't understand," she added.

Noman smells it.

"You've been different since your father died," she said. "Everyone said you'd go under, but you haven't, have you?"

Freddie watched the fire. Each May, the trees were packed with nesting rooks, the ground below nourished by the bodies of the blue-eyed squabs too weak to jostle for scraps. No, he couldn't smell the blood, but the drop on the hem of Tabitha's skirt was there for anyone to see.

"I lost someone this week too," she said. "That's all you need to know."

"Scole's?"

The birds laughed in chorus. Not so ignorant after all.

She was too worn-down to lie. "Shouldn't have told him. Just gave him an excuse to throw me over. I didn't even—I don't know if I'm sad or relieved. It's just never-ending, isn't it? All of it. I mean, they said it would stop. It wouldn't be long and we'd all be together again. But it's all going deeper and deeper and there's so little of me left. Do you feel that too? I can't remember when people stopped saying 'soon'." She dug

362

the poker into the fire, splintering the glowing coals. A gust of wind rushed down the chimney, and the embers flashed in reply. "I think sometimes, what would I give to make it all better again? I see myself turning out my little room, throwing all my clothes and knick-knacks at God, cutting off my hair, pulling my teeth. There must be something He wants. Is that mad?"

"I think..." he ventured. "I think people have always felt that, one way or another."

They both gave a start as the old front door shuddered in its frame. Tabitha rubbed her eyes with her swollen knuckles. "That wind's getting up."

Take your cover! Hold it fast!

The pines heaved and cracked. Nests scattered, throwing twigs and horsehair to the wind. Younger birds, excited by the bluster, took to the air to be tossed about while their parents made for the relative shelter of the Hydropathic at the first warning thrum, deep in the craters of their eye sockets. Under the eaves they clung with armoured feet, puffing up their feathers to repel the cold. Some chose the flint folly, while others fled to the old stables and the laundry outhouse. Squat places, strong places. Servants' places where the crumbs and the gossip spilled freely. Better still was the veranda, where the puppet man made his princess dance. Wide windows, good for spying. The girls hadn't yet pulled the blackout curtains.

She's alone, her with the corn-coloured hair.

Sitting at the piano, coaxing out a melancholy tune. Notes like germs of wheat, light, golden. The rooks snapped them up gladly. She disliked solitude, the Lottie woman. Whenever they saw her, she was sharing a cigarette or telling a yarn. But tonight, James Ferry's death had left her uncharacteristically disconsolate. Poor wee Freddie, so quietly stoic.

Hark at her. Shedding a tear, all over a knave.

As the tune came to its delicate conclusion, a soldier in his hospital blues ambled into the dining room in search of his friends. Lottie cast him a smile and struck out something jauntier:

> *Mr Asquith says in a manner sweet and calm:*
> *Another little drink won't do us any harm.*

The man grinned and covered his mouth for a wet cough. In the eaves, the rooks cackled.

The last search party was coming in for the night, rubbing their cold hands and grumbling about dinner. No sign of the skinny fellow, then. Missus Bailey declared over breakfast that Butler had caught a train and gone to ground, though how he was supposed to stay unnoticed in the bright blue uniform of the invalid soldier, Lottie wasn't sure. As the wind buffeted the windows, the rooks heard Lottie's penny dreadful thoughts. In all likelihood, the poor thing had frozen to death and rolled into a ditch.

She's one of us, her. Sees much. Not enough.

Lottie shrugged the tight spots from her shoulders. Gone were the days when she could hunch at the piano for hours on end. A tipple before bed, then. With any luck, someone would be up for a chinwag by the library fire until she was too tired to do any thinking.

Missus Hardy was an old ally. Scarcity was one thing,

but hospitality was an ancient law, and the stout cook always looked after her favourites. The brandy was being saved for the Christmas cake, but Lottie had always did have a talent for a hangdog expression, and Missus Hardy soon sent her off with a snifter and the briefest of kisses behind the larder door.

We see much. Know much.

There was no one waiting for her in the library, and the pair of old buggers in the gentlemen's billiards room asked her if she was lost. She traipsed up the stairs to the North Wing. The soldiers were in bed watching a film projected onto the ceiling. Someone whistled as a monochrome girl shyly accepted a rose from a tuxedoed cad. All cheap tricks and gurning, she thought, sipping her brandy. She glanced at the nearest men, hoping someone would be receptive to her complaints, but the film shone in their rapt eyes and she hadn't the heart to spoil it.

Resigned to another maudlin evening alone with her glass, Lottie sauntered back to the grand staircase. A pair of VADs came up in the lift, eyeing her with curiosity bordering on impudence. These younger ones had never seen Lottie in her heyday. To them she was a mannish old maid who surely had somewhere better to be, or at least a nice private house where she wouldn't make such a spectacle of herself. Lottie knew when not to bother with overtures. She ambled over to the nearest window to peek around the blackout curtain. The wind insinuated its way through the casement.

Black feathers ruffling in the dark.

The creak of a footstep caught her attention. She briefly wondered if the girls had perhaps come back to ask if she was, in fact, the famous Colonel Crumb. She turned, putting on the Colonel's haughty smirk, to find she was alone. She glanced about. *Sneak up on the half-cut spinster*, she could almost hear them whisper. *Get her to drop her brandy.*

Draping the lightbulbs, the cobwebs fluttered lightly in competing draughts. As a child, Lottie lay in bed with her sisters watching the washing waver by the broken window. Boneless arms animating old shirts. Costumes missing their characters. So many impulses ran through Lottie during those long, chilly nights, but that fear of the dark and of quiet grew on her like mould, impervious to any amount of scrubbing. Only greasepaint did the trick.

Oh. There. Don't move. The young, are they away? Hold fast.

A footstep. Lottie drained her brandy and left the glass on the windowsill. Half the floorboards at Edenwell creaked when you trod on them, and the other half moaned. The steps were close, but moving slowly, lizardly in their thumping, uneven gait. Lottie looked around her at the dark hall, unable to ignore the distinct unease uncoiling at the base of her spine. Turning her head to follow the noise, Lottie could only liken the sensation to being alone in a theatre after dark, knowing that if the ghost light on the stage went out, she could easily blunder over the edge.

The feet were above her, on the stairs.

"No more of that lurking, thank you," Lottie called out. "We've all had enough shocks."

The feet shuffled. Whoever it was had turned their back on her and was making a bid for the next floor. The impertinence of it irked Lottie and she found herself following, if only for the satisfaction of giving the culprit a proper telling off.

The grand stairs coiled up the building's centre like a spine, and from where Lottie stood she could see all the way down into the deserted entrance hall and up into the servants' quarters where no light allowed for further investigation. It was a man; she could tell that much. A plodding figure lost among Edenwell's many corridors. As her eyes adjusted to the darkness, Lottie could make out a narrow body and an incongruously bulbous head, and though he could surely hear her behind him, the man did not turn or alter his course. Almost at the top, Lottie wondered if she hadn't made some kind of mistake.

A blue uniform. Yes, the colour was bright enough, even in the gloom of blackout. Lottie drew breath to warn the soldier he wasn't permitted up here, that Matron would have his guts for garters, and if you got on the wrong side of the staff here, you'd never—

Sharp shoulder blades, diffident posture. No one at Edenwell was as painfully thin. Lottie bounded up the last few steps, her braids bouncing against her back, as Butler struggled up onto the landing.

"Christ man, everyone's been searching for you. We thought—"

She was at his back when he turned. Lottie Mulgrave was not a tall woman, and with her head tilted to peer into Butler's face – inscrutable in the darkness – she again asked herself what she was doing with the staircase yawning behind her and the wind buffeting the old windows, so loud as to almost obscure the tinkling of broken glass underfoot.

The rooks laughed, though their many hearts weren't in it.

Glass?

Flint.

Talons spread and wings fanned, taking a chance on the whims of the wind. A gust broke through the window frames and lifted the blackout curtains, letting in the briefest sliver of moonlight.

Yes, Lottie thought briefly. Like blundering off the dark edge of a stage.

Freddie couldn't bear to return to the service tunnel for Butler's photographic equipment. Call it cowardice, but each time he considered it, he felt that door closing on him and tasted bile. Eustace's room was his own now; Eustace had insisted, bidding him rest while he left in search of dinner. With the blackout curtains drawn and the lamps out, the well-appointed surroundings could have been a cave, but Freddie's eyes adjusted and once again Eustace's portmanteau and crisply made bed were reassuringly discernible. Eustace had lived there so long, the room had taken on his unique scent, like too-strong tea tempered with sweet liquorice. His own cottage had begun to smell different since Fa died. Another reason never to go back.

Butler had spoken of developing photographs at the Front. A cloak and a billycan, Freddie recalled him saying with a grin. If that were possible, Freddie could surely put together a similar setup without ever entering that awful cupboard again, at least until he needed chemicals.

The other option was to send the negatives away for a stranger to develop. That wouldn't do at all.

With a hard tug, he commandeered Eustace's bedsheets. Between the bed, the door and the writing desk, there was a decent amount of space for him to kneel and cover himself entirely in bedding. Plenty of room for his elbows as he mixed powders and fluids like a witch at her cauldron.

He heard the door open as Eustace returned, hopefully with dinner.

"Forgive the mess," Freddie said, muffled by the sheets. He fumbled with the fabric, but there were too many layers over his eyes. Eustace moved slowly, no doubt carrying a tray. Freddie fancied he could smell the oily scent of margarine. *Thick as a duchess' finger*, as Fa always said.

The barest thought of Fa conjured him into the room. His heavy step; the pipesmoke cloud he walked on. Freddie tucked his chin into his chest, squeezed his eyes shut. Would his heart ever stop playing these cruel games? He tugged at the sheets, feeling panic swell in his gut as they tangled and hitched.

"No noise," Eustace said. Freddie felt him kneel before him. His cool hand gripped the back of Freddie's skull, keeping him from thrashing. He was blinkered like a nervous horse, but the sensory deprivation and the proximity of Eustace played a soothing trick on his brain. Freddie felt his body still.

"I thought—" Freddie began.

The hand at the back of his head remained firm. Another came to rest against Freddie's covered cheek, barely touching him. His breath fluttered hotly inside the hood Eustace had created for him.

"What will you give me?"

Eustace's question made Freddie's tongue stutter in his mouth. Eustace's face was a feather's breadth from his own. He could feel it; not see it, thank God. He was afraid to move, to make a sound, to tumble over this precipice. He knew Eustace could see his mouth moving, struggling hopelessly, and yet the younger boy said nothing to put him at ease. He felt Eustace's palm slide down to cup his chin, lifting it, baring his throat.

If ever he'd hoped to speak, there was no chance of it now. The sheet, the face, the firm and open-mouthed kiss. Clinging wet.

Deep in his bowels, something retreated. The wet of algae. The wet of cold game. Freddie scrambled to tear away the hood, scratching at his own clammy, contaminated skin. As he finally wrenched the sheets from his eyes, the figure before him lost weight and mass, gone in an uneven heartbeat, eliciting from Freddie a choked sound that might have come from a snared animal, and not a grown man.

He was quite alone.

A brisk knock at the door. Freddie jolted hard enough to rattle his teeth. Not the true living Eustace he hoped for, but Nick Scole, staring down in mystified contempt at the pile of blankets and Freddie's flushed, distraught face.

"Where's his lordship?" Scole said.

"Finding dinner," Freddie managed.

"You've got him fetching and carrying?" Scole snorted, but the usual glee he took in baiting Freddie was absent. His white Edenwell uniform was a map of creases. Freddie had the distinct impression he hadn't been to bed in some time. "You tell him I'm collecting him at the crack of dawn."

"Whatever for?"

"We have a vagrant problem on the property. I'm taking Moncrieff out to catch the bastard sleeping," Scole said, with all the satisfaction of a problem solved. "Teaching the boy to do his bit, aren't I?"

Freddie's lips were numb; his damp face frozen. "Take me with you."

"You?" Scole smiled, showing tobacco-stained teeth. "This isn't about you, Ferry. This is about young Eustace. We'll make a Hun-hunter of him yet."

Some youthful vestige of Eustace felt like a pirate with Drummerboy clamped to his shoulder. He hadn't encouraged it; the jackdaw had simply hopped up as Eustace left Freddie with the promise of supper. It was comforting, the soft warmth against his neck. If Eustace could build a nest of feathers and hide in it, he might never come out.

A young VAD hurried past, and he made way for her flying skirts. As he neared the kitchens, he detected one of Missus Hardy's watery broths on the air. Missus Bailey and one of her devotees strolled towards the dining room in their evening wear. As they squinted at him and his feathered companion, he fought the urge to stick out his tongue. He could no longer afford such insouciance.

Lost in his thoughts, he almost collided with his sister, hurrying up from the kitchens with a dustpan and a look of sweaty consternation.

"What's wrong with you?"

"The Irishwoman, she fell down the stairs."

"Good God, Miss Mulgrave?"

"I helped get her onto a stretcher, she's—" Phoebe shook her head. "She's like a furnace to touch. Must have fallen into a swoon, wandering about in confusion. And she'd been drinking. What on earth do you have a bird for?"

Phoebe hadn't set eyes on Drummerboy since she killed him, and she showed no sign of recognising him. Eustace laid a finger on his smooth beak, receiving a soft *cronk* in return.

"Will Miss Mulgrave be all right?" he asked.

As another VAD marched by, Phoebe fell guiltily silent. The girl, her harried face smattered with pimples, called out: "Concussion, Moncrieff – memory loss. Come on, this isn't difficult."

"And the temperature?" Phoebe retorted.

"Someone else's problem," the girl said, turning a corner. "I'm on night rounds."

Phoebe contained her annoyance. Snide girls had always wound her up. "You don't want to visit Miss Mulgrave too, do you?" she asked him. "Private Price was understandable, but the last thing we need is you spreading a fever around the place. There's your lungs to think of."

Eustace's jaw tensed. "Don't start."

"Worrying about infection is my job now!"

"Might I suggest a mirror?"

It was a fair observation. His sister's cheeks were ruddy as a slapped backside, and that watery look he noticed in her eyes the day Mister Ferry died had hardened to something glazed and sickly.

"The shock of hard work," she admitted. "I'm not taking time off for rest. I'm already on thin ice with Matron." She glanced at his hands and frowned. "What on earth have you been up to?"

He held them out, nails clogged with charcoal. "Drawing.

We never did draw as children, did we? It wasn't one of Mother's educational obsessions."

"Be thankful she didn't make you practise pianoforte three times a week. What have you been drawing? Your little friend?"

A scowl briefly crossed his face, but he was distracted by something she couldn't guess at, and the petulance quickly passed.

"I find it allows me to think."

Phoebe caught his drift. "You want to talk."

"I need to say I'm sorry. I do know that."

"But?"

"Don't *sigh* at me."

"What else am I supposed to do? You've always been one for picking the worst possible moment. There's just been a serious accident—"

Her tone was gentle enough, even affectionate, but his eyes slid away as he scratched at the tiles with his toe of his boot. Whatever urge had seized him had faded. His moods flared and died like squalls, they always had.

"Was there much blood?" he asked.

"No, thank goodness. Oddly enough, just gravel. Shards of stone. She must have been sprinkling it about. People do all sorts of odd things when they're running a temperature."

Drummerboy flexed his talons, pricking Eustace's shoulder warningly through his shirt.

"I've done awful things to this family," he said.

"We can do this later."

"No, it's true. And I ought to hurry up and spit out an apology, but the fact is, I can't. I can't apologise for what happened," he said, "even though I know it was a terrible thing. I'm still doing

373

terrible things. And I'm sorry for it, but lulling you into a false sense of security is the one thing I can avoid."

With shining eyes, she studied his face. "Love, you're worrying me."

"It's better that you don't know."

"Tosh. I'm your sister. You've always told me everything."

With a wave, he dismissed her. "You're doing so well. Really, a nurse! I'd never have dreamed it. You mustn't let me be a millstone around your neck." He gave a weak approximation of a smile. "Stone. Yes, I want to see Miss Mulgrave's stones. Lead the way."

Like a breadcrumb trail through a witch-infested wood, the Moncrieff siblings followed the shining chips of flint to Edenwell's summit. Eustace hoped his reluctance to mount the servants' staircase would look like nothing more than distress at Miss Mulgrave's misfortune. Phoebe always did tease him for his attachments to odd fish.

They trod carefully. On the servants' landing, Eustace said nothing. In his palm, he examined the flints, knife-sharp and brilliant in the low light.

"Give me the dustpan," he said. "I'll deal with it."

"Don't be silly." Phoebe sniffled, pawing at her sore back. Hard physical work had come as a shock to her, and when she bent to scoop up the debris, she visibly winced.

"I don't want you up here. We don't know what happened."

"You don't think someone pushed her?" Phoebe's look was sceptical. She wiped her nose on her sleeve, and grinned. "Perhaps she saw a ghost."

"Will you *just* allow me to be useful for once?" His shout bounced off the baroque ceiling. Drummerboy jetted off to sit on the lift cage.

Phoebe's stunned eyes brimmed with tears. "As you wish." She dropped the dustpan and brush, crunching over flint as she left him on the dimly lit landing to be useful alone.

Eustace added another future apology to the cairn of them towering in his mind. When his sister was out of sight, he swept a handful of scattered flint into the dustpan. There was too much for Lottie Mulgrave to have sprinkled about herself, even if she had tipsily stuffed the pockets of her dressing gown. Eustace recognised this as the work of an altogether less affable individual.

A thump at the window made him jump. He snatched up the brush, brandishing it with as much authority as he could muster. The blackout curtain wrinkled, moved by hidden hands.

"Who's there? Christ, *Freddie*—"

A flash of feathers brushed his face as Drummerboy flew to his master. Down on the floor, the rangy figure peeped out from behind the bunched fabric, eyes wide with watery panic. "I had to be sure it was really you."

He tried to stand. Something hit the floor and Freddie scrambled to pick it up. Eustace caught the glint of metal.

"Is that a *pistol*?" Eustace glanced around for onlookers, only briefly relieved to find they were alone. That wouldn't work in his favour if Freddie accidentally discharged a bullet into his chest. "Calm down. Lottie Mulgrave came a cropper on the stairs. No, no, she's all right." He paused, doubled back. "What do you mean, really me?"

Freddie's throat worked through a dry-mouthed swallow. "He's inside."

He stood and pushed up the sash. A blast of wind hit them as he got to work, hurling handfuls of flint out into the night with the desperation of a man bailing a lifeboat. Behind him, Eustace slowly approached, mindful of the revolver tucked precariously into Freddie's belt.

Freddie's hair whipped about his face. "Help me," he hissed, scooping flint. "He can't come inside. We can't let him."

"Your hands, Fred."

A network of cuts beaded with blood. Freddie paid the wounds no mind, scraping at the carpet with his fingernails to catch the smallest splinters as the wind billowed in the curtains. Drummerboy clattered from wall to wall in imitation of his master.

"We bolt the doors," Freddie said. "You can have my rifle and I'll use this." He had the pistol drawn, waving it about. "We can't let him in. Not with all these wounded men. They're fragile. He hates to be denied. Give me that."

Eustace had half-heartedly gathered up a handful of flint. Freddie groped at Eustace's closed fist, scrabbling like a rook after a scrap of bacon. Eustace felt nails scoring his skin.

"He took Fa," Freddie said. "And he took Butler, too. You know he did."

"Keep your voice—"

"The Mortons, the monks, the bones in the mines." Freddie gulped, shaking as the wind chilled his flesh. He backed away towards the billowing window, and for a horrific moment Eustace thought he intended to jump. A great gust of wind battered the building, and the roof shingles shivered in response.

"And Fa. And Fa."

As the gun drooped, Eustace went to him, arms wide, hoping his own growing panic wouldn't radiate through him as he carefully wrapped Freddie close. His thin body trembled. When his voice came against Eustace's shoulder, it was barely more than a warm vibration.

"I thought it was you, before. It was perfect. For a second."

"Before?"

A tread on the stairs, and they broke apart. Annie had come up to see what the commotion was, her skirts bunched in her fists.

"Annie," Freddie wheezed. "Lock the doors. Don't go out." With a sigh, he dropped to his knees, a faint passing over him.

The chargirl was frozen, eyes wide at the sight of the blue-eyed jackdaw beating the air above Freddie in agitated circles. "What for?"

Eustace fumbled with the revolver, trying to hide it under Freddie's loose shirt before Annie had a chance to see it and raise hell.

"You need to tell everyone," Freddie panted, eyes rolling. "It isn't safe."

Annie's freckled face reddened. "I'll get Chalice."

"No," Eustace snapped. "Annie!"

But she ran down the stairs two at a time. Freddie's head lolled, supported in Eustace's hands. All around him, splinters of flint, as if Freddie himself were a smashed thing, abandoned there on the floor. His eyelids fluttered as Eustace patted his cheek.

"Shh, your heart. Breathe."

The wind swept over them, bringing Freddie slowly back to

white-lipped consciousness. "Don't let him— Scole. If he tries to take you—" His hands twisted with frustration as the swoon passed, dragging the thought, however important, with it.

Eustace nodded, blandly consoling. "Landslides. I remember."

"I liked Butler," Freddie mumbled. "He was kind."

The thump of boots could only be Scole's. Loping up the stairs, the orderly rushed to the window and shoved down the sash. "What do you think you're playing at? Annie's gone screaming to Chalice. Get up."

"Freddie fainted." With the window shut and the vicious wind locked out, Eustace's voice was suddenly too loud.

"What's this about Butler?" Scole's dark eyes locked with Eustace's. The younger man gave a terse shake of the head, but still Scole caught Eustace's free hand by the wrist. With a sharp twist, he forced Eustace to face him. "You sound? You steady?"

"I swear."

He released his grip only as Chalice came springing up the stairs. The American brought with him a doctor's bag and his habitual smile. The false levity made Eustace's stomach turn. "Fella, what are you doing to me? I can't take all these frights in one night."

Freddie struggled to prop himself up on his elbows. "I'm— fine, I'm—"

Chalice knelt by his side. "Your fingernails are blue, which isn't quite my definition of fine."

Scole stood by, arms folded. "Nothing but hunger, I expect, Doctor."

"I'm inclined to agree with you, Mister Scole, only these fingers also appear to be bleeding." He glanced up at Eustace, watching as Drummerboy made a perch of his shoulder. Having already tended to Miss Mulgrave, the doctor was visibly attempting to put the events of the evening into some kind of formal order. His brow creased when he noticed the evidence of Freddie's fingernails on Eustace's skin.

Eustace fought the urge to hide his hands behind his back. "We were trying to clean up."

Chalice considered this, lips pursed. Brightly, he turned to Scole: "Why don't you take Mister Moncrieff downstairs for a cup of strong tea? Better yet, a warm bath. There's a nasty chill making the rounds, and this floor is like an ice box."

"I want to stay with Freddie," Eustace said, but Scole stepped in and blocked Eustace's view of the patient.

"Miss Healey mentioned you'd missed your afternoon treatment, sir. Follow me, if you please."

The hand on the small of his back left no room for dissent.

The Solarium at night felt twice its true size, empty tubs and sprawling ferns casting long-fingered shadows in the anaemic lamplight. Above them, the skylight took a battering, and Eustace wondered how Freddie's rooks managed in a gale like this. Since meeting him, he worried about the strangest things.

Scole ran the bath. The steam had a mineral tang to it, and Eustace was reminded of home, the way the ozone came in off the sea and gave the fumes of the city an almost animal undertone. Mother used to tell them a great seaweed-covered beast had crawled from the sea overnight, marked its scent, then waded back into the Solent. When he was first sent away to school, he missed her asinine stories with an almost physical longing. Coming home after his first term, he found he could no longer listen to them. Somewhere between cross-country and the cane, he had lost the knack. Freddie was the only person he had ever encountered who still retained that unspoiled freedom. Eustace wanted more than anything to protect that.

His white sleeves rolled up, Scole tested the water's temperature as the pipes chugged and hissed with steam. Eustace wondered what Chalice was doing to Freddie at that moment, imagining sedatives and straps and all sorts of penny dreadful grotesquery. Most likely, the American would be asking about his worries. Of course, the risk was that Freddie might answer.

"Just right," Scole said, straightening up and wiping his hand on his apron. "In you get."

"Is this really necessary?"

"Was any of *that* necessary?"

"He has a weak heart."

"So you took him to see where that old masher cracked her head open like an ice-cream mould?"

The water was sensibly warm, but Eustace's skin was icy, and the burn drew a hiss from him as he sank in. His knuckles stung where Freddie had scored them. He shouldn't be here. He had a duty of care.

Duty duty thassa laugh.

He frowned. With this wind, it was forgivable to imagine spectral voices.

Scole hung behind him, shifting from foot to wooden foot.

"Ferry mentioned Butler."

The water was suddenly colder. "He liked him. That's all it was."

380

"We can't have him getting hysterical. If that bint Annie gets ideas into her head..."

"Everyone knows Freddie's... a little unusual. They'll think nothing of it."

Scole ruminated on this. Eustace longed to twist his neck, look at the man, gauge his expression. Somehow, he didn't dare.

"We've an excursion planned for tomorrow, you and I," Scole said. "Your tramp's gone to ground, what with all these search parties. But I went down to the edge of the wood this afternoon, and you know what I found? Fresh tracks, big ones. And this." Eustace felt something slap his shoulder. A man's boot heel, worn to a wafer. The touch was abhorrent and Eustace shrank into the water. "He's sleeping down there. I reckon I'll take you out for an early morning run. All the better for your lungs. I wouldn't be at all surprised if overnight the laundry room door had been forced open from the outside. Being upstanding young fellows, you and I will investigate – armed, of course – and come upon an unwanted guest making off across the lawn. A scuffle will ensue, I think; these boys always carry knives, and you in your weakened state can't be expected to hold off a great brute like that alone. We'll see you're nicely duffed up – just enough and no more, don't you worry – and then I shall sort him nice and quick."

How like Scole to position himself as the hero. The absurdity of attempting to fight that creature with its crushing club somehow smothered the trepidation Eustace should have felt. He could have laughed were it not for his role in the proposed plan.

"And then?" he asked.

"Before I wrapped up our package, I lifted a few personal effects. Our friend will have them on his person when the police arrive. Buck up! You'll be glad of the experience if you want that sniper's badge. If you ever meant it."

"You know my mother's going to invalid me out."

"I know about *Ridley*, you great simp. Everyone knows about Ridley. He'll take anyone's money. You think the army care about a strongly worded letter? There are men shipping out with rickets every day – scarred lungs, arthritis. You're going. And all the better."

A rifle in his hand and a uniform on his back. His ambitions looked so naïve now, the fantasies of a boy playing dressing up in the garden. He remembered the day Mother's illustrator came to the house to take his portrait, and Phoebe's, and Harry's. A trio of cherubs in their gowns and helmets, laughing, playing, their likenesses sent around the world in a vision of family unity. He never tried to picture his birth mother, not truly. What side was she on, if she still lived?

Scole's words clung to his damp skin. All the better for whom? Eustace was the only person who knew what Scole had done – and what he hadn't. If he were in France, or better yet, deaf and dumb in a soldier's grave, Scole could sleep easier at night. Nausea roiled inside him as he considered what to say, but Scole's breath was hot against his ear and Eustace's head was full of loathsome creatures crawling from the sea, eager to mark their territory.

"You say you're sound."

The water rippled around his ribs. If Scole would only come around where he could see him, talk to him like a man—

A hand on the crown of his head. He was under.

His arms flew up instinctively. One was thrust back underwater by Scole's free hand while the other thumped uselessly against the side of the bath. His eyes, open wide, burned white. Scole's hand twisted in his hair, that wrenching sting he had so often inflicted on himself. Bubbles obscured his vision as he thrashed with all his strength. Eustace tasted bathwater, felt it invade. It was a warning, nothing but a trick to scare him, it couldn't be, it couldn't be—

"You asked for water. I've brought you some."

On his knees in the school chapel, Eustace didn't know what he expected to happen. A lifting sensation? The finality he had been craving these past sleepless months? If Parrish's ghost were to rear up out of the flagstones, clanking and moaning, he might at least feel something.

It occurred to him to pour out a glass, but he had forgotten to bring one. He hadn't thought any of this through; it was all just feelings, battering away at him with no sense of direction.

A feeling. An urge. Eustace was accustomed to quashing both.

"I should have—"

He broke off, the words withering on his tongue. The unmistakable clunk of the chapel door. The pennants waved a greeting at Prefect Hartnoll, followed by the broad silhouette of Rawley. Even in the deep shadows, Eustace could see their smiles.

"Moncrieff, you surprise me," Hartnoll said, full of jovial malice as he stepped down the aisle. "You barely apply yourself. You're equally lackadaisical in games and mathematics. I can't bring to mind a single society you're a member of. But it turns out you're fanatically committed to prayers."

A hundred likely stories sprang to mind, each one curling up and dying before it could reach his lips. The pair came towards him, Hartnoll's eyes raking over the candle, the pitcher, the puddle on the floor.

"What on earth are you trying to achieve?"

Rawley snickered. The boy knew better than to speak until spoken to, but the laughter was too much for him to contain, and when Hartnoll glanced at him he said, "It's water, isn't it?"

"I can see that."

"No, it's water, it's— Don't you remember?"

The realisation bloomed on Hartnoll's face.

"Oh, it's too perverse. Are you bringing libations for your lily-boy, Moncrieff?" He leaned down, hands on his knees, until his face was close to Eustace's. "Only you're a few months late."

Eustace stood. He hadn't realised how cold he had become, crouching in his pyjamas. Hartnoll would want him to beg, he knew that much. That was the sport of it. The prefect wielded a switch like an executioner, punishing the most minor infractions with welts that throbbed for days.

If Eustace were honest with himself, a good thrashing was precisely what he deserved.

"Do you want to see a trick, Moncrieff?"

Hartnoll had a handkerchief. Eustace said nothing. Though his heart throbbed in his throat, the light from the single candle lent the scene a dreamlike detachment. If Parrish's ghost had seen his feeble attempt at an apology, this was surely him spitting it back in his face. And who was he to argue with that verdict?

Hartnoll barked orders and Rawley obeyed without hesitation. They put Eustace flat on his back on the nearest pew. Rawley got down on his knees and pulled Eustace's arms, joining them at the

384

wrist beneath the seat so he was fully pinioned. Hartnoll climbed on top, avoiding Eustace's kicking legs with ease.

"I've never seen this performed," said Hartnoll conversationally. "But I've heard it's awfully effective at making enemy combatants talk."

The handkerchief brushed Eustace's nose with disproportionate menace. It was then that Eustace noticed the pitcher in Hartnoll's other hand. A snippet of dormitory chitchat came to him, an older brother's boast of having learnt a fine new trick in the army...

When Hartnoll draped the handkerchief over his face, he refused to cry out. That was the game, of course. If you met the ordeal manfully, with the minimum of fuss, you passed. Until the next time.

"You're a strange case, Moncrieff," said Hartnoll. "I've never fathomed you out. Come to think of it, when my father was a boy, he boarded with yours here and says much the same thing. Fascinating, really. Because he isn't your father at all, is he?"

The first contact of water was like a punch. Blind and gasping, Eustace thrashed his head, but with Rawley pinning his shoulders and Hartnoll so heavy, it was impossible to squirm away from that searing cold.

And then there was the matter of breathing.

Water in his nose, down his throat. The relentless tickle had him gulping against his will, forcing him to take in more, adding fuel to the icy fire. All the air in the chapel had been sucked away, leaving him to buck and wheeze against the pressure building in his chest, the relentless stream of water a clinging coffin lid bearing down on his face.

He would surely die.

The only honourable thing to do.

Perhaps minutes, perhaps hours. When he woke, it took time to realise that bruises were all that remained of his schoolmates. Hartnoll and Rawley had left him there, with the empty pitcher discarded on the flagstones in a wide, pewter puddle. Dawn light filtered through the arched windows as he dragged himself, raw-throated, shivering, to his feet. The single candle, lit in Parrish's memory, had long gone out.

Cold air: another world. Scole hauled him out by the hair. The orderly was talking, and the hand that had held him under was slapping his shoulder like a friend.

"The Japanese recommend it. Don't they, Mister Moncrieff? One dunk and the body flushes out the toxins."

Did Scole expect an answer? Eustace's arms were free, numb as a stranger's. He wiped his burning eyes and saw the stocky figure of Tabitha Clarke in the doorway, mop and bucket in hand. Her eyes were locked to Scole's, quivering, as if the slightest provocation would send her sprinting from the room.

Scole's voice wore a smile. "What are you doing in here, love? Men's treatments, isn't it? Doctor Chalice won't be pleased to hear you're wandering in, willy-nilly."

Tabitha's palm hovered at her waist, protecting, concealing. "I'm 'love' now, am I?"

"You're my girl. We've been through it all, you and me…"

"You—" she began, bridling at his gall, but as Scole took a step, she drew back. Her eyes darted to Eustace, who still spluttered and shook. "Sir?"

"You won't get any sense out of him," Scole said, slapping Eustace's shoulder in comradely fashion. "That's the point, isn't it, sir? Get the oxygen pumping. Tabby? Tabitha!"

The bucket clattered. She bolted, and he after her, slipping on the tiles.

It took Eustace several minutes to crawl from the tub. Traipsing on shaking legs to the changing room, he found his clothes neatly folded as he had left them. As he ran a towel over his face, he was assaulted by the image of Scole disposing of them. What had been the plan? To drown him and drop him in the dark well alongside Butler? Had there even been a plan? He thought back to that day in Scole's room, his proud speech about killing coldly, without a second thought. Had Eustace really been that wide-eyed fool beside him, listening like a disciple? Fighting back revulsion, he struggled to pull on his trousers. One thought in his head: Freddie.

He stumbled up the stairs. If he were a real man, he would make it his business to find Tabitha and save her from whatever ignominies Scole had in mind for her. His ears ached, the water inside them making the floor bob like a boat at high tide. He lurched up the last few steps, feeling the urge to retch. Goodness only knew how much he had swallowed. It took everything he had not to glance back, half expecting Scole to be loping up the stairs after him, arms outstretched to finish the job.

Muffled voices. He reached the first floor with its Grecian maidens and saw no one. "Miss Clarke?" he called out hoarsely. What could he do for her, with his legs wobbling like a drunk's?

The voice came again, low and plaintive:

"Water."

"Who's that?"

It came from one of the cheap guest rooms. The cry came again, louder, needy: "Please. Water."

Eustace's thoughts drifted muddily across his brain. He had to get to Freddie, but he recognised the voice with a pang of regret. Poor Private Price. All the shock and pity of the accident came flooding over him anew. The door opened with a soft *clunk*. Inside, Price's lumpen figure was bunched up in his bedsheets.

"So... hot."

Eustace went to the nightstand and poured a glass from the jug there, spilling it over his own shaking hands. Price faced the wall, his hands covering his head where that long bruise obscured his features. The stink of sweat and iodine was overpowering. "Take it," Eustace said. "You'll feel better."

Price did not react. He was ashamed, Eustace realised. He felt an uncharacteristic urge to touch the man, to reassure him with that steadfast patience Phoebe seemed to possess in abundance. As he neared the bed, Eustace realised Price was slighter than he remembered. The poor man was fading before his eyes.

"Water," Price moaned. "Please."

Eustace held out the trembling glass, urging Price to roll over. Price's arm slid from his face, revealing the livid trench of bruised flesh. "Moncrieff..." he breathed, eyes rolling white with fever. "Will you hold my hand?"

Eustace shot back from the bed, slamming into the closed door. The glass dropped from his slack hand, spraying water all over the floorboards. The figure of Lawrence Parrish, spiteful schoolboy, rolled over to beseech him with pleading eyes. Parrish, petty and spotty and so terribly unlucky; Parrish who only wanted a glass of water.

With a cry, Eustace half fell out into the corridor. Ignoring the stare of the VAD pushing the evening medication trolley, he broke into a run, thundering up the next flight of stairs to his own room where, to his extreme relief, Freddie had been left to recover. The groundskeeper's son lay on the coverlet, pale but awake, and at the sight of Eustace's dripping hair and flushed face, he blinked owlishly.

Eustace spoke first. "He hasn't come, has he? Mister Scole."

Drummerboy sidled along the headboard, his flinty beak shining.

Freddie shook his head languidly. "Missus Hardy brought soup. We left some for you."

Sure enough, half a bowl of thin broth waited on the bedside table, cold as a stone and just as appetising. The blackout curtain swayed in a draught. They would be safe in here, Eustace told himself, but for how long? Scole's secrets were spreading like a stain. He could feel it seeping under the door.

He went behind his dressing screen and started throwing clothes into his suitcase. Freddie, propped up on his scrawny elbows, watched him.

"What do you want to keep from the cottage?" Eustace asked. "We can fit a decent bit of luggage in your van. We can sleep in the back. There's the New Forest if we head back down to Hampshire. Or the North – Yorkshire is enormous, isn't it? If we keep moving, no one will find us. And when the war ends…"

In his head, he and Freddie were tiny figures bouncing around the map like flies trapped between windowpanes. What did they do to cowards who fled their letters of Notice? Let alone an absconding murderer. Eustace couldn't believe his own thoughts. They felt like the thoughts of someone else, the thoughts of someone he once would have spat on.

With a bundle of shirts over his arm, he went to the door and double checked the lock. There would be master keys somewhere in the Hydropathic, of course, and Scole had the means, but the chest of drawers was sufficiently weighty to pin the door shut. Drummerboy gave an anxious *chacka-chack* as Eustace strained to push the furniture into place. Freddie's bitten lips were pale.

"What's happened?"

"Something. And if we don't leave now, it'll be something worse."

"I didn't think you meant it before," Freddie said. "Leaving. I've never— I don't know how I'd—"

"Fred, when my Notice comes, I'll have to leave you here." He sat on the bed, feeling Freddie's worried eyes on his face, searching for the secrets he couldn't bear to unload. The rag-and-bone thing in the wood was the least of his worries. "I never listened – not to you, not to anyone. I used to talk about duty, but I've lost the knack. It was like a trick I was playing on myself, and now I've forgotten how. All I know is, I can kill as many filthy Hun as I like, but it won't do any good without you to come back to. And I want that. To come back. I never did before."

The wind buffeted against the window. He hugged his knees, waiting for Freddie to stop chewing his lip and speak to him. An age passed before Freddie brushed a lank strand of hair from his glassy eyes, quietly absorbed.

"If Scole touched you, I'll kill him."

"Please. I don't want to hear those words from you. I only need you to trust me." Every time Eustace blinked, it was there inside his head: Butler's thin, smiling face; his meagre weight wrapped in a sheet like a bundle of broken branches. Eustace's hand went to his head, to tug on his wet hair, make it stop. Where once the gesture had offered release, now there was only empty pain. "I want to be honest with you. I should have done this long ago."

"You told me already. The boy at school, cracked his head…"

Eustace winced. "Not that."

The wind rose, howling in the old eaves. To Eustace it sounded as if the storm were in the room with them, rattling around inside the wardrobe and under the bed.

Trams rattled along the seafront, shuttling early evening revellers out to the amusements at Southsea. Dockers in heavy boots traipsed home to their wives. Eustace nipped between them in his cross-country kit, his breath puffing hot against his chest as he watched his footing over the tracks. It was a sweaty day in early September, and the heat gave the sea the green smell Eustace associated with long walks on the shingle with Phoebe. They hadn't strolled like that for years, not since he was sent to school.

His sister had spent the afternoon choosing a new blouse for Mister Bachmann's arrival. Bachmann, one of Father's school companions, ran a canning business in Southsea and was in the market for an office monkey; a little creature to rustle papers. Mother must have gone on one of her missions, telling everyone about her clever son who'd had a terrible run of bad health and simply needed an opportunity.

Eustace picked up the pace, jogging in the direction of the promenade with its herds of strolling couples. Bad health. He wasn't the one who'd broken his head on that fireplace. Though sometimes, he felt a crack in him, a seam running along the centre of his scalp that tingled like marching ants when he caught Father's eye over the evening paper. That investigative look. Who are you? From where do you hail?

Beside a news kiosk, three girls in breezy dresses teased the seagulls with bread. The gulls crowded them, flapping and strutting, and the girls shrieked with delight as their shoes were pecked.

Eustace leant against the sea wall, breathing hard. On the hazy horizon, a schooner glided. He shouldn't be this tired; at school he ran cross-country with barely any effort, letting his long legs do the work while his mind slipped its tethers and drifted away.

Mister Bachmann and his kingdom of tin cans. He would be at the house before long. Would Mother have Cook serve Bachmann's corned beef? Eustace wondered sourly. A job for life. He could taste it: over-salted, barely palatable.

The girls had attracted quite the crowd. To Eustace, they floated on a lake of gulls. The kiosk was smothered in posters: theatre bills, showbands, ferry timetables, tinned meat, tinned cocoa, tinned milk, and the ubiquitous bugle boy with his rallying cry: Another call – more men and still more until the enemy is crushed.

There was a scream as one of the girls felt a gull skim her bonnet. The news vendor laughed.

"He's saying thank you."

"Thank you!" cried the girls, hurling crumbs into the air. "Thank you!"

———

392

"I hope you plan to bathe."

Harry caught Eustace as Mary the maid let him in, his shining skin prickling. Harry never could resist crowing in front of the staff.

He bathed diligently and dressed in the suit Mother had laid out for him; the good one. It sagged a little since his recent troubles. In the hall, he caught his sister returning from town.

"What do I look like to you?" he asked.

She paused, turned, the long line of her skirt barely moving with her body. "Your tie is askew."

"Blow the tie. I mean if you didn't know me. If you had to… form an opinion."

She looked at him, head cocked, her small mouth working on unshareable thoughts. "I wish you wouldn't put me on the spot."

"Tin cans, Phoebe."

"Tin cans, Eustace. Fix your tie."

"I imagine in many ways, managing a business is comparable to plotting a book. A juggling act. Only I do it once a year and you do it every day."

Mother had a gift for small talk. She sat at Father's side, modestly attractive in one of her nicer evening dresses, though nothing so extravagant as to spoil the image of the gentle lady author. With her easy smile and attentive manner, she knew how to make men feel important, and Bachmann was no exception. He wasn't quite the walrus Eustace had imagined, but he was old and plain, with a steel moustache that made a boot brush of his top lip, and when he dipped his spoon into his soup, it clanked tediously against the china.

"I was never one for storybooks, madam," said Bachmann. "Always a builder, as a child and as a man. Sandcastles, wooden blocks…"

"Tin cans are very stackable," muttered Eustace.

Across the serving dishes, Phoebe sent him a look, not entirely of reproach.

"Eustace always excelled at mathematics," Mother said, one of her fictions. "I understand a logistical enterprise such as yours requires a firm grasp of statistics and suchlike. Quite beyond me, I'm afraid." Mother looked to Eustace, silently begging him to show some enthusiasm.

Bachmann let his spoon strike his bowl and took a long sip of beef broth. "My wife has no head for figures, either, madam. I find it's a common fault among ladies. Quite forgivable."

"And where is your wife this evening?"

"Olivia has no flair for socialising. If it isn't a headache, it's a chill, or a touch of hayfever. No, she remains at home where she is most comfortable. Though, I must say, she is missing out on some most excellent oxtail soup."

Father sipped his wine without pleasure. He had welcomed their guest with a swift pumping handshake before settling into cloudy silence offset by the occasional noise of agreement. This was Mother's evening; he was merely the man with the contacts. But Father's silences had their eddies and pulses. Like tides, they governed the direction of the household. In all his years away at school, Eustace had never forgotten to keep one eye on his father's demeanour, calculating and recalculating with each evolving expression. When Father spoke, the pictures on the walls listened.

"I understand the Navy have renewed your contract, Bachmann."

"There was a bidding war, but Admiralty made the sensible

decision in the end," Bachmann smiled. "Gone are the days of fast, cheap and poisonous."

Eustace's scalp tingled. Between two fingers, a single strand was nothing, but the sting it gave when he drew it out and held it there, tense and singing, brought him back to the table. Bachmann was watching him, dully appraising. Eustace wondered what he saw.

The hair came away. Eustace fancied he saw blood glistening on the root, but it was only the reflection of the claret decanter as Mary the maid filled their glasses.

"Now then, young man," Bachmann began. "Your father was telling me your schooling was regrettably cut short."

"Eustace suffered a terrible chill," Mother cut in. "You've never seen the like. We were all braced for the worst, weren't we, darling?"

Eustace wouldn't quite agree with that assessment. After Hartnoll's handkerchief trick and a night on the wet chapel floor, Eustace's severe cold was blamed on sleepwalking. Likewise, his behaviour. In the end, he wasn't sent down; merely asked politely to leave.

Bachmann turned to Father with an overfamiliar expression Eustace was coming to despise. "You were never one for chills at school, were you, Moncrieff?"

"I was a robust boy. One had to be."

"Those long nights in the dormitory, burning books to keep warm..." Bachmann laughed. "Didn't do us any harm!"

Father drank his replenished wine in silence. Bachmann was a thoroughly decent fellow, Father said; a fine example of what hard work and a dash of ingenuity can do for a man. But in Bachmann's presence, Father was uncharacteristically cowed. Bachmann was a year or so older than Father, Eustace understood.

"Those nights," Bachmann shook his head happily. "Cold. Hard. Formative! Do you ever think about – what was his name? Senior

395

Prefect, monster on the rugby field."

"Molyneaux." Father's voice was guarded.

"Molyneaux! Caned the life out of us. But what a fine fellow. Went on to do well in the civil service, I believe."

"I daresay."

Father had finished his claret and was pouring another. It was ground into him, Eustace realised with disappointment – deference, blind and unquestioning. His implacable father brought to heel by an unremarkable boor.

He pulled another hair, dark against the tablecloth.

"Your husband was forever getting himself into bother, Missus Moncrieff," Bachmann went on, leaning closer than he ought. "Did he ever tell you the story of Molyneaux and the cistern?"

Mother smiled, intrigued. "I don't believe so."

"You won't believe this, of course, but Moncrieff over there was once what we called the runt of the litter—"

"Hardly a dinner table story, Bachmann." Father's hard gaze was one his children knew well. Eustace's stomach tightened. Glancing at Phoebe, and even Harry, he knew the hurried arithmetic they were performing.

"Don't be coy, man," Bachmann chortled. "It happened to the best of us. Eustace, tell us: what does a prefect say when he needs an errand run?"

Bachmann expected a response. Eustace noticed the brown gobbet of soup clinging to his moustache.

"'Boy'," he replied. "He shouts 'Boy, boy, boy, boy, boy', and the last boy in earshot to rush to his side gets the task."

"Quite right. An exercise in punctuality. Any boy habitually last to answer the call can expect a good hiding. I trust you were never caught short?"

Rarely. Eustace was tall and fast and learned to shove smaller boys out of his path. But the hot slash of Hartnoll's cane was as familiar as games or chapel.

Phoebe interjected: "But what about boys who are naturally slower? Sickly boys, or with injuries from games? Father says—"

Bachmann made a droll noise, as if a child had said something charmingly ridiculous. "My dear," he said. "That sort must learn. Moncrieff certainly did, after Molyneaux had his way with him."

Father's dangerous look had lost some of its power. Unfocused, he fingered the stem of his glass. "You were there, too, as I recall."

"Quite right! The noise you made drew the whole county. Young man, tell me: what do you know about the art of knot-tying?"

"Nothing," said Eustace.

"Shame. Prefect Molyneaux was a devil with knots. Hogties, they were his speciality, weren't they, Moncrieff?"

Bachmann was half drunk, Eustace realised. The man was impervious to the second-hand uneasiness crawling across the table on insect feet. Eustace tried to think of something to say, some smart comment to derail the conversation, but Bachmann was steaming ahead.

"It was a rainy spring evening, as I recall. Molyneaux was in the common room, chatting at the fireside with his usual cronies. One of the Prefects remarked it would be nice to have a spot of tea. Naturally Molyneaux stood up and called out 'Boy! Boy, boy, boy, boy, boy!'" Bachmann thumped his fist on the table, rattling the cutlery. "The entire room flooded to his side. Boys dropped what they were doing, tripped over each other – anything to not be the boy to reach his side last. I managed it with no trouble at all, being nearby when the cry went out, but your husband, madam…" His shoulders bobbed with mirth. "Poor Moncrieff was sauntering into the common room just as the last 'Boy!' went out. Every time! Like a curse."

Phoebe, sensing Bachmann's reckless course, came to Father's defence. "That's certainly not the Father we know. The most punctual of men."

Bachmann scraped the dregs from his bowl. "Molyneaux saw to that, didn't he, Moncrieff? The water cure, he called it. Down in the cellar under the laundry, the old cistern. The servants still used it then, so there was only a loose wooden covering for convenience. The opening was about two feet across; plenty big enough to drop a man in. Or a boy."

Mother said something under her breath. Watching her husband, her amiable expression had drained entirely. Bachmann, finishing his wine, noticed.

"Don't take fright, madam. He was easily fished out. Molyneaux's ropes saw to that. Hogtied, he was — hands and feet. What a sight!"

Eustace knew that cellar. The wooden covering had been replaced by a safer, more permanent grate of iron since the school's adoption of indoor plumbing, but the cistern overflowed one wet winter, and the earthy smell of the frigid groundwater seemed to permeate their food, their clothes, the very pages of their books. He shivered to think of that dark opening yawning before him, his hands bound behind his back, swinging on the end of a rope as the water drew closer to his helpless face. And the laughter, ringing against the slippery bricks. He could almost hear it.

"Thank you."

Eustace flinched out of his reverie. It was only Bachmann, recognising Mary for replenishing his wine. Across the table, Phoebe caught his gaze, silently asking if he was all right. He looked away.

What kind of boy had his father been before that moment? What did he lose down in that dark cistern?

There was a hot stone in his mouth.

"What kind of name is Bachmann?"

Mother's eyes flicked up, full of warning. "Eustace…"

"A pertinent question," said Bachmann. "My family is of Swiss extraction."

"You could change it. Lots of German-sounding families are doing it." Eustace ventured a guileless smile. "You wouldn't want anyone getting the wrong impression."

"I think—" Mother began.

"The Bachmann name is bound up in the brand, young man." Their guest's voice was steady, but through his overlong moustache Eustace could see the hardening sneer. "As a potential employee, you surely understand."

Seeing an opportunity to ingratiate himself, Harry agreed. "My brother knows little of the real world, Mister Bachmann. I'm afraid fairy-story absolutes are more his line."

"Harry, didn't you say Mister Bachmann's daughter has been going to meetings with conchies?"

Under the table, a boot connected with his shin. Phoebe, if he had to guess. Harry would save his fury for later.

Brightly, Mother said, "Eustace, would you mind popping downstairs and reminding Cook not to put toasted almonds on my fish course? She always forgets my little preferences."

Eustace had no intention of moving. The hot stone in his mouth was sweet against his tongue, like spite.

"Conscientious objectors? Marion would do nothing of the sort." Bachmann bridled, but the look he cast Harry belied his words. Harry glared at the tablecloth, seething to be so wholly caught out.

As Mary came round to collect their empty bowls, Eustace gave a slow, feline blink. "I'm glad to hear it, sir. I mean, how would that look? With your Hun name."

Father pushed back his chair and stood. "If you cannot conduct yourself with decorum, Eustace, I suggest you take your eccentric mood elsewhere. But not before offering Mister Bachmann a sincere apology."

Mary made a quick exit, china jangling in her arms. Eustace fixed his gaze on his place setting, the mirror-shine of the fish knife offering back his own serene face. "I'm doing my duty."

"I will not repeat myself."

Bachmann's laugh rolled over him. "Steady, now, Moncrieff. The boy is playing patriot. And why not? When the police rounded up the German butchers and the Hungarian tailors, my wife wrung her hands in sympathy, but I told her – and I stand by it – duty does not sleep, Olivia. We took our eye off the German war machine, and look what good it did us."

"Up," said Father.

He had always thought of his father as a great edifice of furniture, immovable and polished, yet now, standing almost chest-to-chest, there was a boy between them, dripping and frightened out of his wits. A boy like that could slip beneath a mahogany sideboard and never be found. Eustace balled his fists as he stood.

"I don't want a job pasting labels on tin cans," he said. "I'm going to stand up to German aggression. You taught me that: duty comes above all else. An Englishman's creed." He hiccupped, soup coming up his throat in a sour spurt. "It's all you've ever drilled into me, at home, at school, on the rugby field, in the nursery. I don't care what either of you has to say. I don't care, I don't—"

"Out."

Harry balled his napkin and threw it on the table. He was making fulsome apologies in Bachmann's direction. Mother got to her feet. All the work she had put in to arranging the position, wasted. She kept up a cheerful front, as if some crumb of Bachmann's favour might yet be salvaged. "My fault, entirely mine – the doctor did say this might happen if you pushed yourself too hard. Spirits running high, rich food. Eustace, go to your room and don't think about coming out until you've composed a full apology. My dear Mister Bachmann—"

"Dear Mister Bachmann who almost drowned your husband."

"Don't be absurd!"

Despite the taste of vomit, he laughed. "All right. Stood idly by, cheering while someone else almost drowned your husband. What an employer. What a role model. What a fine alumnus—" Eustace grunted as Father seized his collar. Tripping on his own feet, he was propelled backwards towards the door, seeing little but the blank, perspiring face of his father. "I'll join up the moment I can. Anything to get away from all of you. And if you try to stop me, why, I'll drag out this table and these chairs and all our furniture into the garden and I'll put a match to them so the bloody Kaiser can see us all the way from Berlin. And when the airships come, I shall jump up and wave and say 'Here we are, Kaiser Bill! Blow us to smithereens!' And I hope he obliges."

"Get out," he heard Harry say. "Get out of this house."

"I heard the call, Father! I won't be last to answer."

The slap was sloppy, too hard across his mouth, sending teeth cutting into lip. An iron tang and a flash of thorns behind his eyes, and he was on his father like an animal, like Prefect Hartnoll with his cane, like a boy flinging himself on an outstretched sheet, hoping to fly. When his teeth connected around flesh, he saw colour for the first time in months.

Hands on his shoulders, his wrists, his neck, dragging him from the room. Blood in his mouth, two distinct flavours. Somewhere, his mother's voice, high and sweet – "Please, we're all overexcited" – and then, like a breeze on his slap-hot skin, Phoebe:

"Mother. It's Mister Bachmann."

Slopped wine on lacy table linen. The mahogany armrest of Bachmann's chair was all Eustace saw as Harry clamped him by the neck and dragged him away. Phoebe later said it was the queerest thing. She had never seen the like and hoped never to again. Half the man's face, from jowl to brow: a landslide.

EIGHTEEN

Things Shown Me In The Pit. III.
*Pencil on Edenwell watermarked
writing paper. May 1917.*

Crossed wrists, open hands. In one, a speckled egg. In the
other, the skull of a small bird, the curve of the cranium
mirroring that of the egg. The wrists are bound with a rope of
plaited black hair.

NEITHER OF THEM wanted Freddie's leftover soup,
though they ached to be fed. Freddie scooped a meagre
sliver of chicken into the spoon and coaxed Drummerboy to
take it. His beak tapped cleanly, once, against the silverware,
like a trap snapping shut.

The bed was wide enough for two. They lay top to toe,
studying the ceiling.

"The doctors blamed shock. A stroke can take a healthy man,
but one as sedentary as Mister Bachmann only needed so much
stimulation to bring one on. He was keen to tell his story, with

what limited powers of speech he retained. Soon everyone knew. Marion broke it off with Harry, of course. A flock of madmen and deviants, they called us. An asylum in all but name." Eustace cleared his dry throat. "I rather liked that, privately."

Beside him, ankles together, Freddie was neatly corpse-like. "All those flags in your chapel at school. Hanging there, lined up. I bet that was something." With one crooked finger, he traced an invisible pennant waving like the ear of some prehistoric pachyderm. "We should make our own flag. Just ours."

In spite of the hollow sensation in his gut, Eustace smiled. "Stick it on your van. Like pirates. So when we're thundering down the streets people will say 'Who's that?' and some clever dick'll say 'Why, that's *them*. Haven't you heard?'"

"A flock of…"

"Madmen and deviants."

Freddie's face creased into a smile. He looked sick; a faded print. "I've been feeling… strange impulses. I was thinking… waiting for you here… how hungry I am and how hungry I'll be tomorrow, and I thought about the rooks just sticking their faces into dead squirrels and I was right jealous. Why not, I thought? What's stopping me?"

Eustace watched as Freddie tugged at that full lower lip. The last vestiges of pink vanished between the pinching fingers, leaving flesh a fish-market blue.

"When we're camping in the New Forest, I'll hunt rabbits for you. Insist on cooking them, though."

Drummerboy, blue eyes flashing, ruffled his chest plumage and screeched.

"He don't like that wind," Freddie said. It rattled the casement, tripping over the roof and down the chimneys as

404

if the Hydropathic were nothing more than another hollow skeleton lying in the brecks, sandblasted and whistling. But it wasn't empty, Eustace thought as he shifted on the bed, tucking his long limbs in behind Freddie's, one arm around his waist, hard and warm. It had this.

Eustace shuffled, saturated in sleep and sweat. He could feel Freddie against him, smell the grass-and-brown-bread signature of him, and even without blankets he was burning. The room was like sweltering summer come early. Freddie's body gave a shudder, shoulders sharp against Eustace's chest.

"Fred?"

"Hmm— no. Nono."

"Fred, it's all right."

"He's— I'm— NO!"

The shout awoke Drummerboy, who had bedded down on the floor in Eustace's discarded coat.

Eustace shook him. "You have a fever, Fred. Water. I'll get you—"

Freddie's limbs awoke before his brain, thrashing in Eustace's hold. "W-window."

Eustace slid from the bed, his clothes sticking to his skin. With the blackout curtains drawn, the room was a deep hole, and he felt his way to the window, following the wail of the wind. When his hands touched cloth, he pulled back the curtains and pressed his palms to the glass.

Hot, like skin.

From the bed, he heard Freddie's drowsy mumble. "Is it the dawn?"

By the time they pushed the chest of drawers from the door and ran outside, the folly was a column of flame. The door had succumbed entirely, revealing the piled chairs and billiard tables inside, too far gone for anyone to save. Outside, logs were piled against the walls, burning alongside broken ploughs, brooms, and blunt club-like shapes Eustace belatedly recognised as bones. How anyone had lit such a bonfire in this wind was beyond his understanding. He saw antlers glowing within the stacks, their branches furious as coral.

In the black inscrutable sky, rooks hollered.

Freddie hopped about, trying to tie his bootlaces. He toppled, landing on his arse in the mud. "The blackout," he shouted over the din of the wind.

The folly would be visible across the county; help would come. It was useless trying to put it out themselves. Eustace couldn't get within twenty feet of the building without covering his face against the spitting wood, sending firefly rockets spinning out into the darkness.

Freddie's face was turned to the cloudbank. There was no sign of helpful rain. Only a crowd of rooks and crows and magpies whirling on the currents, specks of coal against the thick pile of the clouds. Drummerboy clung to his side, taking what shelter he could.

"Something's wrong," Freddie shouted. It wasn't dawn that had drawn them out; he knew the fire wouldn't fool the birds, crafty as they were.

There was an invisible caul over Eustace's head. It was the intimacy, he told himself. The shock of telling Freddie the whole ghastly story. He scratched at himself as the roof caved in, the bishop's mitre collapsing in a shower of sparks until only the jagged crown of supporting beams remained. *Lofty, aren't you?* Harry had said. *So sure you'll make it through. You're no better than the others.*

"What others?"

He spun on his heel. Scole's white uniform was half buttoned where he'd flown out of bed. "What others? You did this? We had a plan, for God's—"

A great *snap* interrupted him as one of the burning bones blasted in two.

"Water," Scole yelled. "Get to the stables – there's buckets. You too, Ferry, you useless swine. What are you playing at?"

On his feet, braced against the driving wind, Freddie had remembered Butler's camera. He fumbled with the lens, extended the bellows, and took two snaps directly into the firelight. He was winding the tiny key as Scole shoved him, barking orders.

"In this wind it'll spread. Water. Now!"

Freddie only stared, his blue eyes round and filmy as marbles. Clinging to his shoulder, Drummerboy's cry broke through the wind's relentless howl. A danger call.

At Scole's back, Eustace refused to leave. "You didn't believe me," he shouted.

"Water, you halfwit!"

"I said he wasn't like other men."

"This was your man?" Scole latched on to the information. His eyes darted over the burning furniture, and then to the Hydropathic, wondering why no one else behind the dark windows had stirred. "The one who did for Jenks?"

Freddie's glazed eyes focused in horror. "You told him?" The words were stolen by the wind.

All the harried rage drained from Scole's face. In its place, Eustace saw the shrewd excitement of a man about to seize a rare opportunity. He wiped sweat from his brow, clapped his hands.

"Guns," he said.

Freddie's shaking hands turned the key in the cottage lock. The door creaked open to a flood of Fa-smell, immediately torn away by the ravenous winds. Scole pushed past into the dark parlour. Above the fireplace, Fa's rifle was quickly commandeered.

"Ammunition?"

Freddie fetched the box, eyes down. The light of the blaze filtered through the curtains, casting the room in a Martian imitation of the dawn. Even under the roof, Freddie could feel the circling of the birds, crying out their coded warnings.

Freddie pressed his own rifle into Eustace's slack hands. "You're better than me," he explained. Eustace was poised to protest when he saw the fever throbbing in Freddie's cheeks. *What are we doing?* he silently pleaded, but Freddie tucked his cheek into Drummerboy's feathers, cool and soft, and Eustace received no answer.

Scole paced. "Same as we said, Moncrieff. Everything. When it's done, I rough you up a bit, make it believable. You behave, and you'll have nothing to worry about. Ferry, you wait here. You see that clock? Five minutes, you understand? Then you go hollering to Chalice. A tramp did this, you tell him. A bleedin' madman. Me and Moncrieff gave chase. Five minutes, no sooner, you hear me?"

"Won't do no good."

Blood bubbled hot over Freddie's lips as the back of Scole's hand smacked him across the nose. Eustace sprang up, but Scole thrust the younger boy against the fireplace, sending Fa's china ashtray in pieces across the floor.

"You want to hang?" the orderly bellowed. "Both of you, you say what I tell you and nothing else, or by God you'll rue the day. You—" He jabbed the butt of Fa's rifle at Freddie. "Five minutes. You didn't get a good look at him before he belted you. And you, Moncrieff. Find your stones and load up. Show me where this sorry sod hides himself."

With a final look from Eustace, they went out into the night. Freddie untucked his shirt. As Drummerboy chattered, high and anxious, he inspected the chambers of Butler's service revolver and found them to be full.

The fire's illumination turned the lizard-skin pines of Choke Wood a fleshly red. As they stepped over the rope fence and edged their way into the trees, Eustace's feet vanished into bracken. Scole insisted they did not take the path. *He* would expect them to, he explained. He. As if they were discussing a man like any other, with thoughts and sense.

Mister Ferry's rifle slipped in Eustace's sweaty grasp. "We can't. Mister Scole, we can't."

"Shut it. Think about those traps."

"One was... there, roughly. Where the hill leads down to the well. Another was... up there, I think, I—" His teeth chattered. The wind cut through his clothes. "You don't understand."

"If you go soft on me, boy, they'll be bringing up two bodies from this wood come morning." Stepping over a protruding root, Scole shot him a grin. "Folk'll talk about this night for years. You and me."

The orderly's excitement was cresting. In the distance, the holy well emerged. Eustace recognised its crumbling columns, made distinct from the trees by their eerie stillness. It could be anywhere, their quarry. Where did it crawl from when it felt the urge to crush squirrels and hedgehogs? Did it rest? What if they found nothing, he thought. Where would Scole turn next? Eustace chanted a silent prayer that Freddie had ignored Scole's instructions and woken Chalice right away. They could still take the Albion van. Just drive away, dream up an alternative history where boys slept soundly in dormitories and fathers couldn't die. How far would they have to go? The Noman surely wouldn't follow them. What more did they have to give?

Scole stopped and held up a fist. Eustace blundered into his back and received a shove in return. Scole pointed. Beyond the spring, the tent where Mister Jenks had bedded down leaned drunkenly against a tree. The door flaps were secured against the wind, and inside, despite the light of the burning folly, a candle shone through the canvas.

Freddie's arms were alive with pins and needles as he pulled himself along, tree by tree. He skirted the woods, grateful for the wind's chill against his burning face, and turned his eyes to the sky. The birds ignored him, circling madly as the residents of Edenwell Hydropathic at last spilled outside, drawn by the fire. A human chain was forming; men with buckets, their pyjamas flattened against their bodies with the wind's insistent pressure. VADs scurried, counting heads, while lights appeared at windows; blackout be damned. Freddie thought he saw Chalice, his fair hair bright in the fire's glow. He felt a pang of sympathy.

Easing his way along the rope fence, he could relax his eyes and see down into the bowl of Choke Wood, recognise its familiar gullies and impassable banks. Scole in his white uniform was a beacon. Of Eustace's dark overcoat there was no sign, but he could feel him there. *A good sniper just can*, he always said. And like a good sniper, Freddie felt that invisible thread tying him to Scole's back, tightening with every step.

"Freddie!"

The girl's voice caught him by surprise. He grasped at a branch to steady himself, rattling one of the danger signs he and Fa had so meticulously strung up weeks ago.

Tabitha Clarke was in her nightgown, coat and boots. Her mousy hair blew about, lit from behind by the flames.

"Freddie, where have you been? There's been a headcount."

"It's not safe here," he said.

"Fire brigade's on the way. Doctor Chalice is—" She blinked, backtracking, still half asleep. "That was the first thing you ever said to me. 'Don't go into the woods.'"

He glanced back. The white ghost of Scole had drifted away. He cursed under his breath.

"You should go," he told Tabitha. "Help the old people."

"You're bleeding."

He blinked, feeling the clag of damp eyelashes. Yes, bleeding. In the sky, the rooks hailed him.

"It's Nick. Isn't it?" Tabitha's blunt jaw was set. "I woke up cold in my bed with a feeling, as if— Is this him as well?" She pointed at the blaze, billowing smoke as the soldiers heaved bucket after bucket of healing Edenwell water onto it. "Of course not. Of course not, my God." She screwed up her eyes and wiped them with her fists like a child. "I get so tired. So tired. And he's always—"

Her words were sliced in half by a shriek. Freddie spun, following her wide eyes into the trees behind him.

Nothing but the pines whipping in the dark. Pointing, Tabitha stumbled back.

"I swear," she said, "I swear, I'm not making it up. Standing there, there— Freddie, no! Don't follow him!"

The thread around his heart tweaked with sweet pain. He jumped over the rope and into the wood.

Outside the tent, they trod a path of carrion. Squirrels and hedgehogs and toads and the zigzag skins of adders crunched underfoot. Scole stalked ahead, rifle at his shoulder. Through the weathered canvas, a shape was clear in the candle's flicker: a man, hunched and still. A sleeping tramp to anyone who didn't know better. Eustace caught himself: how could they be sure it wasn't? Scole's broad body was taut with adrenaline. Lord Kitchener could be waxing his moustache inside and Scole would still pull the trigger.

Eustace kept his rifle trained on the tent's opening, though the muzzle wavered as his boots slid in mud and other things he forced to the back of his mind. A throb in his temple and sweat in his eyes. Scole stopped dead. The older man caught his eye: *Be ready.* Eustace sucked in a shaky breath, tasting the rust-and-dust reek of game.

"Out you come, sunshine!"

Scole didn't wait for a response. He kicked open the flaps, and with an animal yell he fired once into the pungent little den, knocking over the candle.

Dark. Eustace's ears rang high and loud, and he clenched his teeth against the powder blast blown into his face by the wind. Scole was shouting, he registered dimly. The orderly had him by the lapels, shaking him. As Eustace's eyes adjusted, Scole's face loomed into view, spraying him with hot spittle.

"You did this!"

Dazed, deaf, he looked over Scole's shoulder and into the tent. No tramp, no bedroll, no signs of life but one.

Eustace had never seen Scole afraid before.

"You *did* this."

There, packaged neatly in tied-off trousers, khaki puttees and a regulation round-toed field boot: a man's lower leg.

Scole's fear spun into rage. He swung the rifle at Eustace's head, but the boy was already in flight, stumbling headlong through the billowing sea of ferns. Away from the tent, away from Scole's bellowed threats, away from the smoke of the burning folly, down into the roots and needles of Choke Wood. In his panic, he floundered in the dirt. He half rolled, half slid down a gulley, hearing Scole's distant curses as the orderly blundered through the wood in pursuit. A shape welled up behind his eyes; that truncated leg, like a slab of lumber. He squeezed his fingers into the dirt, seeking the reality of pain and cold.

The rifle. His fingers brushed something smooth, and he heaved himself up to grasp the stock when feathers swiped his cheek. Something flashed past, a blur of black and white.

413

Drummerboy, shrieking a warning. Instinctively, he retracted his arm.

Chunk. With a spray of pine-tasting dew, the iron trap snapped shut.

Aghast, Eustace stared at the gleaming teeth, so obvious now, grimacing beside him in the undergrowth. A device like that would take his arm and crack it like kindling.

He stood like a foal, finding himself overlooking the holy well. The ring of stones was black in the sluggish dawn.

"Eustace!"

Not Scole's voice, but Freddie's. His heart leapt, then fell. There was a woman with him, struggling to keep up on short legs. The pair were downhill, Freddie leaning against one of the columns, forehead to the cold stone, his chest visibly heaving. Tabitha, Eustace noticed with a grim smile, wielded a stick for all the good it would do her.

Her voice was monotone with fear: "Mister Moncrieff, it's not safe, sir."

Eustace struggled down the hill. He refused to look at the water. He could not afford those memories. Ripples billowed slowly out across the black surface as he hurried to Freddie to clasp him by the shoulders.

"You look rotten."

Freddie raised a finger to the sky. "Listen."

Through the thrashing canopy, Eustace saw them, revolving constellations of rooks and magpies and jackdaws sending their raucous signals into the smoky sky. As eerie as the sight was, it was nothing compared to the glow of fever on Freddie's pale cheeks. "I'm getting you out of here. Miss Clarke—"

Freddie's hand on his, clammy but strong. "They're talking again."

Eustace met his blue eyes, shining with a zealot's intent.

"They say" – he smiled, swallowing down smoke – "it isn't summat you give. It's summat you *owe*."

"What is?"

A shot rang out. Tabitha shrieked as slivers of the well's stone peppered her nightgown. Scole lurched down the path, his white uniform a mess of sap and earth.

"A conspiracy, is it? The bitter little bitch and a couple of—" He cursed as he dropped the round he was attempting to feed into the rifle. "Playing your parlour tricks. Don't you turn away from me, girl! He's been singing, hasn't he?"

The rifle in Eustace's sweaty hands gave him courage. He stepped up, blocking Scole's view of Tabitha. "Miss Clarke," he said, in a steadier voice than he had any right to. "You should go."

"No, Miss Clarke should stay," Scole crowed. "Why don't we invite dear old Mister Butler too, as we're all such pals?" Eustace averted his eyes, earning a bark of laughter from Scole. "Or has the gentleman guest not been quite honest in his version of events?"

A fresh torrent of wind tore through the canopy. The well's surface stippled as dead wood and needles rained down, and Scole rapped the stone rim with the butt of his rifle.

"Visitors, Butler, mate. You remember our Eustace. He's the one who took your feet."

Pushed by the wind, Freddie gently tumbled down onto the well's rim. He sat, dazedly craning his neck to watch the birds turn their urgent circles under the clouds. The implication of

Scole's words failed to penetrate him, but Tabitha's shoulders were rigid.

"Butler? The missing man?" she said, eyes darting from the well's black depths to Scole's grim visage. "The one everyone's searching for, you— Nick?"

"Waste of good boot leather, my girl." Scole jerked his chin in Eustace's direction. "Ask him."

Up at the Hydropathic, the men had the fire almost under control. Voices carried; shouted orders and the names of those unaccounted for. Eustace thought he heard his own.

How fortunate to simply disappear.

He swallowed dry.

"I kept my promise of silence, Mister Scole. For all my word is worth, which, well..." He shrugged. "It's all just shades of cowardice, isn't it? Let Miss Clarke go. She's done nothing." With reluctance, he turned to Freddie, who, despite sitting with his knees to his chest, swayed in the wind like a straw poppet. "I was going to confess my part in it one day, but... not like this."

Whatever reaction he had dreaded, it never came. Freddie's gaze drifted over the pines as if listening to someone else. He plucked at his lip; his thoughts – whatever language they were – remained his own.

Tabitha, meanwhile, choked on dry tears. "You're playing a trick on me. You're always playing tricks on me." She searched Scole's face. "You'll *hang*."

Scole fed a fresh round into Fa's rifle and shunted the bolt decisively. "Lay down your arms, Moncrieff. You'll only do yourself a mischief."

"It's not safe here," said Eustace.

"That was an order, boy."

416

"We should leave. He's—"

"Your tramp? Your mother's not the only one who can spin a tale. More fool me, believing you. But now you've gone and put me in a difficult position." He levelled the rifle at Tabitha. With her nightgown whipping around her legs, the chargirl stared down the barrel, moon-eyed as a pigeon caught in a lamper's beam. "Put down your rifle, Mister Moncrieff, like a gentleman."

Eustace felt the core of himself melting, as if he might sink into the soil. With glacial slowness, he held out the rifle, feeling the burn in his bicep as Scole motioned him closer, keeping his sights on his former sweetheart.

"She doesn't know anything," Eustace promised, "not really. Just a vengeful girl, like you said. Who will believe her?"

Scole's voice was a dangerous mutter. "Do I fancy spending the rest of my days calculating those odds?" He let his sights waver, tracing an invisible line from Tabitha's pale face to her breast. "What do you think, eh, Ferry? Can I trust her? Can I trust you?"

The bright *chacka-chacka* of a jackdaw cut through the clearing. As the groundskeeper's son stumbled to his feet, Scole yelled out for Freddie to stay where he was, but he was answered only by Freddie's guileless laugh. With his sweat-sheened face and billowing hair, he looked like a madman, teetering on his tiptoes to follow Drummerboy's swooping course around the well.

Scole looked to Eustace, who watched with equal bemusement. The white ensign of Drummerboy's wing flashed between Scole's weapon and Tabitha's stunned face. He chattered merrily as he ducked and dove.

"You're a liar," Freddie laughed. He called to Scole: "Listen! What a liar you are."

Freddie lurched towards them, tripping on his own boots. In catching him, Eustace dropped his rifle, and he felt Scole kick it into the bracken as Freddie pressed his mouth to Eustace's ear and whispered something drunken and strange. Drummerboy chirruped a goading song, his splayed talons skimming Scole's head. The orderly swatted at him, trying to keep his aim on Tabitha.

All their eyes were on the sky. Tabitha, too, threw back her head to watch the mounting swarm of birds.

Scole kicked up a clod of dirt, spattering Tabitha's nightgown. "Move, all of you! Together. Where I can see you." He jabbed with his rifle, but Freddie's laughter drained the order of any authority. Scole's face screwed into an ugly mask. "What's so bloody amusing?"

"It's you," he said. Heavy in Eustace's arms, Freddie shivered as the wind lashed his heated skin. "There's nothing they don't see. All your boasting – nothing but a puppet show."

"Call this fucking bird off!" Scole ducked as Drummerboy sped past his nose, cackling in full voice. The distraction allowed Tabitha to dart away, her nightgown billowing as she vanished behind a tree. Scole bellowed after her. "You'll never make it, my girl. I'm faster than you. I can— Jesus! It cut me. The bloody flea-bitten—"

Freddie grinned into Eustace's neck. "Drummerboy says it's time you come clean, Nick. Folkestone? Waiting for the boat? An accident, like a car running off the road or a boiler exploding. And Butler knew, so Butler had to go." He caught his breath. "You've never been to France. You've never fought the Kaiser. You've never done any of it."

Drummerboy's cackles rang out as Scole fired into the air

with a roar of frustration. Freddie allowed Eustace to gently lower him back onto the well's rim, half swooning as he was. "You strung us along for years," he chuckled, wiping tears. "Folkestone!"

"You shut your mouth!" Scole screamed. He struggled with his rifle, fumbling to reload. Eustace was frozen, his heart hammering – *do something do something* – when Tabitha's stocky white form reared out from her hiding place. She had Fa's old rifle by the barrel, caked in muck where Scole had kicked it into the undergrowth. Eustace could only watch as she clubbed Scole with it, a decisive smack to the back of the neck.

Scole fell on his knees with a grunt. Though spirited, the blow had only stunned him.

Standing over Scole, Tabitha was ashen with rage. "You said you took a gun turret," she said. "You said your medal—"

"Everyone spins a yarn," Scole snarled, struggling to stand. His rifle had tumbled out of reach, the rounds scattered all over the clearing, indistinguishable from stones in the dark.

"You said you understood."

"Them up in the North Wing, half their stories are a pack of lies. I wore the uniform. I was as good as there." Upright at last, a wave of giddiness sent him staggering to the nearest pine. He clung to the scaly bark. "Butler – he was an accident. And what about these two malingerers? What do you think your sainted Thomas would say about them, eh?"

The jibe blew away with the rest of the dry leaves. Tabitha's eyes shone cold.

"So what's your plan, Nick? Three more accidents?"

Scole grinned against the rising pain. "I could ask the same of you, my girl."

The rifle was heavy in Tabitha's hands. She had never used one before, Eustace realised. She ran her fingers along the unfamiliar stock, glancing down in search of the trigger. Before Eustace's cry could warn her, Scole's fist slammed her jaw. The chargirl sprawled in the dirt, a dark torrent of blood already flooding down her chin. She could only watch as Scole tore the weapon from her arms.

"I've made a mess of your teeth, my girl, and for that I'm sorry." Scole was conversational as he checked the chamber for rounds. He levelled the barrel at Tabitha's heaving chest. "But I'll not hang."

"*Tum-ti-tum, rom-de-pom.*"

Drummerboy came shrieking down into Scole's bewildered face. From his beak came Mister Jenks' voice, a stream of those inane mutterings Scole so despised and thought he would never hear again. Flinching away from the jackdaw's splayed talons – "*Dee-dum-dum!*" – the orderly whipped around in time to see Eustace barrel into him at full tilt. The rifle was sent flying. Scole was heavier than expected, only staggering a few feet, and as his fists lashed out – at Drummerboy's tail feathers, at Eustace, at anyone within reach – Eustace was distantly aware of his ears ringing, gunpowder bitter on his tongue.

Scole was falling. Toppling backwards, arms wheeling, backwards into the thick undergrowth.

Freddie lowered Butler's revolver and tucked it into his belt.

Tabitha was the first to reach Scole. Eustace ran to her side, not knowing what he might find, the bracken was so high. Freddie remained at the well, listening to something private up in the clouds.

"Oh God," Tabitha slurred through broken teeth. "Oh, good God."

Scole was alive, his right arm bloody where he clutched it. But it was the vicious gleam of iron that held Eustace's attention. Clamped around Scole's leg – *through* it, in a display of butcher's hooks – were the jagged teeth of one of Mister Ferry's traps. No blood issued from the ruinous wound. The iron had smashed straight through Scole's prosthetic, reducing it to splinters. Humiliated and trapped tight, Scole kicked and tugged.

"Ferry, open it. Open it, damn you!"

High in the canopy, the birds hushed.

Eustace was babbling, reassuring Tabitha: "It's all going to be all right. He fell. He fell in the trap and we were rushing to help him, and in the mud Freddie simply slipped. Freddie never meant to hit him, you mustn't…"

He trailed off. Although Tabitha faced him, she wasn't looking at him. There was a smell. Something hot dribbled down the inside of Tabitha's thigh.

Behind the well, in the oval alcove where monks once displayed their gilded statues, something dark unfurled.

Freddie's blue eyes drifted down from the sky. He saw it too: rags, stiff with filth, came sliding down over the stones beside him. They trailed in the water like weeds. It had been there all along, Eustace realised. He had thought the ripples nothing more than the wind.

Legs. Arms. A neck too frail for such a bulbous head.

Tabitha's bloody mouth hung open, transfixed by the long impossible ugliness of the figure lolloping towards them. Scole, oblivious, continued to rant and thrash.

That shuffling, sullen step. A high, cracked sound escaped

421

from Eustace's lips as the creature paused near Freddie. Its head inclined in the older boy's direction, that mess of picked bone peering down with silent interest. Freddie held himself with inexplicable composure, his lips pressed tight against the taste of wet animal pelts bristling on the air.

He met Eustace's eyes. *Go.*

Eustace could only manage a terse shake of the head.

With whatever powers of perception it possessed, the creature assessed the four figures before it. It appeared to recognise them, as much as a predator acknowledges a lower being, and as the orderly persisted in thrashing, a deep creaking emanated from its bundled chest like that of a struggling ship.

Scole had managed to loosen one of the straps on his false leg when the uncanny stillness of the air – the weight of it, bearing down on him – pricked at the hair on his arms. He looked up.

"What in God's—"

"Shh!" Tabitha hissed. Instinct, something wise in the blood, roused too late. The creature looked to the fallen orderly, and then at Tabitha. The chargirl was incapable of movement as, like a bending oak, it bowed to better smell or hear her. She kept her mouth as tightly closed as her swelling face would allow, straining back to evade the touch of that flapping greatcoat.

Like opening one's eyes underwater. Or letting out a breath and watching it bubble and rise. With trance-like intuition, Eustace realised it wouldn't hurt her. He glanced at Freddie as they both stepped warily closer. He, too, felt it.

It was reading her.

Reading, and reflecting.

They smelled high poultry in fresh baby linen; heard the

tattoo gun singing out its memorial hymn; ran their fingers down the black-edged letter delivered by a pimply boy who wouldn't meet their eyes. Their ears ached with the unremittent din of the factory. The copper tang of the shells permeated everything they ate. They knew that one day those monstrous eggs would crack apart, meting out pain and fear and something like justice. They stored that knowledge under their skin: cold sustenance in their grief and somehow a new grief to carry, too. They hid their bodies in loose blouses and retained the habit when their monthlies returned. Another kind of burial. They saw the smiling American doctor and felt their hackles rise when he promised a new beginning. They saw Scole, a man in white. Perhaps. Perhaps.

As this vision flickered across their shared consciousness, the whole filthy body of the creature drained to a luminous cotton pallor. Shoulders wide as a door, protracted elbows fit to draw blood; the crude approximation of the Edenwell uniform was no more human than one of Freddie's boyhood sketches. The head retained its featureless enormity, wobbling absently as the change came over it, guzzling all Tabitha had to give. Flashes of older things sparked and died: dripping cathedral silverware, mourning brooches of plaited hair, a garland of papers wrapped in cheap ribbon, scrawled with petitions petty and great. Epaulettes studded with skulls: avian, canine, foetal. An axe of rare green stone germinated in its belt and wilted into ash. Woven baskets of antlers hung from its arms, dull with mineshaft dust. The longest remained, a great thorn erupting from the creaking figure's hooded scalp.

Tabitha could do little but stare up into the creature's greedily snuffling visage. In her half-dreaming state, her bloody lips worked around a single word, surging to the surface of her brain. All the dragging years of suffering and guilt and quiet forbearance existed inside this being slouching before her, snorting hotly through the gaps in its non-face as if she were meat. And the animal part of her that kept her alive – kept her eating and sleeping, kept her moving when there was nothing to move for – released her from her stupor and animated her tongue.

"A gift," she told it.

She snatched Butler's revolver from Freddie's belt and shot Scole in the face.

The wind seethed through the pines, bringing a flesh glut of smoke from the bonfire, forcing their stinging eyes shut. The creature lurched towards Scole's body and wrenched it free with one tug. The artificial leg remained between the trap's iron teeth. Like a soldier with a knapsack the creature slung the body over its shoulder, and with no further interest in the three people watching, it trudged heavily towards the well. With Scole's arms swinging over its back, they watched as it waded into the water and slowly allowed itself to be taken by the depths, leaving the surface an immaculate mirror of clouds and trees.

Sailing down on the smoky thermals, Drummerboy was the first to find a voice:

Thank you.

Eustace had never known a gale like it. Tumbling out onto the Edenwell lawn with Freddie weighing on one arm and Tabitha on the other, he had to fight every step. With the disappearance of the creature, the birds had resumed their circuit of the skies, crying out in a continual crackle audible even over the weather. The wind fed the folly's flames. In the stubborn glow, Eustace saw faces he knew: the soldiers Sandhar and Thorpe hauled water from the fountain, passing slopping buckets to Katie Healey and a row of underdressed VADs. Chalice led the charge, his sleeves rolled to the elbow as he sweated in the blaze. Of the fire brigade there was no sign. Would they send women, Eustace wondered distantly. Father had made many a joke about the ladies-only firefighting crews with their absurd helmets and flapping skirts. Phoebe would love the chance to see them in action.

His stomach twisted. "I can't see my sister."

"Don't feel well," said Tabitha. She dropped into the grass, content to rock there with the fire shining in her round eyes. They left her, safe as anyone else at the cottage door with the fretting chickens.

Putting one foot in front of the other was the limit of Freddie's capabilities. "I was— fine this morning," he panted. "Yesterday? What day is it?"

Eustace feigned a smile. "A touch of fever. My mother would recommend a stiff whisky and bed with a mustard poultice."

"Whisky... sounds acceptable."

Eustace feared whatever sickness had seized hold of Freddie would take more than a stiff drink to resolve.

They hobbled over the vegetable furrows and irrigation trenches, passing the spot where poor Mister Ferry had died. No thoughts, Eustace told himself. Thinking would bring ruin.

"I need a doctor!" he yelled, but the wind carried his words away before they could reach the crowd. Freddie slipped in the dirt. He fell heavily, limbs akimbo. Like a discarded malkin, he appeared to feel no pain. Eustace waved for attention while Drummerboy, puffed up with alarm at the encroaching storm, snuggled into Freddie's coat. Freddie cupped his hand, shielding the jackdaw.

"You've been a good boy," he said, smiling down into Drummerboy's blue eyes. "And you came back to me, didn't you? You came back." His brow crinkled, hearing something. He turned to the breckland, to the sky. "Oh."

The birds converged on the horizon where the clouds were at their heaviest. Eustace followed Freddie's look to the east where the fledgling dawn was crushed by the low cloud cover. Blown in from the coast, Eustace surmised; some North Sea squall. The flat landscape seemed to roll on for ever, barren, ancient. People had scratched out lives there for thousands of years, hunting, foraging, building their shrines and abandoning them to the Norfolk winds. A dizzying thought. Eustace could almost see the years unwind before him in the dark, as if something were approaching from the crackling maelstrom of birds.

Drummerboy's beak parted, showing a red slit of tongue.

Tiny lights strafed across the horizon. Like no lightning Eustace had ever seen, fireflies tracing fault lines through the clouds. They drifted closer, framing something, lighting it up in split-second increments. He heard it before he saw it: a thing as vast as an island in the sky.

Eustace felt the change in air pressure as the birds went surging out over Choke Wood. His ears popped, his head cleared. A deep tremulous drone was growing. Its advance stately, a slow and sinuous thing propelled by the wind, nipped at uselessly by a pack of – Eustace squinted.

426

Aeroplanes.

Smooth as a whale, the zeppelin was the largest thing Eustace had ever seen. His brain rebelled at the sight. Nothing so monstrously swollen could float in the air. Like flies, three planes from the airfield at Snarehill clung to its grey sides, pelting the gondola suspended under the balloon. As the zeppelin drifted closer, Eustace saw tiny figures inside battling to regain control from the assailing wind.

Freddie's cheeks shone with tears. "It's beautiful."

At the Hydropathic, people stopped what they were doing. Like Eustace, they were rooted to the spot, open-mouthed at the sheer scale of the craft. Windows opened and guests leaned out to listen to the deep whirr of the propellors like some atrocious flying beetle.

The folly was a burning beacon.

The zeppelin was losing altitude, drawing more spectators out into the gravel driveway in dumb awe. Eustace grabbed Freddie under the armpits and hauled him to his feet, dismayed to find him weak and pliant.

"Find your sister," Freddie said.

"I'm not leaving you."

"Listen." He held up a finger. The crackling din of birds formed a wall of sound, and Freddie struggled to be heard above it. "He isn't satisfied. You understand?"

The zeppelin loomed over the gates at the far end of the drive. The fighter planes bombarded it with bullets, themselves thrown about by the wind. Bright tracer bullets bounced off the gondola while others smashed through the glass. The craft lurched in response, continuing to lose height.

Freddie gave him a feeble shove. "Find Phoebe."

"What about you?"

"I'll be waiting."

Eustace shot Freddie a look of promise and charged across the lawn.

"Get out of the building!" He waved as he ran, trying to crack through the hypnosis the zeppelin had on the assembled VADs. His sister was nowhere to be seen. Small as she was, she could be lost in a crowd of any size, and as more guests came milling out of the building to stare, the chances of finding her dwindled. "Run!" he cried. "Into the fields, run."

He looked back. The lawn was a black canvas, but Freddie's shape – perhaps? He hoped? – was making its laboured way out to the stables. An explosion rocked the earth and he tripped backwards over someone's foot as a flash of heat and light hit him a second later. The zeppelin was releasing its bombs indiscriminately, trying to gain altitude as the weather forced it lower and lower. The gondola was almost grazing the treetops.

At last people were moving. Some spilled out onto the lawn. Others fled inside, for shelter or to collect possessions. He saw a flash of red hair as a white cap fell.

"Phoebe!" he yelled as Annie the chargirl came screaming outside and he lost sight of her. He caught Annie's skinny shoulder and spun her around.

"Get as many people as you can out into the fields. Darkness, Annie. It's aiming for the light. Go!"

To his amazement, she turned back inside without hesitation. She brushed past a big man, somehow immaculate in a blue suit, carrying a frail woman in his arms. When the woman saw Eustace, she hailed him.

"He's here," Clarissa called out. "Isn't he? I feel his greed."

"My sister! A tiny girl, red hair. Please."

Hiram shouted, "Inside."

Clarissa's filmy eyes widened. "Help him, Hiram. Set me down here."

"Clarissa, it's—"

"This is my house. I shan't be driven out a second time." She clutched the cross at her breast. "Hiram, do not let that beast touch this boy's family as he did mine."

Hiram only hesitated for a moment. He laid Clarissa gently on a bench and kissed her soft white hair. "Move aside!" he bellowed at the guests dragging luggage through the portico, and in their trance-like state, they did.

"She was with the singing woman," said Hiram. "Up there."

Inside the marble reception, they felt the heat as another bomb tore up the lawn. They thundered up the stairs, passing Annie and a pair of VADs helping the injured men down. Somewhere, the voice of Missus Bailey could be heard, demanding someone unlock the wine cellar, the only safe place to be.

Hiram pushed Eustace up the last few steps, pointing breathlessly to one of the guest rooms overlooking the front lawn. The door was ajar, and for a moment Eustace hoped Phoebe had already fled, but when he saw Lottie Mulgrave on the bed, her mouth slack in unconsciousness, he knew his sister would never have left her. He half fell into the room to find her standing motionless at the window.

"Phoebe, we have to go!"

Drowsily, she blinked. "I had... the most horrid dream."

With placid eyes, she stared at the approaching zeppelin, a

black leviathan trailing fire in its wake. They had minutes at most. Eustace threw his arms around her waist and picked her up. Hiram had Lottie in his arms, cradling her bandaged head.

"What are you waiting for?" he said.

The zeppelin's deep inhuman drone rumbled through the window frame, punctuated by the incessant spitting of the aeroplanes. All around the balloon, birds swarmed like specks of coal dust. They were attacking it, Eustace realised. Hundreds, perhaps thousands of black corvid shapes converged on the approaching craft with one shared intent, ramming their breaks and claws through the fabric. For a moment Eustace could envision the vast craft simply crumpling, sinking to the earth as harmlessly as a paper bag.

Phoebe gave a small laugh. "Aren't they clever?"

He didn't have a chance to answer. In a bloom of white light, the zeppelin erupted. The skeleton of aluminium was black against the flames, a photographic negative. Dazzled by light and heat, Eustace watched, mesmerised, as the dying zeppelin picked up speed, thrust towards the Hydropathic by the explosion's force.

"Run!" Hiram roared.

The staircase was a thousand miles long. He barely drew breath as he dragged Phoebe down, down, vaguely aware of Hiram's large figure beside him and Lottie Mulgrave's yellow braids flying. If they headed for the front doors, they would meet the zeppelin on impact. With a yell, Eustace led them to the door at the back of the tiled reception, into the cool tunnel strung with lamps. Phoebe shook free from her trance just as they poured into the laundry outhouse. "What is happening?" she shouted, just as a great shudder passed beneath their feet and the sound of crushing brick and glass swallowed their screams. The lights sputtered out.

True to his word, Scole had forced open the back door to imitate a prowler, and it swung in the wind, beckoning them into the acrid night as the Hydropathic's grand portico took the full force of the zeppelin. All was light now, day-bright, as the fire consumed the building behind them.

Survivors drifted around them like snowflakes in a storm. There were snowflakes, Eustace realised distantly – specks of ash. Funny, he thought. For all the holy water coursing beneath the earth, in the end Edenwell was destined to burn.

"You there, stop!" shouted Hiram. He waved down a van as it careered across the cobbles. At the wheel, Freddie's face was pale with concentration as he kept the engine from stalling. Eustace's heart chanted: *Freddie. Freddie. Freddie.* Drummerboy, clinging to his master's lap, shrieked a greeting. Phoebe threw open the back doors and helped Hiram ease Lottie Mulgrave's prone body inside.

"Any more wounded, miss?" Freddie shouted.

Phoebe said, "We need ambulances. All our equipment was inside. Go!"

"You're not coming?" Eustace hopped into the passenger seat.

"My duty is here." She wiped the sweat from her eyes. Her apron came away black. "No more stunts, you hear me?"

Eustace looked to Freddie. "You can drive?"

"I can make it go and make it stop." He swallowed down a laboured breath. "Fa taught me."

Two thumps from the back: Hiram was ready. Freddie put his foot down and they roared out onto the ruined lawn. They couldn't take the driveway; from the fountain onwards, the land was a scorched trench the width of a small street. The folly was gone, the white portico as much a ruin as the holy well. The heat was almost unbearable. Everywhere, men and women in various states of undress staggered, stunned and aimless. Eustace held onto his seat as they swerved around a crater, smashing through a row of bean canes. He prayed Hiram had a decent grip on Lottie. Up ahead, an inadequate fire engine was at the gates, and a man had jumped down, trying to open them.

"My God," the fireman hailed them. "What happened here?"

Eustace swung down to help him. "The Kaiser sent us a present."

The gates parted and the fireman scrambled into his vehicle once more. "Back up, son. Make way." He waved. "I said make way!"

But the Albion van didn't move. Eustace rushed over, thrusting his head into the cabin. "Fred, back up, he can't get through."

Freddie's rheumy eyes were fixed on the road behind the fire engine.

"Freddie, what is it?"

He wordlessly shunted the gearstick and reversed, letting the fire engine go roaring past. When Eustace jumped into the passenger seat, Freddie pointed.

"There."

The fire had blunted his eyesight, and he squinted into the comparative darkness of the land beyond the wreck of Edenwell. Hillocks of heather and parched grass thrashed in the wind. Against the horizon, trees swayed like gaunt revellers.

Eustace's mouth worked, dry and gritty, about to articulate the need to press on for help when the breath caught in his throat like a bone.

There.

Framed by the old gateposts, it came loping out onto the road. Rags hung slack from the emaciated body, somehow untouched by the pounding winds. Eustace was acutely aware of Freddie's tortured breathing as they stared at the slouching figure, basking in Edenwell's destruction as a child relishes burning a Guy he built from straw and sackcloth.

Freddie knocked on the partition. "In the back, sir, hold fast." He turned to Eustace, his face so vivid with fever Eustace could almost have missed the affection glowing there, soft but ardent. "Take Drummerboy," Freddie said, cupping the bird in his inky hands. "Gently now."

"Are we reet?" said Eustace, fighting the tremor in his voice. After everything he'd done, after catching Freddie in the cascade of misfortune that followed wherever he went, how could they be?

Freddie placed Drummerboy in his lap. He smoothed his palm over the bird's warm head, letting a stray finger rest on Eustace's knuckle for just a moment.

"We're reet."

The gears crunched as he let the engine rise into a full-throated growl, then slammed his heel on the pedal. The Albion van bumped down the drive, gathering speed through the gateposts of shining flint. The figure stood firm, its face barren as ever, and as they bore down on it, flooding it with light, Eustace wondered at all the names it must have gone by, all the personalities loaned it by those who laid eyes on it, bargaining

433

with it, offering up their gifts these past few thousand years. In that jumble of bone he saw a shining puddle on chapel flagstones, frail ankles protruding from blue cotton trousers, Mary the maid in tears as she cleared away Mister Bachmann's untouched cutlery. Visions pecked at him, threatening to overwhelm the memory of that radiant look in Freddie's eyes.

He turned away.

Glass sprayed his face. Drummerboy shrieked as the van bucked hard, as if shoved by a great unseen fist. Scattering glass and churned-up dirt, the van careened off the road and into the grass where it came to a lurching standstill. The windscreen had shattered completely, leaving an empty frame. Eustace's clothes were studded with shards. When he stretched his aching body to look at the road behind, there was nothing but tyre tracks.

Hiram scrambled out of the back, his fine suit in disarray. "What happened?"

Eustace reached out for Freddie, feeling his hands slide off the steering wheel to rest in his lap. He too glittered with glass. When Hiram reached the driver's window, he sighed.

"I will drive."

It was only when Hiram opened the door and gently slid his arms under Freddie that Eustace realised something was amiss. He rushed to Hiram's side as he lifted Freddie from the van and took him to the cool grass.

"What's wrong with him?" Eustace knelt, feeling Hiram's big hand pat his shoulder. "You're leaving? Now?"

"We must get help for the others."

"Freddie." Eustace shook him, but met no resistance. "Freddie, wake up."

As Hiram climbed into the driver's seat, Eustace cupped Freddie's face in his hands. Drummerboy stood on his chest, tugging at the buttons on his shirt. Eustace managed to heave him into his lap. His body moved weirdly.

"Freddie, come on. Don't play silly buggers, Fred. We have pyramids to build."

Freddie's lips were pale as lavender.

"Somebody help us!"

He was one voice in a hundred. Hiram eased the van back onto the road and sped off towards Thetford. With a wail, Eustace struggled to his feet, hoisting Freddie's bony body over his shoulder. When he reached the Edenwell gates, the smoke had thickened to a hanging smog. The VADs were occupied with the wounded; no one tried to stop him as he hobbled in the direction of Choke Wood. He remembered that first time, coming up with Freddie out of the trees, Freddie dripping and apologising. He could hear himself babbling: "Any minute now, almost there. Hold on. Hold on."

When he reached the wood, he almost fell, rasping against the smoke. The little groundskeeper's cottage, by some absurd miracle, stood untouched. Freddie would be relieved. All his drawings and ledgers, safe.

"Did you hear me, son? You're going the wrong way."

Eustace cried out when a stranger seized him. The man was coated in soot.

"His heart. He needs—"

"All right, steady now," said another stranger. "And you, are you hurt?"

Blue uniforms. Soldiers restrained him. He dropped into the dirt with Freddie beneath him, covering him, protecting him. One of the men pressed his fingers to Freddie's bare neck. Eustace saw him shake his head. He heard a sound come keening out of himself like an animal ensnared.

"Water. I have to—"

"The fire brigade's here, son. You rest now."

He struggled as the soldier inspected his head for wounds. "You don't understand. *Water*. Drummerboy! Drummerboy, go!"

A flash of white feathers and a clear *chakka-chakka*. Eustace watched as the little bird shot down into the whipping trees and disappeared.

One of the men wiped his brow with a filthy sleeve. "If he's all right, we need to go."

"Help me put this one with the others."

They made to take Freddie. With a yell, Eustace clung to him, kicking at their questing arms. In the sweat-damp folds of Freddie's shirt, Eustace's shaking hands touched steel and he snatched up Butler's service revolver without a second thought. "Leave us!" he screamed. The interfering men sprang back, arms spread in supplication. To his relief, they backed away without further persuasion.

It came from the sky. A cold spray, heavenly in the glare of the fire consuming Edenwell. Walking away, the men looked up. Above their heads, a piebald jackdaw hovered, beating his wings with desperate intent. Sparkling droplets hit Eustace's upturned face, a fine rain taken directly from Edenwell's holy spring. He fell aside, letting the droplets rain down on Freddie's fragile body, so still against the woodland floor.

"Please," Eustace whispered. "I'll give anything."

1942

CAIN'S CHEMISTS WAS devoid of customers, and for that he was glad. With his collar turned up against the drizzle, he let the door swing shut, tinkling a bell to summon the shopkeeper from the back room.

Old Cain was wiping his hands on his apron. A chemical tang clung to him, and in the gloom cast by the taped-up windows, he could be mistaken for a hoary sorcerer hobbling out from his summoning circle. "Ah! Hello again. Thank you for your patience, sir."

"I would have been back sooner, only I've been on duty for…" Eustace blinked, trying to trace days and nights divided by cat naps on the station settee. "Well, I never know when I'm needed."

Mister Cain brought up a package from under the counter. "It's been a pleasure to work with film this old. Takes me back to my first Butcher's Midge. They've enlarged beautifully, if I may say so."

He slid the envelope towards his customer, who regarded it with less enthusiasm.

"Forgive me for prying, sir," Mister Cain ventured, "but I must ask…"

437

Eustace met Cain's eyes. His greatcoat, the ambulance insignia, so brazenly conchie, drew comments. *I am a Quaker*, he had become accustomed to saying. *My place is with the wounded and displaced. And furthermore, buzz off.*

"Yes?" he said coolly.

"How did you do it?"

With a brief hesitation, Eustace slid the photographs from the envelope and studied each one, keeping them close to his chest. The shopkeeper leaned against the counter, watching those weary eyes travel over detail and shadow, betraying no emotion.

"Only…" Cain went on, "I've a passion for photography myself, sir. There's a great deal that can be done, trick-wise, but these are sophisticated, very sophisticated, particularly for twenty-year-old equipment. I said to my wife this morning" – he chuckled, a touch awkwardly given the unsettling subject matter – "since developing these I've been able to think of little else."

"They're not mine."

"Oh?"

Familiar sights, memories he had tried to smother with distance and work and as little sleep as he could stand. Seeing those buildings, those pines, made his lungs ache; a slow drowning. "I didn't take them. My friend, he—" Somehow, Eustace felt compelled to put words to it, clipped and protective. "Influenza, so they said."

"Pity. I would very much have liked to have heard about his process, sir. Are you familiar with the Cottingley fairy photographs? Fooled a great many people, back in the day. A pair of little girls clipped fairy pictures from books and stuck them in the ground with hatpins—"

"Fairies aren't my line, no." Eustace had little patience for the man's chatter. His nostrils twitched against phantom smoke as he regarded the photograph on the top of the pile.

There you are, you old devil.

He replaced the photographs inside the envelope, rubbing the strip of sealant with a lightly trembling thumb. "I still have his things. My friend's. Boxes and boxes, actually. You *accumulate*, don't you? And next month, I'm going overseas. Issued tropical kit, so God knows where we'll end up. I thought before I went I ought to— And now I have, so." He straightened up. That schoolboy slouch was a timeworn habit. "Mister Cain, thank you for your work. Would you kindly destroy these for me?"

The shopkeeper frowned in surprise at the proffered envelope. "Even the negatives, sir?"

But the bell above the door was already tinkling as Eustace Moncrieff strode out into the encroaching evening.

Mister Cain was flipping over the "closed" sign for the night when his customer returned, coat tails flapping.

"I'm sorry," said Eustace. "I'll keep them. Of course I'll keep them."

Mister Cane smiled. He could never destroy such artistry. As he bid the ambulance driver farewell, a thought came to him.

"You must take a camera, sir. If you end up in North Africa, you might see the pyramids."

At the door, Eustace paused. The drizzle had thinned to a fine spray, plastering stray curls to his glassy brow.

"Yes," he said, having tucked the envelope into his breast pocket. "I'd like that."

439

EPILOGUE

Kodachrome photograph, black and white:
c.1943. In an arid landscape, Eustace
Moncrieff is seen in silhouette throwing seed to
a jostling flock of birds. A pencil inscription on
the photograph's reverse reads "E + Egyptian
laughing doves". With arms open and face
tipped to the sky, he could be at worship.

THE CHARRED REMAINS of Edenwell Hydropathic and its outbuildings were left to decay until Forestry England acquired the land in 1922 to combat the scourge of post-war unemployment. The Hydropathic, along with all the old farms and tenements Freddie knew from boyhood, were bulldozed to make way for labour camps populated by lonely veterans returned from the Front in varying states of infirmity and distress. We can only imagine what Alfred Ferry would have made of thousands of impoverished men being transplanted to the brecklands, clearing the parched ground and preparing it for the production of much-needed timber.

Today, the Edenwell site is buried inside the largest man-made pine forest in England, stretching over almost 50,000 acres. The windswept heathlands and fern-choked thickets of Freddie's imaginings are all but gone, though the birds remain.

We are indebted to the Moncrieff family for the preservation of the Ferry papers.

DR FRANCIS BYATT,
Norwich Academy of Art and Anthropology
Alfred Ferry: A Centenary of Strange Illusion

ACKNOWLEDGEMENTS

This book is dedicated to Edward, Fred, and Bill Urry, my cousins who died together at the battle of Gallipoli along with their brother-in-law Arthur William Richardson. It's thought they are the only set of three brothers who died on the same day in World War One.

Edenwell Hydropathic never existed, but all propaganda quoted in this book is real, as are most of the locations and some of the people. I consulted too many sources to list here, but I'd recommend the oral history project All Quiet on the Home Front. Dozens of outsider artists' work inspired the character of Freddie. I recommend Jessica Yu's documentary *In The Realms Of The Unreal*, *The Electric Pencil: Drawings From Inside State Hospital No. 3*, and Jamie Shovlin's *Naomi V Jelish* project.

I have so many people to thank for their love and support. This is by no means an exhaustive list.

Very special thanks go to Samer Nashef at Papworth Hospital for upgrading my heart during the writing of this novel. I want to thank all the incredibly kind and hardworking hospital staff who patched me up and got me through cardiac rehab, my friends and family who rallied round when I was at my most disgusting, and all the fellow patients and morphine-generated shadow people I met along the way. Protect the NHS at all costs.

I thank Gabriel, as always, for all manner of invaluable support and encouragement ("I wrote a bewk"). Dad for the same, and for helping me come up with a suitable ending for Eustace.

Dan Carpenter at Titan for being a patient and thoughtful editor in the face of this hefty brick. George Sandison and Dan Coxon who championed this book – and me – from the start. I'm incredibly grateful.

My dog Brontë for accompanying me on cemetery walks where we harvested names from gravestones and were yelled at by families of rooks. My other dog Brando who joined the family during the latter editing stages and fought the War On Distractions firmly on the side of distraction.

All my Patreon patrons for their continued support and friendship. The Discord sickos for the pandemic trauma-bonding. Helen and Steve for the genealogy. And Rachel for pursuing woodland horrors with me since 1990.

About the author

VERITY HOLLOWAY was born in Gibraltar in 1986 and spent her childhood following her Navy family around the world. Always on the move, dealing with the effects of her connective tissue disorder, Marfan syndrome, she found friendly territory in fantasy, history, and Fortean oddities. She is author of the novels *Beauty Secrets of The Martyrs* and *Pseudotooth*, the graphic novel *Gore*, and *The Mighty Healer*, a biography of her quack doctor ancestor. She lives in East Anglia where she edits CloisterFox Zine in a house crammed with Victorian medical antiques. Find her on Twitter: @verity_holloway